Anonymous

Arius the Libyan

A Romance of the Primitive Church

Anonymous

Arius the Libyan
A Romance of the Primitive Church

ISBN/EAN: 9783744771139

Printed in Europe, USA, Canada, Australia, Japan

Cover: Foto ©Andreas Hilbeck / pixelio.de

More available books at **www.hansebooks.com**

THE LIBYAN

A ROMANCE
OF THE PRIMITIVE CHURCH

NEW YORK
D. APPLETON AND COMPANY
1889

ARIUS THE LIBYAN.

BOOK I.

CHAPTER I.

LOCUS IN QUO.

A LONG time ago, Etearchus, King of Axus, in Crete, married a second wife (as many better men have also done), and she persuaded him to get rid of Phronime, the pretty daughter of his former spouse. Thereupon Etearchus agreed with a merchant of Thera that he would take Phronime away in his ship and let her down into the sea. The merchant, true to the letter of his bargain, did let her down into the sea, but true also to that natural tenderness toward a pretty woman which inspires the breast of every man who is fit for anything in this world, he quickly drew her up again by a rope which he had fastened around her lissome waist for that purpose, and conveyed her safely enough to Thera.

There Phronime met another man, Polymnestus by name, a descendant of the ancient Minyæ, who also had a keen eye for feminine beauty, and him she married. By this Polymnestus our Phronime gave birth to a man-child, who grew up to be a terrible stammerer, and was therefore called Battus.

And afterward, when Grinus, the Theran king, made a pilgrimage to the oracle of Delphi to see whether the oracle would tell him some remedy for a fearful drought which then afflicted all the land of Thera, Battus the Stammerer went along with him to see whether the same sacred oracle would tell him some remedy by which to cure himself of stuttering. To both of these suppliants the oracle made the same answer, and this answer was as follows : "FOUND A CITY IN LIBYA !" But they did not know where Libya was, and were, therefore, very low-spirited about finding any cure for the drought and for the stammering ; until it chanced that upon their home-ward voyage they fell in with an ancient fisherman, Corobius by name, who had once been driven by storms upon the African coast, and he undertook to pilot them to Libya.

And afterward, it was about 630 B. C., Battus the Stut-terer went with a colony to Libya, and founded there the city of Cyrene, almost ten miles from the Mediterranean, nearly two thousand feet above the level of the sea, with the grand Barcan mountains rising between it and the great desert of the same name. From this colony afterward sprang (Pentapolis, the Grecian five-cities) Cyrene, Bernice, Arsinoë, Barca, and Apollonia.

Thus far testifieth Herodotus, the father of history, who, if not always entirely trustworthy, is certainly no greater liar than the rest of the tribe.

Battus became king of all Cyrenaica, and his descend-ants, by the name of Battidæ, did rule that land, and

maintain the prosperity of Cyrene through eight generations, until the Ptolemies of Egypt conquered the country,
and under their patronage Apollonia, the seaport, became
the chief city.

It would be a great error to suppose that because Cyrene
was on the northern coast of Africa, and near the vast and
arid Barcan Desert, it was therefore an unpleasant seat. On
the contrary, it may well be doubted whether a more delightful locality can be found on earth. All Pentapolis is
remarkably healthful and pleasant, especially Cyrene and
its vicinity. The lofty mountain-range slopes gently away
to the very sands of earth's middle sea, the waters of which
temper the heat of the climate, while the high mountains lying farther inland ward off the hot blasts of the
desert. In Cyrene, and between the city and the sea, a
luxuriant soil produces almost every fruit, flower, and
grain known to both tropical and temperate latitudes. The
grand fountain of Apollo, which the Arabs of our age
call 'Ain Sahât, gushed up in the very midst of it. The
mean temperature is 85° Fahr., and the variations thereof
are gradual and insignificant.

In the year 26 B. C., Apion, the last lineal descendant of the Egyptain Ptolemies, bequeathed the city to the
Romans.

Cyrene, so happily situated, became noted, not only for
its prosperity and salubriousness, but for the intellectual
life and activity of its inhabitants. It long possessed a
famous medical school; it gave to fame Callimachus, the
poet; Carneades, the founder of the new academy at Athens; Aristippus, the disciple of Socrates; Eratosthenes,

the Polyhistor ; and Synesius, one of the most elegant of ancient Christian writers.

Not far from beautiful and prosperous Cyrene, on one of those gentle declivities which were washed by the waters of the Mediterranean, there was, in A. D. 265, a comfortable stone farm-house, pleasantly located in the midst of a considerable tract of cultivated lands. The farm faced a small bay and the limitless sea northwardly ; southwardly the high range of the Barcan mountains rolled grandly away, their nearer slopes inclosing the farm between the highlands and the bay, and imparting to the beautiful place a most attractive sense of quiet and seclusion from the busy world. The house was one story high, containing seven rooms, and the ground plan of it was exactly the outline of a cross, there being four rooms and a portico in the length thereof, and three in its greatest width.

At this house, in the last-named year, was born a man-child, whose fate it was to become one of the grandest, purest, least understood, and most systematically misrepresented characters in human history—Arius the Libyan, the Heretic—whose fortunes, good and evil, whose experiences, heterodox or orthodox, shall be followed in these pages with genuine love and admiration, with profoundest pity also, and yet with a sincere desire to deal justly with his grand and beautiful memory, seeking to "nothing extenuate nor set down aught in malice."

CHAPTER II.

THE family resident at the Libyan farm-house consisted of only the swarthy Egyptian Ammonius ; his young wife Arete, who, although an Egyptian, had somehow acquired a purely Greek name, a fact which indicated vast influence that the great Grecian city of Alexandria had long exerted over Egypt ; and an old female domestic that had belonged to Arete's mother during even her girlhood, and was called Thopt, the abbreviation of some ancient Coptic name, the letters of which still served to point out the fact that in her infancy she had been dedicated to the service of some one of the gods of the Nile.

The tropical sun was just rising along the Libyan coasts, when old Thopt came into the apartment in which sat Ammonius awaiting news of his wife, bearing in her arms a creature that was swaddled up in such innumerable bandages that it looked like a new and diminutive mummy, and, presenting this pygmy to the father, the old woman said : "It is a man-child, and a fine one ! But he hath a forehead like a ram."

And Ammonius carefully but awkwardly took the parcel into his own hands, and looked upon it with curious

emotion, whereupon the manikin began to cry so suddenly and vigorously that Ammonius would have let it drop
upon the floor if old Thopt had not seized it just as the
lapse began.

"How fareth the little man's mother ?" said he, "and
may I not go in to see her immediately ?"

"She rallieth from her trial wonderfully," answered
old Thopt, "and even now inquireth after thee."

And the great, rough, swarthy man went into his wife's
room, and, bending over her, he kissed her with exceeding
tenderness : "May the Lord help thee, mother," he said,
"for thou art mother now, and doubly dear to me !"

"Bless thee, husband !" said Arete ; "and remember
that thou hast promised me that, if the babe should prove
to be a boy, thou wouldst have him educated for the ministry of Christ. May the Lord raise him up for his own
glory !"

"Amen!" replied Ammonius, fervently. "I did so promise thee, Arete, and will so do if the Lord will. Already
our pleasant farm is so famous for its excellent cattle, that
whereas I did call the house Baucalis because, when the
wind bloweth from the east, the water runneth through
the narrow entrance into the little bay, with a murmur like
the gurgling of wine from a bottle, the neighbors call the
place Boucalis because they say that no land in all Cyrenaica
produceth more or better cattle. So, little mother, thou
need not fear but that with the cattle and with shipments
of corn to Alexandria, whence the merchants transport it
unto Puteoli and Rome far across the sea, we shall be able
to give thy boy all proper training to become a presbyter,

or even a bishop, if he liveth and showeth a godly disposition."

"And thou wilt never let the love of gain, nor of worldly honors, grow upon thee until thou shalt repent thee of this purpose, and so determine that it would be better for the boy to betake himself to business affairs and acquire wealth rather than to serve God wholly?"

"Nay, verily," cried Ammonius; "for the matter lieth nearer to my heart than even thou knowest, Arete."

"For what reason, then, good husband?"

"I have often told thee, little mother, that I was a boy in a temple on the Nile, dedicated to Amun, or Ammon, as mine idolatrous name doth signify, and that at an early age I fled therefrom and betook myself to the river and to the sea, and did prosper so that I got first an interest in a ship, and afterward the sole ownership thereof, and made many long and prosperous voyages. I have told thee, also, in all details, how, on a voyage from Alexandria unto Italy, the storm drove us upon a rocky island where our destruction seemed imminent, until, while we all were momently expecting death, a quiet and almost unnoticed passenger, who had come from Antioch unto Alexandria and was journeying with us to Puteoli, did pray for us to Jesus Christ, and stilled the storm, and so saved the ship and all our lives. I have often told thee how this good Bishop of Antioch did lead me into the knowledge and love of Christ, and how I sold my ship and cargo, and gave one half of my property to the Church, that other Egyptians might be converted, and with the other moiety bought this farm, having known the pleasant coasts of Cyrenaica for many years ; and then returned to Alexandria to bring thee hither that we might as stewards of the Lord manage this estate together. But I did not tell thee that when the bishop asked me whether I experienced any vocation for the preaching of the word, and I did tell the holy man that neither natural gifts nor education fitted me for that sacred calling, I did then vow to the Lord that if any son were given unto me I would teach him as far as I might be able to do in the love and learning of the gospel, and would send him unto Antioch to be more thoroughly in-structed. So thou seest, dear little mother, that not only thine and mine own inclinations, but also mine obligation given unto God, bindeth me to bestow upon the boy all the teaching I can give unto him, and to afford to him every reasonable opportunity for greater learning. And I pray that he may escape the physical infirmity which, even more than the lack of learning, hath kept me from the public ministry of the word ! "

"It is a strange and perplexing thing," laughed Arete, "and yet amusing. For all the Christians of our region rely upon thy strong good sense and modest learning in every private matter, whether of business or of religion ; yet it seemeth so pitiful that, if thou standest upon thy feet to speak to any assembly, thou dost straightway begin to jerk and wriggle like a serpent, and to hiss and stammer so that thou canst not talk intelligibly, although thou hast more brains and learning than many who are eloquent."

"I long thought it to be my duty to try to overcome these physical defects, but, if at any time my heart is deeply moved, I can not talk, and it is useless to try it any more. We shall strive both by teaching and by prayer to train the boy better."

"Dost thou not remember, Ammonius, that evening in our boat upon the dear old Nile, what a distressful time thou didst endure in thine attempt to ask me to become thy wife ?" And the little woman laughed and laughed until her eyes were full of happy tears.

"Yea," answered Ammonius, "nor indeed do I think that I did ever ask thee at all. I did, after many efforts, get thee to say what words thou wouldst have a man use who loved thee and wanted thee to be his wife, and all I could do was to cry out, 'I say that to thee, Arete—I say all that and more !' and in mine embarrassment verily I could utter nothing else !"

"But," laughed the little woman, "afterward I did make thee say the words over and over again, albeit I might almost as soon have trained a parrot to repeat them."

"But I trust thou hast never regretted the trouble thou didst take in teaching me how to court thee," said Ammonius.

"Nay, verily," she answered, "but I think it was the most amusing courtship that hath ever happened."

And, while husband and wife pleasantly conversed, old Thopt brought the child back to his mother, and announced that Christian women from other farms along the coast had come to offer their congratulations and any assistance that might be needed. It was singular to observe that while the adjacent country, from Apollonia to Cyrene, and all around, was settled by Egyptians, Greeks, Jews, and Romans, and while some women and girls of all of these nationalities, during the next few days, made visits of sympathy to the family at Baucalis, none came except those who were known to each other to be Christians, no matter what their nationality might be. Practically the faith of Jesus had broken down all ethnic, social, and political barriers among those who professed it ; and the only class distinction which was recognized at all was between those who were Christians and those who were not. The persecution, which had begun seven years before under the Emperor Valerian, had raged in Libya as fiercely as in any portion of the Roman Empire, and, although intermittent in its character, there had quite recently been cruelties enough, extending in some instances to martyrdom, chiefly at the instigation of Jewish and pagan priests, to render it necessary for the Christians to conduct their religious rites and social intercourse with a certain degree of secrecy, and to preserve their ancient means of instantaneous recognition in constant use, so that, when a Christian might meet any one who was not familiarly known to him, an almost imperceptible sign served as a challenge by which he was instantly enabled to tell, without an inquiry or a spoken word, whether the stranger might be a Christian or not. Of course, if any one came who failed to recognize the sign, another movement, almost as imperceptible, served to warn all Christians present that there was one near them who did not profess their faith ; so that there was little danger in their usual intercourse with each other or with their pagan neighbors.

On the eighth day after the birth of the boy, a few Christians assembled at the farm, and the services of a presbyter of Cyrene were procured. They first engaged in singing and in prayer, and then a portion of the gospel was read and the communion administered, after which the child was baptized. Preparatory to this ceremony there was quite a discussion among them as to the name by which the boy should be baptized, the young mother being desirous to call him by the name of some of the holy men who had suffered martyrdom for Jesus, or had otherwise become especially dear and honored throughout the Christian communities. To this the fatal objection was urged that such a selection of a name might arouse evil-minded neighbors to the fact that there were Christians among them, and so render the family unnecessarily and perhaps dangerously obnoxious to the malice of any who might ever harbor ill-will against them. Ammonius insisted upon calling the boy after the name of a Roman who had been his partner in the old sea-faring days, and whom he had highly esteemed, although he might be still a pagan so far as Ammonius knew; and so the child was finally christened "Arius."

"It is almost the Greek name of the god of war whom the heathen worship," said the presbyter.

"He shall be a warrior," answered Ammonius—"a soldier of Christ; and the military designation is not inappropriate."

"It is almost the name for a ram!" said another.

"I desire him to become the leader of a flock," said Ammonius, "and the name is well enough."

"It is almost the name of one of the signs of the zodiac," said another.

"I pray that the boy's thoughts and hopes may be fixed upon celestial things," said Ammonius, "and the name is well enough."

"It almost signifies that he shall be most lean and spare," said yet another.

"I would not desire him to look like a glutton or a drunkard," said Ammonius, "and surely the name is well enough."

"It may signify 'entreated' or 'supplicated,' or 'execrated,' or 'accursed,'" said the presbyter, "and is certainly a strange name."

"I would ever have him sought after by the good and hated by the evil," answered Ammonius, "and I will not change the name. Let him be called Arius. Besides," he added, "what is in a name? Mine own idolatrous name signifieth 'dedicated to Am-un,' yet I hope ye take me to be a Christian. I call the farm Baucalis, from the murmur of the waters on the garden shore, but ye call it Boucalis, because it breedeth good cattle. Arius!—what doth it matter whether it meaneth this or that? I know it for the name of an honorable man and faithful friend, and, if the boy become what I hope to see him, he shall make both the name Baucalis and Arius loved and honored by the faithful everywhere. If he turneth out ill, a prouder name might be disgraced by him; therefore let him be called Arius."

And so the babe was christened.

"I perceive," said the presbyter, after the religious

services were ended and all of them partook of suitable refreshments and engaged in conversation, "that thou hast fixed thy heart upon having this child devoted unto the service of our Lord. It seemeth strange to me that, having such a pious desire for him, thou that art learned and intelligent hast never thyself sought to preach the gospel of our Lord!"

"I might truly have rejoiced so to do," answered Ammonius, "but that the python's influence prevented me."

"The python!" exclaimed the presbyter; "why, brother, what can the serpent have to do with thee?"

"This," replied Ammonius. "Some time before I came into the world, at Alexandria, to which great city strangers resort from the four quarters of the world even as unto imperial Rome, there came certain priests out of India to witness the ceremonies of a great festival in honor of a new Apis, and in their train certain jugglers who wrought various wonders, and carried with them immense pythons which they had charmed and rendered harmless. While my mother stood on the propylon of our house, watching the vast procession, one of the pythons, that had its tail entwined round the neck and body of an Indian passing below, suddenly sprang up out of its coil erect, and brandished its hideous head before my mother's face, so that she fainted thereat with terror. When I came into the world she was horrified at being able to trace out in the conformation of my head and face the similitude of the cobra; and with many prayers and offerings she had me early dedicated to Ammon, thinking that perchance the idol might remove the peculiarity of my features which made me loathsome in her sight by continually re-calling the fearful image of the python. As I grew older, this conformation largely faded out, but all my life, when-ever my feelings or passions are aroused, involuntary action of the muscles runneth from the feet upward, and maketh me to writhe like a serpent, and throweth a sibilant sharp-ness into my voice, so that anything like public speaking is well-nigh impossible to me ; and I am compelled to master all emotions and to preserve a perfect serenity of mind, in order to avoid this serpentine appearance which is distress-ful to some and fearful unto others, and am compelled to speak in the slow, methodical manner thou hearest. But for this affliction, I would gladly have entered into the public service of the Master. God grant that my boy in-herit not this strange malady ! Pray thou for him."

"Yea, most gladly and earnestly will I," said the pres-byter. "But repine thou not, my brother; for, although thou preachest not publicly, thy godly walk and conversa-tion are a living sermon, which all who know thee must ponder with delight and edification."

And afterward the presbyter departed, and all who had attended the service went each one his own way, with sincerest benedictions upon the little family of Baucalis, and warmest sympathy with the earnest desire of the par-ents that their babe might live and grow up to be a min-ister of Christ.

CHAPTER III.

Soon the ripple of excitement caused by the arrival of the young Arius at the Baucalis farm passed away, and the life of the dwellers there resumed its wonted quiet. Ammonius, generally bareheaded and naked from the waist up and from the knees down, as the custom of the country was, his olive skin glistening with healthful perspiration, pursued the various labors of the farm, and his wife attended to the fruits and vegetables nigh the house; and old Thopt prepared their food, and did the washing which their simple style of living rendered necessary; and both women devoted the hours not otherwise employed to the manufacture of woolen, cotton, and linen goods for domestic uses. Neither Jewish, Greek, nor Roman women generally adopted the luxurious manners and elegance of dress and ornament common to noble or opulent Egyptians; and those Egyptians who dwelt in the agricultural portions of Cyrenaica, especially those who were Christians, followed the simpler manners of the same classes among their neighbors. At the Baucalis farm everything about the house was scrupulously clean and neat, manifestly de-

2

signed for comfort and convenience, nothing for ostentation. In the business of the place, out-doors and in-doors, there was never seen any of that driving spirit which indicates a thirst for accumulation, but all duties were prosecuted as if reasonable diligence were esteemed to be both a duty and a pleasure. At the end of a year's labor Ammonius would have felt no concern at all if he had found that he had not gained a single coin beyond the sum requisite to pay taxes, but he would have experienced a humiliating sense of shame and unworthiness if the occupant of so fine a farm had failed to have enough and to spare for every call of charity, for every reasonable claim upon his hospitality, or for liberal contribution to every work in which the Church was interested. Corn, wheat, and barley, variously prepared for table use, a large variety of fruits both preserved and fresh, and many kinds of vegetables, formed their chief food. Fish of choice kinds, and in great abundance, was in common use, and domestic fowls were raised by all. The consumption of flesh was not an every-day thing with these simple and healthful people. Twice, or, at most, thrice a week neighbors would club together and kill and part among themselves a kid or sheep. Beef was little used among them, and was raised for market chiefly. Swine's flesh they never used, and they wondered at the Roman appetite for coarse, strong meat dishes. The light, pleasant wine made everywhere along the coast was in general use among them all. The every-day dress of both sexes was cotton cloth, a short kilt reaching from the shoulder to the knee, and over this, when not actively at work, a loose gown covering the person from neck to ankle, and confined at the waist with a girdle or sash of bright-colored cloth. They had garments of finest wool and linen for extraordinary occasions.

In this region the Christian communities were not formally organized upon the communistic basis of the primitive Church, because all of them were in a nearly equally prosperous condition, and there were none among them who were "poor" in the sense of requiring assistance. The few that were in any way incapacitated for earning a livelihood were related by ties of blood to one or more families, able and always willing to afford them every needful comfort and assistance. But no Christian family was ever known to refuse anything for which a needy person asked, in money, clothing, food, or whatever they possessed ; and in this respect it made little difference what might be the religion or nationality of the applicant. To refuse to give to one that asked would have seemed to any of these Christians to be a wicked, almost sacrilegious, violation of the very words of Jesus : *"Give to him that asketh, and from him that would borrow of thee, turn not thou away."* They regarded all property of Christians as in the ownenership of the Church, and themselves only as stewards intrusted with the management of this or that portion thereof. Hence every call of presbyter or bishop for assistance to less fortunate communities, and every individual application for aid, was gladly and promptly responded to ; and they regarded it as part of their profession of faith to find some healthful occupation for every one that was able and willing to do anything for the common good. In the cities of Cyrenaica were many Christians engaged in

multiform avocations, but even there the Christian communities were so temperate and diligent that few among
them wanted anything; and the union of the faithful furnished such a perfect safeguard against the ills of life that
they were not only able to care for those of their own
number who might be overtaken by any calamity, but
were always able and willing to afford assistance to foreign
communities less fortunately situated, when requested so
to do. In short, all and far more than modern "poor-
laws," Masonic, Odd-Fellows', and other eleemosynary associations, marine, life, and fire companies, have been
enabled to do toward the amelioration of the condition
of the unfortunate, was far more perfectly accomplished
by these Christian communities, that recognized as a
matter of faith the principle of all human charity which
extends beyond mere alms-giving, *that the average prosperity of the community should extend to each individual
thereof when overtaken by any misfortune*—a redeeming
principle which Jesus and his apostles taught in its most
perfect and effective form as the "communion of saints,"
the partnership or fellowship of the holy (κοινῶνια των
ἁγιῶν); community of property and rights among all who
believe; a principle which good men have been vainly
seeking to restore in some form ever since the subversion
of Christianity, in the fourth century, by the agency of
numberless nugatory statutes and associations; a divine
truth which in its Christless forms of "communism,"
"socialism," and "Nihilism," now threatens the very existence of law and order throughout Christendom; a system
perhaps impossible to any government which recognizes

the legality of private-property rights, and is therefore committed to Mammon-worship.

But these Christians had learned a higher truth than any known to human laws : they were the owners of nothing ; they were only stewards of their Lord's goods ; the wealth which they accumulated and held for the common good was to them "true riches"; the wealth which any individual held for himself and his own private aggrandizement was the "mammon of unrighteousness." Hence no Christian could be in want while the community was prosperous; no community could suffer while any other communities accessible to them by land or sea had anything to spare ; and the faith of Christ made the general prosperity of all Christians insure the individual prosperity of each one; so that there were no "rich" and no "poor" among them.

Plato's dreams of a perfect community ("Republic") admitted human slavery—Jesus Christ taught the freedom, equality, and fraternity of all men : Sir Thomas More's "Utopia" abolished marriage, and proposed to hold women in common—Jesus Christ elevated marriage into a sacrament; denied man's right to "hold" woman at all; proclaimed freedom and equality *for her* also, repudiating the universal idea that she was a chattel, and teaching that she is a soul endowed with the same rights, duties, and responsibilities as are inherent in the soul of man. Modern reformers propose to "divide" out all property, and limit individual acquisitions thereof; but Jesus proposed to divide out nothing, and to limit nothing; but, that all things should be accumulated, owned, and used in common, as every one hath need, just as air, and sunlight, and the boundless sea are common. The word " catholic " (κατα ὁλος) was unknown to Jesus and the New Testament; the word "common" (κοινος) was the key to all of his teachings, social, spiritual, and political.

The only relation which these Christians sustained to the " government " of Cyrenaica, or to that of Rome, was to pay the taxes demanded of them ; and they had no concern as to who might be emperor or proconsul, except so far as these rulers might be disposed to persecute the Christians, or otherwise. They paid taxes, to avoid giving offense, even as Jesus himself had paid tribute, although born under Roman rule, and not a "stranger," and not liable to pay tribute ; but they never acknowledged the Roman authority in any other way. It would have been an ineffaceable stigma on the character of a Christian to summon another Christian before a civil magistrate for any cause ; they would not "go to law before the heathen." If any differences arose between any, they left it to some of the brethren to consider the matter and adjust it ; and they considered themselves bound to abide by the settlement reached, by bonds of faith and love stronger than human statutes can be made. If any became careless of right and duty, or actively wicked, his nearest friends remonstrated with him, and, if he refused to abandon his sinful course, the presbyters reproved him ; and, if this proved ineffectual in working out the needed reformation, they brought the offender before the Church, and either succeeded in drawing him back into the right way, or, if he proved incorrigible, they simply refused henceforth to fellowship with him, and held him as a publican and a sinner. They never had recourse to any temporal penalties to enforce the law of Christian brotherhood; knowing that no one who refused to be controlled without the use of force was a Christian, they publicly disowned him, and that was the end of it. For they had been taught from the beginning that the essential difference between the kingdom of heaven and every other kingdom established upon earth consisted in the fact that human governments recognize private property-rights in estates, rank, offices, prerogatives, and seek to enforce these legal, fictitious rights by temporal penalties,. contrary to reason and justice; while Jesus denounced all such private rights as Mammon-worship, and all statutes enacted to enforce them as lies of the Scribes and Pharisees; and never fixed, and never authorized his apostles to fix, any temporal penalties whatever. They understood perfectly well that the necessary and inevitable result of all law-and-order systems is to produce a ruling class at the top of every political fabric to whom all of its benefits inure, an oppressed or enslaved people at the bottom upon whose weary shoulders rest all of the burdens and the waste of life, and between these extremes ecclesiasticisms and an army (always on the side of the ruling classes and against the multitudes) seeking to adjust their mutual legal rights and duties by the agency of bayonets and prayer—a system of laws creating fictitious rights, creating legal offenses by the disregard of these pretended rights, and denouncing legal penalties. But they knew that Jesus died as much for the children of Barabbas as for the offspring of Herod; and that every statute, custom, or superstition which attempts to make one of the babies "better" than the others is a fraud on our common humanity and a violation of the law of Christ. For the kingdom of heaven was organized upon the basis of community of rights and property among all who believe, thereby removing all inducements to commit such crimes as treason, larceny, and fraud, which exist only by force of the statutes creating and punishing them; for civilization itself is the parent of all crime except murder or lust, which might sometimes occur from the mere ebullition of brutal passion and instinct in low and base natures. Hence those Christians, who "called nothing they possessed their own," regarding themselves as only stewards of the Lord's goods, held by them for the common good of all believers, had no use for the Roman government or any other, and cared nothing for it except so far as taxes and persecutions, imposed or omitted, might affect the temporal welfare of individuals and of the communities of which they were members. They were citizens of a kingdom in but not of the world, desiring to be at peace with all worldly kingdoms. They knew that Jesus proclaimed a good news or gospel for the poor, the very foundation-stone of which is the absolute equality, liberty, and fraternity of man; and they learned from the same divine Teacher that kings, lords, nobles, all personal and class distinctions among men, are the mere creation of legal fiction, sustained by unjust force, like slavery and piracy, and do not exist in the nature of things or by the will of

God; and that these laws are everywhere only the utterances of selfishness crystallized into the form of statutes, customs, or decrees, government over the people being nothing more nor less than an organized expression of faith in the ancient lie that private property (in estates, rank, or prerogatives) is the one thing sacred in human life, and that laws and penalties are necessary to maintain it; which faith is the idolatry of Mammon, the only paganism that Jesus denounced by name, and declared to be utterly antagonistic to the worship of God.   They understood, therefore, that in place of attempting (as all human legislators have ever done) to provide a more perfect law-and-order system for the protection of private rights, our Lord designed to abolish all private property, and with it all the unjust laws and penalties by which the worship of Mammon is maintained.   Hence, in place of teaching to men a better slave-code than the world had known before, Jesus taught freedom for all men. In place of teaching a more effective art of war, he proclaimed the gospel of peace, love, justice.   In place of ordaining only more wise and just regulations for governing the intercourse of men with their female chattels, he elevated monogamic marriage into a holy sacrament, and applied to man and wife alike the same divine law of personal rights, duties, and responsibilities.   In place of teaching better laws for the government of men by other men as erring, sinful, and selfish as themselves, he taught that all such laws and government are unnecessary to any people who believe that there is something more sacred, higher, and holier than private rights, and are willing by faith to renounce all human, statutory advantages in order to acquire divine truth.

So in beautiful Cyrenaica, while Greek and Roman, Egyptian and Jew, concerned themselves about politics, and struggled for offices, and toiled beyond measure for useless gain, the Christian communities pursued the calm and even tenor of their way, meeting on every Sabbath for religious services and instruction ; closing each week-day's labor with a pleasant formula of evening prayer ; training up their sons and daughters to despise all the false statutory and customary distinctions and vanities of worldly life "after which the Gentiles seek" ; teaching them to seek knowledge, especially the knowledge peculiar to their faith ; to love all men, especially the brethren ; and to regard this earthly life as but the threshold of a higher, holier, and more perfect state of being that lay only a few brief, fleeting years away from every one of them. And so, while the sun arose and set ; while the harvests were grown and garnered ; while the pure and fadeless sea lapsed along the fertile garden of the Baucalis farm, and new lives came upon the stage of human action, and older ones were gathered into the rest appointed for all the living, peace and plenty, charity and love, purity and truth, blessed the dwellers at the stone cottage by the seaside.

CHAPTER IV.

FINE TRAINING FOR A CHRISTIAN MAN!

THE boy Arius increased in stature, and learned, even before he had learned the alphabet, to think that he knew and loved the Lord. For from the time that he could talk, daily, after the little family had completed their healthful tasks, they spent an hour in repeating to him, and in teaching him to repeat after them, some simple passage out of the New Testament, so that the child had memorized a whole gospel before he had learned to read the written text, and become familiar with the general course of the Old Testament Scriptures, particularly with the salient and beautiful narratives wherewith the sacred word abounds. After he grew older his father taught him both to speak and write the Latin and Hebrew equivalent of every word in the Greek text; so that Arius acquired the three languages together. The father watched with intense and painful anxiety to ascertain whether the singular affliction which his mother's terror of the python had entailed upon himself had been transmitted to his son, and rejoiced to see that, while some unmistakable traces thereof appeared in the boy's voice and manner, they were so slight as not

only not to be unpleasantly obtrusive, but were even attractive, as perhaps every marked peculiarity, which is of
a graceful character, is attractive in a man.

At twelve years of age, Arius was an unusually tall and
slender lad, peculiar in the shape of his bold, shaggy head,
peculiar in the length and litheness of his shapely neck,
peculiar in the mesmeric luminosity of his dark and tender
eyes, and in the singular but incisive sweetness of his voice.
He spoke, wrote, and read Greek and Latin with fluency,
and was well informed in the Hebrew tongue ; and yet he
was scarcely conscious of the fact that under his father's
wise and careful training he had been a student almost
from his infancy, so steadily, easily, and gradually, had he
progressed in the acquisition of knowledge.   The New
Testament written on parchments in the uncial text ; the
"Pastor of Hermas," which, in those days, was thought to
be of almost apostolical authority ; and copies of some of the
letters of Polycarp, Irenæus, and Clement, were almost the
only books which Ammonius owned, as the cost of a library in those days was enormous.   From these they would
read a few verses at a time, and translate them into Latin
as they went along.   A presbyter at Cyrene loaned them
the Old Testament, from which the boy copied and memorized such parts as his father directed him to learn, as
having the directest bearing upon the life and doctrine of
Jesus.   The boy did his full share of labor in all the working of the farm, and took the bath daily in the little bay on
which it fronted (as in fact all the family were accustomed
to do), and at night father, mother, and son, read and trans-
lated from the Scriptures ; and occasionally the boy was

made to stand up and repeat by rote the Apostles' Creed, the Paternoster, the Prayer of Agur, the son of Jakeh, Paul's beautiful hymn in praise of Agape, or some other favorite passage, sometimes in one language and sometimes in another. In these little recitations, as often as the boy's feelings were enlisted, there came a peculiar and fascinating sibilation into his voice; his hand, chiefly the right hand, would move and wave with a strange, easy, vibrant motion, almost as if it involuntarily strove to accentuate the syllables of the sonorous text; his head would dart up and lean slightly forward from the long and shapely neck, like the crest of some splendid cobra, peering forward toward the hearer, and his dark eyes dilated with a strange mesmeric light; and altogether the lad had a very peculiar and impressive appearance. But these slight hereditary traces of the python's influence were never unpleasantly obtrusive, and the father did not think it to be necessary to impose upon the son that life-long self-restraint and self-consciousness which, in his own case, had been requisite to guard himself against serpentine manifestations of emotion. But his own long and careful effort and study in this respect qualified him to impart to the boy a marvelously distinct and peculiar accentuation, which made every word he uttered as clear and perfect as a pearl—as distinct and resonant as trumpet-notes.

But while Ammonius was thus cautious and diligent in training his son to acquire critical exactness in his knowledge of the philology and history of the sacred text, he was not the less anxious to imbue his mind with the very spirit that distills upon the faithful heart out of the words of uncorrupted truth. This he strove to do by continually spurring the boy's intelligence to seek for the real significance of our Lord's life and teachings, the differences between his philosophy and ethics and those of other renowned moralists and teachers; the essential differences between the kingdom which Jesus established in the world and all worldly kingdoms; the great fact, indeed, that Jesus taught not only the purest ethics in a few sweeping principles which cover the whole range of human life and experience, but taught also social and political truth essential to the establishment and maintenance of human rights and liberty. Yet the man's instructions were not dogmatic; they belonged to no sect or system of religion or of philosophy; they consisted chiefly in exciting in the mind of the youth an honest desire to know the truth, and of questions and suggestions designed to aid him in discovering it for himself. The manner of instruction generally pursued by Ammonius may be gathered from one or two of their evening exercises, like the following.

The boy read this passage : "*Now when John had heard in the prison the works of Christ, he sent two of his disciples, and said unto him, Art thou he that should come, or do we look for another? Jesus answered and said unto them, Go and show John again those things which ye do hear and see : the blind receive their sight, and the lame walk, the lepers are cleansed, and the deaf hear, the dead are raised up, and the poor have the gospel preached unto them. And blessed is he whosoever shall not be offended in me.*"

Then said Ammonius, "What lesson dost thou understand to be taught in this place, Arius?"

"Obviously it teacheth," answered the boy, "that John desired to know of Jesus whether he might be 'he that should come,' that is, Christ. In place of answering the question directly, he pointed them to the miracles which they saw him even then performing, as if he knew that these wonderful works would be sufficient to satisfy John of his divinity. This and other passages seem also to show that miracles are the only proper evidence that can be offered that Jesus is the Christ."

"All that is on the surface," answered Ammonius, "and is well enough. But canst thou see nothing deeper in the words? Is there nothing strange in the answer of Jesus that provoketh inquiry, or needeth comment? Read the passage again, Arius, and see what else thou canst find in it."

Then the lad reread the passage very carefully, and he said : "The blind receive sight : a miracle ; the lame walk : a second miracle ; the lepers are cleansed : a third miracle ; the deaf hear : a fourth miracle ; the dead are raised up : a fifth and greater miracle. It seemeth strange to me that our Lord should add, as if it were a greater miracle than all the others, and the crowning proof of his Messiahship, the fact that the poor have the gospel preached unto them. Is it a fact, father, that before the coming of Jesus the gospel had never been preached unto the poor? Was the Jewish scripture only for the rich?"

Ammonius smiled, but answered : "The rolls of the law, the Jewish scriptures, were read on the Sabbath-day in every synagogue, and both the rich and the poor were required to be present and hear it. Perhaps the gospel

of which Jesus speaks was not in the Jewish scriptures, or
else was only taught in laws and prophecies which the
Jews had not correctly interpreted."

"But it could not have been our gospel," said Arius,
"for no part of the New Testament was then written. I
wonder what this gospel was ; and why it was good news
to the poor rather than to the rich ; and why our Lord
said that whoever should not take offense at the gospel was
blessed. Why should any one take offense at it ? Why
did they crucify him for proclaiming it ? Why did the
chief priests and rulers of the people so bitterly hate the
gospel ?"

"If thou wilt follow up these questions and learn the
true answers thereto," said Ammonius, "thou wilt get
hold of a fine, large truth ! "

"Wilt thou aid me therein ? "

"Yea, so far as I am able to do so ; and to that end I
ask thee if thou canst tell what reason is repeatedly given
in the gospels why the Pharisees 'were offended' at our
Lord's teachings ; why they 'derided' him ; in a word,
why they hated him and his gospel ? "

"Yea ! The reason that is always given for their hatred of Jesus is that they were 'covetous' ? "

"Dost thou think that the fact that they were rich
and covetous could account for their rejection of their own
scriptures, which showed them the Messiah plainly, and
in which they all believed, unless the gospel which Jesus
taught in some way antagonized their legal right to their
property ?"

"Nay, verily," said the boy. "The gospel must have

interfered with their property, or the fact that they were 'covetous' would not be given as the reason for their hatred of Jesus."

"Then let us examine what this gospel was that was 'good news to the poor.' Dost thou remember any other place in which the same words occur ?"

"Yea," answered Arius. "It is written in Luke : *"And he came to Nazareth, where he had been brought up : and, as his custom was, he went into the synagogue on the Sabbath-day, and stood up for to read. And there was delivered unto him the book of the prophet Esaias. And when he had opened the book, he found the place where it is written, The spirit of the Lord is upon me, because he hath anointed me to preach the gospel to the poor : he hath sent me to heal the broken-hearted ; to preach deliverance to the captives ; and recovering of sight to the blind ; to set at liberty them that are bruised ; to preach the acceptable year of the Lord. And he closed the book, and gave it again to the minister, and sat down. And the eyes of all of them that were in the synagogue were fastened on him. And he began to say unto them, This day is this scripture fulfilled in your ears."*

"Now canst thou find the place in Isaiah referred to in the text ?"

"Yea," replied Arius ; "it readeth as follows : ' *The spirit of the Lord God* is upon me ; because he hath anointed me to *preach good tidings.*"

"Stop," said Ammonius ; "thou seest that the 'gospel' is the same thing which the prophet calleth 'good tidings ?'"

3

" Yea," answered the lad, "but whence cometh this expression of 'the acceptable year of the Lord,' and what signifieth it ?"

"It cometh from the statute of the year of jubilee, set forth at large in the book of Leviticus. When thou shalt examine this statute fully, thou shalt find that it is emphatically a law against private property, providing that debts expire every seventh year, and that all Israel was prohibited from seeking to make gain every seventh year, and from saving what they had already made. Thou wilt see that it was a statute restoring all real estate every fiftieth year to the original possessors thereof, and providing for the release of all prisoners, the manumission of all slaves, the cessation of all oppressions—a year of joy to all that were poor and afflicted. Thou wilt see that Isaiah, and other prophets also, foretold that this great and acceptable year of jubilee was simply a type of the condition, social and political, which should be established permanently in the kingdom of heaven : and that our Lord declared that this prophecy was fulfilled in himself. Thou wilt find, if thou shalt grasp this one truth in its fullness, that the gospel which was good news to the poor was simply the fulfillment of the prophecies concerning Christ— the permanent establishment of 'the acceptable year' ; and that the Pharisees, who were rich and 'covetous,' hated the gospel because it required all who believe to hold all rights and property in common for the good of all ; and they preferred their own selfish aggrandizement to the common good of all ; and thou wilt see that the chief priests and rulers of the people conspired together to crucify Jesus, not because they ever doubted his divinity and Messiah-ship, but because they worshiped Mammon more than God. For the same reason, Rome, that welcomed every heathen superstition under heaven, and built a Pantheon for all the gods, persecuted the Christians from the very beginning, because the gospel of our Lord is eternally opposed to Mammon-worship, war, slavery, polygamy, and the princes and powers of the earth—a kingdom in which Christ only is king, and all men are brethren."

"And it must have been hard for a rich man to enter the kingdom of heaven," said Arius, "only because he had to consecrate all earthly possessions to the common Church, and abdicate all human titles and prerogatives."

"Yea," said Ammonius, "that was the property-law laid down by Jesus; and it was verily easier for a camel to go through the eye of a needle than for a rich man to comply with the law. But thou shouldst trace this truth through all the laws of the Jews, through all the prophecies and through all the parables of Christ; and thou wilt then understand how the law was a schoolmaster leading men to Jesus. Thou wilt understand how it is that in the Church all are free, equal, and fraternal, while in all other kingdoms there are kings, princes, lords; masters, and slaves; the rich and the poor; and universal selfishness, pride, ambition, usury, extortion, licentiousness, oppression, and wrong; and thou wilt more and more love and worship our blessed Lord for establishing the only system upon which true liberty and true religion ever will be possible for the masses of mankind."

Then the bright, patient, hopeful student resolved that

4

he would never cease to read and to ponder upon the fullness of the gospel until he had thoroughly explored all
the possible bearings of the divine, social, political, and
spiritual system of our Lord upon human life, and its relations to all other kingdoms organized on earth. The lad
had learned more than the meaning of an isolated text;
he had found a broad principle that rests at the very basis
of all profitable reading and interpretation of the sacred
word.

And in this sort of school he learned the wisdom of the
primitive Church.

CHAPTER V.

A PAGAN HERMIT, OLD AND GRAY.

AT the age of sixteen, the lad Arius was very thoroughly informed in knowledge of the kingdom of heaven as that knowledge had been taught in the Church from the very days of Jesus and the twelve. In those days the only written authorities relied upon by Christians were the four gospels and the Acts of the Apostles. The letters of Paul, especially those written against Judaism, the epistles of Peter, of John, of Jude, of Hermas, Irenæus, Polycarp, and others, were held in high esteem as the deliberate utterances of wise and pious men ; but even the humblest Christian never hesitated to quote the gospels and the Acts against any of them with whose opinions he was dissatisfied. The wilderness of creeds and dogmas which in later times grew up out of these epistles was entirely unknown to primitive Christianity ; yet the perusal of them was advantageous to the young man in many ways. The journeys of Paul aroused in his active mind a keen desire to know more of the world, and of the religion, manners, and customs of other nations ; and the knowledge that Ammonius had acquired of different lands and peoples, both by his sea-faring observations and by such reading and

conversation as circumstances had rendered possible to him,
seemed to have been absorbed by his son in the long years
of constant and affectionate intercourse between them;
and this was no small stock of information, for the Mediterranean was then in every sense the "middle" sea, the
highway of the world; and it was impossible for a shrewd,
intelligent ship-owner and sailor like Ammonius to navi-
gate its waters for years without being brought into personal contact with men out of every nation under heaven.

In the same way the lad had almost unconsciously acquired an intimate knowledge of the fauna and flora of
Cyrenaica, and in fact of Northern Libya, and could name
almost every plant, animal, bird, and insect in the vicinity
of Baucalis; so that even at this early age he had laid the
foundations of future acquisitions in every department of
knowledge that was in any way accessible unto him, and
had acquired a sturdy habit of independent thought and
examination about everything that came within the range
of his observation.

On Sabbath evenings (the word Sunday was then unknown to the Christian world) he loved to wander along
the sea-shore, or through the wooded mountains that everywhere around Baucalis rose up from the water's edge and
rolled away like gigantic and immovable billows high and
higher southwardly toward the great Barcan plateau.

On one bright afternoon he had wandered farther west-
ward than ever before, going far beyond the limits of the
land appurtenant to the farm. He was weary with climb-
ing over the endless hills, and reclined to rest upon a projecting rock beneath an ample shade of forest-trees, and

gazed away over the calm and brilliant expanse of the
peaceful Mediterranean.   But not long had he rested there
when his quick ear caught the sound of slow and measured
footfalls as some unseen person paced slowly back and
forth upon a diminutive plateau that stretched still farther westwardly along the mountain-side.   The intervening
foliage hid the person from sight, and, the lad's curiosity
being aroused by the presence of a stranger in a spot so
secluded, he quietly went forward, and a few steps brought
him to the place where this little stretch of level ground
had been carefully denuded of trees and seemed to be cultivated as a garden.   Then he saw a tall, gray-haired, vener-
able-looking man, with downcast eyes, and slow, deliberate
step, coming in his direction along a narrow walk that led
directly through the cultivated land.   Almost at the same
instant the aged man perceived him also, but quietly pursued his way, and, when he had come near, Arius respect-
fully bowed and saluted him.   The ancient returned his
salutation, and added words which the boy did not understand, but the lad said, in the Greek tongue, then in common use throughout Cyrenaica : " I think thou speakest
the language of Egypt, which I do not comprehend.   If
thou wilt speak in Latin or in Greek, I can understand
thy wishes or thine orders."

The old man gazed at him in astonishment, but answered in the Greek tongue : " Surely thou art an Egyptian !—and in the course of a long life I have never met
with a son of Egypt that could not speak his mother-
tongue if he could speak at all ! "

" Yea, sir," answered Arius, " I am altogether a son of

Egypt, although born on an adjacent farm, but my parents
would never use that language, and, while they carefully
instructed me in Greek and in Latin and in Hebrew, and
in the Aramean tongue of the Israelites now in use, they
would never permit me to learn an Egyptian word."

"Strange enough!" said the ancient. "Dost thou
know any reason why thy parents thus forbade thee to acquire the primitive and wonderful old speech of the land
of Kem ?"

"Yea, sir," answered Arius. "I have heard my father say that in his childhood he was placed in a temple
and dedicated to Ammon, and that when he grew older he
liked neither the temple nor the god, and fled away to
follow another course of life ; and I think that he believed
the language of the Nile region to possess some peculiar
power over every son of Egypt, and that to preserve me
from that influence, whatever it may be, he desired of me
that I would never seek to learn that speech—at least not
for many years to come."

"And thy father was wise," cried the ancient; "for, if
ever the powers of darkness gave any gift to man, it surely
was the strange language of the dwellers by the Nile.
Centuries before there were any such peoples as Greeks and
Romans, centuries before the Israelites became a nation,
so long ago that the universe seems growing old since
then, and the earth itself hath nodded out of the line on
which the mighty pyramid was built up to point to the
polar star, even then, boy, the language of Egypt was a
perfect instrument of thought, adapted with superhuman
cunning to the purposes of idolatry, with rhythms and in-

tonations in the utterance of it, that prick the sensuality
of human nature like a goad, and deaden conscience with
some mysterious, witch-like power which the intelligence
can no more resist than the charmed bird can escape the
python's fascination, and no more explain than it can explain why the iron touched by the magic stone pointeth
for evermore unto the north. It is the natural language
of sensualism and idolatry, and ought to be blotted out of
human speech. I tell thee, lad, thy father was wise to forbid thee from seeking to acquire that fearful tongue!"

"But thou art thyself an Egyptian," said Arius, "and
I suppose thou hast long used the wonderful language
which thou dost condemn."

"Yea," answered the ancient, "but the speech I use is
the hieratic form, invented by the priests for the very
purpose of keeping their souls free from the polluting
power of the popular forms of speech, to which a pure
thought or expression is well-nigh impossible. But didst
thou come hither to seek me out," asked the ancient, "or
was thy coming accidental? What is thy name? Of
what religion art thou? Why hast thou come to me?"

The old man spoke hurriedly and apparently with much
anxiety, and the boy could not conjecture the cause of his
manifest excitement, but after a moment's reflection upon
the bitter and strange denunciation of man's ancient
speech, and the subsequent things spoken by his companion, he replied in singularly musical and persuasive
tones, the mesmeric light burning in his eyes, the bold,
peculiar head erect and slightly bending forward toward
him whom he addressed: "My name, sir, is Arius; my

coming hither is purely accidental, as I supposed this
mountain-side to be entirely uninhabited; my religion is
that of our Lord and Saviour Jesus Christ!"

"Thou art a Christian," said the ancient, in tones of
great astonishment; "so young too, but clear, bold, and
settled in the new faith, as thy voice and manner undoubtedly proclaim. I am much pleased with thee, boy. Come
thou with me, where I dwell alone, for I desire to speak
with thee more fully. Wilt thou not come, Arius?"

"Willingly, sir, if the distance be not too great," replied the lad.

"It is very nigh," said the ancient; and then he turned
and followed the path west for, perhaps, fifty yards, and
then the path led southwardly for about the same distance,
and stopped at an abrupt and densely wooded elevation in
the side of the mountain. Arius saw that a rough but substantial stone wall formed the outside of a room that was for
the most part composed of a cavity under the rock; and
having passed through a door, on each side of which was a
long, narrow window admitting light into the apartment,
the ancient said: "Here is my dwelling, Arius; come
thou within."

The room was nearly twenty feet square: the floor was
smoothly covered with dry, white sand, procured perhaps
by pulverizing sand-rocks taken from the mountain; there
was a wooden table in the middle of the apartment, above
which a huge oil-lamp was suspended, and a smaller table
upon one side, upon which rested a complete service of
beautifully fashioned earthen plates, cups, pitchers, dishes,
and similar articles. There were several large and com-

fortable chairs made of huge reeds curiously interwoven, and a couch constructed of the same material, and covered deep but smoothly with lamb-skins, dressed with the wool on. Everything about the place indicated a rather coarse but genuine comfort, even to the presence of several beautiful goats that came with their kids to the door and gazed in at the old man with confidence and affection, as if he were a familiar and trustworthy friend.

"Be thou seated, my son," said the ancient, "and, if thou wilt eat, I have here goat's milk, bread, and dried fish and fruits in abundance."

"I am not an hungered," answered the lad, "but partake of the bread and milk to honor thy hospitality," which he did, and found both excellent. "Thy very palatable bread," he said, "is the same with that made at my home by Thopt, and is, she saith, the same that priests at Memphis always preferred to eat."

"Even so," replied the ancient, "and at Memphis for many years, indeed, I did eat thereof, and learned there the manner of the preparation of it."

And, when the lad had finished his slight repast, the old man said : "Thou art a Christian, boy ; in what, then, dost thou believe ? Tell me briefly, what dost thou believe ?"

Then the lad stood up as he had been accustomed to do at home : the fine but peculiar head involuntarily erected itself upon his long and shapely neck, and drooped a little forward, a strange, scintillant light gleamed in his sweet, dark eyes ; his elevated and extended right hand waved gently from side to side like the *báton* of a music-master, and his musical, penetrating voice rang out clearly and incisively as he said : "I believe in God, the Father Almighty, and in Jesus Christ, his only-begotten Son, our Lord, who was conceived of the Holy Ghost, born of the Virgin Mary, crucified under Pontius Pilate, dead, and buried ; the third day he rose from the dead, and ascended into heaven, and sitteth on the right hand of God the Father Almighty, whence he shall come to judge the quick and the dead. I believe in the Holy Ghost, in the holy common Church, in the forgiveness of sin, in the resurrection of the dead, and in the life everlasting. Amen !"

"So thou believest !" said the ancient. "But why dost thou say ' only-begotten ' son? Are not all men the sons of God, even as the Greek poet saith, ' For we also are his offspring?' "

"Yea !" answered Arius, "all men are his sons by creation, and some of them by adoption—Jesus alone by generation ; he was 'begotten,' not made."

"True ! true !" said the ancient; "so teach the gospels, which I have here with me. So thou believest ! When didst thou learn this faith, thou whole Egyptian ; and dost thou never doubt it?"

"I know not when I learned it," answered Arius ; "I was learning it from my mother when I lay helplessly upon her breast ; I was learning it from my father when he dandled me upon his knees ; every day and hour of my life I have learned it more and more ;" and then, involuntarily rising upon his tiptoes, like a python standing upon its tail, with his head erect and bending slightly forward, and sparkling eyes agleam, he exclaimed, "and I was never such an idiot as to doubt it at all."

Then, as if modestly conscious of some impropriety in such demonstrative utterances in the presence of one so aged and venerable, he sank lower upon his chair with an ingenuous blush.

"O glorious certitude of youth and hope!" said the ancient, mournfully. "O bold, triumphant faith, fitting its possessor for happy and jubilant exertion in the accomplishment of all life's aims and purposes! Thou wast 'never such an idiot as to doubt it!' But I, that have seen nigh fourscore years of misery, do doubt it much and painfully. I that have mastered all the arts, science, and religion of ancient Egypt—a land that was wrinkled with age centuries before the era of old Moses; I that know both all that the priests of Kem ever taught the people, and also the higher and more recondite forms of ignorance in which the priests themselves believed—I verily know nothing! I can scarcely believe in anything save universal spiritual darkness, for which no day-spring cometh, and universal wretchedness, for which there is no cure. O wretched man that I am, who shall deliver me from this body of death?"

The bloodless hands were clasped upon the ancient's aching breast, the noble gray head was bowed with hopeless sorrow, the weary eyes seemed dim with long and bitter anguish. Arius gazed upon him with astonishment and sympathy. Then the grand gifts of every born minister of Christ, the missionary's yearning to instruct, the physician's longing for the power to heal and to strengthen, moved in the boy's heart, and once more he sprang to his feet, and with extended hand that quivered with emotion like the python's tongue, and tearful, scintillant eyes, and head bent forward from the long, lithe neck, and a strange thrill in his vibrant musical voice, he cried : "Who shall deliver thee ? Surely Jesus Christ, our Lord ! He saveth even unto the uttermost all that come unto God by him. Believe and live !"

"So ! so !" said the ancient, in tones of hopeless weariness. "Believe and live ! Believe and live ! 'He that believeth on me shall never die ! He that believeth on me, though he were dead, yet shall he live again.' O new, strange faith, hidden through all the dynasties like the Nile's undiscoverable source, yet ever hinted at in the few high, arid, half-intangible truths in which the priests of Ra believed ! What if it be true ? What if the spiritual dualism of the first cause, which the priests gradually elaborated into the splendid pageantry and elegant mysticism of Hesiri-Hes, and the offspring Horus, has at last become an actual truth by the incarnation of the spiritual Son of the one God that is necessarily a spiritual hermaphrodite ? Through the long centuries the priests secretly sneered at the polytheisms which they taught to the people, and they did believe in one God that was utterly unknown to the masses of mankind, for whom they had neither name nor symbol ; and they conceived him to be a dual entity, containing in himself the fullness of double spiritual sexhood ; and they stood in awe of some grand revelation which they supposed would some time be made to mankind when this one, almighty, hermaphrodite spirit should 'beget' with one side of his spiritual nature and 'conceive' with the other, and incarnate its son in flesh, and save man by assuming human nature. This they saw foreshadowed in Hesiri-Hes ; this was the mystery which the priests perceived in every Apis, the emblem of one 'hidden' like the fountains of the Nile; for in the hieratic language Hapi, which is 'hidden,' signifies both the sacred river and the sacred bull ; for this they prepared the mummy that a body might be ready for the returning soul when 'the hidden' should be revealed ; this, the sacred scarabæi dimly intimated, and this was the secret mystery that lurked beneath the veil of Hes that 'no mortal hand hath lifted.' Some such glorious revelation must have flitted past Greek Plato's vision, when he longed for a clearer statement of the will of God to men, and prophesied the coming man. This was the grand thought of Moses, the monotheist, when in the same breath he denounced all forms of polytheism, and yet designated the one God whom he worshiped by a name which is the plural number of a Hebrew noun"; and, as if he had forgotten the presence of Arius altogether, who sat listening to this strange monologue with silent wonder, the ancient continued the unconscious utterance of his fervid meditations : "So hath it been throughout the world with every ancientest form of all original myths ; for while Assyria and the Medo-Persians and other comparatively modern nations, and afterward the Greeks and Romans, borrowed only the lower, vulgar forms which the Egyptians had fashioned for popular use, in China Chang and Eng symbolized the original conception of one dual God that afterward degenerated into anthropomorphism ; and in India Indra and Agni, a primitive conception that antedates Brahma, Siva, and

Vishnu, by countless centuries, and is the burden of the ancientest and uncorrupted Rig-Veda, bears unequivocal testimony to the same primitive conception ; and the Buddhas taught that they were, perhaps believed themselves to be, earthly manifestations of the spiritual self-conception of one dual God : for polytheism was never the original form of any primitive nation's faith, and every people that began with paganism borrowed from some older nation in which the original faith had already been degraded. Strange ! most strange ! Oh, if it could be proved ! If it could only be proved that Jesus of Nazareth is, in very truth, the incarnation of that which was to be ' begotten ' and ' conceived ' of the one dual God, and born of a woman into the world, how grandly would the fact vindicate the primitive utterances of all human faith, and translate its vague but splendid dreams into a glorious reality ! It must be true ! Surely it must be true ! For among Egyptians, Chinese, Indians, and Jews, this original faith preceded all idolatries ! "

Then, buried in profoundest meditation, the old man ceased to speak. But after a time he roused himself, and looking upon the astonished youth he said : " And thou believest all this ! thou hast ' never been such an idiot as to doubt it ! ' Happy art thou, boy, if thou shalt preserve unfalteringly and unquestioningly thy serene and all-reliant faith."

But the lad's sturdy independence of thought asserted itself, and he answered : " Nay, sir ! I have professed faith in none of the things of which thou speakest. I believe in one God and in Jesus Christ, his only-begotten Son, and in the Holy Ghost. I believe not in Hesiri-Hes, nor in Chang and Eng, nor in Indra and Agni, nor in any gods which Moses denounced as falsest idols. Nor in Jupiter, nor Venus, nor Mars, nor in any of the gods that came into fashion with the heathen long since Moses died."

The ancient smiled approvingly, and replied : "Thou art altogether in the right, my son. Many of the gods in which the nations believe were born long after the records kept by the Egyptian priests began ; but all were born of the myths which Egyptian, Chinese, and Indian priests wove about the grand, primitive conception of one dual God. The idolaters of other lands received in various forms the mythologies which the priests wove about the most ancient, simple faith, which was primarily the same for all, only the children of Abraham refused to add anything to the original conception, clinging obstinately to the primitive monotheistic idea ; and yet Moses designates the one God by his name of *Adonai*, the plural number of a Hebrew noun ; and when the one God speaks of himself he uses the words 'we,' 'our,' and 'us' : *Let us make man in our own image and likeness*. Thou seest that it would be contrary to reason that the original utterance of every faith should be the affirmation of God that was one, and yet more than one, unless the divine being is spiritually hermaphrodite, having a double spiritual sexhood. Thou seest that, if this were not so, Moses could not have used the plural number to designate one God. Thou seest that, if it were not so, the only act possible to God would have been creation, not generation ; and thy faith in 'the only-begotten Son' must have been false ; and the very ancient-

4

est forms of faith would have been demonstrated to be merely impossible falsehood—impossible, because there can not be a falsehood which does not originate in and grow out of a truth; for falsehood is a perversion or misconception of the truth; for falsehood is not that which hath no existence, but is the wrong statement or conception of that which doth exist. If it were not so, my son, thy faith in God the Father, Son, and Holy Ghost, would be merest polytheism, for three are not one, nor is one three; but the three may be one divine nature and family. For the one God was always conceived of by the primary faiths as a dual being, possessed of both elements of spiritual sexhood perfectly; and 'begotten' is a proper thing to say of one side of the dual God, and 'conceived' is a proper thing to say of the other; and so thou mayst believe, without any imputation of polytheism, in Christ, as a being 'begotten,' not created; 'conceived,' not made. Would that I knew that Jesus of Nazareth is he!"

"This learning is entirely new to me," said the lad. "Perhaps it is higher than I am yet able to comprehend. I believe in just precisely what the gospels say, no more, no less; that Jesus is the Christ, only-begotten Son of God, conceived of the Holy Ghost, before there was a creation, and born of the Virgin into the world long after God by him had made all things that are created. But, with thy profound knowledge of all these mysteries, how is it that thou thyself dost not believe? Who and what art thou, thou ancient, learned, yet unhappy man, whom may our Lord soon bless and save?"

"I love thee, boy, but I am old, and now too weary to

talk more with thee.   Wilt thou not come unto me again ?
I desire to live in seclusion as I have done for years, and
beg of thee to speak of me to none ; but come again thyself whenever thou canst ."

"I will return upon the seventh day hence," said
Arius, "and speak of thee to none except my father's
family, and thou wilt not be annoyed by them.   And so
fare-thee-well, sir, and may the peace of God come upon
thee !"

"Amen !" said the ancient, "and farewell !"

CHAPTER VI.

FLOTSON OF THE MIDDLE SEA.

IN the evening of that day upon which Arius en-
countered the strange old eremite upon the mountain-
side, draggled skirts of clouds swept across the northern
horizon, and distant lightnings gleamed upon the waves.
During the night the storm came nearer and nearer, and
before sunrise the wind roared wildly over the Baucalis
farm, and the troubled sea broke in foam and thunder
for many a league along the coast. All day the tempest
raged, but with nightfall the clouds broke away, although
the turbulent waves continued to roll and tumble on the
coast, and the angry waters gurgled through the narrow
entrance into the little bay upon which Baucalis fronted.
The dwellers at the farm watched the magnificent display
from their open windows, but saw no sign of any ship be-
labored by the storm, and, after their usual religious exercises, retired to rest, thankful that there seemed to be no
wreck along their coasts. During the night the sea ran
down, and when Arius, early in the beautiful morning,
went to the garden's edge beside the water, there was only
a gentle swell perceivable upon the bosom of the deep, and
a faint murmur of the waters crowding into and out of the

narrow opening of the bay with a gurgling noise from which the farm derived its name. The lad pursued his usual occupation, until his attention was caught by a sound under the bank below him, as if some one gently and regularly struck upon the rock; and the boy then stepped forward, and, parting with his hands the fringe of shrub and weeds that grew upon the verge of the land, he gazed down into the waters of the bay, and at once discovered that the unusual sounds were made by the striking of the ends of some spars that composed a small raft against the rock, with the rise and fall of every wave. He also saw that two long spars or fragments of a ship's mast had been fastened across two others so as to form a small square between them, and that a large bull's hide was securely stretched over this square, leaving the four ends of the timbers extending beyond it. He also saw the outline of a human form lying supinely upon the hide, and of a smaller figure, with its head resting upon the other, both covered over with a bright-hued woolen quilt.

The lad called loudly to his father, who was at work in an adjacent field, but at a considerable distance from him, and, as soon as he had caught his attention, Arius sprang down the bank to ascertain whether the persons so quietly lying upon the raft were still alive. The ends of the timbers projected far beyond the hide upon which they lay, and the boy found himself in deep water almost at his first step from the shore; but he had been accustomed to daily baths in the bay from childhood, and without fear or hesitation he boldly dashed in between the projecting timbers toward the hide on which the bodies lay. The noise he

made in calling Ammonius, and in dashing through the
water, roused up one of the sleepers on the raft, and she
slightly raised her head, and with her hand threw back
the woolen covering, and Arius saw the swarthy face of a
young Egyptian girl of twelve turned upon him with
wide-open, wondering eyes. The other form was that of
a woman, but she neither spoke nor moved, and Arius
thought she must be dead. But the girl did speak, and
the boy thought she used the Egyptian tongue, although
he could not understand her words. Then he said,
"Maiden, canst thou speak in Greek."

A swift gleam of intelligence broke over the child's
wan face, and she joyfully answered : " Yea ! for in Alexandria Greek is the common speech of all, whether they be
Romans, Egyptians, or Jews ! "

" Art thou wet ? "

" Yea," she said, " soaked in salt water for I know not
how long ; but I have slept soundly, and mamma has not
even yet waked up."

" If thou art so thoroughly wet already, a little more
water will not hurt thee ; so put thine arms about my
neck, hold fast, and I will carry thee to land."

" But mother ! " she cried ; and then becoming frightened that she did not awake, she kissed her passionately,
saying : " Mamma ! mother ! wake up ! We have drifted
to the shore ! "

Then the poor lady murmured words that neither of
them could comprehend, but she made no attempt to
move, and seemed to be talking unconsciously. Then
Arius took the girl's hand in his, saying gently : " My

father will soon be here, and together we can take thy mother from the raft. Come thou with me. "

Then the girl raised herself up into a sitting posture, and Arius, holding to the spar with one hand, with the other drew her down into the sea beside him, saying: "Now put up thine arms and hold on tightly; it is but a few feet to the shore."

And the girl said, "I can swim as well as thou, but I am weary and cold and hungry, and will put one hand on thy shoulder." And when she had done so the boy went hand over hand along the spar, and drew himself and her rapidly shoreward, until his feet rested firmly upon the bottom, and then he caught the child up in his arms and lifted her up to the dry ground.

By this time, Ammonius, coming with all speed, had reached the bank above them, and at one swift, intelligent glance comprehended the scene in all its pitiful details; then he sprang down the bank beside them, and said unto Arius, "Doth the woman yet live?"

"Yea, father, she was talking even now; but I scarcely think she knew what things she said."

"Run thou unto the house swiftly, tell thy mother, and bring hither a saw."

And the boy sprang up the bank instantly and ran homeward. Then Ammonius spoke kindly to the girl, saying, "How farest thou, little maiden?"

And the child said: "I am well enough, but wet and hungry. But mamma is ill. Please bring her to the land."

"Yea, maiden; soon will my son return with a saw,

wherewith I can saw off two of the timbers where they cross the other two, and so draw the raft up close to the land, and then lift thy mother gently and safely to the shore. Dost thou understand me, child ?"

"Yea," she answered, "and I see that it is best to wait. But I want my mother; she is sick indeed."

Very soon the agile youth returned, bringing the saw with him, and Ammonius immediately swam out to the bull's hide, and sawed away two of the timbers at the intersection thereof, and quickly drew the raft close up against the shore, and took up the quilt and cast it to Arius, telling him to spread it out upon the ground, and in his strong arms lifted up the unconscious woman and bore her up the bank and gently laid her upon the quilt. Soon Arete and old Thopt joined them; and Arius and his mother took each an end of the quilt upon which the woman lay, and Ammonius gathered up the other two ends, and they bore her gently but swiftly to the cottage; and old Thopt took the girl's hand in hers and followed them as quickly as her growing infirmities permitted.

Arete and old Thopt stripped the poor lady of her elegant apparel that was soaked through with sea-water, and rubbed her vigorously with woolen cloths, clothed her with warm woolen gowns out of Arete's wardrobe, and gave her hot tea made of such shrubs as were known to their simple domestic pharmacy. The sufferer manifestly got much relief from this treatment, but it was only too apparent that the terrible exposure to which she had been subjected had taken hold upon the very roots of life in her beautiful but delicate frame. Her unconscious murmurs were uttered in the Egyptian tongue, and, no sooner had old Thopt heard it, than a strange excitement seized her, and she answered the lady in the same strange speech, crooning over her like a mother over a sick child, or more like some affectionate animal licking its wounded young; for the Egyptian speech evidently shows the syllabication into articulate sounds of thoughts that were primarily expressed in signs and grimaces — the translation of brute means of communication into words; and its original rudimentary form is as direct and unveiled in the expression of passion and emotion as the actions of an animal could be.

The maiden, Theckla, having been well rubbed, well clad in dry garments, and well fed with hot soup and viands, seemed almost free from any ill effects of her long exposure upon the raft; and, being assured that her mother was tenderly cared for, rapidly recovered her strength and spirits.

The famous medical school at Cyrene educated many men in all the learning of a profession which was then in its infancy, and so thoroughly infested with charlatanism that even the most eminent professors of the art of healing commanded but small respect among intelligent people; and the Christians especially had no faith in their pretended ability to cure disease. In ordinary cases they trusted to careful nursing, and the curative power of nature in people whose freedom from vice and whose simple, healthful manner of life gave the patient every chance of recovery, without the use of incantations, charms, and poisons, which then constituted the chief resources of professional pharmacy; and in desperate cases they anointed the stricken one with oil, obtained the prayers of the Church in his behalf, and calmly awaited the issue; having neither any inordinate love of life nor any distressful fear of death, and looking upon even a fatal issue of the illness as a change that was often better than recovery—a happy release from the cares and uncertainties of earthly life, that was neither to be too rashly sought for nor too anxiously avoided. Hence the women at the farm themselves assumed the care of their interesting patient, and gave her constant and affectionate attention, but no drugs except such simple remedies as were in common family use, of all of which old Thopt had a very thorough knowledge. The old woman believed that sound and refreshing sleep is the secret of health and longevity, and that no one would die so long as this blessing was obtainable; and hence, in her opinion, the poppy was a panacea. The bark of certain species of the willow she knew to be good against malarial fevers, and this was her favorite remedy in every disease which manifested a remittent or intermittent form. She had no hesitation in declaring that the lady would be ill a long time, and that whether she would live or die must depend upon the vital forces she had to draw upon; for old Thopt had always remained at least a semi-pagan, and, if there was any Christianity in her, it was inextricably tangled up with the remnants of the old religion which she had learned in her home upon the Nile. She loved her mistress passionately and devotedly, just as a faithful dog might have loved, and she refused to accept the freedom offered to her by Arete when, under the influence and instructions of Ammonius, that lady had become a Christian; because one of the fixed and immovable articles of her ancient creed was that many Egyptians were created to be slaves, and that she was one of them; so that it would have been a measureless impiety for her to set up herself to be free. If she had any hatred of the new religion, it grew out of the fact that that faith undertook to abolish the relation of mistress and slave between Arete and herself. She had not undressed and washed her patient without immediately perceiving that she was one of that aristocratic class who had come into the world to enjoy all of its advantages, and to be waited upon by slaves, as was demonstrated to old Thopt's satisfaction by the fineness of her kilt, girdle, and gown, and by the delicate pink-color of her flesh beneath it; and the old woman would as soon have thought of organizing a rebellion against Anubis, the jackal-headed god himself, as to have thought of withholding proper reverence and care from the superior being who had been cast upon her guardianship. So that the Christian charity of Arete and the inborn sense of duty and obligation which generations of inherited servitude had made second nature in old Thopt combined to secure faithful and untiring care in behalf of the sick woman, and one or the other of them was in attendance upon her day and night.

But as Ammonius had carried her from the raft to the land, and on the way up to the house, he had heard her utter unconsciously, in the Egyptian language, disjointed sentences which caused him much anxiety; and, as soon as her immediate wants had been attended to, he charged the family that they were not in any way to apprise the

lady that she had fallen into the hands of Christians until
such time as he might deem it proper to instruct them
otherwise ; but that they should be as diligent in their care
of her as if she had been the sister of them all.   Before the
close of the first day's watching beside her patient, Arete
found ample reason, in the lady's feverish revelations, for the
injunctions which her husband had given concerning her.
She talked almost incessantly: now of her home in Alexandria ; now of the rulers of Egypt; now of her husband
Amosis, and of her daughter ; now of some special mission
which Amosis had undertaken at Rome ; now of the fearful
tempest ; now of a desperate struggle upon the raft between
her husband and some one else, in which both had fallen
into the sea together.   The substance of this disjointed
and feverish babbling left no doubt upon Arete's mind that
the lady's husband was in the service of the rulers of
Egypt, and high in the confidence of both the priests and
of the government; nor that he was a bitter adversary of
the Christians ; nor that, when overtaken by the tempest,
he was on his journey to Rome, to obtain from the Emperor larger authority to persecute the Christians, even to
extermination, in Egypt and throughout Northern Libya.
She gathered also that when the officer and his wife and
child had betaken themselves to the raft as their last hope
of safety, some one, seeing that all order and discipline were
lost, inflamed by a guilty passion for the beautiful woman,
had leaped upon the raft with them as it was leaving the
vessel's side, and that a desperate struggle had occurred between the husband and the intruder, in which both had
fallen into the sea ; and that the lady herself regarded the

very name of Christians with detestation and horror, and fully sympathized with her husband's purpose to persecute them; and she had expected him to reap great and rapid advancement from his zeal against the churches. And, although not unconscious of the element of danger lurking in their intercourse with such a conscientious hater of Christianity, Arete felt even larger compassion for her beautiful patient's pagan darkness than for her physical illness; but she fully realized the propriety of her husband's caution upon the subject.

And so the weary days went by, and on the sixth morning the fever broke, and left the poor lady with restored consciousness, but physically as weak and helpless as an infant.

During these days, Arius and Theckla had become fast friends. She was a beautiful child, but an Egyptian of the aristocratic class. Her hair, which was as black as jet, curled profusely all around and over her shapely head in luxuriant masses. Her forehead was low and broad, the face a perfect oval from the full temples to the point of the plump, delicate, projecting chin, while the small, full-lipped mouth was red as a cherry, the upper lip notably short and voluptuous. The black, arched, delicate eyebrows nearly met at the root of the high, straight, delicately chiseled nose, and the large, dark eyes, soft, black, and fathomless, free alike from fire and languishment, were of a kind found nowhere on earth except along the Nile—full, wide-open eyes that seemed calm and untroubled as the sightless orbs of any sphinx, yet full of mystery as is the old, old land of Kem. Arius soon discovered that the girl was remarkably bright and quick, but that she could neither read nor write, all the instruction she had ever received (and she had been very carefully taught) having been communicated by oral teaching. Her native tongue was, of course, that of Egypt, but she spoke Greek with fluency, and Latin also, but with difficulty and hesitation.

On the evening of the day on which she had been rescued from the waves, the boy and girl were playing and chatting together in the shade before the cottage. The sun was just sinking beyond the distant mountain-range, when the girl said, " Do you go at sunrise or at sunset ? "

"Go whither ? " said Arius.

"Why, to worship Mentu, or Atmu, of course ! Do you not worship ? "

" Worship whom ? " asked Arius.

"Oh," she answered, " old Ra, or Ptah, or Hesiri-Hes, or the other gods, any of them you prefer ? "

" I do not worship any of them," said Arius.

" Perhaps, then," said Theckla, " thou art an atheist, and hatest all of the gods ; and that is very wrong. For papa says that the atheists are little better than the Christians themselves, and that it is owing to their evil influence that so many young people in Alexandria are growing up to believe in nothing. But, blessed be the gods, I have been brought up in religion ! "

"And which of the gods dost thou love and worship most ? "

"I love none of them surely, but I fear and worship Ptah, Ra, and Hesiri-Hes, the cross old things ; because mamma says that they are the most respectable ; and

I fear them much, especially the terrible, implacable, pitiless Ma-t."

"But do you not think," said Arius, "that you would rather worship some loving, compassionate, and holy deity, whom you could love, and obey because you loved him?"

"Oh, that would be funny, would it not?—for a girl to fall in love with a god! I never thought of such a thing before, but I believe," she added, with an arch glance at Arius, "that I would like a really nice handsome boy better than any of the plebeian gods!"

"What dost thou mean, Theckla, by saying 'the plebeian gods'?"

"Oh, I mean the new-fangled deities that have come into fashion during the last two or three thousand years —the cheap, low-priced divinities worshiped by the slaves and by the mechanics, like Sebek, the crocodile-headed, and all that contemptible crowd. Mamma says that we— that is, the nobility, you know—ought not to pay any attention to any of them except the dreadful old gods, like Ra, Ptah, Hesiri-Hes, and the other ancient divinities; because our own family is older and more honorable than any of them except the high, dreadful old fellows that have lived forever. Still, boy, thou hadst better worship even the wretched Sebek than to be an atheist or a Christian; for papa says so."

Then the boy's heart yearned to tell the beautiful pagan of the God in whom he believed, but, remembering his father's caution on that subject, he chose rather to avoid further conversation of the kind, and started off toward the bay to take his evening bath.

"Whither goest thou?" asked the little maiden.

"I am going to the bay to take a bath, as I do daily."

"That will be fine sport," she cried, "and I am going with you!"

And Theckla sprang to her feet, and ran along beside him. The boy reached the water's edge, and, casting aside the loose gown habitually worn about the farm, he plunged into the bay and struck out from the shore, the play of his limbs being almost unimpeded by the close-fitting under-garment reaching from the neck to midway of the thigh; and instantly the young girl, whom old Thopt had arrayed in the short, sleeveless kilt and long gown which the women usually wore, threw off her outside gown and plunged in after him, exclaiming: "Oh, it is nicer than Lake Mareotis! But I have swum with papa from the great Pharos to the Kibotos in the little harbor of Eunostos!" and she swam after the boy as gracefully as a mermaid. Soon she caught up with him, and, having placed her little hands upon his head, she suddenly straightened out her arms with all her strength, and raising herself up with a lithe and joyous spring above him, with all her weight she plunged his head down far beneath the surface, and swam laughingly away. The boy came up instantly and pursued the fleeing maiden, and as soon as he could catch up with her, which was no easy task, he said, "Thou shalt go under too, Theckla!" but she was so excellent a swimmer, and so quick and active, that for a long time she baffled all his efforts to get her head beneath the waves. She laughed and struggled, and defied him, and exulted greatly that he was not able to give her such a ducking as she had given him, until, at last, he wound his long arms around her, pinioning both of hers, and, clasping her to his bosom, stood straight up, and they sank together until his feet touched the bottom, from which he sprang upward to the surface. Then the lad kissed her and released her, saying, "Wilt thou dip me again, Theckla, or hast thou had enough of it?"

But the girl clasped her hands above her head, threw herself suddenly downward, and for a moment her little feet flashed above the water as she dived, and instantly afterward she clasped the boy's legs in her arms and pulled him again beneath the surface, and rose above the waves before he had recovered himself. And so they sported in the calm waters of the bay until the twilight began to thicken over the valley, when they started for the shore, and the girl swam beside him as lightly as a gull, and, having thrown their long gowns around them, hand in hand they walked back to the cottage.

Theckla's first inquiry was of her mother, and, finding that she continued ill, she obstinately refused to leave her after it grew dark, even for a moment, but stretched herself out upon the couch beside her and slept until morning.

So it was every evening. During the day-time Arius was her favorite companion, but she seemed to have an unconquerable aversion to darkness, and would not leave her mother's side while it continued. Ammonius told them to let her have her own way, as terror of the dark hours was part of the old religion in which she had been raised.

5

CHAPTER VII.

THECKLA FINDS ONE GOD AND HEARETH OF ANOTHER.

So passed the days away, and Arius and Theckla became as firmly bound to each other as if they had been raised together all their little lives. On the second day after her coming, Arius had resumed his usual tasks in the garden and in the fields ; and when he came home at noontide she seemed rejoiced to see him, and demanded with playful imperiousness, "Where hast thou been all the morning, Arius ?"

"I have been at work in the garden," replied the boy.

"At work !" she exclaimed ; "digging with thy hands ? Why, thou art not a slave !"

And the boy answered, laughing merrily : "Nay, I call no man master ; I am as free as any Cæsar !"

"Why, then, dost thou work ? Verily, I thought that none but slaves and mechanics ever labor."

"But thou dost greatly err. It is true that some Greeks, Romans, and Jews, suppose that none ought to labor except those whom they call 'vile' ; or rather they call all who labor 'vile,' but I do not accept their monstrous definitions, having been thoroughly taught that the only man who is free is he who lives by his labor without dependence upon relatives, or upon the offices which are distributed by the favoritism of the dissolute and wicked creatures whom they call emperors, Cæsars, proconsuls, and such titles; and I am free-born, and will maintain my liberty."

" Why, then, dost thou toil ? "

" Because we need to toil in order to live comfortably and independently, as we are not rich, and do not desire to be so; but I never will be any man's servant. And, also, because it is noble and right to toil in some way, and every one who is not idiotic, deformed, or afflicted, is unfit to live unless he follows some honorable and useful vocation."

" Thou art the very nicest boy I know," she said, " but it seemeth so strange to me that thou shouldst labor with thy hands, and shouldst talk as if thou didst believe that it is good and not degrading to do so. I never heard such things. But I will go with thee this afternoon and see what thou doest."

" Thou mayst do so," said Arius, " and thou mayst help me with my work if thou wilt."

But the little maiden held up her hands that looked like delicate wax-work, and laughingly cried out, " Even with these hands ? "

" Yea," said the boy, merrily, " even with those, tender and pretty as they are."

So after the midday meal, when Arius went back to the patch of onions at which he was at work, Theckla accompanied him, and stood awhile watching him as he dug up the tubers.

"What is to be done with these?" she asked.

"They are to be gathered up into little heaps, and carried hence to the house, and stored away until wanted."

"Why, I can pile them up for you," she cried, and straightway she began to gather the onions up as fast as the boy dug them, saying: "I wonder what mamma would think if she knew I was learning to work? But it is good, and I will help thee every day."

"Thou shalt not weary thyself," said the boy, "and thou shalt quit as soon as thou dost desire to do so."

But she would not stop, and continued at the task for several hours, until it was completed, seeming to be delighted with her newly discovered ability to be of use.

"What other work hast thou to do?"

"Nothing else, Theckla, except to take some salt to the cattle in the pasture, beyond the field, and thou mayst go into the house. I will not be long absent."

"But I will not go to the house, Arius; I will go with thee, and see the large-eyed beasts."

"Come on, then," said the boy, and, taking up the bag of salt which he had brought from the barn, he led the way along the shore of the little bay until they had passed beyond the field, where they came upon the edge of the pasture-land, and there Arius scattered the salt along a great trough of wood, to which some of the cattle had hurried up as soon as they saw the boy, and others came one after another, until more than a score were contentedly licking up the salt; and among them a fine bull-calf that was peculiarly marked. The kindly-treated herd were tame and fearless, and, as soon as young Theckla

saw the bull, she gazed at him with the most intense interest, and ran up to the animal, crying out, excitedly:
" Lo, the god ! the god ! the beautiful young Apis !"

" What dost thou mean now ?" said Arius.

" Why, boy," she answered, joyously, "thou art
the most fortunate boy that ever lived. Seest thou not
the god—the sacred bull—the beautiful young Apis ?
Seest thou not the black-colored hide ; the triangular
white spot upon his forehead ; the hairs on his back
roughened out into the form of an eagle ; the crescent
white spot upon his right side ? Oh, if he hath a knot
under his tongue in the shape of a scarabæus, the sacred
beetle of Ptah, he hath then all the marks that reveal the
bull to be a god ! Wilt thou not look under his tongue
and see ?"

The boy gazed upon her with mingled pity, amusement, and contempt. He had read and heard of the worship of idols and of beasts, but had never before witnessed
an actual exhibition of such idolatry. "Why, Theckla,"
he answered, "the bull is no more a god than thou art a
cow. I am amazed that so sensible a girl should be capable of such folly as to think this beast a god."

" But he is an Apis, Arius, and the priests of the temple at Memphis would give thee his weight in gold for
him. They would come hither in a royal procession to
carry him hence ; they would keep him for forty days at
Nilopolis, and for forty days at Memphis, and the noblest
of the women in the city would go in naked and worship
him ; and he would be fed like a great king as long as he
lives, and when he dies he would become an Osor-hapi, a

great god, and would secure thy soul. Surely the priests must know that he is a great god, or they would not build such grand temples in honor of Apis, and worship him with such magnificent and costly ceremonies and processions. I verily fear that thou art an atheist, Arius, but I have been raised up to be religious, and I know."

"Theckla," answered the boy, "I can take a goad in my hand and drive this sort of a god whithersoever I will; I can catch his tail in my hands and twist it until he shall bellow with pain. If thou wilt hold out to him an ear of corn in thine hand, he will follow thee about like a dog; and thou callest the beast a god! Theckla, I am verily ashamed of thy foolishness."

But the young girl looked gravely at her companion, and said in tones of solemn warning and reproof: "Arius, thou dost not believe in Ra, Ptah, Shu, Seb, Set, Mentu, Atmu, nor in Hesiri-Hes; and thou dost laugh at the sacred Hathors, and thou dost mock the bull-god Apis! —Boy, dost thou believe in anything? Or art thou an atheist?"

"Yea," cried Arius, laughing, "I believe thou art the brightest and the prettiest little pagan in the world; and some time I shall explain to thee what I believe, and convince thee of the folly of thy polytheistic and idolatrous notions. But not now, for thy god and the other beasts with him have salt enough, and we must return home."

They went back along the bay-shore, and the sun was nigh the tops of the distant mountains; and Arius, walking a little in advance of Theckla, heard a sudden plunge into the water, and looking back he saw the little maiden swimming boldly out into the bay, and immediately he plunged in after her. They swam, dived, raced, scuffled, and sported in the pure and healthful element until twilight began to gather over the lowlands, and then, hand in hand, they wandered back to the cottage, Theckla going immediately to her mother's apartment, whose side she would not leave so long as the night lasted—a horror of darkness being incident to the Egyptian religion, derived, perhaps, from the grand midnight ceremonies of the Memphian priests in which annually with torches and processions, and weird and impressive wailings, they celebrated the world-wide search of Isis for the dismembered body of the consort whose mangled limbs the hatred of the evil Seth had scattered about the earth.

Theckla wanted to tell her mother about the wonderful young Apis, but old Thopt peremptorily enjoined silence upon her, and forbade the sick lady to talk in her present excessively debilitated condition. For it was manifest that her recovery was exceedingly doubtful, and that even the slightest excitement or effort might be fatal to her. She lay quietly enough, and while she recognized Theckla, and seemed to understand the few Egyptian words spoken to her by Arete and old Thopt, which were carefully limited to repeating to her that she had been very ill, and must remain entirely quiet, and neither talk nor even think, she seemed almost to have forgotten the shipwreck and the loss of her husband; and the two women who watched her devotedly even doubted whether she knew that she was away from home. They looked forward with great anxiety to the time when she might grow strong enough to

shake off this healthful lassitude of extreme exhaustion, and
realize her unhappy circumstances.   But the recent past
seemed to have been blotted out of her memory, and she
lay quiet and uncomplaining, apparently content with her
surroundings ; and the anxious nurses carefully avoided
everything that could even by chance arouse her drowsy
intelligence, and renew the consciousness of grief that
seemed to slumber in her brain.

The Sabbath-day came round again, and, with the rising
of the sun, young Theckla bounded out of her mother's
room, calling aloud for Arius.   It was usual on the Sabbath for the family at Baucalis to go to some house of a
Christian in the vicinity, where would be gathered together
a small assemblage of the faithful for religious services, or
to have the neighbors assemble at the farm for the same
purpose.   On this day, however, Arete and old Thopt
would be necessarily detained at home by the illness of the
Egyptian Hatasa ; and Ammonius, who still thought it
prudent, both upon her account and upon his own, not
to inform her that she was enjoying the hospitality of a
family belonging to the hated sect that was everywhere
spoken against, and that was persecuted throughout Libya
even more bitterly than elsewhere in the Roman Empire,
ordered that Arius should take charge of Theckla for the
day, and determined himself to go to the assembly, in
order to consult certain of the brethren about his future
course in reference to his involuntary guests.   Arius then
informed his father about the singular recluse he had met
with upon the mountain on the preceding Sabbath, of his
promise to visit him upon that day, and asked his permis-

sion to go, saying that he would take Theckla with him if his father had no objection to suggest, and would invite the singular and learned old man to visit them. To this Ammonius readily gave his consent, and Arius thereupon told Theckla of the facts, and invited her to accompany him, to which she enthusiastically assented. The farm vineyard produced a wine almost identical with the famous Mareotic, which was praised from the mouth of the Nile to Athens and to Rome. It also produced figs, pomegranates, apricots, peaches, oranges, citrons, lemons, limes, and bananas, which the Christians commonly called the "fruits of paradise," because in that latitude they were in season the whole year through. It also produced various melons, among them a delicious watermelon, yellow on the inside, lotus, and olives. In their garden, also, grew the rose, the jasmine, the lily, the oleander, chrysanthemums, geraniums, dahlias, helianthus, and violets, and they could raise almost every vegetable known to both tropical and temperate zones.

Arius procured a basket, and enlisted the services of old Thopt by telling her that he was about to visit an ancient Egyptian hermit who dwelt alone upon the mountain, and desired to take him a lot of good things to comfort his loneliness; and that kind-hearted creature soon had a few bottles of excellent wine, some bread-loaves of finest flour, and quite an assortment of choice fruits, both preserved and fresh, packed into the basket, the whole crowned with a beautiful bouquet plucked by Theckla's dainty fingers. Arius, bearing his basket, and followed by the agile girl, pursued his way along the little bay until he had passed by it westwardly, and then began the long but gradual ascent of the mountain, upon a small plateau of which dwelt the aged eremite. In less than two hours they had reached the plateau in front of the hermitage, and soon beheld the ancient seated near his own door, his weary eyes gazing far away over the brilliant expanse of the Mediterranean. The approach of the two young people caught his attention, and with a genial smile the old man welcomed them. Taking the girl's hand in his own, he murmured: "She is a bright and lovely child, and a true daughter of Kem " (the Black-land). He spoke in the Egyptian language, which he knew Arius did not understand, but the girl answered in the same tongue: "Yea, father, I am from To-mehit" (the North-land), "and was born in Alexandria."

Then the ancient said with surprise: "How is it that thou speakest Egyptian, when thy brother knoweth no word of the strange old language? Or *is* he thy brother?"

This he said in Greek, and Arius answered, "Nay, she is not my sister, but is a guest in my father's house."

Then he succinctly narrated the story of the rescue of Theckla and her mother from the raft. The old man listened with much interest to the boy's graphic recital; and then, turning to Theckla, he said: "Child, art thou, too, a Christian like thy friend Arius; or art thou still in bondage to the false and fearful gods of Kem?"

Then the girl showed in her speaking face her loathing and abhorrence for the very name of Christ, and turning hastily to Arius she cried: "Art thou, then, a Christian? Belongest thou to that accursed and criminal association?

Oh, say it is not so, or I will never, never love thee any more!"

But the boy drew himself up proudly and answered: "Yea, Theckla, I am a Christian, thank the boundless mercy of God! And, when thou shalt have learned what it is to be a Christian, I trust that thou wilt follow Jesus thyself, and love me and all other Christians more and more. For verily we are not such a people as thou hast been taught to believe us to be, any more than our bull is a god, as thou didst suppose."

"I do not very much believe in Apis," she said, "but the common people do. Ah! Arius, I am so sorry to hear this thing of thee! Why, if my mother had known that ye were Christians, she would sooner have died upon the raft than have gone into thy father's house, or to have suffered any one of you to touch her with your hands. Oh, I am so vexed to find that thou art connected with such a people!"

Then said Arius: "Thy mother is well cared for; and thou must let her know nothing until she hath become stronger; thou wouldst only distress her by informing her of the fact of our being Christians, and it could do no good to tell her."

Then the girl drew nigh to him with tearful eyes, and crossed her little hands upon his shoulder, and leaned her head against them, and, looking up into his eyes with sorrow and tenderness, said: "Ye have been so good and kind to both of us, that I can not help loving all the people at thy home, and I do love thee, although thou art a Christian; but it is a terrible thing;

for papa says that to be a Christian is worse than to be an atheist."

These things all occurred in a moment, and the ancient, seeing that it had not been the purpose of Arius to inform the maiden concerning his religion, and that he himself had unwittingly brought about the disclosure of the fact, said unto them : "Come within and be seated, my children ; I desire to talk to both of you."

And, when they had gone within, Arius set his basket upon the old man's table, saying : "I have brought unto thee wine, bread, and fruits, as a token of my reverence for thine age and learning. I desire to be friendly with thee."

The old man seemed to be much touched by the boy's speech and manner, and gently answered : "I thank thee, truly, and far more for thy kind words than for any gifts. Not often do the ancient enjoy the friendship of the young, although nothing else on earth can be more pleasant unto them."

"But the heart of a Christian needeth renewal," said Arius, "if it be not always both young enough to sympathize with the youngest, and old enough to sympathize with even the very oldest. The very core of our religion is the *Agape*, a love which is not measured by age nor accident, but goeth out freely to every one that needeth it."

The old man looked upon the boy with wonder, saying : "That is beautiful, indeed ; there is no such truth in any other religion."

And the girl said, "That is good and strong, Arius, although it be a Christian dogma."

Then the ancient said : "I desire that ye will listen to

me carefully for a moment, and thou especially, Theckla. Children, I am nigh upon fourscore years of age. My name is Am-nem-hat. In mine infancy I was placed in the great temple at Thebes, and dedicated to the service of Amen-Ra, Mut, and Kuhns, the Theban triad. My family was ancient and honorable in Egypt, and their influence and wealth opened the way for me to all priestly honors and learning. I remained in that temple fifty years, during twenty-five of which I was a priest, and I gradually mastered all the wisdom, learning, and mysteries of the priesthood, until my fellows determined that I should be elevated to the highest rank in the sacerdotal service, and I was ordained and inaugurated to be high-priest at Ombos, where I continued for five-and-twenty years longer. The triad which throughout all Egypt is worshiped as Hesiri-Hes, and Horus, we at Thebes worshiped as Amen-Ra, Mut, and Kuhns, and at Ombos as Ptah-Pukht and Imhotep. But, while during all these years I exercised the functions and exhausted the learning of the priesthood, I forever sought after Ma-t, the Goddess of Truth, she that in her own hall, in the lower world, is called Two Truths, by whom the dead are judged.—Dost thou know something of the fearful Ma-t, young Theckla?"

"Yea," answered the girl, with a perceptible shudder, "I know her well, and tremble at the dreadful thought of her! So wise! so hard and pitiless! so tearless, and yet so just! The terrible Ma-t, without mercy, incapable of love, unmoved by hate, implacable, emotionless, the fearful judge, the Truth!"

"Then listen to me, child! I worshiped through all

these lonely years as a faithful, conscientious priest, and memorized the book of the dead, and studied the mysteries of medicine, of astronomy, and of mathematics, and sought unceasingly to know the awful Ma-t! Dost thou think that I am one who ought to know whether any of the gods of Kem are true or false?"

Then Theckla fell upon her knees before the ancient priest, and lifting her little hands to him she cried: "Yea, father, thou knowest! Ancient, honorable, learned priest, thou knowest! Teach thou Arius to believe in the three great gods, to seek the awful Ma-t, and to abandon the pernicious Christian faith, for thou art wise! thou knowest all the truth!"

"Listen then, Theckla. Five years ago, driven by the quenchless curiosity of an unsatisfied but earnest soul, I caused to be brought before me one who preached to men of Jesus Christ of Nazareth, because I had heard that these Christians were irreclaimable from the errors of their superstition, and I desired to test the question whether they could be persuaded to return unto the old religion. I kept him with me many days, while we discussed these things, and then sent him from me unconvinced. And afterward I fled from the temple secretly, in an open boat, in which I had placed my most valuable possessions, and floated down the Nile. Thence I wandered along the coast to Alexandria, where, for a great sum, secretly I purchased all the sacred writings of the Jews and Christians, and, after many days more of wandering along the coast, I found this spot and have since then dwelt here alone, still seeking for the truth. For—art thou listening to me, Theckla?—a horror of great darkness had fallen upon my soul. I know that Amen-Ra, Mut, and Kuhns, are not true gods! Apis is nothing but a bull; Anubis is only a jackal; Sebek is a crocodile and nothing more; and even the most ancient gods, if there be any truth in them at all, are only the visible emblems of some higher truth which the very priests have forgotten, if, indeed, they ever knew it. I have hoped and half expected to find that this unknown truth, this 'hidden' thing which is not Hapi, might be that which the Christians promulgate; but this I do not know. Nevertheless, my child, I tell thee that the gods of Kem are no true gods; and I counsel thee to learn of Arius that which he believeth! For falsehood is not profitable; and I realize that all my days have been consumed in learning and in teaching only errors; and it is sad and terrible."

Both of them heard the old man's confession with awe and sympathy, and when, overcome by strong emotion, he had ceased to speak, Theckla gave way to a passionate burst of tears; but, as soon as she could regain her self-control, she turned to the ancient and with strange earnestness exclaimed, "O Father Am-nem-hat, high and honorable priest, hast thou, too, become a Christian?"

"Nay," replied the old man solemnly, "I have only learned the bitter lesson that the gods of Egypt are all false: I have not found a true God yet, if any such there be."

"Thou shalt yet find him," cried Arius, "to the joy and consolation of thy spirit, and thine old age shall be filled with the peace of God that passeth all understanding; for he that seeketh findeth, and to him that knocketh shall it be opened."

Then they were all silent for a time. Then some of the kids came up to the door, and Theckla, oppressed with the sadness and solemnity of the last few minutes, sprang up, crying out: "O the pretty, happy kids! May I go out and play with them?"

And the old man, with a pleasant smile, answered, "Yea, my child, if thou wilt not leave the plateau."

And Theckla bounded out of the house, and was soon engaged in a lively romp with the sportive young goats.

CHAPTER VIII.

WHO IS ΠΑΡΙ?

THE absence of Theckla gave Arius the opportunity he desired to call out from Am-nem-hat a fuller expression of certain theological ideas suggested by the ancient during their first conversation, the remembrance of which had been the subject of frequent meditation ever since; and the boy said: "Since I last saw thee, Father Am-nem-hat, many circumstances have combined to prevent me from giving to the things which I heard from thee that careful consideration which I desired to bestow upon them; yet I have pondered much upon those philosophic views which thou didst utter concerning the dualism of God. I desire to hear more fully thereof; for although I know that Christianity is, for the most part, a practical, experimental thing, concerning the heart and the life of a man rather than a philosophical or theological system, concerning which Jesus himself had naught to say, as if he preferred to leave dogmas and ceremonies to the Scribes and Pharisees, so that it is possible for one to be a genuine and faithful Christian with little knowledge of philosophy or of science, yet it behooves the young especially to seek for information concerning every question that can arise out of the faith."

6

"Thou must understand," said Am-nem-hat, "that I do not assume to be a teacher of thy religion. Being set free from the bondage of Egyptology, and left, as it were, without any religion for the last five years, I have given much time and study to Christianity, reading the Scriptures, of course, by the light of all that I have learned of other systems, and seeking only to discover the truth. There is one thing, which I had long supposed to be true, which recent thought and investigation seem to establish beyond any great room for doubt. That thing is the fact that the old Egyptians believed the human spirit to be of divine origin, engaged throughout earthly life in a warfare between good and evil, and that its final state was determined after death by a solemn judgment rendered according to the deeds done in the body. This warfare continued through all the dynasties alike until during the eighteenth dynasty, the priesthood, fearing that the principle, or god of evil, was about to triumph, got together and obtained a royal decree, ratified by the sacerdotal order, to banish Seth (the evil god) out of Egypt, and out of the religion of Kem; but this action failed to have that salutary influence which had been expected from it. The fact itself was, perhaps, the most singular one in Egyptian history; but our sacred records leave no doubt that the royal and sacerdotal authorities united in a solemn decree for the banishment of Seth, in order to secure the future safety of the human soul. I have just as little doubt that originally they believed in one supreme God, who was conceived of as a dual being, combining in himself both the poles of spir-

itual sex-hood perfectly, and giving birth to a third divinity, by which the triad, that is constantly repeated
under different names, was made complete. Hence I declared to thee that nothing could save the Christian faith
from the imputation of polytheism except the assump-
tion that the God of the Christians, like the original
myth of all primitive faith, hath in himself a double
spiritual sex-hood, of which Christ is the Son, 'begotten,'
not created; 'conceived,' not made; divine, because as
the son of man is human, the Son of God must be divine. If this is not true, then the Christ of these Scriptures, no matter how pure and exalted he may have been,
was either a created being, or else he was only a mere
appearance, a mere *simulacrum* of Deity, a pious fraud,
who merely *seemed* to live among men, and to die for
their justification, but did not do so in reality."

The old man paused at this point, but the boy, keeping steadily in view the matter which had aroused his
own interest in the conversation, said, "But are there
any proofs of the divine dualism and trilogy of which
thou hast so confidently spoken?"

"I think so," said the ancient, "but the original idea
has been overlaid and hidden for countless centuries by the
myths and symbolisms and external ceremonies devised by
ancient priests to express them for the common people,
until the priests themselves perhaps only dimly perceived
the original truth, and regarded the symbolism itself as
true—a most bare and flagrant idolatry. For when, at
some indefinite yet very remote period, religion became
blended with government and the priests sought rather to

control public affairs than to maintain a true worship, the religious idea became so degraded that the sun, which was originally only the symbol of a higher, unseen God, was mistaken for a God itself, and worshiped as such; and this degradation increased with ages, until finally any one who could build a sculptured sarcophagus, and pay for the embalming processes, ritualistic prayers, incantations, charms, and ceremonies, was declared to be in Hesiri justified. According to the inscriptions on the sepulchres, no rich man was damned, and respectability on earth and salvation after death were dependent upon money alone. There was nothing to be done in the way of restraining one's self from evil, nothing to be done in the way of active benevolence. The chief business of an Egyptian's life was to acquire sufficient wealth to build a costly tomb, and the most expensive event in a man's experience was his funeral. Hence the rich were all saved, and the poor were mostly condemned, without regard to personal character and action. Yet all the while the most pious and learned of the priests clearly perceived, even through the mists of error, superstition, and selfishness, which debased the ancient faith, the primitive truth that God was one—a dual being that was to become a triad by the generation of a Son."

"I think," said Arius, "that I comprehend the argument; yet I desire to hear the proofs of this divine dualism more explicitly stated."

"The proofs thereof, derived from the dualism in the original faith of the most ancient races (as the Egyptian, Indian, and Chinese), and from the fact that the monotheist Manes, or Moses, called his one God by a name which is the dual or plural number of a Hebrew noun, have already been suggested to you. But, in the ancient religion of Egypt, this dualism pervaded the whole system everywhere. There was even a dual name for everything—the one common, the other sacred or hieratic. The ancient name of Egypt, 'Kem,' signified both the 'Black-land' and also the 'black man' or people. The local name, Mizraim, was a dual word, signifying both upper and lower Egypt, in which 'To-mehit' was the north-land, and 'To-res,' the south-land, and the sacred name of the river, which the Greeks call the Nile, was 'Hapi'; and the same word was applied to Apis, the bull-god; and in both cases the word was used to denote 'the hidden,' 'the concealed,' the source of the Nile being believed to be undiscoverable, and the being of whom Apis was originally the symbol being yet 'hidden,' 'unrevealed.' No matter where, or by what name, the one supreme, self-existent, self-productive Creator of all things was worshiped, he was originally worshiped as a dual entity, a double god, at once father and mother of a third manifestation that was always a son. Primarily Apis, 'the hidden,' 'the concealed,' simply meant that this third person was yet unrevealed; but just as Ra (the sun), originally the symbol of the one God, became substituted for God himself, afterward Apis becomes the real 'hidden' thing, of which he was primarily only a symbol, and his spiritual form seems to have become Horus. Yet Ra is rarely associated with a female consort; but, when he is so, it is always with a female Ra, and never with an inferior being. But, even after this idolatry be-

came established, the higher priests preserved the original
idea of a dual god, to be made a triad by the generation of
a son ; and everywhere in Egypt, no matter by what local
names their gods were called, this trilogy was affirmed
in every temple.   The very essence of the ancient Egyptology, therefore, is the idea of one dual god, that becomes
a trilogy by the generation of a son.   The same thing is
true of the most ancient form of the Indian and Chinese
polytheisms.   Thou must perceive, therefore, that in the
original faith of all the primitive nations, the divine being
is Father-mother, which is one dual God, and a son.   If,
therefore, the Christian religion presents the idea of a spiritual dualism made a trilogy by the generation of a son,
it maintains the very idea of the Deity, which is the core
of all the primitive religions—Egyptian, Indian, Chinese,
and, I think, Jewish also."

"If thou art not weary," said Arius, "I would desire
much to hear thee declare how these views, which are entirely new to me, agree with thy reading of our sacred
books."

"I will cheerfully state the result of my investigations," said the ancient, "again reminding thee that I read
them only as I have done the sacred books of every other
people known to me, and not as one having any especial
authority to declare the meaning thereof."

"I know perfectly well as to that," said the boy, "but
desire to know what thou hast found therein in reference
to this opinion of thine."

"I have found first, as I have already suggested, that
Moses, who was a monotheist, and a bitter enemy of all

polytheistic ideas, constantly uses the plural number of a Hebrew noun to name the one God in whom he believed. According to the prophetic portions of the Jewish scriptures, I find that the Son of God was to be born of a virgin, and the trilogy was to be manifested to man by the incarnation of this son. Now, in the sacred books of the Christians, the four called Gospels, Christ is always called the Son of God, and Jesus is called Christ. Uniformly that which stands in the same relation to God that was attributed to the earthly manifestation of the divine nature by all original faiths is the Christ; that which in the Christian system occupies the same relation to the divine nature which was borne by the feminine side of the dual God of all the original faiths is called the Holy Ghost. This expression (Holy Ghost) occurs two hundred and twelve times in the New Testament, and in every instance the words are in the Greek neuter gender, which expresses nothing as to sex. The common declaration concerning Christ is that he was 'begotten' of God: a man is begotten of his father; he was 'conceived' of the Holy Ghost: a man is conceived of his mother. My interpretation, therefore, must be that these scriptures teach us that the one God is a divine dualism, a double spiritual Being, the Father-Ghost, and that the Christian trilogy is completed by the generation of a son of this Father-Ghost which is one double God; and that as far as sex-hood can be predicated of a spiritual nature, Christ, the Son, is a spirit begotten and conceived of God his Father-Mother, by whom the worlds were made, and who was afterward manifested in the flesh by assuming human nature. This is what thy

scriptures teach me : I know not whether it be true ;
but it is a glorious statement of that which was the
original faith of all primitive peoples before mankind
lapsed into idolatry ; for every high-priest in Egypt assuredly knoweth that polytheism was not the first faith
of men. "

"But," said Arius, " is not the Holy Ghost called 'he'
in the paragraph from John which readeth—'And I will
pray the Father, and he shall give you another Comforter,
that HE may abide with you forever ; the Spirit of truth ;
whom the world can not receive, because it seeth HIM not,
neither knoweth HIM : but ye know HIM, for HE dwelleth
with you and shall be in you ' ; and in that passage which
readeth as follows : ' But the Comforter, the Holy Ghost,
whom the Father will send in my name, HE shall teach you
all things' : and do not these readings conflict with your
idea that the name of the third person in the Christian
triad expresses nothing as to sex ?"

" I think not so," answered the ancient, "because it is
evident that in these places the only thing that can be
meant by the ' Holy Ghost ' and the ' Spirit of truth ' is
the Paraclete, the Comforter ; and while the Greek word
for comforter is a noun of the masculine gender, the words
' Holy Ghost ' and ' Spirit of truth ' still retain their neuter form, although put in apposition with it ; and the pro-
nouns ' he ' and ' him ' take their masculine form from
the word comforter, and not from the words Holy Ghost
and Spirit, which are always neuter, and express nothing
as to sex. Besides this, I do not find anywhere in the
scriptures any characteristics which are essentially mascu-

line ascribed to the Holy Ghost, and I do find many which are essentially feminine."

"Wilt thou state any other argument, if there be any, that maintaineth this grand idea of a dual God that becometh a triad by the generation of a son ?"

"There is another," said the ancient, "which is conclusive to my mind that the doctrine of thy scriptures is as I have stated it. In Genesis it is written that God said, 'Let *us* make man in our own image'; and, also, it is written, 'Male and female created he them.' It seemeth to me that this 'image' and 'likeness' hath a deeper signification than the mere similitude of man's character to that of God can convey. God is a spirit, according to these scriptures, and no resemblance can be imagined between human beings and him in regard to physical constitution. So far as the characters constituted the 'image and likenes,' the books show that it would include only the first man on one side, and God the Father on the other. But the words are generic : 'us' and 'our' the triad, on one side, and 'man' (that is 'male and female,' the human race) on the other, and I suppose the 'image and likeness' spoken of is one found in the essential nature of man, in his constitution and relations. For as in heaven, so in earth ; in both, the trilogy includes Father, Mother, Son : trinity is family ; and the essential point of the image and likeness between the human and the divine subsists in the fact that human nature necessarily exists as a triad—father, mother, son ; just as the divine nature must do. This seemeth to me to be the only ground from which it is possible to predicate divinity of Jesus Christ without in-

volving the whole Christian system in the mazes of polytheism ; for if he be divine otherwise than in this fact of
generation, there must be more than one God. In strict
accordance with this view, I have observed that in those
nations which are ignorant of this feminine aspect of the
dual god, wives are degraded—are mere chattels, mere
slaves; in others, that (like Egypt) recognize the divine
feminine nature, but hold that she is inferior to the masculine element of this dualism, wives are tolerated, are
not shut up in seclusion, are not mere slaves and chattels ; while among the Christians alone who hold the
absolute equality of Father and Spirit, womanhood is
glorified and made honorable ; and Jesus himself elevated marriage almost, if not altogether, into a religious
sacrament."

"The views you present seem very like the truth," said
the boy, musingly, "and they are certainly grand enough
to be true. But they are entirely new to me, and I shall
not fail to give them such study and meditation as my
sense of the magnitude of the subject involved may demand. I have never heard any discussion upon the nature
of the relation of the three persons of our Christian trilogy."

"I think," said the ancient, "thou wilt find that it is
a mere mistake to suppose that there are three, for the sacred books teach me that there are only two, the Father-
Ghost, or double God, but one only ; and the Son of this
one God. The perfectest flowers in nature are hermaphro-
dites."

"But wilt thou inform me whether any perfect, self-producing creature, possessed of animal life, hath ever been discovered ?"

"Never," answered the ancient. "The partial realization of such a condition, the rare approximations thereto, which have been curiously noted by Egyptian priests for centuries and myriads of years, have been universally regarded as a deformity, and not as a perfection. Yet the priesthood say that the fact was perfectly realized, according to Moses, in the case of the first man; for the first woman was not created as the man was, but proceeded out of him; and the account given by Moses afterward means just that. I could say many things upon this matter indeed, but for the fact that the oath of secrecy, taken at every step of his progress in the sacerdotal life by every Egyptian priest, was vast and solemn; intended to cover his whole future life, and secure his silence under every possible mutation of his own fortune. The sphinxes, with wide-open eyes and sealed lips, and faces that are inscrutable and calm, revealing nothing that might show a trace of any passion, emotion, thought, or purpose, and yet full of intelligence and power, are the perfect symbol of the Egyptian priesthood; and I know not just how far these obligations are binding upon me."

"I will not question thee," said Arius, "but will endeavor to profit by whatever thou mayst be at liberty to declare."

"Thou mayst some day find use for the fact that was well known to the priesthood, who were the repository of all knowledge in the land of Kem, that in the embryonic or fœtal life, both in animals and in man, there is abso-

lutely no distinction of sex. Up to a short period prior to
its birth, it is impossible to determine whether the offspring will be male or female—from which fact it seems
to follow that sex is not a primary or essential function of
animal existence, but dependent upon conditions during
gestation which centuries of investigation have failed to
disclose.   Dost thou remember how bitterly the sacred
books of the Israelites, from Moses down, denounce Baal,
and Ashtaroth, and the star-god Remphan, and all the secret rites of the national religions of all other people except their own, the Egyptians included ? Hast thou observed that many of the ceremonies which other nations
practiced as part of religion are denounced by Moses as
crimes punishable with death ? Hast thou observed that
throughout the Jewish scriptures, and especially throughout the Pentateuch, there are bitter and vindictive laws
and customs devised for the express purpose of segregating
the Israelites from all other peoples, for building up, as it
were, a wall of partition between them and all other nations—and this, notwithstanding the fact that it would
have been natural and right for Moses and his people, if
they believed themselves to be in possession of the truth,
to seek to impart that truth to others, and so procure the
universal acceptance thereof ? Hast thou marked the fact
that the missionary spirit, which was the glory of every
other religion, so as to create continual wars undertaken
for the sole purpose of forcing other peoples to adopt the
religion of the conqueror, was constantly repressed by the
Jewish laws and branded as a crime ? And hast thou
ever reflected upon the real signification of these facts ? ”

"Yea," answered Arius, "and I have been taught that
God, by Moses, so commanded the Jews in order to preserve the peculiar people from being seduced into following after strange gods, and adopting the idolatries which
were everywhere believed in.   For the idolatries thou hast
named, and every false religion which had for its symbol
a moon, a cow, a cock, or any symbol intended to indicate
the fecundity of Nature, was only the worship of that very
mystery of sex of which thou hast spoken such strange
things, the deification of lasciviousness, the apotheosis of
sensualism."

"They finally became so, indeed," said Am-nem-hat,
sadly, "when the original truth became thoroughly corrupted ; but it was not so in the beginning.   For if thou
wilt keep in mind the fact that the original faith of every
primitive nation held the true God to be a dualism that
was to become a triad by the generation of a Son ; if thou
wilt remember that this Son was also held to be Hapi, 'the
hidden,' 'the concealed,' 'the unrevealed,' even as unto
this day the high-priest of every temple in Egypt will declare unto thee ; and, considering these things, thou wilt
not surely say that the grand roll of Egyptian priests,
stretching back for more than thirty centuries of recorded
history from this age of ours, were all mere sensualists.
On the contrary, thou wilt see in these singular rites and
ceremonies, even in their present degraded form, the signs
and symbols of a deathless longing in the hearts of that
grand, pure, holy race of sacred priests, and of a search
prosecuted over land and sea, through heaven, and earth,
and hell, during all the fruitless and slow-gliding centu-

ries, by every art, science, and resource known to men—a
longing and a search after Hapi, 'the hidden one,' 'the
concealed Son,' 'the unrevealed Saviour,' for whom the
whole creation groaneth—a sublime spectacle, sad and grand
enough to move a god to pity! For while the crowd see
only a splendid pageant in that annual festival in which,
with torches and with magnificent display, the priests and
the whole population at Memphis wander over the city,
the river, and the lake, seeking in earth, and fire, and
water, for the dismembered body of the dual god, thou
wilt find among them aged, pure, sad, learned men, who
see in the same grand spectacle the perpetual memorial of
their world-old search for Hapi, 'the concealed'; and, if
thou couldst gaze into their shut, silent, sorrowful hearts,
thou wouldst see all the faculties of soul and spirit exhal-
ing in a yearning prayer that he might come! and at the
gate of every temple thou wouldst find the priestly symbol, the Sphinx, the sleepless watcher, cut out of imperish-
able stone, 'gazing right on with calm, eternal eyes,' till
Hapi come!—for such is the true signification of Hesiri-
Hes, whom the Greeks call Osiris-Isis! And even in the
later and more degraded worship of the bull-god Apis,
while the common crowd see only the apotheosis of sensualism, as thou hast called it, in the fact that, when a new
Apis is discovered, devout women at Memphis, during
forty days, expose themselves stripped naked to the gaze
of the sacred brute, the sad-faced priests realize that the
endless and unavailing search to discover Hapi, 'the concealed,' had sometimes been prosecuted by unlawful means,
against which Moses, in the Jewish scriptures, denounced

the penalty of death.   And the period of forty days was purposely chosen in order to cover by a few days, in both directions, a lunation of the moon ; for the worship of the moon-god universally connected the lunations of that planet with the sexhood of women.   But thou wouldst greatly err if thou shouldst believe that in its original, undegraded form, this worship was sensualism ; for it began with some new effort to wring out of the mystery of sex the secret of Hapi, 'the concealed'; and was glorified by the fact that it was part and parcel of the weary, world-old search after him !   Oh, will he ever come ?"

Then the boy sprang to his feet, to the very tips of his toes, his right hand vibrating, his head erected and bent forward, his dark eyes gleaming with mesmeric light, his whole form and face glowing with passionate and quivering emotion, and he cried aloud : "Thou art pious and aged and learned !   Thou teachest me much !   But I will also teach thee something !   As surely as thou livest, Hapi, the Hidden, whom thou callest the desire of all nations, hath already come in the flesh, and his name is Jesus Christ."

"Perhaps so, perhaps so," said the ancient, mournfully.   "But the priests of Kem, during the past three thousand years, often imagined that they had found him, and as often met with bitter disappointment.   The Sphinx still watches with unwinking gaze for the solution of the mighty problem, and the old are difficult to convince."

But at that moment Theckla burst in upon them, flushed and weary with her romping with the goats, crying out, "O sacred Hapi, I am so hungry and so tired !"

Then the old man spread out a linen cloth upon the table, and, at his desire, Arius and Theckla placed thereon the table-ware and the dainties taken from the basket which the boy had brought, while he took from a little spring nigh his hermitage a jar of cool, refreshing goat's milk; and they three did feast right joyously.

CHAPTER IX.

THE DEMOCRACY OF FAITH.

It was indeed a singular thing to hear, the usual conversation of those young people about religious questions upon which the greatest minds of subsequent ages have spent their force without exhausting them; but it should be remembered that everything like exact science was then in its infancy: all that was actually known of medicine, chemistry, geology, geometry, geography, botany, and even of mathematics, could be very quickly learned; and around this narrow limit of ascertained truth spread a boundless wilderness of vagrant speculation, in which the seeker after learning might wander a whole lifetime without ever being able to add one single valuable fact to the stock of knowledge; so that religion, whether Christianity or paganism, was universally regarded as the one thing that might most profitably be learned and known; and education, even from infancy, consisted in acquiring the knowledge of it: and this education was among the heathen chiefly objective, handling the visible, tangible symbols of a superstition which possessed only the most meager elements of subjective truth and power, except, perhaps, for the higher priests who had been

7

initiated into mysteries unknown to the common people; while among the Christians the process was almost reversed. Christianity had no objective life, except in the person of Jesus Christ; and the subjective power which it possessed upon both intellect and consciousness had no assignable limits, inasmuch as it seemed to make the martyrs almost insensible to physical pain, and yet could produce a moral sensitiveness so acute that to be conscious of willful deception might work the death of the body, as in the case of Ananias and Sapphira when they lied to Peter about the consecration of their property to holy uses. This education among the Egyptians, especially among females of the higher classes, was chiefly oral, but among the Christians the young were taught both orally and by the written text.

One of the strangest and yet most logical results of the Christian teachings and practice (and one which has been, for very sufficient reasons, ignored by the theologians) was to develop a radical and uncompromising spirit of democracy throughout the Christian communities or churches. The early Christians uniformly held that they, as Christians, belonged to a kingdom which was in, but not of, the world—a kingdom for which no earthly potentate had right or power to legislate; and this living faith loosened the bond of allegiance and dissolved the sense of obligation as to all human authority, and was the negation of the lawfulness of temporal government over the subjects of the kingdom for which they recognized no king but Christ. While, for the sake of peace, they were willing to render unto Cæsar the things which are Cæsar's, by paying taxes to that government under which they lived, and by even yielding ready obedience to all laws and customs which did not come in conflict with the higher law of the kingdom, the rights of conscience, they universally regarded these laws as extraneous to their own organization, foreign statutes, imposed upon them from without; and, being solicitous to render unto God the things which are God's, they steadily abstained from any participation in the affairs of government, and quietly assumed the right to judge for themselves whether any law, regulation, or custom, prescribed by the sovereign power, or other human authority, was or was not such as they might conscientiously obey. And, while they would no more have thought of holding office under pagan rulers or of participating in their legislation and government than they would have thought of accepting the priesthood of a heathen temple and participating in its idolatrous worship, they obeyed all laws alike, except such as conflicted with conscience, and these they refused to obey in the very face of persecutions, torture, and death. But this fearless assertion of the rights of conscience necessarily involved the right to sit in judgment upon all human laws and the powers that ordained them, and to determine for themselves whether the law was lawful. That helpless spirit of blind obedience to the decrees of despotic governments which characterized the pagan peoples was, therefore, impossible to the Christians. In the very teeth of universally established law and custom, they steadily refused to bear arms, to own slaves, to seek any legal redress in civil courts, to follow

the law of their domicile in regard to the ownership of
property or the succession to estates of the deceased, just
as they refused to sacrifice to the gods, or to call any
man master. Under the same lofty conception of the
rights of conscience, in lands where women were bought
and sold like cattle, they refused to practice polygamy;
and in lands where female chastity was unknown and
plural wives and concubines were esteemed to be the in-
signia of honor and influence, they clave fast to that
monogamic marriage which Jesus had elevated into a holy
sacrament; and while throughout the world women were
regarded as slaves, as domestic chattels, or, at the very
best, as an inferior race and a necessary evil, so that the
birth of a female child was looked upon as a household
calamity, the Christian faith that the Holy Ghost conceived Christ before he was born of a virgin and manifested in the flesh, glorified and exalted the dignity of
womanhood and maternity, and created the idea of personal responsibility, rights, and duties for both sexes
alike. The logical tendency of Christianity was, therefore, to originate the idea of personal liberty for all men,
unknown to the world before; to repudiate the heathen
doctrine of the divine character and right of kings; to sit
in judgment upon their laws, and to intelligently obey, or
refuse to obey, them; in a word, to cultivate and exercise, as a matter of religious faith, that spirit of personal
independence, both of action and of thought, which we
in later times denominate democracy, the concrete form
of which was the election of deacons, presbyters, and
bishops by the people unto whom they ministered.

But this habit of independent thought did not tend as in later times in the direction of ecclesiastical schisms; because, if any one embraced a doctrinal error, either it was maintained by him as an individual opinion; or if a mistaken zeal led him to proclaim it publicly, and seek thereby to bind the consciences of other Christians, the matter soon came to the knowledge of the churches, and, when the Church assembled to consider the alleged error, the Holy Paraclete directed the counsels of the assembled bishops and presbyters, so that their deliverances were infallibly correct, and were universally accepted as final. So that, during the first three centuries, no heresy could survive the condemnation of a Christian council, and no learning, zeal, and genius could give to heresy such vitality and power as to seriously threaten the peace of the Church. Even Peter could not force the observance of the rite of circumcision upon the free Christian communities; and the heresies of Menander, Cerinthus, Nicolaus, Valentinius, Marcion, Tatianus, Blastus, Montanus, Artimon, and others, perished almost as soon as they had been condemned.

It was perfectly natural, therefore, that while both Arius and Theckla were almost children in many respects, they should both be far advanced in religious learning, each of them in harmony with one of the separate systems under which they had been reared; and that they should be, in many attitudes of thought and feeling, a pleasing enigma to each other. The girl, although brimful of bright and pleasing fancies, had all her life been accustomed to accept as truth whatever was taught to her as

such, and the very basis of her training had been implicit
and unquestioning obedience to authority without reason,
so that she had never, perhaps, attempted to exercise an
independent thought, judgment, or inquiry about any
question of religious, political, or social life, her existence
having been passed in strict and unconscious conformity
to rigid Egyptian customs, into the molds and forms of
which she had been fashioned from her infancy.   The
illness of her mother, which left her to the freedom of
thought, expression, and action, characteristic of every
Christian household, was a new and intoxicating experience
to the girl ; and, whatever else it might be possible for her
to become, it was manifestly impossible that she could ever
again resiliate into the moral and social mummyism of
ordinary Egyptian female life.   The bondage of Egypt
was broken.

But the boy, fixed and immovable in his faith in the
few salient and all-important doctrines covered by the
Apostles' Creed, as that creed was taught during the first
three centuries, as to everything else, had been freed by
his training from the shackles of authority, and so unconsciously enjoyed and exercised "the liberty of the
gospel" in which he had been reared by questioning, in-
vestigating, trying every phenomenon—social, religious,
and political—that came within the range of his observation and experience.

Am-nem-hat imagined that in these two youthful but
well-instructed young people he beheld the living incarnation of the opposing civilizations under which they had
been reared ; and it was a pathetic and beautiful thing

to see with what eager intentness he noted almost every inflection of their voices, every expression of their countenances, almost every peculiar turn and change of their thoughts, while he encouraged them to talk, hardly caring what might be the subject of their conversation.

At the beginning of their little feast the ancient said: "Arius, if ye Christians have any custom of thank-offering, prayer, or libations, before ye partake of food, I would desire to have thee perform or repeat it now."

Then answered Arius: "We make no libation or offering, nor are we restricted to any set formula for returning thanks to God; but generally we repeat the Πατὲρ ἡμῶν."

"Wilt thou do so now?"

Then the boy said, "Yea, gladly"; and, while they watched him narrowly, he solemnly said: "Our Father, which art in heaven, hallowed be thy name: thy kingdom come: thy will be done on earth as in heaven. Give us daily our daily bread; and forgive us our debts as we forgive debtors: and let us not be led into trial, but deliver us from trouble: for thine is the kingdom, and the power, and the truth, forever."

Then said Am-nem-hat, "Theckla, what form of worship hast thou been taught to observe before partaking of thy daily food?"

And the girl said: "On solemn occasions, our fathers make libations; but it is not according to Egyptian customs, or religion, for a female to meddle with any sacred rite, beyond her own private devotions, as thou, O priest, must assuredly know."

"Dost thou know the reason, Theckla, that woman is

thus excluded, not only from participation in the sacred rites, but from every place that is inconsistent with the idea that she must of necessity be either a slave or a domestic pet, having right to existence only as the appanage of a man upon whom she is dependent as slave, wife, or daughter?"

"Nay," she answered; "but I have been so taught, and, therefore, it must be right and proper."

"I will tell thee, Theckla, for it is verily a thing which every female ought to know. The reason of it is that the original idea of God was that of a dual being, equally divine and glorious in both aspects of his double nature. But nearly all nations, as they sank deeper and deeper into idolatry, degraded the feminine conception of this dualism, and some of them utterly lost it. In Egypt they have held Hes to be consort of Hesiri, and, although inferior to him, yet entitled to great honor. Hence the Egyptian women have never been shut up, kept in seclusion and ignorance, and esteemed only as slaves or as chattels, as is universally the case among nations that have entirely fallen away from the divine truth. But I tell thee, Theckla, that the religion of the Christians alone maintains the absolute equality of the Godhead, by maintaining the Holy Ghost, the Mother of Nature, to be consubstantial with the Father, and hence it alone elevates woman to her true position, and endows her with responsibility, respect and honor, rights and duties; so that, although all men on earth should reject and curse the Christ, every woman, who is true to herself and to her sex, should cleave unto him in spite of pain and even death itself. Do thou remember these things, Theckla; and, when thou shalt see with what respect, honor, and love the Christian husband treateth his wife and daughters, remember thou that the vast difference between them and other men, in that regard, ariseth not out of any difference in the nature or disposition of the individuals, but out of the difference in their religion only; for that faith regardeth women as persons, not as things. Forget not these truths, Theckla! for, whether it be true or false, Christianity alone hath ever done justice to womanhood, wifehood, maternity; and the woman who does not love and follow Jesus betrayeth herself and her sex."

"Surely thou, also, art a Christian!" said the young girl.

"Nay," answered Am-nem-hat; "I say not that to thee! For I can not understand what it is to be a Christian. But, having carefully studied this religion as I have done all others known among mankind, I do solemnly assure thee that it is the only one on earth that is fair and just to chaste and intelligent women. For it teacheth that the equal, consubstantial Holy Spirit conceived a Saviour that was virgin-born; and it so serveth to redeem all womanhood from centuries of contempt and degradation; for no man who hath an intelligent faith in Christianity can ever regard woman as the mere instrument of his pleasure, or as the mere slave of his will, but as a friend, helpmate, and companion, worthy of love, honor, and respect; so that, whether it be true or false, every woman should cleave thereto, because it is for her, at least, temporal salvation. For Christianity differeth as radically

from all other religions in regard to the esteem in which
it holdeth women as it does in regard to slavery and
to the poor. And while the rich and the great may hate
this system because it would deprive them of the social
and political precedence which every other religion maintaineth for them, the slaves, the poor, and the women
should never forget that Jesus Christ is the truest friend
they ever had on earth."

Then said Arius, "Father Am-nem-hat, why art not
thou a Christian, having views of our religion that are so
wise and just?"

And the old man answered: "That thing, my son, I
can not tell thee, nor can I comprehend it for myself. I
can not understand what is the precise attitude of mine
own spirit toward Christianity. Canst thou instruct me?"

"Nay, verily," said Arius. "In my heart I yearn for
the power to say something that might open thine eyes
unto the light; but my small knowledge and experience
serve not to enable me to understand how it is possible
that one so aged and so wise, so well instructed in our
Lord's own teachings, can fail to be a Christian. But
my father was an idolater in his youth, and he is learned
in our religion. If thou wilt go home with us, thou shalt
be received with honor and affection, and he, perhaps, can
give thee aid. Wilt thou not go?"

"I thank thee much," said Am-nem-hat. "But the
way is long, and the mountain steep, for one so old as I.
And besides, it seemeth to me that, if human knowledge
and patient thought could extort any final truth out of the
mute lips of Nature, even I could have made her speak!"

"But," said the boy, "the tree of knowledge is not that of life. Even the most ignorant and depraved find peace in believing, and I have met with none so wise as thou. If thou wilt come to us, I will bring hither on to-morrow a she-ass, gentle and sure of foot, which my mother is accustomed to ride, and will walk beside thee to our home, if only thou wilt come."

"Yea," cried Theckla, "thou must surely come ! For I will tell my mother that I have met the high-priest of Ombos, and she will long much to see thee."

Then Am-nem-hat, as if overpowered by their persuasions, replied : "Ye are both so kind to an old and lonely man that I can not resist your entreaties, and will even do as ye desire; for ye know not what pleasure the old may derive from the polite and hearty attentions of the young."

Then the two young people bade the old man a kind farewell, and, with the light heart of youth and health, took their way homeward down the mountain. And when they had come to the edge of the pasture-land they met with some of the cattle, and among them was the young bull-calf whose peculiar markings had so excited the wonder and superstition of Theckla; and Arius cried out laughingly: "Lo, Theckla! there is thy god, and thou shalt ride home upon the back of the beast."

And he cut a long withe and fastened it upon the horns of the bull, and led up the gentle beast, and, seizing the young girl in his arms, he lifted her astride of the fat, round calf, and led him along. And, when Arius mocked and ridiculed the young Apis, the girl joined in his merriment, and he was glad to see that she was fast losing all superstitious reverence for the brute, and for all the other pagan deities; for her growing contempt for Apis necessarily struck at her reverence for the whole system, of which a bull with a black hide, a triangular white spot on his forehead, a spread-eagle in the hairs of his back, a crescent white spot upon his side, and a knob like a scarabæus under his tongue, was so important a part.

When they had reached that part of the pasture which was nearest to the house, Theckla sprang from the animal's back, and, with some lingering doubt of his divinity still troubling her mind, she said: "Arius, I really wonder whether the Apis hath a knob under his tongue in the shape of a scarabæus? Wilt thou not look into his mouth?"

"I know not that," said the boy; "but, if he hath not a rather odd-looking spot under his tongue, he is the only bull-calf I ever saw that hath it not; and I suppose it would be easy to irritate and inflame this spot until it would look like a natural knob about as large as a good, lively beetle."

"I had never thought it might be possible for the priests to so deceive any one," said Theckla.

"Perhaps they did not do so," answered the boy; "but they may have been deceived by the cunning of those who had such beasts and desired to sell them."

Theckla sighed, but her reverence for Apis and for all of his mysteries was utterly gone forever.

CHAPTER X.

FAITH AND PHILOSOPHY.

DURING the time that Arius and Theckla had been absent at the hermitage of Am-nem-hat, a great change had occurred in the condition of the Egyptian lady, Hatasa, at the Baucalis cottage. Early in the morning she had fallen into a profound slumber, but before noon she had awakened suddenly, and in a moment afterward the whole house was filled with her bitter wailing. All at once the terrible sense of loss had overwhelmed her mind with impassioned force, and in heart-broken tones she repeated the name of her husband over and over again, and momently called aloud for "Theckla, darling Theckla! Where is my daughter, my only child?"

Then with great tenderness Arete told her that Theckla was well and happy, and would soon return with her own son, with whom she had gone to visit a near neighbor. The poor woman's grief seemed hopeless and unendurable. At one moment she would yearningly lament the loss of her husband, and at the next reproach the gods of Egypt with his destruction, and then, perhaps, pray to them in tones of hopeless supplication. "O Ra and Thoth!" she cried, "ye murderous, heartless gods, that have so cruelly bereft me, have pity upon Amosis, whom ye have snatched away to the under-world! O merciless and fearful Ma-t, that hast never had compassion upon any mortal, thou terrible Two Truths in thy dark halls sitting, unmoved by sorrow or pain, in the gloom of mournful Amenti, soften once thy stony heart, that thou mayst feel the sharpness of our earthly woe, so that thou judge not mine Amosis until I have builded his sarcophagus. O thou Hesiri-Hes! that cometh nearer to our human life than other dreadful deities, restore my husband's body to the land, that with due honors and uncounted cost I yet may have his mummy-rites prepared to smooth his pathway through the under-world!" Then, seeming to realize the uselessness of any prayer in the absence of the ceremonies of a funeral, she moaned in hopeless grief: "O terrible! to be cut off in youth, with no sarcophagus builded, and no mummy-cloth—cast off alone and friendless, into the darkness of Amenti! O fearful fate! to be called up for judgment, like a pauper, before the merciless, unsparing Ma-t!"

And so she would cry, as loudly as her feebleness permitted, until exhausted nature enforced silence upon her wailing lips.

"She calleth upon the ancient, fearful gods of Kem," said old Thopt, in a half-terrified whisper to Arete.

"She is without God and without hope in the world," whispered Arete. "May the compassionate Lord pity her and bring unto her the consolations of his grace!"

"My heart weeps for her," whispered old Thopt; "for the Egyptians are not as the Christians are. They have a shuddering horror of death, and it is to them the sum of all possible wretchedness."

And so the weary hours passed slowly, and, at last, came Theckla and Arius home; and the girl, bounding into her mother's room, cast her arms about her and kissed her passionately. And when the mother broke out into renewed wailings, the daughter said: "Nay, mother, why dost thou lament so bitterly? Surely thou art much better now, and father will soon return to comfort thee. Cheer up thyself with the hope of speedily returning health and strength."

"Alas! alas! thy father will return no more!—no more! Ah, nevermore!"

Then with startled, wondering eyes, the young girl gazed into her mother's face, crying out: "What meanest thou? He hath always come back from every absence joyously; why sayst thou 'No more—ah, nevermore,' so sorrowfully? Surely he must again return to us!"

Then it seemed apparent enough that these Egyptians had such an awful terror of death, and the girl had been so carefully guarded against all knowledge thereof, that she could scarcely realize what thing was meant thereby; for the Egyptians said nothing of "death," but only, "He hath gone hence," or "He is the Hesiri justified."

"He is dead, poor child!" moaned the mother, "swallowed up forever by the cruel, unrelenting sea! Thou wilt see his face, and hear his voice, and spring to meet his fond caress no more," she wailed—"no more!"

"Is he, then, the Hesiri justified?" she asked, a nameless wonder and terror taking hold upon her soul.

"Oh, thou wilt break all my heart!" she answered. "He hath died without a sarcophagus and the mummy-cloth. How shall he, then, dare to meet the dreadful Ma-t in the dark hall wherein she sitteth as the Two Truths, judge of all the dead?"

Then the full desolation of her father's awful fate, and of her own mighty loss, for the first time swept her young heart with terrible distinctness, and, sinking down beside her mother, the girl blended her broken-hearted wailings with the woman's bitter cries.

"Leave them together," said Arete, and she and old Thopt quietly withdrew. And she informed Ammonius of the sorrowful condition of their guests, and, with her dark eyes full of sympathetic tears, she said, "It is a harrowing grief, and I was so young when I became a Christian, and view death so differently from them, that I know not how to offer consolation for such sorrow."

"Thou shalt leave them alone for the present," answered Ammonius. "The Egyptians have no consolation except those which their erroneous faith buildeth upon the sarcophagus and the mummy-rites — all external consolations — of which, in such a case as this, they are deprived. Let them alone. Perhaps the Lord will show us some way to aid them, or their violent grief will wear out itself in lamentations. All thou canst do is but to wait and hope."

The long night passed wearily away. Arete and old Thopt divided the watches thereof between them, as

they had done ever since Hatasa came to Baucalis, to
see that she wanted no attention which kindness could
supply; but neither of them knew how to utter sooth-
ing words unto a grief that seemed so hopeless; for the
religion of Egypt contained no word of comfort for such
grief, and the beautiful idolaters were ignorant of that
of Jesus. All that mother and daughter knew of religious faith kept forcing back upon their broken hearts
the dreadful conviction that the soul's condition after
death depended upon the building of a sarcophagus and
the preparation of the mummy, in accordance with the
rites prescribed in "The Book of the Dead"; and in
such a case as this no mummy-rites could be paid unless the corpse could be recovered; and, although the
sarcophagus might be builded, they did not know but
that the father and husband whom they loved might be
judged by the awful goddess Ma-t before this work could
be completed; and none of the exceptions made by their
religion in favor of those who fell in battle for the
rulers of Egypt, or who perished by shipwreck, applied
to the case of Amosis, for he had lost his life in a private quarrel after the shipwreck had happened. Their
hopeless sorrow was pitiful, indeed; but the young girl
fell back upon a final truth when she kept repeating to
her mother, over and over again, her own convictions in
such words as these: "Thou knowest that he was a good
and upright man, doing only what he did believe to be
right and just, and surely the greatest God of all, by
whatever name he may be known, will be most merciful
to him without a sarcophagus or the mummy-rites."

8

And so the young idolater, not knowing the law, but doing by nature the things which are written in the law, became a law unto herself, and the unknown God, whom she did ignorantly worship to that extent which was commensurate with her faith, revealed himself unto her; and even from this unreasoning hope they both drew something of comfort. And during the night Theckla informed her mother of her visit to the old eremite Am-nem-hat, and of his having been priest at Thebes and high-priest at Ombos; and how ancient, wise, and good he seemed to be; and that he had promised to come to the cottage on the following day, and expressed the hope that out of his vast stores of wisdom he might be able to bring forth some truth that would yield them surer consolation; and this also somewhat comforted that bitterly smitten pair.

And early the next morning Arius went to the abode of Am-nem-hat, leading the she-ass on which his mother was accustomed to ride, and, having got the ancient comfortably seated upon the jennet, he led her down the mountain and unto the cottage of Baucalis safely, where all were awaiting the arrival of the priest to whose visit Hatasa looked forward with vague but earnest hope. And, when the old man had come, Ammonius, with great respect and tenderness, assisted him to dismount, and led him unto the house. And, having most kindly received him, they told him of the sorrowful woman, and how anxiously she had anticipated his coming, and he said, "Let me go unto her at once."

And, when he had entered her chamber, he stood in the

middle of the floor, and, with his raised and extended arms crossed at the wrists in likeness of a cross (for the cross is ages older than Jesus), he looked upon Hatasa, saying: "Whatever God is greater than Ra, whatever God is wiser than Ptah, and whatever God is more merciful than Hesiri-Hes, and more just than Ma-t, by whatsoever name the great God of all ought to be known among men, I invoke him to bless and comfort thee, O daughter of affliction. May that truest and highest God lift up the light of his face upon thee and give thee peace!"

Then, sitting down beside her couch, he took her hand in his, saying kindly, "Daughter, what is thy name?"

"Hatasa," answered she.

"Art thou of Alexandria?"

"Yea," she said. "But my family were of Thebes, where lived and died my father Ahmad, and my grandfather, Butau, and many generations more."

"Butau, of Thebes!" said the old man. "Hast thou, then, never heard of Am-nem-hat, priest at Thebes, high-priest at Ombos?"

"Surely so," she answered. "For the same wise and holy priest was the brother of my grandfather Butau, the great general, and I have often heard my parents speak of the sacred priest with reverence and pride."

"I am that Am-nem-hat, and thou hast found a kinsman in whom thou mayst implicitly confide."

Then seized she his hand, and, kissing it, she cried, "I do rejoice thereat, and welcome thee as kinsman, and as sacred priest most pious and most wise."

Then she poured out to him the burden of her heart,

and asked him if there was any hope, her husband having builded no sarcophagus, and having had no mummy-rites. And the old man answered mournfully, "Daughter, as an Alexandrian, thou shouldst know the vast temple of Serapis which standeth before the magnificent street, two hundred feet wide, in Rhacotis, the western and Egyptian quarter of the city—the grand and beautiful temple which containeth the statue of the god that was brought thither out of Pontus?"

"Yea, father," answered she, "from childhood I have known the holy temple well."

"And didst thou also know the wise and pious Raphnath, high-priest of that temple, who died there some fifteen years ago?"

"Yea, verily, I remember him quite well."

"He and I were boys, at Thebes, in the great temple together. All his lifetime we were friends. When he felt that his physical powers were failing, and that the end of his long and holy life was fast approaching, he sent unto me to come to him and spend his last days with him; and so it happened that I was at Alexandria when the ancient high-priest died. We did talk much and often of our long religious lives; much, of our learned ignorance; much, of the destiny of the human soul; much, of the truth. When I did ask of him whether he had any special request to make concerning his own funeral rites, he answered me in some such words as these: 'Nay, my brother. Let the obsequies be simply conducted, but in accordance with the rites and ceremonies prescribed for a priest's funeral by 'The Book of the Dead.' For although both thou and I be well aware that the sarcophagus is naught, and the mummy naught, and that no rites nor ceremonies which men can devise in any way concern the soul after death, yet, because the law and order system of Kem hath been for so many centuries built up on these vain things, I desire that the usual forms be all observed at mine own funeral. Although surely no high-priest of Egypt ought to think that it can make any difference to the soul how, or when, or by what means, a man may depart this life, or whether any funeral rites are paid or not; for thou knowest that the true purpose of religion is to control the living, and that the dead are far beyond the reach of human agencies.'

"'On what, then, dependeth thy soul's condition in the other world?' I said.

"'Surely,' he said, 'upon nothing that any priest can do or leave undone, but upon whether the man hath done his duties well according to the best of his faith and knowledge.'

"And afterward, and almost in the hour of his dissolution, I said unto him again, 'Brother, how farest thou?' And he answered me, saying: 'The light of life within me burneth low and flickereth. It will soon go out. But I fare well and peacefully.'

"'And thou hast no fear of awful Ma-t, my brother, and of the silent hall wherein the Two Truths judge the dead?'

"And smilingly he answered me: 'Nay, Brother Am-nem-hat. No man attaineth to the high-priesthood in Egypt without having learned that the things of which thou speakest are for the people—not for the higher priests—part of the system which we administer, not final truths for us. For I know, as thou also knowest, that above and beyond the grand Egyptian triads, there must be some supreme God over all whom we ignorantly worship; who is patient because he is eternal, and merciful because he is all-wise; and having all these years discharged, as faithfully as human frailties might permit, every duty that came under my hand, I look away above the gods of Kem, and trust myself unshrinkingly in the hands of the unknown God, in whom we both believe.' And, almost in the same moment, the old man quietly departed.—Daughter, for thee and for thy great sorrow there is no consolation in the religion of Egypt. All of the consolation I can offer is to tell thee plainly that the things which the high-priest Raph-nath declared unto me upon his bed of death are true; and, as the sum of all my learning and priestly life, I say unto thee that thou canst do nothing else for thyself, nor for thy husband, nor for any human soul, except to cast thyself and him upon the mercy of the unknown God, hoping and believing that all is for the best."

The old man's voice was tremulous, and his grand, pure face was full of compassion as he uttered these words in tones of inexpressible and uncomplaining sadness, and with impressive earnestness.

"And this is all?" she cried—" all that the old religion of Kem, stripped of its outward, ornate forms and ceremonies, has to offer to the broken-hearted?"

"Yea," answered Am-nem-hat. "This is all, indeed. And it is little; and the prevailing sadness of all wise

men grows out of this ; yet the heart that loves and trusts
may find that even this is enough to reconcile it to the
grand and pitiless course of nature. So saith the philosopher Seneca : 'We shall adore all that ignoble crowd of
gods which ancient superstition hath gathered together in
a long course of years, only so as to remember that their
worship is rather in accordance with custom than with
reality or truth.' And again he saith, 'The God is near
you, is with you, is within you' ; and again, 'There is no
good man without God.'

"And Epictetus also saith : 'If you remember always
that, in all you do in soul or body, God stands by as a witness, in all your prayers and your actions you will not err,
and you shall have God dwelling within you.' And he
saith : 'Great is the struggle, divine the need ; it is for
kingdom, for freedom, for tranquillity, for peace. Think
on God ; call upon him, thy champion and aid, as sailors
invoke the great twin brothers in the storm. And, indeed,
what storm is greater than that which ariseth out of powerful semblances (appearances of evil), that drive reason out
of its course ? What, indeed, but semblance is a storm itself ? Come, now, therefore, remove this fear of death, and
bring as many thunders and lightnings as thou wilt, and
thou shalt soon perceive how great tranquillity and calm are
in that reason which is the ruling faculty of the soul.' And
he saith further : 'Thou must be absolutely resigned to
the will of God. Thou must conquer every passion, abrogate every desire.' And one greater, sadder, diviner than
them all, even Marcus Aurelius, the Stoic Emperor, declareth : 'Surely life and death, honor and dishonor, pain

and pleasure, all things happen equally to bad men and good, being things that make us neither better nor worse, therefore are they neither good nor evil.' And he saith of every man: 'Thou hast embarked, thou hast made the voyage; thou hast come to shore; get out. If, indeed, unto another life, there is even there no want of gods; but if unto a state devoid of sensation, thou wilt cease to be held of pains and pleasures.' And he saith: 'Then pass thou through the short space of time conformably to Nature, and end the journey in content, just as the olive falls off when it is ripe, blessing Nature that produced it, and thanking the tree on which it grew; . . . accepting all that happens, and all that is allotted, and finally waiting for death with a cheerful mind.' And so I say unto thee: No man can do more for thee, for thy husband, or for any human soul, than to fall back upon the mercy of an unknown God, and seek for peace in the grand hope that all is for the best."

"I can not live on that," she murmured. "O my husband, all my heart yearns after thee, and it will break within me unless I can find some clearer, higher assurance of the mercy of Egypt's gods for thee, or of this dim and terrible unknown whom Am-nem-hat declares to be in truth the only one. I can not live in this void uncertainty and darkness! O Amosis, my husband! O ye cruel gods!"

"These good people among whom I find thee," said Am-nem-hat, "are followers of the new God, Jesus Christ, a sect that is everywhere spoken against. I have, however, a very favorable opinion of Jesus and of his religion, and I take it for granted that thou dost not know the truth concerning them. Perhaps they could teach unto thee some consolation for thy sorrow."

"The hated Christians!" she cried out, bitterly. "Why, when my lord Amosis lost his life, he was even then upon his way to Rome to obtain from the Emperor power and authority to extirpate the impious and terrible association from Egypt. If they had known this fact, perhaps I had been already reconciled, or at least silenced, by the icy hand of death."

"Nay, nay, mother," cried Theckla. "That is but an unjust thing, for they knew from the first, and from thine own unconscious talk, that father desired to destroy them all; and the lad Arius, their son, charged me that I should not tell thee until thou wert stronger; for that it might distress thee, and could do no good. He is a true-hearted boy, and I think a wise one also."

"And they have treated their known enemy with more than sisterly care and kindness," said Hatasa. "Surely it is most strange!"

But Am-nem-hat said: "I have seen the Christians tortured, decapitated, burned at the stake, and have heard them even with their last breath pray to their God to forgive those who punished them with such torments. It is a new and most strange religion, and possibly it might do thee good. No gods of Kem can aid thee in thy sorrow."

"I wish that I could see the boy," she said.

And Theckla sprang up quickly, saying, "I will bring him unto thee."

And thereupon she went forth of the room and sought

Arius until she found him; and she said, "Arius, my mother desireth much to speak with thee concerning thy religion."

And the boy said, "I go unto her gladly, and may the Lord direct me what to say unto her!"

And when the boy had come into that room where she was, Am-nem-hat said : "I have discovered that Hatasa is the granddaughter of my brother, and she seemeth very dear to me, that am childless. Thou knowest the great sorrow for which I have been able to offer no consolation, except to bid her cast herself upon the mercy of the unknown God in some way, and seek for him if by chance she might find him, and obtain mercy. For neither faith nor philosophy, as I have learned them, goeth one single step beyond where this dim, uncertain light guideth the soul, and we must therewith be content."

"But," moaned the stricken woman, "this chill and shadowy uncertainty will drive me mad. My soul yearneth after my loving, noble husband.—O boy, if thou knowest anything that bringest comfort in the very face of pitiless Death, speak thou to me, and speak thou truthfully; for I am sore afflicted and without hope! *How*, when all the gods of Egypt fail me—how can I trust the mercy of a strange and unknown God?"

Then the God-ordained minister stood up before them, and with that strange, continuous, rhythmic motion of the hand, with his fine head erect and bending toward her from the long and shapely neck, his luminous eyes agleam with strange mesmeric light, his voice sibilant, tremulous, incisive, began to preach his first little sermon in a way that grace and training made natural unto him : " Trouble not thine heart, O woman, with any thought about the gods of Egypt, for I tell thee that the unknown God to whom all men turn in time of sorest trial and sorrow, even as Am-nem-hat hath declared unto thee, is no more unknown, but is one God over all, blessed for evermore, and hath revealed himself unto men through his Son, our Lord and Saviour, Jesus Christ, who loved us, and hath borne all of our sins upon himself, that we by faith in him may so be free ; for, to them who believe in Jesus, life and immortality are brought to light in the gospel, and for them death hath no sting, the grave no victory.—What name do ye Egyptians give unto the burial-place of your dead ?"

The boy paused, and looked upon her, demanding an answer with his eyes.

" We call it sarcophagus," she replied.

"Yea," he continued, "sarcophagus! The devourer of human flesh ! But we Christians call it cemeterion—a sleeping-ground ; because we know that Jesus arose from the dead for our justification, and know that all they who sleep in death shall rise again ; for so our Lord hath taught us. Thou complainest that the light of nature is dim and chill, and giveth thee no certain guide nor hope ! Thou moanest that the course of nature is stern, pitiless, implacable ; teaching only that one must submit to the inevitable without hope ; a forced resignation in which there is no comfort ; an iron stoicism which teaches us to endure pain bravely but furnisheth no compensation for sorrow ; the obedience of a slave who knows that it is impossible to resist and foolish to attempt it ; not the faith and love of a

child that obeys because he loves, and bears chastisement
meekly because he knows that infinite wisdom and exhaust-
less love inflict it for his good. O woman, listen what
the divine Son of God, who took our nature upon himself
and was in all things touched with the feelings of our infirmities, saith unto thee : 'Come unto me, thou weary and
heavy-laden, and I will give thee rest. Like as a father
pitieth his childen, the tender mercy of our God is over
thee. He that believeth on me shall never die, for life and
immortality are brought to light in the gospel, which is the
power of God and the wisdom of God unto salvation for
every one that believeth.' For Jesus loveth thee ; he died
to save thee and to give thee peace ; and his blood can
cleanse thee from all sin, so that thou mayst be justified by faith, and find peace in believing, and in all times
of tribulation and distress thou mayst find Jesus a present
help and saviour. O woman, sorely smitten ! which one
of the gods of Kem hath died to redeem thy soul ?"

"None," she answered—"none !"

"Which one of them cleanseth thee from sin, and
giveth thee a sure, unfailing promise of eternal life, thereby releasing thee from the fear of death that keepeth mankind in bondage, teaching that death is but a change
through which the conscious spirit passeth into larger
life ?"

"None ! not one," she answered. "I have never heard
such glorious promises from any priest."

"But to make these glorious promises steadfast, abiding, true, the Son of God took upon himself our nature ;
became a man for our justification, and offered up himself

a divine and perfect sacrifice for us, to make atonement for our sins ; and having submitted himself to be crucified by Pontius Pilate, the third day he arose from the dead, whereby we know that we also shall rise. Seek thou for Christ by faith, for in him are joy and peace. In him are hope for all bereavement, consolation for all grief. He loveth thee. He so loved thee as to die for thee ! Come thou to him, and thou shalt learn how kind, and compassionate, and merciful a loving God can be ! For all that hath happened unto thee is not the cruel, blind, relentless infliction of merciless fate, working through nature ; nor is it the vengeance of an angry God upon thee and thy husband ; but is only the wise chastisement of thy Father, God, whereby he seeketh to wean thee away from the love of this vain and transitory life, and to draw thy spirit upward to himself, and to the glory of the world to come. Oh, if thou wilt believe in Christ, thou shalt find before his mercy-seat a refuge from every stormy wind that blows, and peace that passeth all understanding, that floweth as a river, that teacheth thee that these light afflictions, which are but for a moment, shall work out for thee a far more exceeding and eternal weight of glory in that bright world to which we haste. Seek thou for Christ, and thou shalt know how good, and pure, and holy an exercise even thy human sorrow and yearning may become."

Then said the woman : "It is all very beautiful and comforting, and I would know more of it. But tell me where I may find a temple in which these things are taught, and a priest that knoweth them."

Then answered Arius : "We have no temple here ; and

Jesus is our only priest.   But there are bishops and presbyters who preach the gospel, when the Christians assemble
together.   And in every Christian family there are daily
religious exercises."

"Dost thou have such worship here in thy father's
house ?"

" Assuredly ! on the evening of every day."

" And at what place ?"

"In any place that may be most convenient.   In thine
own apartment, if thou wilt."

CHAPTER XI.

"FOR THE WORK'S SAKE."

THAT night, at the request of Hatasa, the whole family assembled in her room, and she insisted upon having them engage in their usual religious exercises, to which she listened with profoundest attention, and with a certain amazement; for it was hard for her to grasp at once the idea that God might be worshiped without a temple, a priest, and a sacrifice; but the fact furnished its own best explanation. And the sorrowful woman soon found herself following with a new, strange sort of interest the reading of the gospel, and the earnest, extemporaneous, sympathetic prayer of Ammonius, in which he pleaded with God not to suffer his dear and sorrowful guests, nor the aged and righteous priest, who had so long sought for the truth, to depart from his abode without having learned by blessed experience how freely Jesus can forgive, and what light and peace his gospel can afford to all who believe thereon.

After the conclusion of these exercises, Am-nem-hat saith to Ammonius, "There are some things connected with thy simple and beautiful religion about which I would question thee when thou shalt have leisure and inclination to answer me."

Then said Ammonius : " Whenever thou wilt ! Even now, if thou wilt go with me into another room, where our conversation may not weary the others."

"Nay," cried Hatasa. "Go not hence, I beg ; for I eagerly desire to hear such conversation."

Then said Am-nem-hat : "I know the Jewish scriptures, and also the new books which the Christians have written ; but I desire thee to tell me plainly what the evidence is of the fact, upon which thou dost continually insist, that Jesus of Nazareth, whom Pilate crucified, is the Christ."

"The evidence is primarily historical and prophetic," said Ammonius, "based chiefly upon the Jewish laws and prophecies concerning him that were written centuries before the advent of our Lord, and that do testify of him."

"Yea," answered Am-nem-hat, "but these proofs only go to establish the coming of a Divine Man, in whom not only Plato and Socrates, who knew nothing of the Jews, but the Egyptians also, and many more, believed. I speak not of proofs that Messiah was to come, but of the proof that Jesus, whom Pilate crucified, was he."

"The evidences upon this point are twofold," answered Ammonius. "One line of proof which is the most satisfying, and which in fact amounts to positive knowledge, is the personal consciousness of the believer, experimental religion, whereby he knoweth that faith, the conviction of sin, the justification of the believer, and all of the phenomena which must necessarily attend the faith, are true. But this highest, most satisfactory, most scientific form of evidence is of course inaccessible to one that believeth not, except by the testimony of those who have personal experience of the truth. The other line of evidence is founded on the fact that the prophecies foretold for centuries just what Messiah should do and suffer when he might come, and we know that Jesus did and suffered just those things—many of them not possible to be done without the Divinity—as healing of the sick, unstopping the deaf ears, cleansing the lepers, restoring sight to the blind, raising the dead, and preaching good tidings to the poor ; all of which things Jesus customarily did, all of which things his followers have done from that day to this ; whereby we know that he is Christ indeed."

"Dost thou mean to assert that the Christians yet work miracles?" asked Am-nem-hat.

"Assuredly," replied Ammonius. "Jesus not only did the miracles himself, but did solemnly promise that, wherever his disciples should continue to obey him in all things, they should be able, by faith in his name, to do thaumaturgical works even unto the end of time ; and they have certainly done so ever since."

"Dost thou really believe that thou hast seen a miracle with thine own eyes?"

"Yea, verily," said Ammonius, "and many of them."

The ancient paused a long time, and seemed lost in profoundest meditation. At length he answered in a tone of inexpressible sadness and weariness : "I was in the temple service at Thebes for nearly half a century, and much of the time a priest. At Ombos I was high-priest for five-and-twenty years, and until some five years ago. I have seen some wonders, indeed, which the people called miracles,

9

but alas ! alas ! I know just how those things were done !
The sun rises and sets, and no man hindereth it ! The
Nile overfloweth its banks, and refresheth all the land of
Kem, and shrinketh back in his accustomed channel ; the
stars in heaven pursue their bright and tranquil way, and
seed-time cometh, and the harvest ; and life and death.
All nature moves on in obedience to fixed, changeless, universal laws, which have been from the beginning ; and I
find myself unable to believe that these laws were ever
violated, or suspended, in order to furnish evidences of
any religion, or for any purpose whatever ; although, no
doubt, good men may believe that such things have occurred."

"And as to that," said Ammonius, "beyond any question thou art right. He hath but a poor conception of our
God who thinketh that, in creating a world wherein he
intended miracles to occur, he did not know enough to provide natural laws by which these phenomena might come
to pass without violating or suspending the established order. But, if I could know that it violates or suspends any
law of nature to raise the dead, I would not believe such a
fact, although I have seen it done. But why dost thou
suppose that the anastasis of the dead is contrary to natural law ? Our Lord hath never said so ; on the contrary,
he came to fulfill, not to violate, the law. Surely thou
canst not declare that any miracle violates or suspends, or
is without law, unless thou canst first truthfully declare
that all laws are known to thee, and that among them
there is none by which the dead might be raised up. But
although thou art wise and learned, thou knowest that Na-

ture withholdeth many secrets yet from thee. Thou knowest that no man hath mastered all her laws; and even those which we know may be weak, and mean, and narrow, compared with those of which we are profoundly ignorant. But we Christians teach that God is not the author of confusion, but of order; that all laws of nature, physical, mental, spiritual, are but the expression of his will, which must be harmonious throughout, and can not be self-contradictory; and that just as he hath made some law by which water seeks a level, and by which heavy bodies tend toward the center of the world, and by which oil and water, that repel each other by nature, will unite with an alkali to make a new creature, just so he hath established laws by which the miracles are done; so that the anastasis of the dead, or any other miracle, must be as purely and truly a natural phenomenon as is the rising of the sun, or the falling of the dew—not so common, perhaps, because these phenomena involve powers and faculties of the human soul that do not act always and automatically as do the laws of physical nature; so neither does one sleep, or talk, or think always, but only when he wills to do so."

"That is a new, strange view of thaumaturgy! Thou sayst 'the miracles are under law'; perhaps, then, other men besides the Christians might be able to perform them."

"I know not to what extent it might be possible for other men to exercise the power of faith which is an essential condition in the working of miracles. I suppose they might do wonderful things, that would bear

about the same relation to our Christian miracles that
their various religions bear to our holy Christianity.
And I suppose that the witchcraft and demonology denounced by Moses were the results of the exercise of
faith in false gods.   But a Christian miracle, depending
upon faith in Christ as a primary condition for the exercise of thaumaturgical power, must remain impossible
to all who possess not that faith.   Thou hast read the
Gospels, and thou knowest the Lord hath said, 'If ye
had faith as a grain of mustard-seed, ye might say unto
this mountain, Be thou removed, and be thou cast into
the midst of the sea, and it should obey you.'   But he
also said, 'Without me ye can do nothing.'"

"I infer," said Am-nem-hat, "that thou thinkest
faith to be the law of miracles; thou thinkest that this
faith is itself a force in nature sufficient for the accomplishment of physical results; and that they who sin-
cerely believe may, by means of this force, even raise
up the dead.   Why, then, are not all the dead raised
up?"

"Thou hast stated the law rather too broadly," answered Ammonius.   "The faith that worketh miracles
must be applied under proper conditions to be of any
avail.   Water, oil, and alkali do not always produce
soap, but only when the proper conditions are observed.
So I suppose that no man could be raised up from the
dead against his will; and, while there be many Christians that have sought for martyrdom, there be but few
that were willing to be raised again, and fewer still that
ever requested the brethren to pray for their anastasis.

because they preferred to depart, and to be with the Lord, which is far better."

"I do remember," said Am-nem-hat, "that many years ago, when Decius was Emperor of Rome, a bitter persecution raged against the Christians at Alexandria. I saw Julian, and Macar, and Epimachus, and Alexander burned at the stake; and truly many seemed to seek for martyrdom rather than to shun it, a fact which we attributed to a certain incorrigible and hopeless wickedness in them, and not, as thou dost, to their assurance of obtaining a better life. I suppose, indeed, that such men as those would not have desired to be restored to a life which they seemed anxious to lose; and it seemeth reasonable enough that, even if it had been possible to do so, they should not have been recalled against their will. Wilt thou not state more fully yet the conditions upon which thou thinkest this thaumaturgy may be exercised?"

"Faith in Jesus is the primary condition," said Ammonius, "but there are also others. Once a man came unto our Lord and besought him to heal his son, saying that the disciples had been unable to do so. Our Lord did heal him with a word. Afterward the disciples inquired of him why it was that they had failed in doing the same work, and he said unto them that it was because of their unbelief. Now thou must perceive that it was not because of their want of faith in him, for they were then following him; so that it must have been because of their unbelief in their own power and authority to do the work in his name. It seemeth, therefore, that faith on the part of the thaumaturgist in his own power to accomplish the miracle in the Lord's name is one of the conditions of thaumaturgy."

"That also seemeth to be a reasonable and proper condition," answered Am-nem-hat. "But are there yet others?"

"It is written that he did not many wonderful works at Capernaum because of their unbelief. He often said to those who asked his aid, 'Be it unto thee according to thy faith.' And from these facts it seems to follow that faith on the part of him for, or upon, whom the work was to be done, and on the part of those among whom it was to be done, was also one of the conditions upon which the exercise of thaumaturgical power depended."

"But," objected Am-nem-hat, "if he was in truth divine, why should he pay any attention to the unbelieving or to the unwilling? Why did he not do the miracles in defiance of them all, as well as if they had been faithful and willing?"

"Because," answered Ammonius, "our Lord teacheth and requireth only a willing obedience and faith. Not God himself will force the human will; for that which is of compulsion hath no morality. It is of necessity, therefore, neither holy nor unholy. A necessary holiness is a contradiction in terms. God's use of sovereignty hath been to make man free. Besides, faith itself is the law of miracles; to have wrought miracles where no faith was, would have been to violate the very law by which he worked, and so to have degraded miracles to the plane of an arbitrary and sporadic exhibition of divine power, instead of leaving them as they are, the highest result of the very highest form of universal law."

"That seemeth reasonable enough," rejoined Am-nem-hat, "and in accordance with my conception of the character of a holy and perfect God. But as I perceive thou clearly comprehendest the Christian system, upon which I have bestowed much thought almost in vain, suffer me to put one other case to thee which seemeth to me to be inexplicable upon any principles which thou hast stated as constituent elements of the law of mira-cles, if thou art not yet weary of my questions."

"Nay," said Ammonius, "I am not weary. Thou mayst ask many things, indeed, which I know not, and can not answer; but, so far as I can give thee any aid, it affordeth me pleasure to answer thee as intelligently as I can."

"The matter is this," said Am-nem-hat. "It is re-corded in thy sacred books that when the apostles were going about Jerusalem, imparting the Paraclete by the laying on of their hands, and working divers miracles, one Simon, a magician, came unto them and offered money unto them if they would communicate unto him the same power, so that he also might become a thau-maturgist. But one of them, named Peter, did bitterly rebuke him, saying, 'Thy money perish with thee!' Now, the apostles had faith; the people who saw them doing all these wonderful works had faith, and were bap-tized by Philip. Simon Magus himself had faith as much as any one of them, and, when Peter rebuked him, with

fear and trembling he besought Peter, saying, 'Pray ye
to the Lord for me, that none of these things which ye
have spoken come upon me.' Now, here seem to have
been all of the conditions of faith and willingness in
Simon of which thou hast spoken, and yet Peter manifestly regarded the desire of Simon as a sort of sacrilege.
Why was this so ?"

"Why," said Ammonius, "Peter declared that his
thought that the gift of God may be purchased with
money was evil; and that his heart was not right in the
sight of God, and that he should repent of his wickedness, and that his very thought showed that he was still
in the gall of bitterness and in the bonds of iniquity."

"That is very true," answered Am-nem-hat, "but his
tender of money to the apostles only proves his apprecia-
tion of the value of the power which he desired to purchase. Peter saith not that Simon was a bad man, but
that this particular thing was wicked; why was it so in
him, and not in them ?"

"Because," replied Ammonius, "it is manifest from
the whole record that Simon desired to purchase this power
for himself, and to use it for his own purposes."

"Certainly so," persisted Am-nem-hat, "but in what
respect was it sacrilegious for him to desire to use the
power for his own purposes, any more than it would
have been to use his brain, or his hand, for his own
advancement; or his learning, or skill, for the acquisition and cultivation of which he had, perhaps, expended
money ?"

"The answer to thy question," replied Ammonius,

"involves some consideration of the very genius of Christianity as a system of divine truth. If, as thou seemest to suppose, the religion of our Lord had been only a system of spiritual truth, it might be difficult to deny that the apostles were selfish, and that Simon was very badly treated. But this is not at all true. Thou knowest that the legislation of Moses was for the Israelites only; that of Egypt for the land and people of Kem only; that of other lands and ages for certain peoples only. But thou canst not have read the scriptures so carefully without learning the fact that Jesus died for all men, and that his truth is designed for all mankind. Thou seest, therefore, that, if Simon Magus could have obtained this power to exercise it for his own purposes, he would have made it the agency by which to gain limitless authority and wealth unto himself, and oppress the poor. Thou seest also that, if any nation or government could exercise thaumaturgical powers, that nation or government would soon become the ruler and the tyrant of the world. Thou seest that, if any church that is in any way connected with, or bound unto, an earthly government, could exercise this power, ecclesiasticism would quickly make mankind its slaves: for manifestly no people could long resist a government that had thaumaturgical power wherewith to enforce obedience to its laws. Thou seest also that if the faith that is effective for miracles could be exercised for any purposes except the edification of the Church and the good of all men, the faith itself might have become a nameless and unappealable tyranny. Nay, if it were ever possible to exercise such power except under such conditions as necessarily and absolutely to preclude the use of it for any private purposes, thou seest that sooner or later, under the influence of inborn selfishness, the thaumaturgists would have made war upon each other, and, in place of seeing nations contending with sword, and bow, and spear, we would have seen them hurling against each other all of the destructive forces of nature, and only chaos and utter ruin could have ended the superhuman strife. It was therefore ordained that the thaumaturgic faith can not be exercised except under conditions which necessarily exclude the use of it for private purposes, and insure its exercise for the good of the common Church only."

"Canst thou specify by what means this restricted use of the power hath been enforced? For it seemeth to me that, if it exists, it must be beyond control."

"In order to exclude all worldly ambitions and selfishness from the kingdom which he established in the world, our Lord ordained that his Church should be a community in which all men are free and equal—brethren only. Hence he ordained, as the fundamental law of the kingdom, that all private rights of property (including estates, rank, offices, prerogatives) should be forever abolished in his Church, and that Christians should hold them all in common. Hence, the kingdom of heaven is an absolute democracy, social and political, based upon faith in Christ, and community of rights and property among all who believe. Of this community the apostles themselves were the divinely appointed type. They used thaumaturgy for the common good only, and not for personal aggrandizement.

The common treasure was put into a bag, and, as if to show the divine scorn of wealth and of all human distinctions that grow out of it, the bag was intrusted to Judas, the only base one of the twelve. It was easier for a camel to go through the eye of a needle than for a rich man to enter the kingdom of heaven, because the law of that kingdom imperatively required the consecration of all that he had to the common good. But, under the power of a living faith, many complied with this law, and the Church prospered. Thus did the bishops that were ordained by the apostles, as Linus at Rome, Polycarp at Smyrna, Evodius at Antioch, and others also. Thus did Paulinus, Cyprian, Hilary, and others. Such has been the law and practice of the common Church even unto this day. For the primary law of the kingdom of heaven demandeth the consecration of all property, and the abdication of all worldly honors, offices, and authority. And Simon Magus desired not part or lot in this kingdom, but his own advantage only. And thou must perceive that thaumaturgical power exercised by such a church must necessarily be for the common good of all, and not for any personal, political, or sectarian purposes; and the faith that worketh wonders must therefore be impossible to any human association except to the church organized upon the foundation which Jesus himself laid, even the communion of the holy; for the liberty, fraternity, and equality, which constitute the socialism and politics of the kingdom, can not exist upon any other foundation. And, of course, thaumaturgic power will vanish even out of the Church if the day shall ever come in which those who believe shall abandon the communal organization of the kingdom of heaven, and establish human statutes as the law thereof."

"I think," said Am-nem-hat, "that thy words remove many of the difficulties which have beset my study of thy sacred books. For I now perceive that the parables of Jesus—a species of literary composition unknown, perhaps impossible, to other men — which I supposed to refer to some spiritual, mystical doctrines, were in fact spoken concerning his Church, or kingdom, in this world."

"Assuredly so," replied Ammonius. "And thou hast done well to characterize the parable as 'a species of literary composition unknown and impossible to other men'; for no other man hath written a parable, nor do I suppose that any man ever will do so. For he spake as never man spake: he spake in parables; without a parable he spake not. The history, the poem, the fable, the allegory, may be used by other teachers also; but the parable is the language of Jesus alone; and no man can handle it but himself."

"I can now understand that strange parable of 'the unjust steward,'" said Am-nem-hat, "although, when I first read the words, 'I say unto you, make to yourselves friends of the mammon of unrighteousness, that when ye fail they may receive you into everlasting habitations,' I did even suppose that Jesus represented eternal life to be a vendible thing, and that his religion, like every other, assured the rich that they could purchase salvation with money—although this seemed to be antagonistic to the general current of his teachings."

"Verily," replied Ammonius, "the words of Jesus would convey no other meaning, if, indeed, the fundamental law of the Church had not excluded therefrom all the private wealth, honors, and authority after which the Gentiles seek. But, if thou wilt consider that the unjust steward is any believer that useth his means, pecuniary, intellectual, physical, for his own aggrandizement, and not for the common good ; that the Lord of that steward is Jesus ; that unrighteous mammon is wealth held by private ownership, and that the true riches is wealth held by common title for the good of all—thou canst then understand how, even upon ceasing to be steward (the end of life), one may make amends for past selfishness and mammon-worship, by giving up his property to the common Church. Thou canst understand how it is just that those who come in even at the eleventh hour to work in his vineyard shall have an equal reward with those who entered early and bore the heat and burden of the day. Thou wilt see that it is true that those who gave up houses and lands for his sake and the gospel's reaped manifold more 'now in this present life' by gaining a communal title in the property of all other believers—an increase which our Lord expressly promises as to all the interests and relationships of life, except as to the wife ; for, while, if one leave houses, lands, father, mother, brother, sister, or children, for the gospel's sake, the severed interests and relationships are replaced a hundred-fold by his admission into the kingdom of heaven, monogamic marriage was and is the law of the Church. And thou canst thus give a practical and beautiful meaning to all that our Lord hath said and done; thou wilt see that the social and political system of the gospel is the only kingdom that can ever banish crime, hatred, and selfishness out of human life, and so regenerate the world; thou wilt see that the Scribes and Pharisees persecuted our Lord because his kingdom excluded war, slavery, private-property rights, estates, rank, offices, prerogatives—of all which things they were 'covetous'—just as the Romans and all other established governments persecute the Christians, even unto this day, for the same reasons. For Christ desireth the brotherhood of men; the liberty and equality of men; and that the average talents, energy, and prosperity of all may insure the common weal; and not that some shall be emperors, lords, and masters, whereby it cometh to pass that many must be slaves; not that some be inordinately rich, and others distressfully poor."

"I will read the gospels and the Acts again in the light of thine instructions," said Am-nem-hat. "But, verily, many passages thereof already come crowding into my mind that bear new and potent meanings; for I perceive clearly enough that Christianity is not only a system of spiritual truth, but also of social and political truth, that is founded upon the faith, and from that basis assaulteth selfishness in its strong citadel of private rights by elevating the common good into a higher thing than private aggrandizement, and separating the people of his kingdom from all personal honors, prerogatives, and wealth, after which the Gentiles seek."

"Thou wilt perceive this all the more clearly," said Ammonius, "if thou wilt reread the gospels with this thought in thy mind ; for thou wilt at once perceive that many passages, which in any other view would seem strongly tainted with fanaticism, or rhapsody, or demagoguery, are precisely the things which Jesus ought to have said if his kingdom was, indeed, a social and political democracy founded upon faith and community of rights and property. For the Jews, who supposed that our Lord would overturn the Roman authority and establish a great Israelitish nation instead thereof, were not any more in error than are those who falsely suppose that he would establish no kingdom at all, and that he taught only spiritual truth, as do the Therapeutæ."

"I am familiar with the work of Philo ' On a Contemplative Life, or the Devout,' answered Am-nem-hat, "in which he giveth a full and succinct account of the Therapeutæ ; but, indeed, I had supposed that he therein intended to describe the first heralds of the gospel, and the practices handed down from the apostles."

"Beyond doubt the Therapeutæ were Christians," continued Ammonius, "but they separated themselves from the apostolical churches in order to lead a more devout life, and they gradually exalted all their conceptions of spiritual truth until they began to despise all temporal surroundings ; and in this they departed from the teaching of our Lord : for there is no teacher of men more free from asceticism or stoicism than is Jesus. He was ever busied about and interested in the common, every-day life of common men ; he was touched with the feeling of

our infirmity in all things ; sympathized in all the joys
and sorrows of those about him, their trials and triumphs,
seeking to lead them, not out of the world, but into a
way of life wherein every pure and wholesome feeling, affection, and faculty of the human heart might find full development, exercise, and satisfaction.   The vast difference,
indeed, between Jesus and the philosophers subsists in the
fact that, while they were ever painfully seeking for rules
and actions by which the select and favored few might attain a perfect human life, he ordained a simple, perfect
system by which to bring the higher, purer life within the
reach of all men, especially the poor."

In such conversations the time passed quickly ; and it
was strange to note with what deep interest the sorrowful
Hatasa, and also Theckla and Arius, listened to every
word, and strove to catch the full signification of every
phrase ; while Arete heard it patiently, as one might listen
to an oft-told but still pleasant story, and old Thopt, as if
she knew little and cared less about the whole matter,
being satisfied that whatever Ammonius and his wife
might do must be right and true.

CHAPTER XII.

On the same day began Arius to teach Theckla letters; for, although the girl had been remarkably well instructed for an Egyptian maiden, all of her tuition had been oral. But, in accordance with her strong wish to learn how to read and write, the boy began at once with the three alphabets, Latin, Greek, and Hebrew, and in a single day she learned all of the letters, and the relative power of each, and in a very short time she could make all of the characters with a sharp point of *keil* upon a leaf of papyrus. Then, as leisure served, he would take a single word, as, for example, "spirit," and would pronounce and spell it in the three languages (*nishema, pneuma, animus*), and she would repeat the three names for the same thing after him, and spell them, and write them down, over and over again, until she had become thoroughly familiar with the letters, the sound, and the form of the written word. The acquisition of a few words every day soon gave her command of a considerable vocabulary in each tongue, and she rapidly learned to associate the words with all familiar objects, and to call them by the right name in either tongue. Then he would select some short passage, gener-

10

erally from the sacred writings, and during the day she would write it over and over again, in each of the languages, while he was absent upon the various duties which pertained to his part of the farm-labor. The girl was continually learning; and it was pleasant to see how soon she began, of her own accord, to select and translate into the different tongues any passage which pleased her. This process of education continued, as we shall hereafter see, during the years which she spent at Baucalis, and finally Theckla became very familiar with the three languages in which the scriptures were then written.

On the next evening after that described in the last chapter, all the dwellers at the cottage assembled again in Hatasa's room, by her request, to hold the usual evening service; for the lady had seldom quitted her bed, and she remained deplorably weak, suffering with continual pain in her lungs, the result, perhaps, of her great exposure during the storm, and of the terrible depression of spirits that succeeded it. All through the pagan world, the only known refuge from hopeless sorrow was suicide, and the idea of self-destruction was ever present to her. Perhaps her maternal affection for Theckla alone deterred her from putting an end to her life; for it was not regarded by the heathen as cowardly, criminal, or even immoral, to seek that refuge from misfortune. Cato did it; Seneca approved of it; Epictetus, Aurelius, and all the great lights of pagan antiquity regarded self-immolation as a matter of choice, and often as an act of wisdom. But, from the moment in which Hatasa had been informed that the kind friends who surrounded her were Christians, she felt a desire to know more of them, and of their peculiar religion, strong enough to give her a new interest in life; and she had requested Ammonius to have the service in her room, and told him that, although she was too weak to take any part in their conversation about Christianity, she desired to hear himself and Am-nem-hat discuss any topic pertaining thereto in which they were interested. So, after the usual exercises of reading and prayer, the whole family remained together. The ancient remarked to Ammonius that during the day he had pondered much upon the things spoken of in their former conversation, and suggested, as a difficulty in the way of the acceptance of Christianity, something like the following: "I can understand how a kind and merciful God might lay down certain rules of action, and require obedience to his laws, under whatever penalties he might choose to impose; but it seemeth to me that to require one *to believe*, as the sole condition of justification, is arbitrary and unjust. Suppose that one hath some natural bent of mind, or hath been reared and educated in some such way that it is hard, perhaps impossible, for him to believe; yet thy books say: 'Believe and live; he that believeth not is condemned already.' Is not this an arbitrary demand for faith; and doth it not do violence to that very autonomy of the will which thou sayest Jesus himself always respected and venerated?"

"Thou dost somewhat mistake the matter," said Ammonius. "The Lord does not demand our faith; he simply stateth an actual fact, which is, that the believer is justified by faith, and that he who does not believe is condemned already."

"I hardly understand what thou sayest: 'he simply stateth an actual fact.'"

"I think thou wilt find that there is no arbitrary demand in it. Our Lord gave no command only because he had power and authority to do so; but he knew what was in man, and gave only such commands as his divine wisdom perceived to be necessary for the welfare of mankind. As to the necessity of faith upon which he insists, the case is thus: All men upon earth are under the conviction of sin, and all alike are forever seeking for some escape from the bonds of this conviction. Thou wilt perceive that this conviction hath no reference to any specific, sinful act; for, perhaps, the best and purest men have always been those who felt it most keenly. ·It is a consciousness of alienation between the human and the divine. . It is a natural, intuitive perception, in the heart of every man, that he is not as good as he ought to be, less perfect than he might be. The universal desire to get rid of this conviction of sin hath filled the world with false and ineffectual religions from the very dawn of time; for all men, in every age and clime, have sought for some form of penance or of sacrifice, some means in faith or work, by which to make atonement and secure reconciliation, and thereby shake off this conviction of sin. Hast thou ever heard of any kindred, tribe, or tongue (or even of any individual), that professed to be perfect, sinless, needing no sacrifice, no atonement for sin—that is, for a consciously sinful condition independent of all specific acts of transgression?"

"Nay," answered Am-nem-hat; "for thou art clearly right in that. All men do by nature bewail their sinful state. Humanity standeth forever like the lepers in Israel, with uplifted hand, crying aloud to heaven and earth, 'Unclean! unclean!' It is a conviction upon which philosophy hath no power. It cometh some time into every human heart, resistless as the precession of the equinoxes, spontaneous as the flowing of the Nile— a natural thing, which a man can no more control than he can reach forth his puny hand and unloose the bands of Orion, or bind the sweet influence of Pleiades, or guide Arcturus and his suns. All literature, all monuments, all ages, and all men, testify unto this terrible truth."

"Now the work of Jesus," said Ammonius, "was not to burden this sick and sorrowful nature with any arbitrary law of faith, but was to provide a way by which this universal conviction of sin might be atoned for — a perfect righteousness and sacrifice available by faith for our justification; to wit, that God was in Christ reconciling the world unto himself. And faith is made the condition, because no other condition could be available for all men alike, whether great or small, rich or poor, learned or ignorant; and Jesus died for all! Thou must see that this faith, instead of being, as thou didst suppose, an arbitrary condition or command, is simply the enabling act, instituted by divine wisdom and compassion, by means whereof we may be able to attain unto reconciliation with God. And without this faith we could never be justified by holy life and works alone, because it is a law of our nature that, just as we become better and purer beings, our conception of the degree of fitness required of us necessarily becomes higher, so that it is impossible for us to get any nearer to it; so that without faith the best men are as much under conviction of sin as the worst; so that without faith it is impossible for us to be consciously justified, because our nature requires a perfect righteousness; and this perfect righteousness and sacrifice must be human, that we may be able to trust its love and willingness to aid us, and must be divine, that we may have faith in its power to save. Hast thou ever heard of any name given under heaven, or among men, which supplies these natural and necessary conditions for our conscious justification and reconciliation with God, and with our own hearts also, except the name of Jesus Christ? If thou hast, please utter it."

"Verily," answered Am-nem-hat, "there is none. No religion of which I have heard professeth to know any."

The old man seemed lost in profoundest meditation, and there was silence in the room, until Theckla said: "Father Am-nem-hat, do thou bid Arius repeat what things he said to me of this matter of faith when he was teaching the alphabets to me this morning. I think it was much plainer than thy learned discoursing with Ammonius."

"Yea," said Am-nem-hat, "I beg that Arius will do so, for I much desire to hear thereof."

The boy blushed vividly at being so called upon in

the presence of his elders, but, at a sign from his father, he stood up before them, saying: "I did not suppose the talk of persons so young could interest those who are so much older and wiser, but, as ye desire to hear it, I can almost repeat it. As Theckla and I were running over the alphabets, in order to get the sound of the letters and the form of the characters, she came upon the letter 'A' a second time, and she cried out: 'Oh, I know that one; it is Latin A, Greek Alpha, Hebrew Aleph.' And I said unto her, 'Theckla, how knowest thou that the characters stand for these sounds?' and she answered, 'Thou didst tell me so, and I did believe thee, boy, and that is how I know it.' Then said I: 'Theckla, thou learnest the alphabet by faith only. If thou wert naturally constituted so that thou couldst not believe, thou couldst never learn anything not tangible to thy senses. If thou wert by nature even indifferent between faith and non-faith, thy progress in the acquisition of knowledge would be slow and painful. Thou shouldst therefore learn, from the learning of these alphabets, that faith is the first, most inevitable act of intelligence. Thou shouldst learn that belief precedes knowledge always, that Faith is the elder sister and leadeth Knowledge by the hand, and that without antecedent faith it is impossible to learn and to know anything except what is palpable to the senses; just as it would be impossible for thee to learn these alphabets without faith.' And thereupon Theckla did pinch mine ear, and laugh at me, saying, 'That all seemeth to be true and plain enough, thou odd boy, but why art thou preaching at me now?' And I did answer: 'Because, thou dear sister, some time thy faith may be demanded for another alphabet than this, even the alphabet of spiritual life; and, when that day shall come, I would have thee remember that just as all human knowledge is builded upon the basis of faith only, so it should not seem a hard thing unto thee that God hath fashioned thy nature so that thou must be incapable of learning even the alphabet of everlasting life except upon the very same condition of faith only. Faith precedeth all knowledge; believe and obey, and finally thou shalt know.' I think this was about what was spoken between us concerning faith."

"And it is most wise, beautiful, and instructive talk," said Am-nem-hat, "and serveth to complete the powerful utterances of thy father upon the same lofty and interesting subject. I do thank thee for repeating it."

Then spake Hatasa, saying to Ammonius, "Suppose that one hath died without having known the truth concerning Jesus, and without having exercised this faith, is there no hope for such a one?"

The trembling voice in which she spoke, and the look of timid, doubtful entreaty which accompanied these words, touched every heart, and made them all feel that by "such a one" the poor lady meant her young and gallant husband Amosis, whose memory seemed ever in her heart.

Ammonius answered: "I do not know whether I could make thee understand fully the views which we Christians entertain about such a case as thou hast sug-

gested, but we believe that there is hope for such a
man. The great apostle Paul was Saul of Tarsus, and
for a long time he did persecute the Christians because
they were Christians, yet he declareth himself that he
acted in all good conscience before God, believing that
it was his duty to do so, and he afterward became the
great apostle and a glorious martyr. I doubt not that
there are among those who now persecute the Christians
some good and just men, that would follow Jesus unto
death if they could know him as he is. The conviction of sin, we know, hath no reference to any specific
transgression, nor hath the forgiveness of sin. Whether
an act be a sin or not dependeth largely upon the intent
with which it is done. Now, when the heathen, who
know not Jesus nor his divine truth, do yet live just and
righteous lives according to the best light and knowledge they possess, and die without the consolation of the
faith, the benefit of the atonement accrueth to them in
some way, we know not precisely how far, nor to what
effect ; to all such, indeed, and especially to such as have
some living Christian relative or friend that taketh upon
himself the rite of baptism for the dead ; for, if they have
not the law, they are not judged by the law, but by their
works and righteousness under the law which they have."

"How is that ?" said Hatasa, with breathless interest.
"Thou sayest a living Christian may be baptized for the
dead ?"

"Assuredly," answered Ammonius. "The apostles
so taught, and the Church hath always so practiced. If
any Christian hath a relative that died without knowl-

edge of Jesus, and such Christian doth believe that the deceased was a just and righteous person according to the measure of light given unto him, and was such that he would have followed our Lord if he had known sufficiently of him, such Christian may receive baptism for the deceased, and the dead shall reap benefit of this vicarious faith and obedience, how and to what extent hath never been clearly revealed unto us."

"There is hope in that!" cried Hatasa. "There is consolation in that. Thy Lord must have been full of human love and pity to make provision not only for his friends, but for those good and just men, also, who have ignorantly been his enemies."

"Yea, verily," answered Ammonius. "He loveth all men; his mercy endureth forever; his loving-kindness is stronger than height, or depth, or life, or death, or any other creature, as thou mayest assuredly know for thyself if thou wilt believe on him."

Then Am-nem-hat said : "There is much in this religion that taketh fast hold upon both the heart and the mind; for it verily seemeth that Jesus seeketh not to impose a system upon man that is in any respect external to man, but rather that he seeketh to show unto man such spiritual food as is most divinely suitable to satisfy that hunger of the soul wherefrom the whole world suffereth already; and he seemeth to propose nothing as matter of faith which was not already a conscious want and need of nature : so that his teachings ought to be accepted as at least the highest utterance of philosophy if even not as divinely true."

"Thy profound criticism of the spirit of our religion striketh very nearly to the heart of the whole matter," said Ammonius. "For the world yearned after God whom it knew not, and Jesus plainly declareth that unknown God whom men ignorantly worship. The world groaned and sorrowed under the blind conviction of sin, and, wherever men acquired a local habitation and a name on earth, there they had their holy places also; and in some way—often in a crude and ignorant way, often in a gross and sensual way, often in a heathenish and cruel way—they sought, by sacred rites of penitence and sacrifice, to atone for their wrong deeds done; but the wrongs continually repeated themselves, and the unavailing religions left the world's heart like a troubled sea that can not rest. But Jesus saith the sin for which ye suffer is not a wrong thing done at all; these wicked deeds of yours are not sin, but are the outcroppings of the sin that lieth back of all your deeds. Can a bitter fountain send forth sweet waters? Doth an evil tree bear good fruits? Do ye gather figs from thistles? Cease now your world-old and unavailing efforts to regenerate the heart by the vain expiation of your wicked deeds. Purify the fountain, that the waters thereof may be sweet. Make the tree good, and its fruits shall be good also. For sin is non-conformity to the will of God, and your evil deeds are only the evidences of your enmity against him. So, when the blind yearnings of the world's heart after peace had made sacrifices, not only of every beast and creeping thing upon the earth, but of men also, he saith: 'All these things ye do in vain, for your righteousness must exceed that of the Scribes and Pharisees, or ye shall likewise perish. I am the Light, the Truth, the Way—the Lamb of God that taketh away the sin of the world—a perfect righteousness and sacrifice once for all offered for the sin of men. Believe in me, and ye shall be saved; all other sacrifices are in vain.' So every yearning want of the heart is met and satisfied in Christ. All other religions under heaven condemn actions which they suppose to be wicked, and prescribe certain forms of expiation for such as they suppose to be expiable; but Jesus proposes to pardon, not so much the sinful act as the sinner, the sinful nature out of which the act ariseth, and to regenerate this nature so that it will hate what it believes to be wicked, and love what it believes to be holy. For Christ atoneth for all sin, and the act of faith is to personally appropriate the benefit thereof to each one for himself."

"True," said Am-nem-hat, "and I undertake to assert that no other religion in the world hath so represented sin to be want of conformity to the will of God, rather than an evil deed; and in this whole matter of sin and the forgiveness thereof, thy religion differeth from paganism more radically than even in the doctrine of one God it differeth from polytheism."

And in this and such like conversation the evening wore away until bed-time came, and they separated for the night. The family at Baucalis did not speak or think of these matters as of mere abstract theories of truth, or of philosophy, but as actual, living verities. The Christians felt their religion to be the only real life. They regarded all earthly pursuits, passions, and pleasures, as mere incidents of existence, and religion as the one controlling and all-important thing. Their pleasant home was to them a merely temporary station on the highway whereby they were journeying to a better land ; the flesh was only a tabernacle which the spirit must soon forsake ; all that pertained to it was for a brief season only ; the real life was only begun during their occupancy of this earthly tenement ; Christian faith was to them the one thing real and permanent, and earthly existence was of little consequence except as it might stand related to eternal interests. Hence there was a freshness, a vigor, a sense of reality and earnestness, in their way of thinking and speaking of such things, that demonstrated their religion to be no beautiful, speculative philosophy, but a hard, experimental, and all-controlling fact. And so every night during that week the dwellers at Baucalis assembled in Hatasa's room, and passed long hours in the discussion of all the salient points of Christianity in a friendly, careful way, as if, indeed, they had a mutual interest in ascertaining the truth, especially concerning all those ideas upon which the antagonism between Christianity and paganism most plainly appeared. To set down all the various conversations in which they engaged would indeed be to write a treatise upon primitive Christianity, a work in which, perhaps, no interest would be felt in an age in which that system no longer exists upon earth, and is utterly unknown to all except a few self-poised, fearless, unpopular antiquarians, who have been eccentric and independent enough to exhume that ancient religion from

out the accumulated *débris* of fifteen centuries of ecclesiastical "progress" which flourisheth over its ruins even
as the vine ripens and the roses bloom over the wreck
of buried Pompeii. Yet we can not resist the inclination that moveth us to write out our notes of one other
evening's conversation that happened between this Christian family and their pagan guests.

CHAPTER XIII.

ON the next evening, after the conclusion of their usual daily services, the ancient Am-nem-hat began the conversation which occupied their attention during that meeting by saying to Ammonius: "Thou didst observe that the future state of just and good men who died without any sufficient knowledge of Christianity to lead them to embrace that faith 'hath never been clearly revealed unto us.' Is it not true also that the future state of all men hath been left almost entirely unrevealed? I ask thee this, because I have found myself altogether unable, from my readings of the sacred books, to locate heaven, either anywhere in this world or in any other sun or star. And either I have utterly failed to comprehend some of the things which I have carefully read, or else the scriptures leave this future state in a very misty, uncertain, indefinite condition. Wilt thou inform me how this matter may really stand?"

"Thy reading is in no respect at fault," replied Ammonius. "Our Lord hath left the future life altogether unrevealed, not only in respect to the locality thereof, but also in every other respect. Types and figures are used in reference thereto, whereby we know that it shall be eternal and blest; but, beyond this general assurance of exalted happiness and unfailing duration, we are not informed. To each Christian soul it will undoubtedly be the best that is possible for him : the place, the development, the environments thereof, and all else that belongeth thereto, are unrevealed."

"I know not whether it would have been more pleasing to have some definite knowledge of that future life; that is, I can not tell whether the system of religion would or would not appear unto me to have been more perfect if all had been revealed by it, or whether it is wiser and perhaps even more pleasing to have left it thus vague and undefined, with a general assurance of its beatitude," said Am-nem-hat, "yet I could wish that something tangible and satisfying were revealed in reference thereto. Why, thinkest thou, was it not more fully revealed ?"

"I know not," answered Ammonius, "but I feel certain that it was purposely left as a thing to be held by faith, and not in knowledge. Either it may have been because it hath not yet entered into the heart of man to conceive what that life may be, so that human speech could not convey any adequate knowledge thereof; or, if it were possible to do so, the overpowering glory and splendor thereof, if definitely grasped and understood, and already realized, might render us impatient of this mundane existence, and too indifferent to all the duties and obligations thereof. I think, indeed, that those very Therapeutæ, of whom Philo speaketh, were to be censured for an unwarranted attempt to realize, in this present world, a spiritual life which our Lord expressly reserved for the future; an effort, indeed, necessarily impossible to succeed, and perhaps injurious both to these anchorites and to other men also. For the purpose of the gospel is not only to justify and save all who believe and obey it, but the declared purpose of our Lord is to regenerate mankind by the agency of his own kingdom; and surely it tendeth not to the accomplishment of this purpose to have Christians withdraw themselves permanently beyond the reach of common life and experience; so that it is manifestly an error to suppose that, because they have the assurance of a superlatively better life beyond, Christians should for that reason despise the life that now · is. And, in accordance with this view, thou wilt find that the Church forbiddeth any man to go out of the world (by suicide) as the heathen commonly do; forbiddeth any man to seek for martyrdom, as many had done; and forbiddeth any man to flee from· that place in which he was converted into the mountains and the deserts : because the kingdom of our Lord must exist in the world—not out of it—for the regeneration thereof."

"But he saith himself," suggested Am-nem-hat, "'My kingdom is not of this world.'"

"Verily," replied Ammonius. "And his kingdom is not 'of' the world, but is 'in' the world. Not surely a kingdom founded upon the social, religious, and political laws and customs of the world, like other kingdoms; but, not the less, a kingdom for men living in the world, and founded on its own social, religious, and political economies. And this temporal, earthly kingdom, established

11

by our Lord in the world, is the very essence of the gospel, the most important part of the truth which he revealed to men."

"That is new to me," answered Am-nem-hat, "for I had supposed that the religious idea chiefly handleth the affairs of man with reference to the future life, and that his temporal condition is the affair of government, unto which he is kept in subjection by the sense of duty and obligation which religion supplieth."

"And thou art manifestly in the right as to all governments that exist or ever have existed among men, except only the kingdom of heaven. How many governments have existed in Egypt?"

"I know not that," answered the ancient. "Our records cover thirty full dynasties before the second Persian invasion, which occurred seven centuries ago, but each of these dynasties represents more than one Pharaoh, and several of them a great many; for government is not a permanent thing, and some form of revolution ever lieth in wait for it, as a tiger in a jungle watcheth a man to spring upon and strangle him."

"And how many governments have existed among other peoples and nations during the thousands of years covered by the records of thy land of Kem?"

"I know not that," said Am-nem-hat; "they are unknown and innumerable."

"Therefore," answered Ammonius, "each one of them must have contained, in its very constitution and nature, the seeds of its own dissolution; and, so far at least in human history, the science of government hath learned no secret by which to secure permanency for itself."

"The inference thou hast drawn seemeth to follow necessarily and undeniably from the known facts."

"And what hath been the net result of the science of government among all the peoples and nations of whom thou hast ever heard?"

"Misery!"

"Yea!—But state the net result of government in political or in philosophical terms!"

"State it for thyself; I desire to learn of thee."

"Hath not the net result of human government everywhere, in all climes and ages and among all men, been only to produce, or develop, a ruling class at the top of every social and political system, unto whom all the blessings of the government and civilization are given by law; an oppressed or enslaved people at the bottom, upon whose weary shoulders rest all of the burdens and the waste of life; and between these two extremes, some religious system and some armed force, seeking to adjust the correlative legal rights and duties of the high and the low, the rich and the poor, the class that ruleth and the class that is ruled over, by the agency of religion, so long as the religious sentiment serveth to keep the people in bondage, and by sword and spear when superstition faileth? Add to this result the fact that women are everywhere slaves, or chattels, legally lower and more debased than their husbands and fathers, no matter what position the men may occupy; and have we not plainly stated, in this terrible formula, the net result of the

science of human government to which it infallibly leadeth, and from which it hath never escaped ? If thy large
learning hath ever taught thee the name and location of
any nation or people of whom this is not true, wilt thou
now declare it ?"

"I can not name such a government or people,"
answered Am-nem-hat. "For history is but a dreary
record of unceasing strife—among the fortunate for precedence and power, and among the poor for existence;
and during the struggle it hath evermore happened that
the women have been trampled into the filth and mud.
I know not the reason thereof, but the fact is fearfully
true."

"Doth it then seem to thee that to have ordained some
system by which this net result of the science of government may be avoided; some truth by which war and
slavery that have cursed the life and labor of every people under heaven, may be abolished; some social and
political organization by which the false and cruel distinctions maintained by accidents of fortune, birth, rank,
or by even genius and extraordinary abilities, between
the rich and the poor, the great and the small, the feeble
and the wise, may be utterly removed; and by which
womanhood, wifehood, maternity, shall be redeemed from
slavery and elevated to such a place that men can no more
degrade them without consciously degrading themselves
also; some divine and human law of brotherhood among
men by which the race shall attain to liberty, equality,
and fraternity—dost thou think that to devise and establish such a system is a work worthy of a God ?"

"Yea, verily! most worthy of a God; perhaps impossible even unto him."

"This very system hath our Lord ordained; it is the kingdom of heaven upon earth; it is the common Church of Jesus Christ whereby the regeneration of mankind must be secured."

There was a long silence after this, during which all seemed to be pondering on what Ammonius had said, and it was finally broken by Arius, who spoke as follows: "I do not get all of thy meaning. Why is it true that all human governments of necessity result in the slavery of the many to the few, and in their own ultimate destruction? Why can not wise and good men organize some form of government that may secure both permanency for itself and the prosperity of the people. also?"

"Yea, tell us that," said Am-nem-hat, "and also inform us by what means Jesus designeth to avoid in his kingdom the net result which seemeth necessarily to overtake all human governments sooner or later?"

"The same considerations," said Ammonius, "may furnish an answer to both questions. But first let me ask of thy great learning, Am-nem-hat, whether any man hath proposed, or even conceived, of some form of human government which hath never yet been tried among mankind?"

"I think not," said the ancient. "Both Plato and Aristotle have indulged in the attempt to define all the possible forms that government might assume; but, even in the political dream which Plato calleth 'The Republic,' he faileth to specify any form or machinery of government which hath not been repeatedly tried and found to fail; only the results he dreams of are imaginary; the government he devised hath been vainly experimented upon by others."

"The Greek philosopher erred in his delineation of an ideal government both by omitting therefrom the power of faith as the controlling principle thereof, and by denying the sanctity of monogamic marriage. His 'Republic' is, therefore, nugatory, for liberty can not exist in any community at all unless it exists for all alike; and polygamy denies the liberty of half the human race by enslaving women. But thou truly sayest that every possible form of government hath been tried among men, and that all of them alike have failed to secure either permanency for themselves or the welfare of the people. Thou must see, therefore, that the universal failure of government dependeth not upon the form of it, nor upon the age, or clime, or nation in which it existeth; nor upon the religion, language, laws, nor customs of the people; for all forms of it have failed alike, in all ages, among all peoples, under all imaginable religions, languages, customs, and laws. Seemeth this conclusion to be just and true?"

"Yea," answered Am-nem-hat, "I can see no escape therefrom whatever."

"Then it surely followeth," said Ammonius, "that whatever may be the cause of this universal failure of government, it existeth in all of them alike, and worketh the destruction and failure of them all, independently of the form, religion, laws, customs, or other things in regard to which they differ one from another ; for the cause of this failure must be common to all of them. Seemeth this conclusion a valid one to thee ?"

"Verily," said the ancient. "The cause must be one common to all governments, or else we might find somewhere a government in which this cause did not exist and operate ; and so find a government that possesseth permanency and secureth the welfare of the people. But there hath never been, and is not, such a government on earth. The cause of failure must be common unto all."

"Wilt thou draw from out the store-house of thine erudition, and show unto us one law or custom that is common to all human governments ? For in that one thing, whatever it may be, we shall assuredly find the sole cause of the failure of governments, and of all the tyranny, injustice, oppression, and wretchedness, that maketh human life a burden to the masses of mankind."

"Thou must state the law or custom that is common to all governments alike, for thyself," said Am-nem-hat, "for they differ almost inconceivably in form, religion, language, laws, and customs ; and I recall none which is common to every human government."

"All human governments," said Ammonius, "have one thing in common : they agree in one pernicious law and custom which is the cause of failure in them all ; for all human governments alike maintain the legal right of individuals to acquire, hold, and transmit private property-rights in estates, offices, prerogatives ; even in women and in slaves. This is the idolatry of mammon, of which all nations arc guilty, the only idolatry which Jesus ever denounced by name, the only one that opposeth his kingdom with a potent logic based upon selfishness. Many arc learning to hate this idolatry in respect of the royal offices : even the debased Romans scorn the name of 'king,' and call their master 'imperator,' the commander of the army; some tribes hate it in its application to men, and own no slaves; the Scythians and some other nations deny the right of property in women, and take but one wife. Jesus Christ denies the right of private property, not only in women, slaves, offices, and prerogatives, but in houses, lands, and everything else. Hence the property-law of his kingdom imperatively demandeth the transfer of all that the believer hath unto the common Church; this sacrifice is hard to make if one hath great possessions, and, therefore, it is hard for a rich man to enter the kingdom of heaven. No rich man doeth this except under the power of a dominant faith which teacheth him that the thing which is best for all believers is best for him; and that the common good is better than self-aggrandizement. No sane man doubteth that the political economy of Jesus would bless the world, if men would adopt it; but not many great, not many wise, not many rich, not many noble, come into the kingdom, because selfishness revolts at the sacrifice of real or imaginary advantages, secured to them by mammon-worship. It is emphatically the gospel, the glad tidings, for the poor, and it is a regeneration that beginneth at the bottom, not at the top, of every social system. All human governments are founded upon the idolatrous faith that private rights of property are the sacredest thing in human life, and that government over the people is necessary to protect it. Jesus denieth this faith : he saith that liberty is better than wealth, equality better than rank, fraternity better than power. He, therefore, in his kingdom, abolisheth private rights of property in order to reach something that is infinitely higher and better for all men ; and he summeth up human life, laws, governments, all that pertaineth to man's social condition, in one short sentence which containeth in itself the ultimate truth of all social and political economy and wisdom : 'Ye can not serve God and Mammon.' And the Pharisees hated Jesus only because they were 'covetous'; and the Romans and other nations persecute us even unto death because they know that the triumph of the kingdom of heaven is the overthrow of all government over the people ; and they love power, and wealth, and rank."

"How wouldst thou punish crime if all human governments were thus abolished ?" asked the ancient.

"There would then be no crime to punish," answered Ammonius. "For human statutes, growing up out of the idolatry of private rights of property, both create and punish crimes. There could be neither treason nor war in the absence of government ; and all other crimes, which in some shape are the out-put of the idolatry of mammon, would cease with the false social and political systems which generate and nourish them. Crimes are, and for nearly three centuries have been, utterly unknown among the Christian communities."

"What, then, standeth in the way of the triumph of the kingdom of heaven?"

"Naught except the selfishness of men intrenched behind the strong rampart of private property-rights— the one thing against which our Lord hath declared undying and uncompromising enmity."

The old man sat in silence for a long time, and his grave and noble face showed the traces of many conflicting emotions. Finally he said: "Thy son did once ask me why I am not a Christian, and I could not answer him, nor do I know. But Arius thought that thou mightst understand better than either he, or I, the exact attitude in which my soul standeth toward Christ and his religion. Canst thou tell me what the trouble is?"

"Then," said Ammonius unto him, "thou mayst believe that Jesus is the Christ; thou mayst believe that his religion is divinely true and perfect, best for thee and for mankind; thou mayst believe that he is ready and willing to accept and save every one that cometh unto him by faith; thou mayst believe that he will so accept and save thee whenever thou wilt come unto him thus; thou mayst believe and purpose that thou wilt come—but all this maketh no man a Christian! The thing which maketh thee a Christian is the voluntary surrender of thine own will to the will of Jesus; to abrogate all in his favor; to accept his will as thine only law. And this he saith thou canst do if thou wilt; no man on earth, no angel in heaven, can do this thing for thee, nor force thee to do it for thyself; nor can any enginery of earth or hell prevent thee from doing this thing if thou wilt. It is a matter between thee and thy Lord only; and thou and he must transact it. But if, freely and voluntarily, with a full purpose of heart and mind to obey Christ only, thou makest this grand surrender of thyself to him, the light, and peace, and blessedness which he imparteth to those who truly love him shall be thine own forever. Wilt thou have this man Christ Jesus to reign over thee?"

Then a glorious beauty shone from the old man's countenance, and his eyes grew bright with happy tears, and he exclaimed joyously: "I make this surrender now; the light breaketh in even upon my soul; it is as plain as the noonday sun: 'Glory be to God in the highest, and on earth peace; good-will to men!' The truth for which all my life long I have so vainly sought cometh unto me as to a little child. And it is pure, satisfying, beautiful! 'Praise the Lord, O my soul!'"

"'Except ye be converted, and become as little children, ye can in no wise enter into the kingdom!'" said Ammonius.

"And all men, great and small, wise and ignorant, young and old, meet upon an exact equality before our Lord," said the boy Arius; "for God is no respecter of persons."

CHAPTER XIV.

THE BLIND RECEIVE THEIR SIGHT.

THE next day was the Sabbath again, and Christian families from the region round about Baucalis, to the number of some four hundred, assembled at the cottage for religious services. Some of them came on foot, some on horseback, and some of them in boats along the coast. Am-nem-hat informed the presbyter, who came to preach for them, of his desire, and that of Hatasa and her daughter, to be received into the kingdom of heaven. He also informed him that, at his cottage in the neighborhood, he had a considerable sum in gold and silver, which he desired to give to the Church, or in some other way consecrate to holy uses ; and that the Egyptian ladies had property in Alexandria, all of which, or such portion as he might advise, they wished to use in the same way. The presbyter informed them that such a desire was natural and commendable in every one that sought to be a Christian ; but that for the time being they must remain as stewards of their own estates, because the Christians of that region were all prosperous and needed nothing, and there was no application for aid from other communities. He further told them that, as soon as it might be considered safe for them to do so, the Christians of the vicinage purposed to erect a church for the accommodation of the numerous brethren around about, and that whenever they might enter upon this work the opportunity would be given to them to aid therein; and that, if any calamity should overtake another Christian community, in any part of the world, whereby they might be brought to need assistance, he would inform them of it as soon as the bishops communicated such facts to him; but that at that time there was no way in which the money could be used.

Early in the morning Arius and his father had set up some poles in holes in the ground already made to receive them, and had stretched strong cords from them unto the eaves of the cottage, and had unrolled and fastened thereon a canopy made of wide cotton cloth, which formed a shelter from the sunshine; and, while some of the congregation sat within the house, the greater part of them found places on the outside under the awning. Hatasa had her couch drawn up beside the open window, from which she could see and hear all that might be done. Theckla was here, there, and everywhere, making friends with nearly all the girls and boys that attended, and especially with one little fellow of twelve years of age who was stone-blind. In the course of her sympathetic talk with this lad he informed her that his parents had brought him there to have the Church pray that his sight might be restored to him.

"How long hast thou been thus blind?" asked Theckla.

"I do not know," said the boy. "I remember that

I could once see, and the world was beautiful to me, and the people, and many things. But it has been so long since then!"

"Dost thou believe that their prayers can cure thy blindness?"

"Assuredly," said he, "whenever the Lord will."

"Why, then, hast thou not sought the prayers of the Church before this time, if so thou believest?"

"My parents wished not to have the miracle wrought on me until they thought me to be old enough both to understand how great an affliction loss of sight is and to remember the means whereby I regained it—if, indeed, the Lord will at this time grant our request."

"And thou surely wilt love Jesus much if he shall hear thee, wilt thou not?"

"Yea, will I! Indeed, I love him now with all my soul; but if he restoreth my sight unto me I could work for him far more when I am older; and chiefly for that reason do I pray for his mercy in this matter."

"And I shall pray for thee, also," said Theckla.

And she told Hatasa and Am-nem-hat about the boy, and they looked amazed thereat, but said nothing.

By nine o'clock in the morning all had assembled whom they expected; and, having set a watch on the only practicable road that led down from the mountains to Baucalis, to give them timely notice of the approach of any whose coming might endanger them, the exercises of the day were inaugurated with singing and prayer and the reading of the gospel. There were a wonderful simplicity and directness, both in songs and prayers. If

Jesus Christ, the Saviour, Friend, and King, through whom their worship was addressed to God, had been visibly present regarding the manner of their devotions, the whole service could not have been more earnest, simple, and direct. If, indeed, he was not present, they thought and felt otherwise; and the sense of his presence was as real and actual unto them as if, on raising their eyes, they could have looked him in the face; and this unquestioning faith gave a strange sense of life and vividness to all of the exercises, the progress of, which Am-nem-hat, Hatasa, and Theckla watched with joy and eagerness.

The presbyter preached with great simplicity and earnestness, describing the love of Jesus and the triumphs of the faith, and in the peroration his address swelled into a glorious pæan of victory as he declared the steadfastness and faithfulness of certain Christians who had recently suffered martyrdom in other places, telling them that no man could foresee how soon some of them also might be called upon to tread the glorious path by which their brethren had been perfected in the Lord, and transferred to eternal felicity. But, looking into the flashing eyes and rapt faces turned upon him from every side, he deemed it prudent to give them solemn warning that the crown of martyrdom was not to be officiously sought after, any more than it was to be avoided by unfaithfulness; but that they must be alike ready to live unto Christ, or to die for him, as the providence of God might determine to be best for each of them.

Then he said that if there were any present who had

not before publicly professed their faith in Christ, and desired to do so, the Church would then witness their good confession ; and thereupon Am-nem-hat and Theckla both stepped forward and gave their hands to the presbyter. The presbyter then briefly stated to the people the facts which he had learned in regard to the past life and experience of the ancient, and the recital thereof at once rendered the old man an object of respect and affection to all of them. Their interest was enlisted by the exceptional fact that an aged and learned pagan priest had found the Saviour precious to his soul. Then Ammonius sent forward Arius and bade him relate to the assembly the story of the shipwreck of Hatasa and Theckla, and of their desire to become Christians ; and the boy narrated the circumstances so vividly, and with such unconscious force and eloquence, that they twain also were welcomed into the hearts of all those Christians, and the sense of strangeness and restraint that naturally affects the mind at our first meeting with those whom we have not seen before was at once dissolved by the influence of fraternal interest and affection.

Am-nem-hat having signified his desire to be baptized by immersion, they all repaired to the shore of the little bay, where, with appropriate ceremony, that sacred rite was administered. But, owing to the debilitated condition of Hatasa, she and Theckla received the same sacred rite, after suitable explanations, by having the water sprinkled upon them at the house.

Many of those who were present, and especially those who had come in boats, brought prepared food with them, and soon this was distributed over clean cloths spread out under the trees, and all of them did eat together with gladness, as if it had been one large and loving family—Arete and old Thopt being diligent to supply from their own stores everything that was needed or had been forgotten.

Then in the afternoon the congregation was again assembled, and they engaged in singing and prayer. The presbyter informed the people that a blind boy had come, with his parents, to ask the prayers of the Church that God would restore his sight, explaining the reason why they had not sooner done so, very much as the boy had stated to Theckla, and saying that they should first partake of the holy communion, and afterward pray for the lad's recovery. Then this rite was administered; and all of them engaged in prayer, the presbyter leading and the people making occasional responses. And even while they were so engaged the lad sprang to his feet, and, throwing his arms about his mother's neck, he cried aloud: "O mother, I see! I see!—Brethren, thank God for me, for my sight is perfectly restored!"

And the presbyter changed the form of his words from supplication into praise and thanksgiving; and, when he had finished, many pressed forward to congratulate the lad upon his miraculous cure; and afterward, when they went away, he went also, seeing as well as other boys.

Then later in the evening, having first agreed upon the place of their next meeting, the congregation received a benediction at the mouth of the presbyter and quietly dispersed. But almost every head of a family first came unto

12

Am-nem-hat and unto Hatasa and Theckla, and urged
them with great kindness to come unto their homes and
abide with them as long as might be convenient.

But, before the presbyter departed, Hatasa requested
that he come unto her, and of him she asked concerning the baptism for the dead ; and having diligently inquired of her concerning the character and manner of life
of her husband, and having heard her firm declaration of
her belief that he was one who ever sought to do that
which he thought to be just, right, and true, so that if
he had sufficiently learned of Jesus he would have been
a Christian, the presbyter administered to her the baptism
for the dead, from which the poor lady derived a strange
and unmeasurable satisfaction and peace.

But Hatasa did not recover any strength, and the next
day she was weaker than ever, and the next, and so on
from day to day. She requested them to hold services in
her room every evening, and seemed gladly to engage with
them in prayer. But she said that she had no power to
will or to wish that she might continue to live. She
dreaded the pain and weariness of a lingering convales-
cence, and she said that the only earthly care that had
troubled her was concern for her daughter's welfare, and
that she would never separate her from her newly discovered but precious Christian friendships, and did not wish
her to go among their pagan kindred. She informed Ammonius that there was much property in Alexandria that
now belonged to Theckla, and asked him what disposition
should be made of it. Ammonius at first said : " Let it
go. Theckla shall lack for nothing ; and riches are a

snare to the young." But, upon considering that the estate would go to the pagan kindred, and never to the Church, unless the legal right of the girl thereto was asserted, he sent unto Cyrene for a proper officer, who came and took the depositions of Hatasa, Arius, Thopt, and Theckla, as to the shipwreck of Amosis and his family, and as to the identity and parentage of the maiden, to be laid before the orphans' court at Alexandria. She also made a written request that Theckla's relative Am-nem-hat should be appointed guardian of the maiden's person and estate, with her friend Ammonius to succeed him if the aged man should die during Theckla's minority. And, having accomplished these things in due and proper form, she began to fail more rapidly, and about midnight sank peacefully into rest, almost her last request being that she might be buried in the "sleeping-ground" of the Christians of that vicinity.

And, when Theckla saw that she was dead, the wild sorrow of her heart broke out in almost the very same words that her mother had used upon the death of Amosis, and she cried: "No more! no more! Ah, never more!"

But Ammonius said unto her, "Come hither, daughter!" And, when she had come, he laid his hand upon her head and he asked, "Art thou a Christian?"

And she answered, "Yea, I love the Lord."

Then he saith: "That is well, my child. But, if thou art a Christian, use not the vain and despairing lamentation of the heathen. Thou shouldst not think nor feel as they do when they cry out in their bitterness, 'No more.' Thy mother leaveth thee not forever, child. She hath only gone before thee by a little space at most, and thou shalt go unto her again. So the Lord whom thou lovest doth solemnly promise thee, and thou must never distrust his promise or his love."

"But I loved my mother! I must weep for her."

"Yea, daughter, weep as much as thou wilt. That is but natural and proper. So perhaps thou wouldst weep if she had gone to Alexandria, leaving thee behind; yet thou wouldst take comfort in the hope that she would come to thee again. So now she hath gone to Jesus, and is safe with him, and thou must take comfort in the hope, nay, in the very certainty, that, while she returneth not, perhaps, unto thee, thou shalt soon go unto her. And thou, being a Christian girl, shalt not vex thy heart with the hopeless sorrow that the heathen feel."

And the girl was comforted indeed, and her pleasant faith aided the buoyancy of health and youth in helping her to weary down the sorrow that followed the loss of her young, beautiful, and beloved mother; because the power of that faith brought the world's Consoler very near, and Death to her was shorn of his greatest terrors.

It was agreed among them that Theckla and Am-nem-hat should reside permanently at the cottage. The old man and Arius soon brought all of his possessions from the hermitage, even to his favorite goats; and, some of the neighbors assisting them, they built another room of stone, into which the ancient's manuscripts, his furniture, and his accumulation of coin, were all safely stowed away. And, all things having been thus satisfactorily arranged, the old

man was conveyed in the boat around to Apollonia, and
thence he took shipping unto Alexandria, where he produced before the orphans' court the depositions and
other papers committed unto him by Hatasa; and, as guardian of Theckla, leased the houses which she owned in
the city, and received and brought back to Baucalis with
him some elegant personal effects that had belonged to
Hatasa; her relatives consenting thereto without much
opposition, and stipulating only that, if the girl should
die, they were to be immediately informed of the fact;
and that, if she should live, she was to come to the city as
soon as she became of age.   They were all pagans, and
the old priest would have gone almost any length to avoid
placing his young and beautiful Christian ward within the
range of their influence.   And, having transacted all things
necessary, in a very few days the old man returned gladly
to Baucalis—a place to which his heart seemed bound by
stronger and more beautiful associations than had ever
come into his long and lonely life elsewhere on earth, not
even excepting Thebes and Ombos, nor his own quiet
hermitage upon the mountain-side.

And the aged priest at once installed himself as the
tutor of Theckla; and he taught to Arius, also, such science and literature as then were known unto the wisest
men of Egypt; but some things he continued to learn
from the boy himself.

And so the next four years glided quietly away, during
which the routine of their peaceful lives pursued its usual
course; and in their flight Arius became a tall and graceful youth of twenty; Theckla grew into a blooming and

exquisitely beautiful woman of sixteen ; for in the ardent Libyan latitudes the girls grow quickly into womanhood. These years made small changes in Ammonius and Arete ; they told lightly upon the venerable Am-nem-hat, whose pure and quiet life had been favorable to longevity and to the preservation of his faculties unimpaired even unto an extreme old age ; and Thopt herself bore the flight of time quite well, becoming almost imperceptibly more fixed and rigid in all her actions and opinions, and more and more impressed with the idea that Christianity was an excellent and beautiful thing for wise and perfect people like those among whom her lot was cast, and might even have suited her if it had not sought to abolish the relation of mistress and slave between herself and Arete, "contrary to nature and to common sense," she said ; but that old grudge she could never entirely get over.

CHAPTER XV.

DURING these four years a great change had occurred in the heart and in the person of beautiful young Theckla. There came a gradually developing fullness and roundness over her whole form; the sharp, angular lines of childhood faded away in the softer curves of maturity; a deeper color bloomed upon her peachy cheeks; a sweeter, more unfathomable light burned in her dark, soft eyes; the delicate pink hue under the skin, which in all Egyptians of the higher classes, whose complexions are untanned by a hard life and constant exposure, proves the ancient race of the land of Kem to be consanguineous with the Aryan rather than with the Nigritian family of man, became more clearly and deliciously defined; and a sort of intangible self-consciousness grew up within her heart which intuitively led her to keep her hands off the boy companion whom she loved as a brother, and, without understanding why she did so, she ceased to romp and tumble around with him as she had been accustomed to do during the first year of her residence at Baucalis. In place of casting aside her gown and plunging into the waters of the bay with him, when she went to bathe, she went alone, or

with Arete. Yet there was not the slightest tendency to
prudishness in this gradual withdrawal of that tactual fa-
miliarity with Arius which had characterized her first intercourse with him; but, without ever having been talked
to or lectured at on the subject, her chaste, pure soul
instinctively drew from the very spirit of the gospel lessons
fine boundaries of feeling that made her unconsciously
observe even the most delicate bounds of maiden modesty.
But this retiring somewhat within herself—this ceasing
from the outward, demonstrative signs of trust and affection—was physical only: for the boy and girl grew daily
nearer and dearer to each other; grew daily more trustful
and confidential with each other; and daily became more
and more identified in interest, thought, and feeling.
They talked not of love any more than an affectionate
brother and sister would have done, but the affection that
united them to each other seeped down dew-like to the
very roots of life in both. Ever his care and watchfulness
for her grew more tender and respectful, and ever the smile
with which she acknowledged his constant little attentions grew more bright and trustful; and, from this basis
of evenly developing physical, intellectual, and spiritual
progress and perfectness in both of them, their souls
leaned unto each other, and mingled in an affection as
chaste, strong, and intimate as human nature knows,
growing together day by day, and attuning themselves to
perfect concord in all the utterances and aspirations of
their beautiful and happy lives—a human love that was
impossible to pagan civilization, and is almost impossible
to ours, but that flourished in its almost divine sweetness .

and beauty in the primitive Christian communities, side by side with thaumaturgy and the graces of that spiritual life which hath almost become a dream unto the world rather than a blessed reality.

So those four years passed fleetly and pleasantly away, and Arius was now a very tall but graceful youth of twenty, and Theckla was an exquisitely beautiful woman of sixteen, when Ammonius told his son that the time had come at which he desired him to go to Antioch in Syria, and pursue his studies with the Bishop Lucanius, for four or five years, preparatory to his ordination as a presbyter —if, indeed, his heart was still set on preferring to be a teacher and a preacher of the gospel to all other vocations; whereupon the young man at once answered that no earthly inducement could lead him to abandon the ministry, for which he had always considered himself set apart; and immediately the family began to make preparations for the young man's departure.

On the evening before Arius left Baucalis, he and Theckla wandered along the shores of the little bay, until they happened to come unto the spot at which she had been rescued from the raft, and the girl said: "Even there thou didst bring me unto the shore, Arius. It seemeth to me to have been ages and ages ago; and yet the time hath passed so pleasantly!"

"Yea," said Arius, "yet it is only four years since then, and, after to-morrow, it may be as long a time before I see the dear old farm again, or thee. Theckla, wilt thou forget thy friend and our happy life at Baucalis, and all the things which made us blessed here so long?"

"Nay," she said. "Life opens wide before us both, Arius, as we stand here upon its threshold—wide as the sea out yonder, and unknown. But Baucalis will always be the dearest place on earth to me."

"Theckla," said the young man, taking one of the girl's hands in his, "I love thee truly and tenderly. When I shall have finished the course of study at Antioch, I desire to come for thee and claim thee for my wife. Dost thou love me, Theckla, so that thou couldst be happy as my wife?"

And the girl laid her head against his shoulder, and, raising her dewy eyes to his, she said, "If thou so lovest me, Arius, I would be the happiest woman in the world to be thy wife."

Then the young man kissed her tenderly, and said: "Theckla, let this be a covenant between thee and me before the Lord, that when I shall have finished the studies required at Antioch, I will come for thee, and thou shalt be my wife."

And she answered: "Yea, Arius! Let this be our covenant."

That was all of it—quiet, simple, truthful; based upon the very highest mutual love, respect, and trust; but no grand ceremonial that human pride ever imagined, or human lips pronounced, could have any more thoroughly bound and consecrated them unto each other for life and death than did that simple, heart-felt covenant. For in those days, and in the Christian communities, marriage was not of compulsion, or of trade, convenience, ambition, but of free, intelligent choice; and among those people the equally shameful blasphemies of adultery and divorce were utterly unknown.

So, upon the next morning, after a tender leave-taking all around, in which even old Thopt commended him to the guardianship of God, Arius, accompanied by his father, loaded his boxes into their little boat, and they made their way unto Apollonia, at which port they took shipping for Alexandria, whence immediately they went in another ship unto the sea-port for Antioch, and thence to the ancient city wherein they "were first called Christians."

Ammonius recalled to the mind of the Bishop Lucanius the fearful storm in which they two had met more than twenty years before, which interview had been the medium of the Lord's mercy unto him; and was most gladly and affectionately welcomed. Ammonius informed the bishop that, having been precluded from the public ministrations of the word by his own physical infirmities, he had made a vow to dedicate the first son that might be born unto him to the service of God, and had, therefore, brought unto him his only child, a lad not altogether ignorant of the gospel nor of letters, whose heart was set upon doing the Lord's work, to profit by his experience and instructions. And the lad pleased the bishop greatly; and, after some conversation, Arius was admitted into the school, or class of young men whom the bishop taught, as a deacon in the church immediately under the charge of Lucanius; for the bishops of those days were not lords or princes, but were presbyters, who had their own congregations, and who, from zeal and learning, age and experience, were intrusted also with an advisory superintendence of some other presbyters and churches, and especially with the training of young deacons for the ministry.

And the next day Ammonius resumed his homeward journey, and in due time reached Baucalis without accident or delay.

On the very same evening that Arius and Theckla had plighted their troth unto each other, the young man took the girl by the hand, and, having led her unto his parents, told them of the new relationship established between them, and Ammonius and Arete gladly accepted the maiden Theckla as their daughter; and she abode with them for two years longer, constantly aiding in all household duties, and likewise pursuing such studies as Am-nem-hat advised; and especially practicing the art of writing upon papyrus, and upon parchment, and upon vellum, until she had satisfied herself that vellum was altogether the best material for a certain purpose which she had in view, and that her own handwriting had acquired sufficient precision and neatness for her contemplated task; and then she announced her purpose of removing to the city of Alexandria, and occupying one of her own houses there, if only Am-nem-hat would go with her and make his home at her abode. This purpose she mentioned to the whole family one evening after their usual religious services, whereupon Arete said: "Why wouldst thou leave us, daughter? Art thou not happy at Baucalis?"

"Yea," replied Theckla. "Thy home hath been a haven of rest and happiness to me, and I could be happier here than elsewhere in the world; but in two years more our Arius, of whom the bishop writeth such loving things, will be a presbyter; and I go hence unto Alexandria because, before the time expires, I wish to make with mine own hand a perfect copy of the scriptures for our young presbyter, and also wish to build a church for him, that when he leaveth the bishop he may have a church and a congregation, and a perfect copy of the sacred word ready for him; and thou knowest that at Alexandria I may even find original manuscripts of both gospels and epistles from which to transcribe my copy. What less than this, indeed, wouldst thou have me do for our most dear young presbyter?"

And they all, seeing that she had made a matter of conscience of these two purposes, ceased to oppose her design; and not long afterward she and Am-nem-hat were taken in their little boat unto Apollonia, by Ammonius; and thence they went by ship to Alexandria; and, after a speedy and pleasant voyage, they cast anchor in the little harbor of Eunostos; and thence removed straightway unto one of the nine dwellings which she owned in Rhacotis, the Egyptian quarter of the city. Here, with the aid of six years' accumulated rents from her handsome estate, the young girl quickly furnished her home in the most comfortable manner, and had a room carefully furnished for Am-nem-hat, and another in which the manuscripts were to be kept, and in which they might prosecute their studies; for the aged grand-uncle and the young maiden had almost come to sustain to each other the relation of dear companions and fellow-students rather than that of teacher and pupil. Very soon, also, with the aid of the old man, who possessed a critical knowledge of such matters, she procured a large quantity of the finest vellum, and began her self-appointed task of transcribing the scriptures for Arius. And afterward she sold (through her guardian) five of the nine houses which she owned, for a large sum, and having carefully selected a plot of ground suitable for the purpose, she bought it, taking the title thereto in the name of certain persons whom she knew to be Christians, upon a secret trust for the common Church, and after many consultations with Am-nem-hat, and with the bishop and with other friends, she began the work of building a beautiful and substantial church ; and, with the making of her careful and accurate copies of the scriptures and the building of the church, both she and Amnem-hat found themselves constantly employed. For, although at that time there was no open and public persecution of the Christians, it had not long ceased, and none knew at what moment the caprice of their pagan rulers, stimulated by the hatred of Jewish and pagan priests, might blaze out into a general and merciless war against them ; so that their meetings were quietly held, and the erection of churches was carried on without show or publicity ; and generally, indeed, parts of the buildings were used as a school for the children of Christians ; and many a church was saved from destruction by the fitful and uncertain hate of the populace and priests, by being taken for a school rather than a church. And there were few who desired to be known as Christians, except to persons of like faith, though none hesitated to declare this faith at any peril, when called in question about it.

The city of Alexandria, which was founded by Alexander the Great, about 322 B. C., was, at the date of our story, one of the most populous, wealthy, and intellectual cities in the world. Situated twelve miles west of the Canopic mouth of the Nile, its walls were washed on the south by the placid waters of Lake Mareotis, and on the north by the Mediterranean Sea; and it was the seat and center of a vast industry and an almost unequaled commerce. The streets were straight and parallel, and the city was divided into four quarters by two magnificent highways, each two hundred feet wide, crossing each other at right angles, and built up on each side with splendid houses, temples, and public buildings of every kind. A vast necropolis lay west of the city, on the east a mighty hippodrome. In the northeastern part was the Regis Judæorum, or Jewish quarter, wherein the Israelites abode, but their business extended not only through the great city, but throughout the world. The western part was called Rhacotis, the Egyptian quarter, and contained, besides its vast Libyan population and magnificent residences, the great temple of Serapis, and the sacred statue of the god that had been brought thither out of Pontus. But Bruchium, the royal or Greek quarter, was the most splendid portion of the city, containing the palace of the Ptolemies, on Lochias, a peninsula stretching eastwardly, the library and museum, the Cæsarium, or temple of the Cæsars, and the Dicasterium, or court of justice, and other buildings that bore witness to the knowledge of Dinocrates the architect, who rebuilt the temple of Diana at Ephesus. About a mile from the mainland was the little island

of Pharos, on which was a light-house over four hundred
feet in height, that was begun by Ptolemy Soter, 300 b. c.,
and finished by Philadelphus, his successor.   An artificial
mole called Hepta Stadium, nearly a mile in length, connected the island with the mainland, and between this mole
and Lochias was the great harbor, while on the other side
of it was a smaller harbor, called Eunostos (safe return), in
which was an artificial basin known as Kibotos (the chest),
which was filled from and connected with Lake Marcotis
by a canal, another arm of which stretched eastward to the
mouth of the Nile.   Throughout this vast metropolis, in
every quarter thereof, undistinguished by dress, nationality, language, or manners, of almost every race under
heaven, engaged in every avocation except official business
or military services, unknown except to their co-religion-
ists, dwelt the countless members of the Christian Church,
forming numerous communities, or congregations, that,
without any public visible organization, were yet bound
together by bonds of faith and love stronger than any
Roman statutes, or any ties of nature, or any ligaments of
interest or of ambition.   Of course, in so vast a population, an aged man and a young girl would be as indis-
tinguishable to all, except their own small circle of friends
and acquaintances, as any particular leaf in the forest, or as
any wave at sea ; and in such a city, the selfishness of the
crowd, the hurry and confusion of business or of pleasure,
formed a sort of refuge for the Christians ; so that, long
before the period of which we write, almost the first cir-
cumstance which called any public attention to their
numbers was the fact that, under their influence, the

pagan temples were less crowded, and the pagan offerings less rich and free, than had been usual in times past; and, when the fated Israelites had been accused of proselyting the people from the worship of the gods, they defended themselves against the angry priests by declaring that not they, but the Christians, converted men of all nations from the old superstitions, and led them to abandon the temples and forsake the gods.

Soon after their settlement in Alexandria, Am-nem-hat had informed the relatives of Theckla of the young girl's arrival, and they had courteously called to see her, and had invited her to their own homes, and had showed every disposition to receive the beautiful young heiress with favor and affection. But they were all heathens, and her association with them was necessarily limited to formal and distant intercourse; as every visit to the great temple of Serapis, every public occasion, or a birth, a marriage, or a funeral among them, might force her either to countenance their pagan rites and ceremonies, or to attract unto herself an unpleasant and perhaps dangerous attention by refusing to do so. Hence she preferred to maintain only a ceremonious acquaintance with her kindred, and to find her real friendships among the Christians, with many of whom she soon came to be upon terms of social and personal intimacy and confidence.

Among the relatives whom she was almost compelled occasionally to meet, and to receive at her own house, was her cousin Harroun, the son of her mother's sister, who also was a pagan. The young man was of perfect physical organization, like so many of the Egyptian upper class, as

13

beautiful as an untamed leopard, of quick, bright, sparkling intelligence, instinct with passion and appetite, and a
general favorite among the aristocratic youth of Egyptian
society in the city. One of Theckla's greatest misfortunes
and annoyances she found in the fact that this elegant
youth conceived a violent passion for her at first sight, and
seemed resolved to push his claims to the heart and hand
of the young maiden without delay. As soon, however, as
Theckla perceived any intimation of his feelings in regard
to herself, she quietly arranged to receive him thereafter
only in the library, and took care to see that Grand-uncle
Am-nem-hat should be present, so that the young man
never got an opportunity to see her alone. And to prevent the constant repetition of his invitations to her to
visit the theatre, the hippodrome, and other places of
amusement, she told him kindly that it was useless to
offer such courtesies, for, that while it was unpleasant to
refuse them, she could not and would not accept them
from him nor from any one else, having no inclination to
mingle in such throngs, and no need of any amusements
except those which she was accustomed to find in literary
pursuits. Harroun, who had been raised under a system
in which courtship and marriage were, to a large extent,
matters of convenience, and in which a chaste girl was
not supposed to be possessed of any will, but was to be
disposed of as her relations might deem to be proper and
advantageous, thought that he had never seen so shy a
maiden ; but, in spite of her seeming unconsciousness and
manifest indifference, he ceased not to visit her, claiming
the privilege of a near relation in that particular, and

ceased not to show his admiration for her by looks which
were almost loathsome to her pure young soul. For the
youth, like every other pagan, was mostly a brute, a very
beautiful and elegant animal, truly, but not the less an
animal ; a very intellectual and gifted brute, but not the
less brutal ; and his sensuous admiration was offensive to
the girl.   The lofty and pure affection to which she and
Arius gave the name of love would have been utterly
incomprehensible to him as to every heathen.   That to
which they gave the name of love sprang as directly out of
sensuous admiration and preference as does the passion
of the lower animals ; and while she did not comprehend
why his advances were so repulsive to herself, she began to
feel his preference as a sort of persecution, and avoided
him as much as possible.   Yet, as far as a pagan is capable
of love at all, he loved her, and the very fact that he found
her favor hard to win rendered successful pursuit of her
all the more desirable.   To him it seemed a strange and
unprecedented thing that a girl so young, so beautiful,
and so wealthy, should voluntarily renounce all the social
advantages of the aristocratic circle in which her family
moved, and spend her time in seemingly unending studies,
with little or no companionship save that of the grave and
taciturn old man who was never absent from the room
while he was there ; and Harroun gradually learned to
regard his unfailing presence in the light of a personal
injury to himself, so that he soon harbored a bitter preju-
dice against the ancient, that lacked very little of growing
into actual hatred.   But there was nothing tangible about
which to make a quarrel, except the fact that he could

never see Theckla alone, and, as this seemed to be her
own choice, exercised in her own house, there was nothing
for him to do except to submit to it; but his aversion to
the quiet and dignified old man increased in intensity from
month to month.   Finally, he told her in Am-nem-hat's
presence that he had been called away by the public service
in which he was engaged, beyond the cataracts of the Nile,
and would be absent for several months; and that he
desired to have some private conversation with her before
he departed from Alexandria.   The young girl looked
somewhat disconcerted by this request, but she immediately arose, and said unto him, "Let us pass into the
adjoining room, cousin, and I will hear thee."

He followed her gladly, and no sooner had the door
closed behind them than he came close up to her and
began a most vehement protestation of his love. As soon
as there was the slightest pause in the passionate and
rapid torrent of his speech, she said, gravely and calmly:
"Cousin, hear me for a moment.   I have carefully avoided
any such declaration as thou hast begun to make, and
beseech thee to leave it unspoken.   It is useless to say
such things to me, and can only occasion mutual and
unavailing regrets.   Thou art my cousin, and, I trust,
my friend.   There never can be anything else between
us, and it is folly to think otherwise.   Here let it rest,
and let us return to the library, and forget this foolish
episode."

"There is no folly about it!" cried the young man,
passionately.   "We are both young and wealthy, and in
every way suitable companions.   It is very natural and

right.   I am neither an idiot nor a child, and I love thee,
Theckla, and will not be put-aside in any such fashion.
Why dost thou continually avoid me ?   Why hast thou for
months contrived so that I can not speak to thee except
in the presence of strangers, or of that old mummy whom
thou keepest at thy side forever ?   Why dost thou deny
thyself all the pleasures and associations natural to thine
age and social rank ?   Why spendest thou all thy time in
dreary readings, unsuited to thy youth and circumstances,
for the amusement of that selfish old fossil there, who
never leaveth thee for a day nor an hour ?   All this
must and shall be changed ? "

Then the girl drew herself up straight, and, fixing her
dark eyes full upon him, said in calm and measured tones,
" If I give thee a good reason for having avoided thee,
and for having endeavored to escape any such useless
and unpleasant conversation as this one, will that suffice
thee ? "

" Yea ! if, indeed, the reason be a good one."

" The reason, then, is this," she answered : " I do not
love thee ; I do not desire thy love ; strange and incredi-
ble as it may seem to thee, I do not even admire thee in
any way whatever, and thy profession of affection is irksome to me, and the more irksome the more thou dost
insist upon my hearing thereof."

" But thou wilt learn to love me, Theckla," he cried
out vehemently, " and thou shalt give me some reasonable
opportunity to win thy regard !   Ah, I understand it perfectly.   It is the fault of that old grand-uncle, who ought
to have been 'the Osiris Justified' half a century ago.

He hath prejudiced thy heart against me, because he desireth thee to consume thy youth and brightness in ministering unto his desolate and selfish old age. But I swear by all the gods that, as soon as I return home, I will have thy nearer kindred take thee away from him, so that thou shalt take thy proper place among the maidens of thine own age and rank, and learn some more reasonable way of life, and some better views of duty and of happiness than his selfish and exacting age can teach thee! I see that thou art now blinded by this old man's influence, and resolved against the course of reason and of nature; so for the present, fare thee well, Theckla, but remember that I love thee, and that thou shalt yet be mine own."

Then the young man, trembling with rage and disappointment, fled from the house, and for many months the young girl saw no more of him.

Meanwhile, the building of the church was quietly but diligently prosecuted; and, with the most elaborate and conscientious patience, Theckla labored to make an accurate copy of the scriptures, and, through the bishop and other Christian friends, she obtained the use of more than one original epistle from which to transcribe the text. Some months before the date arrived at which Arius was to be ordained, the diligent young girl had the satisfaction of witnessing the completion of the edifice, a splendid and substantial structure, which the bishop dedicated to God by the name of "Baucalis," given unto it at Theckla's request; and a number of Christians who had learned all about the young girl's history, and why and for whom the church had been builded, organized themselves into a community, and customarily held service of singing and prayer therein. And they prepared also a letter, signed by all of them, in which they informed Arius that they had agreed in requesting him to come and be their presbyter, as soon as he might be ordained ; and that, although they knew him not in the flesh, they were ready to receive him with open hearts, first for Theckla's sake, and afterward, they hoped and believed, even for his own. About the same time, also, the young girl completed the copy of the sacred writings which she had made for Arius ; and this labor of love, and of care and patience, included the Old Testament, the New Testament, the Pastor of Hermas, and the Epistles of Clement to the Corinthians, together with some letters written by Polycarp, Bishop of Smyrna, all copied in the uncial Greek text, with minutest care and accuracy. And she had a box made of cedar of Lebanon, with silver hinges and fastenings, to contain the precious parchments, and a silver plate thereon, upon which was engraved the name "Arius"; and, having finished both the church and the writings, she prepared a letter unto him, and put her letter, and that which the Church had written unto him, and the scriptures, into the cedar box, and laid them away safely, awaiting an opportunity to send them to him against the time of his ordination, for the Christians of those days sent no letters or parcels which might show that they were Christians, except by the hands of those whom they knew to be of the same faith.

And this was Theckla's letter to Arius :

"DEARLY BELOVED : Seeing that thou hast devoted thy life unto the service of our blessed Lord, I did meditate much how I also might be able to accomplish some good in his holy name, and likewise gratify thee. I have accordingly, during the past two years, caused to be builded here a beautiful church, which hath recently been dedicated by the name of 'Baucalis,' in memory of our dear old home ; and thou wilt learn, from the letter sent herewith, that our little community desireth thee to be our presbyter. Also, as a token of the great love wherewith thy Theckla loveth thee, she hath written with her own hand a most careful copy of the sacred scriptures, and of some other manuscripts which thou esteemest highly, and sendeth the same unto thee, with the love of thy   THECKLA."

And a short time before the days set for the ordination of Arius, and of other young men who were deacons studying with the bishop at Antioch, the Bishop of Alexandria went unto the ancient city to be present upon that occasion, and by him Theckla sent unto Arius the box containing the scriptures and letters ; and, having so done, the young girl waited the coming of the youthful presbyter, with her heart full of love, and peace, and happiness.

CHAPTER XVI.

AND while Theckla thus awaited, with gladdest anticipations and almost trembling joy, for the consummation of her own happiness, Harroun returned to Alexandria, and immediately began manœuvring to have the young girl taken to the house of his mother, or to some other relative, where she would be thrown into association with those of her own age and rank, and removed beyond the influence of old Am-nem-hat. And immediately thereafter his mother came unto Theckla, and urged her, by every argument and inducement which she deemed most suitable to influence a young and beautiful girl, to abandon the strange seclusion in which she had lived so long, and come to her home, and take her proper place among the best and gayest young people of the city—a society to which she belonged by birth, and which she was so well fitted to adorn. Theckla kindly but persistently refused every such invitation, pleading her orphaned condition, her love of solitude and literature, and her strong aversion to the gay and beautiful but voluptuous life led by the golden youth of Alexandria.

"But Theckla, darling," said her aunt, "if thou dost

not at least occasionally repair to the great temple of Serapis, where all the youth and fashion of the city are often seen, the world will learn to regard thee as an atheist; and I assure thee, dear, that there is hardly anything more injurious to a young girl's prospects than a reputation for singularity or eccentricity in any respect. The world takes it for granted that there must be something radically wrong about every young girl that is in any respect different from others of her own age and rank, or that affects to feel, and think, and act differently from them. Thou must ever sacrifice thine own inclinations to conform thyself to that which is considered the proper thing."

"Why, aunt," said Theckla, laughing, "thy talk of what 'the world' will say and do amuses and amazes me. Not one out of ten thousand of the people of Alexandria knoweth or careth for me. 'The world,' it seems to me, is thyself, and Cousin Harroun, and, perhaps, not a half score besides my relatives; and, while I meddle not with their pursuits, it seemeth to me that it would be easy enough for them to avoid distressing themselves on my account."

"But thy manner of life exciteth unfavorable comment. Thou dost refuse to go into society, and scornest all the amusements, pleasures, and pursuits proper to thine age, and family, and wealth. Believe me, dear Theckla, that no young girl can affect such eccentricities without being visited by the condemnation of society. Thou must leave this ascetic and unnatural life, and live conformably to nature and to custom."

"I suppose," said Theckla, laughing again, "that 'society,' like 'the world,' significth that very small and exclusive circle of rich and aristocratic people to which my noble kindred belong. But surely I can determine what manner of life suiteth mine own feelings, inclinations, and desires as well as any of them might do. And concerning these matters, I will even judge for myself, not seeking in any way to influence their actions or opinions, but abiding steadfastly by mine own."

"Horrible! O Hes!" cried her aunt. "To think that mine own niece, my sister's child, at the age of eighteen, should be unmaidenly enough to hold any inclinations, desires, or opinions except those which are framed for her by the custom of the class to which she belongeth! Why, Theckla, a young girl hath no more business to entertain or handle such things as 'opinions' than she has to handle sword or spear. It is bold, vicious, unmaidenly! Never—never—never utter such an atrocious and barbarous sentiment again! If I did not know thee to be chaste, and pure, and maidenly, such abominable utterances would make me fear that thou art on the road to ruin!"

"I am aware," said Theckla, "that the Egyptians regard all females, young girls especially, as things; but I consider myself as a person, not as a thing at all. Nature hath granted unto me certain rights, privileges, powers of mind and body, and hath devolved upon me certain duties and responsibilities. Thou seest, therefore, that I am unfitted for association with young ladies who are merely things, not persons. Thou seest that such an association might bo dangerous to them; and might interfere with their 'prospects' by rendering them averse to being reared up, to be selected by some 'eligible' youth, or by some rich and influential old man, as a horse or a dog is selected, and then disposed of as any other domestic animal is provided for. And thou must assuredly perceive that it would be most unwise of thee to expose these pretty, proper, feminine 'things' to the dangerous influences of an association with a girl who hath the hardihood to be-, lieve that she is a person, and the boldness to declare that she hath 'opinions,' convictions of duty and of right which she will not sacrifice even to the terrible fear of 'the world' nor of 'society.' It is best, therefore, even to suffer me to live as I desire to do, neither interfering with my relatives in their way of life, nor suffering them to prescribe my own."

The good lady's fastidious notions of "propriety" were fearfully shocked by the young girl's independent character and utterances; and she determined in her own heart to do whatever she could to prevent her son from continuing his pursuit of a girl whose alliance with him would have been so advantageous in every way if she had not been spoiled by such absurd and dangerous opinions.

But the young man Harroun had his opinions also, one of which was that he was almost irresistible; and another, that the "opinions" of any young girl were merely moral or social megrims, which any man of common sense and passable appearance ought to know how to cure or alleviate; and he, therefore, did not admit the possibility of giving up Theckla voluntarily, or of being ultimately rejected by her, although he dreaded Am-nem-hat's influence over her, and began to hate the old man with great intensity; for he supposed that the declaration of personal independence on the part of Theckla, whereby his mother had been shocked, and even frightened, was simply the repetition of sentiments inculcated by the learned and ancient man, the force and effect of which Theckla did not even comprehend. He dreamed not that these very principles of thought and of action might be the legitimate outgrowth of a new religion which had, with undying energy and power, laid hold upon the very roots of her whole nature, so that no change therein was henceforth at all possible, except in the direction of larger life and development. Accordingly, notwithstanding his mother's unfavorable report, both upon his own prospects of successful courtship, and also upon the bold, self-centered, fearless character of the maiden herself, he resolved to visit her as usual, and to prosecute his suit with diligence. He called immediately upon her, and finding that neither Theckla nor Am-nem-hat was at home, with the freedom allowed by his kinship to the maiden, he passed on into the library, intending to tarry there until her return. While he lingered there impatiently, his eye caught sight of a roll of parchment which had been thoughtlessly left lying in the great arm-chair usually occupied by Am-nem-hat, and, to amuse himself until Theckla's return, he picked up the book and glanced at the title thereof. That title was, "The Gospel of our Lord and Saviour Jesus Christ, written by His Servant John."

Harroun started visibly as he read the words; and then a baleful light came into his beautiful dark eyes, and a sinister smile, that made his handsome face look malevolent and cruel, passed over his bright young face. He knew that it was a very grave offense against the law to read or to possess such books, yet, impelled by curiosity, he read a page or two thereof, beginning with the words: "In the beginning was the Logos, and the Logos was with God, and the Logos was God"; and ending with the words, "And I saw, and bare record that this is the Son of God"; but, remembering that he was violating the law by reading this writing, he turned it over in his hand, and upon the back thereof read this inscription: "Am-nem-hat of Ombos."

"So! so!" murmured the young man. "The old and meddlesome idiot hath fallen into the accursed and criminal superstition of the Christians! and from his manner of life is, perhaps, one of the Therapeutæ, as they style their most crazy ascetics, who seldom appear in the cities, or leave the deserts and the mountains. The book itself, as far as I have read, seemeth to have been borrowed from the Neo-Platonists, and is harmless enough, surely. But it is a crime to own or read any magical book of the Christians, and this book is Am-nem-hat's! I think I see a way to rid myself of the pestilent old dotard! Ah! a Christian! A renegade high-priest of Ombos! Manifestly a corrupter of youth! Perhaps sent hither by his accursed associates to seduce the wealthy orphan into the same illegal and abominable association and plunder her of her property. I think I see my way clear before me!"

The young man carefully concealed the manuscript in his clothing, and, leaving word that he had called to see his cousin, but could not longer await her coming, he went straightway from the house unto the temple of Serapis, and requested an interview with the high-priest. And having been introduced into the audience-chamber of the high-priest, whom he greeted with the profoundest obeisance, as if addressing some superior being, he saith unto him, "I desire to know of thee whether the laws now allow the profession of the iniquitous and atheistic Christian faith in this city, or in any part of Egypt?"

And the high-priest answered : "No. The law is still in force which requires the destruction of their magical books, and of their churches, and the punishment of all who refuse to sacrifice unto the gods. But our magistrates and people have become careless and indifferent to these wise and salutary laws which are for the good of religion, and for the preservation of the government, so that the law is not enforced, and even here in Alexandria this illegal and criminal association possess houses in which they secretly celebrate their infamous rites and ceremonies."

"Canst not thou cause the law to be enforced if an extreme case of such crime should be brought to thy notice ? "

"Recently a better feeling hath been manifested in many localities," replied the high-priest. "Tyrannis, bishop of a church in Tyre, Zenobius, of Sidon, Silvanus, at Emisa, have but lately paid with their lives for the crime of Christianity, having been cast unto the wild beasts, and so destroyed. Another Silvanus, bishop of the churches about Gaza, and thirty-nine others with him, have been beheaded. Even here in Egypt, Peleus and Nilus have been committed to the flames, and Pamphilus at Cæsarea. Thou canst remember that even in Alexandria, Peter the bishop, and Faustus, Dius, and Ammonius, have been put to death, and in other parts of Egypt, Phileus, Pochumius, Hesychius, and Theodorus, have been in various ways destroyed. But a false sentiment of humanity protects these criminals; for it hath become a common saying in the city that the superstition is a harmless one, and that the Christians are the most honest, faithful, and diligent servants, tradesmen, mechanics, and agents, that one can employ; and those who cherish this fatal leniency for the accursed sect, themselves neglect the temple services, and gradually drift off into atheism. So that there is a great indifference on the subject of enforcing the law against these criminals; yet I doubt not that, if an extreme case should occur, the people might be easily roused up to seize the malefactors, and the magistrates would hardly dare to resist any forcible expression of the popular will. Of what case dost thou speak as an 'extreme' one?"

Then said Harroun: "There is a man in the city who hath embraced this accursed superstition, and who owneth and readeth the books of the sect contrary to the law. He was for many years a priest of our religion, and was even a high-priest at Ombos. He hath by some sort of necromancy, perhaps by means of his magical books, infatuated and attached unto himself a young Egyptian maiden, an orphan girl, belonging to our own ancient and honorable family, mine own cousin, and he keepeth her shut up in her own house, separated from her kindred, and deprived of all the pleasures and advantages that naturally belong to a noble and wealthy maid of Alexandria. Some years ago he procured himself to be appointed her guardian, and he hath sold five houses that belonged to her, and hath given no account thereof, except to produce the young girl's receipt therefor, in which she saith the sale was made at her request, that she had received the price thereof from him, and had used the same for pious purposes."

"Why did not her relatives interfere to prevent the alienation of her estate?"

"Her father was shipwrecked and lost, and we supposed that the 'pious purposes' signified the use of the money to build his sarcophagus and propitiate the gods, with which, of course, no one would interfere; but this, I lately discover, hath never been done, and we suppose that the man of whom I speak hath persuaded her to use the money for the purpose of building some temple or burial-place for the use of the abominable Christian association."

"Who is this man?" said the high-priest.

"His name is Am-nem-hat."

"Am-nem-hat!" said the high-priest, in amazement, "I know of the man: he was high-priest at Ombos, and, after a long life devoted to the service of the gods, he left his temple secretly to become an eremite — a great, and learned, and pious man! Surely there must be some mistake!"

"There is no mistake about what I have told you,"
14

said Harroun, "for he left the temple to become a Christian, and, from his manner of life, I think is one of the fearful sect called Therapeutæ."

"Hast thou any proof that he hath become a Christian?"

The youth drew forth from his clothing the Gospel written by John, saying: "Here is one of the magical books of the Christians which no reasonable man understandeth. I found this in Am-nem-hat's own chair, in his room, and on the back thereof is the indorsement, 'Am-nem-hat of Ombos.' He will not deny that he is a Christian if charged with that crime. For they never deny it when they are guilty thereof."

"This is an extreme case," said the high-priest. "Besides the corruption of youth and the plundering of this young girl of which thou speakest, it is an enormous sacrilege for a priest to abandon his religion, but infinitely worse when he leaveth religion and adopteth the accursed and inhuman Christian superstition. Leave that book with me and go thy way, but fail not to point out the house when the proper time shall come."

The young man took out his purse, and placed a liberal sum upon the table, saying: "This is for proper prayers and offerings for thy success; but remember that the deluded young girl, my cousin Theckla, must not be in any way molested."

"Assuredly," answered the high-priest, "her near kinship to thine own ancient, honorable, and devout family will be her protection, and I promise thee to reclaim her from the delusion which the witchcraft of this renegade priest hath brought upon her. As for this man who hath so dishonored the ancient religion of the land of Kem, and who might by reason of his former lofty character seduce much people from allegiance to the gods, this man shall surely die."

Then for a few days there was a great running to and fro among the pagan priests throughout the city, and especially among those who were connected with the great temple of Serapis. Great processions were had, at different places, in honor of various gods, the people were vehemently exhorted to greater diligence in their worship, and the Christians were vehemently denounced, so that there was an uproar throughout Rhacotis, and crowds of people rioting through the streets, accompanied by squads of soldiers, and seeking for the dwellings of those who were suspected of being Christians. And, in the language of the historian of those times : "A certain prophet and poet, inauspicious to the city, whoever he was, excited the mass of the heathen against us, stirring them up to their native superstition. Stimulated by him, and taking full liberty of exercising any kind of wickedness, they considered this the only piety and the worship of their demons—viz., to slay us. First, then, seizing a certain aged man named Mitra, they called upon him to utter impious expressions, and, as he did not obey, they beat his body with clubs, and pricked his face and eyes ; after which they led him away to the suburbs, where they stoned him. Next they led a woman called Quinta, who was a believer, to the temple of an idol, and attempted to force her to worship ; but, when she turned away in disgust, they tied her by the feet and dragged her through the whole city, and over the rough stones of the paved streets, dashing her against the mill-stones, and scourging her at the same time, until they brought her to the same place, when they stoned her. Then, with one accord, they all rushed upon the houses of the pious, and whomsoever of their neighbors they knew, they drove thither in all haste, and despoiled and plundered them, setting apart the more valuable articles for themselves, but the more common and wooden furniture threw about and burned in the roads, presenting a sight like a city taken by the enemy. But the brethren retired and gave way, and, like those to whom Paul bears witness, they also regarded the plunder of their goods with joy."

And, on the third evening of this rioting against the Christians, a crowd of people, with soldiers, assembled about the vast temple of Serapis, and the high-priest harangued them against the Christians, and especially against Am-nem-hat, whom he called the renegade of Ombos, a seducer of youth, and a plunderer of orphans; and, the house having been pointed out unto them, the mob surged thitherward, yelling and shouting, and calling upon their idols for vengeance against the Christians, and chiefly against Am-nem-hat, the renegade of Ombos. And they struck with violence upon the door, insomuch that the domestics were frightened, and the old man himself opened the door and said unto them, " What seek ye?"

And they yelled out: " We seek Am-nem-hat, the

traitor to the gods ! Am-nem-hat, the renegade high-priest of Ombos ! "

And, as soon as their clamor somewhat ceased, he said, "I am Am-nem-hat of Ombos."

And when they saw the man's great age, and his calm and dignified deportment, they were somewhat abashed, and they cried out, " It is reported that thou hast forsaken the ancient gods of the Nile, and that thou hast fallen away into the atheism of the Christians."

Then the old man stood up straight and glorious before them, and he said : " Children, for fifty years I was in the great temple of Thebes, and was long time a priest. Twenty-and-five years I was high-priest at Ombos, always seeking for the truth. Then I discovered that the Christians alone know and worship the one true God, and I am with all my heart, soul, mind, and strength, a Christian ! Children, seek ye the same divine truth ; the same glorious forgiveness, faith and light ; the same redeeming love."

And he would truly have borne further testimony for Jesus, but from the outskirts of the crowd the high-priest shouted : "Away with this blasphemer ! To the stake with the old renegade ! " And the mob echoed the cry, shouting out vehemently : "Away with the atheist ! To the stake with the ancient traitor ! " And one of them standing near knocked down the old man with his pike ; and, as many of them sprang forward to seize him, Theckla darted out of the door to his side, and with blazing eyes and extended hands she cried : " O cowards ! brutes ! The disgrace of Egypt, to strike down an old man like that ! Stand back ! "

And the men seemed abashed at the words and manner of the beautiful young girl, and stood irresolute until the high-priest called out, "Perhaps thou, also, art a Christian ?"

And she said : " Yea ! thank God, I am !"

Then all the more they shouted : " To the stake with the old atheist ! The corrupter of our youth !"

And they forcibly pushed the maiden aside, and they lifted up Am-nem-hat, and set him upon his feet, and the soldiers haled him away to the vacant space in front of the great temple of Serapis, where were set up iron columns to which the wealthy visitors thereto were wont to hitch the horses that drew their chariots. And they chained the old man fast to one of these, and soon they built a great pyre round him out of the furniture of which they plundered Theckla's house, and other houses of Christians on that street. And they did set fire unto the pile, and by the first flames thereof Theckla beheld the calm and shining face of the beloved ancient gazing peacefully upon the mob. Then they lighted it in other places, and the girl went near to the edge of the fire, and she cried aloud : "Be thou of good cheer, O father Am-nem-hat ! Thy Lord and Saviour Jesus Christ be with thee now !"

" Yea, daughter Theckla," answered the old man. " But go thou hence ! The Lord is all-sufficient unto me ! Go thou in peace !"

Then Theckla fell upon her knees before them all and prayed aloud, saying : " O Jesus, Son of God, have mercy upon him ! Comfort, sustain, and strengthen him, and receive him into glory !"

And, while she prayed, the fire grew fiercer, and spread all over the dry, combustible furniture of which the pyre was builded. And, while she was praying, a strong centurion came unto her, bearing some incense in his hand, and he said : "Thou invokest the accursed Galilean for him, and seekest by thy strong magic to harden him against the flame ! Take thou of this incense, girl, and cast it into the fire to Jupiter, cursing the malefactor Christ, or thou shalt quickly follow the old renegade !"

Then she only prayed the more ; and the man called another to him, and they seized the young girl, and, swinging her back and forth between them, so cast her through the circle of fire unto Am-nem-hat. And she arose and stood up beside him, and threw her arms about the old man's neck, and did kiss him lovingly, and leaned her head upon the old man's breast, and smiled upon him radiantly. And the idolaters being the more enraged, because they twain seemed to scorn the flames, piled yet other furniture and wood against them, until the greatness thereof hid them from view ; and with a last farewell, commending themselves and Arius unto God, they breathed the cruel flames, and so died. But the pagans continued to pile on fuel until they were utterly consumed ; and the high-priest, coming near, cast into the flame the manuscript of the Gospel of John, saying, "The law requireth all books of the Christians to be burned " ; and the crowd pillaged the house, and found yet other sacred writings, which they brought and cast into the flames ; and there were destroyed the original Epistles of John, which Theckla had copied for Arius.

Now when the centurion and the soldier seized upon Theckla to cast her into the fire, a young man ran forward from the outskirts of the crowd, shouting in terror and in agony, "Not her! centurion, not her!"

But the act was sudden, and before he could reach them, and before they heard his cries, it was done, and the girl was leaning on the breast of Am-nem-hat. And the youth fainted, and, with a wail of anguish, fell heavily upon his face along the ground. And the high-priest, seeing from his apparel that he was a man of rank, leaped forward, and raised up his head, and, looking upon his face, he saw that it was Harroun.

CHAPTER XVII.

CRUCIFIED UNTO THE WORLD.

ARIUS having been joyfully ordained to be a presbyter, and being uninformed of the martyrdom of Am-nem-hat and of Theckla, with gladness of heart and bright anticipations of coming happiness reached the city of Alexandria, and went first of all, as his duty was, to Peter, the bishop, whose return from Antioch had briefly preceded his own arrival. And, after the usual salutations had passed between them, the bishop, looking tenderly upon him, said: "Son, thou hast been ordained a presbyter, and hast been consecrated to the Master's service, and the Bishop Lucanius highly extolleth thy fitness for the holy office. But thou art young, my son, and the Lord hath laid a heavy cross upon thee. Hast thou received any recent news from our unfortunate city of Alexandria?"

"The last news I received was borne by thee when thou didst come unto Antioch bringing a letter from my betrothed, and that from the community, and the casket containing the perfect and beautiful copies of the sacred writings which Theckla wrote with her own hand for me. Why dost thou ask so seriously?"

"I did only precede thee by three days, my son; but upon my arrival heard the news of a sudden outbreak of persecution in which many of the pious were perfected, and their goods despoiled, the recital whereof will pierce thy heart. Thine old friend Am-nem-hat did bravely testify for Jesus even in the midst of the flame by which he was made perfect."

"I loved him much," said Arius, "and his long life hath ended gloriously!" Then a ghastly pallor came over the young man's cheek and lip, and he could only murmur, "And Theckla, bishop?"

"Son," said the bishop, tenderly, "thy beautiful Theckla was also a perfect witness for our Lord at the same time and place with the ancient Am-nem-hat." Then bowed the youth his head upon his hands, and writhings as of some mortal agony swept over him.

"Son," said old Peter, tearfully, "canst thou not say, 'He doeth all things well, and blessed be his name'?"

"Not yet! not yet!" sobbed out the broken-hearted man; "but give unto me the key of the church Baucalis!"

And the bishop called a young deacon unto him, and bade him take the key and guide the youthful presbyter unto that church. And in silence the sorely-smitten man followed his guide until they had reached the door of the beautiful church; then said Arius unto him: "Thou mayst return. Farewell!"

And Arius opened the door and passed within, and locked the door behind him. And it was twilight; and the full moon shed a soft and mellow light through the vast area of the sacred room; and, not far off, the gentle waves of the sea gleamed in the golden sheen, and lapsed away along the quiet coast.

Back and forth, along the great aisle, with slow and heavy footsteps—back and forth, until the long night waned away, and the muffled tread of the sufferer seemed to become regular, unceasing, continuous, as part of the very course of nature itself—all night long, back and forth, wrestling sorely with his sudden, mighty grief, the young man trod the desolate aisle, and his bosom heaved with anguish, but not a single word escaped his compressed, ashy lips. The first faint light of dawn mottled the eastern sky; then the glad sunlight streamed far out along the peaceful sea, and the freshness of the morning laughed from earth and heaven. Then went he slowly unto a window opening unto the east, and the sun was rising gloriously, and then the man raised up his right hand reverently, and, gazing away into the glowing heavens, with trembling lips and broken heart, he murmured : "Yea! He doeth all things well; and blessed be his name !"

But the first great sorrow of his life had fallen upon him ; that which ages a man in a single day ; that which breaketh off and casteth far from him all the brightness and freshness of his youth forever, and setteth him henceforth face to face with the hard and bitter realities of life, making all of the beautiful past only a dim and blessed memory of happiness, the light and sweetness whereof his lip shall taste no more on earth.

The youth was a man now; tried in the furnace of

affliction; exercised by grief; strengthened and hardened and chastened by the bitter cup of woe.

Quietly he departed from the church; with calm, unfaltering tread he went back unto the bishop; and then unwaveringly he asked for, and unflinchingly heard, the pathetic details of the martyrdom. And the kind-hearted old man said unto him : "Son, thou triest thy heart too bitterly. If thou desirest to be alone, I can give thee a room unto thyself, and thou canst abide quietly with me until thou shalt feel better able to assume thy pastoral charge."

"I thank thee much, bishop, for thou art very kind. But God forbid that private grief should ever keep me from a sacred task ! I will even preach to my people in the Baucalis church this morning. For I know "—and then the right hand momently began its rhythmic movement, the mesmeric light gleamed in his somber eyes, the strong, bold head sprang forward upon the lithe, serpentine neck, and, with a light, plaintive hiss in every tone that cut through the hearer's heart, he continued—"for I know that Theckla would even have it so if she could counsel me."

The good old bishop sprang toward and embraced him, crying out : "My son! my son! Thou art of the splendid stuff of which God maketh martyrs ! May he console and comfort thee, and feed thee with the bread of everlasting life !"

For the bishop saw in his haggard countenance the ineffaceable traces of his mighty struggle with that night-long agony; he saw the grandeur and beauty of the imperious will that wearied down the complainings of an aching heart; and the clear, resolute soul that fixed its eye upon the path of Christian duty, not to be swerved therefrom by any earthly agency, and ready to immolate even its sacred hours of grief for the sake of other souls.

Henceforth the fair forms of youth, and love, and hope, would pass him by upon life's lonely pilgrimage almost unrecognized—strangers to him except for some far-off, heart-broken memories. Henceforth upon his chastened hearing the voices of honor and ambition would fall unheeded as the sounding brass or the tinkling cymbal! Only when the stern, cold face of Duty might meet his gaze, henceforth, his spirit would look up and say: "I know thee. Welcome here!" Only when the shrinking forms of human sorrow, and pain, and wretchedness, should henceforth claim his sympathy, his soul would reach forth ministering hands and say: "Ye are old friends of mine! I welcome you!"

And he did preach in the Baucalis church, that very morning, a sermon which was never forgotten by those who heard it. "The love of Christ constraineth us," he exclaimed; then in words that leaped, and flashed, and glinted, ringing distinct as bell-notes, yet all flowing in a strong, even, jubilant current unto a definite purpose, he set before them the loftiest form and manner in which love hath ever showed its power and beauty, in the best stories of pagan mythology and history, in high and glorious examples from the Old and New Testament, and from church history, all brought out like pictures before the

mind, and above them all he glorified and magnified that
love divine of Jesus; then how we are bound, constrained
thereby; unto what end; and, finally, that the necessary
result of this bondage to Christ is absolute freedom as to
all other authority upon earth, higher than any natural
courage or Stoic philosophy could confer. But there was
not even the remotest reference to his private sorrow. All
of them had known Theckla, and the covenant between
her and Arius, and the building of the church for him,
and the transcribing of the scriptures for him by her
hand; and all of their hearts had yearned after him in
sympathizing sorrow; but not one word of self even inad-
vertently found utterance in his clear, cold, steel-like
exegesis of the truth, or in the copious, affluent stream
of exhortation and comfort. He had come to minister
unto them, not to be ministered unto by them; he had
come to help them bear all things, with clear eyes to see,
with open heart to feel and share, with strong, resolute,
uncomplaining spirit to bear all of their sorrows and trials;
his own to be sealed up in his own soul, buried out of
human sight forever. He took all [hearts by storm: instinctively they felt that this young man was thoroughly
furnished unto every good work; they could rely upon
him, they could trust him under all circumstances, in any
emergency. An old Christian in the congregation, who
had been a Roman officer for many years before his conver-
sion, and had faced every form of death upon the battle-
field, whispered to the friend next to him: "What a splendid commander he would have made! He is the bravest
man I ever saw, for, if there had been a streak of weakness,

or cowardice, or selfishness in his nature, he could not have buried his own grief out of sight, and put his whole heart into his work as he hath done."

It was so through all the services of that first day. Quiet, grave, courteous, he discharged every duty of his position without the slightest reference to his own feelings or trials. For, during that night of awful sorrow, he had fully settled all his earthly life. Henceforth the church at Baucalis was to be his home ; the community that might worship there, his family ; he was, henceforth, to have no griefs, ambitions, trials of his own ; no hopes, no fears ; he was to bear the burdens of others ; to love, guide, counsel, and strengthen the souls intrusted to his care ; to do a minister's work, that is, a spiritual servant's work, so long as life might last, and to wait patiently, uncomplainingly, without disquietude or bitterness of spirit, if possible with gladness, until the end might come. Such was the destiny he had mapped out for himself during that night of bitter anguish in the beautiful church ; such was the destiny that upon the next morning, with grand, simple, unselfish faith and courage, he arose to meet.

The thoroughness of this profound self-abnegation was exhibited on the night succeeding that first day's labors, when, in the solitude of his own apartment, he took from out its cedar casket the beautiful manuscript which Theckla's hand had lovingly prepared for him, and made an indorsement thereon, in the Arabic tongue, that it had been transcribed by Theckla, a noble Egyptian lady, who also was a martyr in Alexandria. But he did not write that it was transcribed for him ; his name nowhere ap-

pears on any part of the manuscript; there is not a word
or sign that can by any possibility connect his name or
fate with hers. Arius seemed to him to have been slain
and buried long ago; only God's presbyter survived the
ruin of his life, and stood up in the place of Arius, calm,
strong, fearless, unselfish, and devout.

And this great manuscript, which was the offering of
Theckla's love unto him, hath survived the lapse of ages,
bearing yet upon its priceless pages the indorsement of
Arius. It is known throughout Christendom as the " Co-
DEX ALEXANDRINUS "—" A " of the British Museum, although some later writings have been blended therewith,
and some of the manuscripts prepared by Theckla have
been lost.

BOOK II.

CHAPTER I.

"HIS MOST CATHOLIC MAJESTY."

THE historians, secular and ecclesiastic, have alike failed to do justice to the vast abilities of Constantine the Great. Those who have questioned his superiority to all other Roman emperors (if, indeed, not to all other men) have united in ascribing to accident, to the mere drifting of events, facts which were really the forecastings of profoundest statesmanship, guided by a political sagacity that pierced through to the very core of the whole social and religious life of the vast empire over which he ruled, almost untroubled by the influences of human passions, fears, and faith. On the other hand, those who have felt constrained to give even the slightest credence to his alleged profession of faith in Christ have attributed to religious zeal, enthusiasm, or fears, the most salient actions of a life that was, from beginning to end, dominated only by the lust for dominion, incapable of any creed but atheism, and absolutely content with the negation of the existence of any Being greater than him-

15

self. To those who take a more rational view of his magnificent but criminal career, and who, looking behind the mask of reverence for paganism which he cast aside at precisely the politic moment, in order to assume a false pretense of reverence for Christianity, discern the cool, deliberate atheist, who was ready to profess any creed and foster any superstition that might best serve to smooth the road to absolute power, and make mankind his slaves: to them the astute politician, the successful warrior, the consummate ruler of men, assumes such colossal proportions that, compared with him, Alexander, Cæsar, and Napoleon, seem to sink into the lower grade of butchers and stabbers, only half-taught in the science of government, of which Constantine alone was master. For it is no more certain that he despised and pitied paganism while he was solemnly offering sacrifices to Jupiter, and winning the admiration and love of the Roman world for his imperial piety, than it is certain that he pitied and despised the Church of Christ, even while he was manipulating the faith into a sure and reliable support of the empire; in both courses he only played with the world, giving men any religious toy which the greater part might prefer to have, in exchange for the liberty of which he robbed them so plausibly and successfully that they scarcely perceived his theft, and enthusiastically caressed the royal thief.

The Christians of that age died at the stake, or by the sword, or by wild beasts, rather than to cast a pinch of incense into the sacred fires and say, "Proh Jupiter!" The pagans would have plunged into civil war, and would

have endured or inflicted any pain, rather than acknowledge any feeling for Christ except hatred, loathing, and
contempt.   But Constantine both adopted the cross as a
military standard, and also observed the heathen rites
with customary ostentation and solemnity; having absolutely no conscientious scruples for or against any religion; regarding both the old and the new faiths as
things proper enough for common men, but altogether
indifferent to him; and using both alike as mere instruments convenient for the advancement of his own political purposes.

After he had defeated Maxentius at the Milvian
Bridge, he caused his own statue to be erected at Rome;
and, while the general design and execution of the work
were unexceptionable to his pagan subjects, the image bore
in its hand the symbol of the cross, which, until that
day, had been esteemed to be a badge of crime and in-
famy, as disgraceful to any Roman as the lewd Priapi
of the gardens could have been to the Christians; and
the thanksgiving which he offered to commemorate his
victory was couched in such enigmatical terms that in
applying it to Mars or Jupiter, the pagan did no more
violence to the text than the Christian would do in ascribing it to Christ and God.   So, when, to please the
Christians, he decreed the solemn observance of Sunday, he
inspired the pagans with confidence and respect, by calling the sacred day *Dies Solis* (the Day of the Sun), a
formula of heathendom with which they had been familiar all their lives.

Utterly devoid of faith in anything else except himself

and his own destiny, unyielding in that ambition to exercise dominion which nerved him for the doubtful war
against Maxentius, he regarded both mankind and religion
with pity and contempt, and sought to rule men for their
good and his own glory, by means of any faith which they
might prefer; and hence, as Christianity became more
known and popular, he identified himself with it more and
more, only in order to foster an agency which seemed to be
available in the work of consolidating the warring factions
of the empire and securing the permanency of his throne.
But the gospel of love and peace over which he extended
the imperial protection did not deter him from exterminating the whole race of Maxentius after he had defeated him in battle; nor from the deliberate and politic
murder of Maximin, who was the father of Fausta his
wife, and who had been the benefactor of his father Constantius; nor from the destruction of his wife herself,
nor of his sons; nor from the assassination of the Emperor Licinius and his son, the offspring of his sister Constantia—crimes so infamous and unnecessary that the first
spark of real animosity against the gods of Rome that
ever flashed across the serene and boundless depths of his
almost superhuman intelligence gleamed for a moment
past his consummate and life-long duplicity when the
pagan priests refused all expiation for such crimes; and he
turned away more decidedly to a religion which promises
pardon for every sin : not that he cared anything for the
sacred rites of either church; but because he was the first
Roman ruler to attach any definite meaning to the words
"public opinion," and he desired to maintain the confi-

dence of his people, and also to secure the full benefit of those crimes which he committed to place his own authority beyond the reach of accident.

So thoroughly indifferent to all sense of religion was this greatest of the rulers of mankind that dissimulation was an easy task which involved no conscientious scruples of any kind ; and was so gracefully and perfectly enacted that even Eusebius, the father of ecclesiastical history, himself no ordinary man, was for a long time very thoroughly deceived into believing that the atheistic emperor was God's vicegerent for the establishment of the Christian Church on earth. "Constantine, therefore, in the very commencement" (says Eusebius), "being proclaimed supreme emperor and Augustus by the soldiers, and much longer before this by the universal sovereign, God—Constantine, the protector of the good, combining his hatred of wickedness with the love of goodness, went forth with his son Crispus, the most benevolent Cæsar, to extend a caring arm to all them that were perishing. Both, therefore, the father and the son, having, as it were, God the Universal King and his Son, our Saviour, as their leader and aid, drawing up the army on all sides against the enemies of God, bore away an easy victory." "With choirs and hymns," says Eusebius, "in the cities and villages, at the same time they celebrated and extolled first of all God the Universal King, because they were thus taught ; then they also celebrated the praises of the pious emperor, and with him all his divinely-favored children," including Crispus Cæsar whom he caused to be murdered afterward.

Only the lone and incorruptible seer of Patmos, John

the Divine, foresaw the mighty pagan in his real character, and depicted him in words of scathing denunciation and rebuke which the prostituted Church then failed to understand when the things were transacted before her eyes—a prophetic and apocalyptic view of Constantine and Constantinople which becomes of easier interpretation as the centuries glide away, revealing more and more clearly what things John foretold, that were to follow upon the subversion of Christianity by the most potent human enemy that Jesus ever had, and locating the seat of Antichrist upon seven hills above the sea to which the commerce of the world resorted—a description inapplicable to any capital on earth except the city of Constantinople.

The tentative effort made by Constantine in 312 and 313, when he had used the influence of the Christians against Maxentius, had proved entirely successful, and the great ruler at once began to make inquiries to ascertain to what extent the same faith might prevail throughout the Empire of the East, and how far he might depend upon its aid in subverting the sovereign power of Licinius, who then reigned over the Eastern Empire. For, upon the death of Diocletian, Constantius and Galerius had parted the empire between themselves in accordance with the emperor's will, dividing both the provinces and the legions, which was the first division of Roman sovereignty. Constantine succeeded his father Constantius, and, by the overthrow of Maxentius, had become master of all of the Western Empire, although north of the Mediterranean Licinius ruled Pannonia, Dalmatia, Dacia, Greece, and Thrace ; and, having overthrown Maximian, ruled the East, including Asia Minor, Syria, and Egypt.

But it was always Constantine's set purpose to restore the unity of the empire, and to concentrate the whole imperial authority in his own hand—a purpose of which he never for one moment lost sight, and which is the explanation of his whole magnificent career. The present difficulty in the way was the fact that he had permitted, perhaps solicited, Licinius to sign with him the Decree of Milan, which gave peace to the Church; and this celebrated document had been issued in both their names, by their joint authority, and had been so published throughout the empire. In addition to this was the fact that the Christians universally regarded the defeat of Maximian and the triumph of Licinius as providential, for the former had persecuted the Church, and the latter had protected it in conjunction with Constantine. The public actions of Maximian gave countenance to this opinion: for, while he had great faith in the heathen gods and priests, and had resorted to magic in order to conduct the war with Licinius triumphantly, after he had been defeated in battle "he slew many of his priests as jugglers and impostors, and as the destroyers of his own safety, since by their oracles he had been induced to undertake the disastrous war. Moreover, having heard that Constantine and Licinius were both Christians, he supposed that their success was the result of their religion, and himself immediately issued a decree providing safety for the Christians whom less than a year before he had ordered to be persecuted, by decrees engraved on brazen tablets; he gave them liberty to rebuild their churches, and commanded that all of their property which had been seized and sold under the former decrees should be restored to them. Shortly afterward he miserably died, and Licinius ruled alone."

Licinius was a firm believer in Christianity, and his faith and the decrees of Maximian alike confirmed both himself and his subjects in the opinion that he was under the divine protection.

Constantine was not long in perceiving the greatest political error, perhaps the only one, committed by him, the affixing of the signature of Licinius to the Decree of Milan; but, at the time it was done, human foresight could hardly have anticipated such a wholesale abandonment of paganism, and such an ardent and enthusiastic adoption of Constantine's new ecclesiasticism, on the part of the people, as did actually occur. To have left the name of Licinius out of the decree would have fostered any ambitious views which that emperor might have entertained, by enabling him to set up himself as the especial guardian of the heathen religion, and so concentrating in his own hands all the resources of the pagan world. Constantine was compelled, therefore, either to divide the influence of the Christians with Licinius, or else to array himself and Christianity on the one side, against Licinius and paganism on the other; and he was too wise a ruler not to perceive that such a civil and religious war would be disastrous to both rulers, if not the ultimate ruin of the empire; and, not knowing the vast numerical strength of the Christians, he chose the former alternative. But no sooner had he succeeded in getting all power in the North and West concentrated firmly in his own hands, than he began to seek for means whereby to undermine the power of his rival, and so carry into effect his life-long purpose—the reuniting of the divided empire, and the concentration of all power in his own hands.

The Christians of the Eastern Empire maintained the primitive religion, and persevered in their original opposition to bearing arms in war, and to slavery, and to private-property rights, and so added nothing to the military power of Licinius, except their constantly increasing communal wealth. Licinius simply left the Church at peace, and was not consummate politician enough to use its vast resources in aid of his government, as Constantine had done, by inducing the Christians to abandon the primitive organization of the Church and become Roman subjects in everything except the mere article of faith. When Ulfilas, the Goth, converted his barbarous countrymen, and transformed the fierce and warlike tribes into peaceful and settled peoples among whom war, slavery, polygamy, and private property, were unknown, and among whom no king was recognized but Christ, Constantine declared war against them, and pursued them with fire and sword until they were forced to adopt Roman laws and customs, and agreed by treaty to supply a permanent force of forty thousand young men to the imperial army ; and, after that, he caused Ulfilas himself to be ordained a bishop, and sent him back to his own people to teach the imperial religion instead of Christianity. But this profound and atheistic policy was too deep for the Emperor Licinius ; and Constantine knew well that, according to the primitive Christianity, a whole Christian province would not furnish a single recruit to his rival's legions, since no Christian would bear arms.

Eusebius of Cæsarea, who had prepared the way for Constantine to become the head of the Church in the Western Empire, was the emperor's chosen friend and constant counselor, and the ruler of Rome never forgot that the bishop had, first of all men, invited his attention to the fact that the despised and persecuted Christians constituted already a body of men so numerous, so virtuous, and so prosperous, as to hold the balance of power between any factions which might divide the Roman people just as soon as the legal disabilities which both concealed their numbers and fettered their influence might be removed by imperial favor.

Under the advice of Eusebius, the emperor, in his own name, sent to Anulinus, Proconsul of Africa, a decree most favorable to the Christians throughout that region ; he also made presents of large sums of money to the bishops of Africa, Numidia, and Mauritania, who had been plundered in the persecutions of Maximian ; he also sent a decree ordaining that all church prelates be freed from obligation to discharge any public, military, or political duties and offices ; also, he made a decree commanding a certain council to be held concerning the affairs of Cæcilianus, Bishop of Carthage, and sent to Miltiades, Bishop of Rome, copies of the charges against Cæcilianus ; also, a decree addressed to Chrestus, Bishop of Syracuse, commanding that a council of many bishops, both of Africa and of Gaul, should assemble at the city of Arles, in order to consider and determine certain questions which were disputed among the faithful.

In short, counseled by Eusebius, who never doubted the ultimate overthrow of idolatry, and the ultimate triumph of whatever ecclesiastical system might be established in place of the Christian communities, Constantine zealously strove in every way to identify himself and his government with the new religion, and to hold himself out as the head of the Church, as well as of the state. At the same time he steadily pursued a secret policy of winning to himself the affection and confidence of the Christian subjects of the Emperor Licinius, by the use of agents whom he kept in his own service, in the household of every bishop of the Eastern Church. This zeal in the service of the established ecclesiasticism soon met with the great reward which Eusebius had promised to the emperor; for, throughout the length and breadth of the churches it began to be commonly declared that " Constantine was the divinely-appointed protector of the Christians"; that "God was the friend and vigilant protector of Constantine"; and that "no man could be his equal, and no man could stand against him." Licinius soon perceived the influence of these machinations, and saw that, even in his own dominions, the Christians, and especially the prelates, offered up more prayers for Constantine than for himself — "so that he did not suppose," saith Eusebius, "that they offered prayers for him at all, but persuaded himself that they did all things, and propitiated the Deity, only for the divinely-favored Emperor Constantine."

This treasonable sentiment, of course, aroused the resentment of the jealous Licinius, and more and more developed that estrangement between him and the Christians for which Constantine secretly but zealously labored ; and Licinius sought revenge by fomenting every disaffection which manifested itself against the rule of Constantine in Africa.   But the bishops were as perfect a police force as modern times have ever succeeded in organizing, and kept Rome fully advised of every movement inaugurated by the enemies of the "most Christian emperor."   And Eusebius saith, concerning Licinius, that "when he saw that his secret preparations by no means succeeded according to his wish, *as God detected every artifice and villainy to his favorite prince,* no longer able to conceal himself, Licinius commenced an open war.   And in thus determining war against Constantine, he now *proceeded to array himself against the Supreme God whom he knew Constantine to worship.*   Afterward he began imperceptibly to assail those pious subjects under him who had never at any time troubled his government.   This too, he did, violently urged on by the innate propensity of his malice, that overclouded and darkened his understanding. He did not, therefore, bear in mind *those that had persecuted the Christians before him,* nor those *whose destroyer and punisher he himself had been appointed,* for their wickedness.   But, departing from sound reason, and, as one might say, seized with insanity, he had determined *to wage war against God himself,* the protector and aid

of Constantine, *in place of the one whom He assisted.*
And first, indeed, he *drove away all the Christians from
his house,* the wretch thus divesting himself of those
prayers to God for his safety which they were taught to
offer up for all men.   After this he ordered the soldiers
in the cities to be cashiered and stripped of military
honors unless they chose to sacrifice to demons."

Constantine having craftily succeeded in embroiling
Licinius with the Church, watched with secret joy, until
the enemy whom he wished to destroy followed up this
lustration of his army and navy, which was designed to
drive out the Christian spies of Constantine, with more
strenuous measures; and, in the language of Eusebius,
"at last proceeded to such an extent of madness *as to
attack the bishops,* now indeed regarding them as the servants of the Supreme God, *but hostile to his measures.*"
And as the angry tyrant adopted extreme remedies for
this ecclesiastical treason, "razing the churches to the
ground"; "subjecting the bishops to the same punishment as the worst criminals"; "cutting the bodies of
some into small pieces and feeding them out to fishes in
the sea"; and "destroying others by various modes of
torture and death"—"the whole Christian world regarded
him with horror and detestation, and looked to Constantine for deliverance."

So that the error which the emperor had committed,
in soliciting Licinius to affix his signature to the Decree
of Milan, was not only fully compensated by his consummate skill and artifice, but the Church prayed earth and
Heaven for the destruction of Licinius.   Licinius, irritated

more and more by the wide-spread disaffection of his subjects, espoused the cause of Bassianus, who had married Anastasia, the sister of Constantine, and urged him into rebellion in order to gain larger power; and, Bassianus having been defeated and dethroned, Licinius refused to deliver up the partisans of the fallen Cæsar who had taken refuge in his dominions; and upon this pretext Constantine declared war against him; and in two battles, one at Cibalis in Pannonia, and the other upon the plains of Mardia in Thrace, he defeated Licinius, and so crippled him that he was compelled to make peace, with the loss of Pannonia, Dalmatia, Dacia, Macedonia, and Greece, which provinces were added to the dominions of Constantine, and extended his empire to the extremity of Peloponnesus, leaving Licinius Emperor of Thrace, Asia Minor, Syria, and Egypt.

This war happened in the year 315, and the ambition of Constantine was temporarily sated, so that he then refrained from pushing to extremities the defeated but still powerful Licinius until he might have time and opportunity to alienate the affection and confidence of his subjects in Asia as thoroughly as he had done in Europe. And, besides this, he wanted time in order to subjugate the Goths whom Ulfilas had converted, subvert the Christian communities organized among them on the primitive foundation, and force them to adopt the ecclesiastical system which he had established at Rome, in order to make the Gothic nation an available factor in any future war in which he might engage. But in a few years afterward, having successfully waged war against the Goths, and having seen the influence of Licinius greatly impaired by the persecutions of the Church in Syria and Egypt which he had encouraged and, perhaps, instigated, as well as by that secret diplomacy of which Constantine was master, the Roman emperor deemed that the time had come to destroy Licinius, and restore the unity of the empire, and consolidate all power in his own hands, especially as the great age and unpopular vices of Licinius seemed to presage an easy victory. He accordingly (and without any pretext whatever on this occasion) declared war against the Illyrian emperor; and in the great battle of Adrianople, and in the siege of Byzantium, and in the decisive action of Chrysopolis, in all of which he engaged Licinius with inferior numbers, his vast military genius asserted itself, so that by continuous defeats he reduced the Emperor of the East to the necessity of making an unconditional surrender. Constantia, the wife of Licinius, was the sister of Constantine, and, at her request and entreaties, the conqueror temporarily spared the life of his fallen rival, and banished him to Thessalonica, where he was soon afterward assassinated in some mysterious manner, it being to this day uncertain whether he perished by the order of the senate, by a tumult of the soldiers, or by the machinations of Constantine. But it is certain that the "first Christian emperor" regarded the fact that a man might stand in the way of his ambition, or possibly compromise his safety, as a sufficient reason for putting him to death, even if the unlucky person happened to be his own son.

"Thus the mighty and victorious Constantine," saith

Eusebius, "adorned with every virtue of religion, with his most pious son, Crispus Cæsar, resembling in all things his father, recovered the East as his own, and thus restored the Roman Empire to its ancient state of one united body; extending their peaceful sway around the world, from the rising sun to the opposite regions, to the north and the south, even to the borders of the declining day."

But this greatest statesman, politician, and ruler—this absolute, untroubled, and self-confident atheist—had only "the godliness that is profitable for the life that now is"; for this "Christian" had never been baptized (knowing that an emperor can not be a Christian); and he afterward murdered in cold blood, without provocation, "his most pious son, Crispus Cæsar, resembling in all things his father"; his own wife Fausta, and the youthful Licinius, son of his sister Constantia; just as he systematically assassinated every one whom his calm, merciless, wise policy thought to be possibly inimical to his own safety. But he realized the life-long ambition of his soul, the restoration of the unity of the Roman Empire under his own authority; and did it by the aid of the Christian Church, which he bribed, corrupted, and secularized, until it acknowledged him to be king instead of Jesus Christ.

These historical details, however, anticipate our narrative of Arius the Libyan, to which we must now return.

CHAPTER II.

AFTER the overthrow of the Christian communities which Ulfilas had founded among the Goths, Constantine called Eusebius, Bishop of Cæsarea, unto himself, and began to make diligent inquiries concerning the churches of Syria and of Egypt; and, having obtained all of the information current among the bishops, he entered into conversation with Eusebius, apparently for the purpose of still further satisfying himself upon certain points involved in his investigations.

"Thou sayest," said Constantine, "that, in spite of the persecution in which many bishops and private persons have suffered martyrdom, the Church constantly increases in numbers and influence."

"Yea," replied Eusebius, "but not so rapidly as in thine own dominions; for in most places their services are secretly conducted because of the heathen; yet the truth triumphs everywhere, and the churches prosper wonderfully. The cruel wrongs done unto the faithful excite the interest and compassion of all fair-minded men, and there are always many who seek for fuller information concerning our holy religion, and there are always some at hand ready to impart it."

16

"I would that it were possible for me at this time to occupy the same relation to the Eastern Church that so happily obtains in the Empire of the West. But that seems to be impossible while the Emperor Licinius reigns over those realms."

"Thou art as much beloved by the Christians of the East as by those of Europe or of Africa; and they look unto thee for deliverance, and hopefully await thy coming."

"But Europe and Africa are under mine own hand, and Asia is not; the Church of the East is beyond the reach of my protection."

"Stretch forth thine arm of power, thou favorite of the supreme God, and take it unto thyself. Thou alone art fitted to be emperor, and Asia, as part of the Roman Empire, is rightfully thine own."

Then Constantine gave way to one of those fits of sudden, silent meditation which were not unusual to him, and continued to gaze upon his bishop long and earnestly. At last he said: "The Emperor Licinius is a brave and skillful commander, trained all his life in the discipline of the Roman army. He not only hath yet a solid foothold upon European soil, but he could call into action out of populous Asia double as many soldiers as the Western Empire could put into the field, including the hardy Goths, whom I have added to the military force of Rome. He is no merely titular emperor, but is a consummate warrior, a wise ruler, an able and valiant man, as he hath already proved against both Maximian and myself."

"Thou and God art greater still!" said the bishop, solemnly.

"That might be so upon the land," murmured Constantine, absently, "for many of my legions are veterans, who have followed me through seventeen campaigns without defeat, and the Goths are brave and hardy. But the old emperor's vast superiority is on the sea. For, since Rome ceased to be the seat of empire, the naval establishments of Misenum and Ravenna have been greatly neglected, and the maritime cities of Greece no longer furnish those formidable fleets which made the republic of Athens so famous. But the Emperor Licinius can draw from Egypt and the adjacent coasts of Africa, from the ports of Phœnicia and the Isle of Cyprus, and from Bithynia, Ionia, and Caria, a fleet to which the rest of mankind could offer no effective opposition; so that, if I should be successful on land, the emperor's naval superiority would enable him to carry an offensive war into every sea-coast of Hispania, Gaul, and Italy, cut off all my supplies, and force me to retreat even in the face of victory. It will not do!" he cried, passionately and despondingly—"it will not do! and it requires years to prepare a navy! There must be some other way—some other way!"

What dark and secret thought slumbered in the capacious deeps of that calm, unwavering spirit to which expediency was ever a sufficient justification for any crime that might advance political designs, no man can ever know; but Eusebius at once perceived that the thing which he supposed to have been a suggestion of his own—a temptation held out by him to the emperor and ventured

upon because his zeal for the persecuted Christians of the
Eastern Church made him earnestly desire that Constantine should conquer and protect those regions—had in
truth long been a subject of profoundest meditation in the
emperor's soul ; a most dangerous ambition, which he had
considered in every possible aspect of it.   Neither of these
able men spoke for some time.   Then the emperor said,
musingly : "Would that it were possible for me at this
time to occupy the same relation to the Eastern Churches
that so happily obtains in the Empire of the West !   But
there must be some other way—some other way !"

Eusebius perceived from the repetition of these words
that they in some way contained the particular matter concerning which Constantine desired him to speak ; and he
shuddered at the unwelcome thought of what might possibly be required at the hand of some bishop of the Church
by the implacable and unscrupulous emperor ; but, not
fully comprehending the drift of the royal mind, he answered : "It would be easy to attach the bishops and their
congregations unto thyself as thou didst those of Africa,
by secret aid to the churches, and by kind messages unto
those who have experienced the tyrant's cruelty ; for already all Christians regard thee as divinely raised up for
their succor, and they are comforted by the hope that,
when thou dost rule the world, the gospel shall be as free
in the East as it is in the West."

"But that is a mere sentiment," answered Constantine.
"The Christians are not soldiers ; in the East they refuse
to bear arms, or to recognize an earthly ruler.   Surely
thou dost remember how difficult it was to bring them

over to any active support of mine empire even in the West."

"Yea, verily! But thou mayst gradually assume direction of the Church there as thou hast done here : by largesses to the bishops ; by calling councils in thine own name to settle clerical differences ; and by training them, as thou hast done here, to regard thee alone as the real source of both ecclesiastical and political authority ; and so by degrees control them as thou wilt."

"I have meditated over all of that," said Constantine, "and the great difficulty in the way of its accomplishment grows out of the fact that any attempt to interfere in the trial of charges against bishops or presbyters, whether upon accusations of personal misconduct, or of erroneous doctrine, within the dominions of the Emperor Licinius, would be regarded by him, and by his subjects, as an unwarrantable interference in matters which do not concern the Empire of the West ; and such a course would only inflame and consolidate those whom I prefer to divide in sentiment."

"But," said Eusebius, "if the question in dispute should be one, not between the members of some particular community, or locality, but between almost the whole body of the Christians in the Western Empire on the one hand, and almost the whole body of the Eastern Church upon the other, could there be any impropriety in calling a council of the whole Church, East and West, to consider and determine it ?"

"No," said Constantine. "If there were only such a question, the way would be laid open at least for a beginning. But how couldst thou ever create such a question?"

"The question, or rather the questions (for there are two of them), are already created—the East upon one side of both, and the West upon the other."

"What are these questions?"

"One is a great dispute concerning the proper time for the celebration of Easter; and the other a most subtile controversy concerning the nature of Godhead and the relation of the Father, Son, and Holy Ghost; a dispute in which Hosius of Cordova leads many bishops and presbyters upon one side, and Arius the Libyan as many upon the other."

"Arius the Libyan!" cried Constantine, with sudden wrath. "The Libyan serpent! The ram of Baucalis! a presbyter of Alexandria! By thundering Jove, I will yet crush that hard, stubborn, fearless nature, for he hath been more in my way than even the Emperor Licinius himself! Curse the man! curse him!"

Eusebius gazed upon the emperor in mute astonishment. He knew that Constantine possessed an almost supernatural knowledge of all political movements and persons, even in the remotest corner of the empire over which he reigned, but he had never even dreamed that the mighty emperor had heard so much as the name of the gaunt, unsocial, self-denying, and inflexible presbyter of the Baucalis church at Alexandria, in the dominions of Licinius.

"Knowest thou the man?" he asked with unconcealed astonishment.

Constantine had already regained his usual calmness, and in placid tones replied: "I have never seen Arius, but have constantly and often heard of his dangerous and revolutionary teachings, and of his rugged, implacable, unyielding character. He hateth me without any cause, except that I am emperor, and scorneth every favor I was inclined to show him. I even tendered unto him the bishopric of Alexandria, which Alexander now holds, but he refused to accept it, for no other reason than that he supposed his advancement to that high place to have been procured by the influence of mine agents in that city."

"I regret that he is not thy friend," answered Eusebius; "but wilt thou instruct me how a presbyter could teach dangerous and revolutionary doctrines? Perhaps such teachings might furnish matter for which the Church might suspend him from the office of presbyter, and silence his utterances."

"I do not think so," answered Constantine. "He teaches that a Christian can not be an emperor, nor bear arms in war; and that to take sides in a struggle between any earthly governments is to betray the Christ. He teaches that no Christian can hold slaves, own private property, or recognize Roman and Egyptian laws and customs in reference to marriage and divorce. In a word, he still rigidly adheres to that primitive Christianity, the prevalence of which would soon render all government over the people unnecessary if not impossible, and which, as thou knowest, it was so difficult for us to guide to right and reasonable action even in Rome and in other parts of the West. But his primitive and fearless teachings have reduced to the ghostly form of a mere sentiment all the active aid I had expected to obtain from the Christians of Syria and of Egypt. The fleet, the mighty fleet, which putteth all my coasts at the mercy of Licinius, ought to have been mine own, and would have been but for that Libyan serpent who paralyzed the arms of willing Christians by his accursed teachings."

"But," said Eusebius, solemnly, "these teachings were the very doctrines of our Lord, and Arius hath proclaimed nothing but the truths of the gospel, and for three hundred years no Christian man hath owned a slave or claimed private title to property, or lifted up a weapon even in defense of the faith for which he does not hesitate to die." And the bishop's fine face darkened, and his heart twitched as if some transient gleam of lightning had revealed before him a bottomless pit that opened down to perdition ; and for a moment he half-way felt that he had lost his own soul by juggling with the empire in the name of Jesus and for the glory of the Church.

While he stood in painful meditation, the emperor continued : "Yea! doubtless this was the primitive system ; and, thoroughly permeated with its new and radical principles, Arius seeketh to enforce them. The African ram, bold, self-confident, aggressive ! the Libyan serpent, agile, beautiful, tameless, and dangerous ! scorning all earthly ambitions as trifles unworthy of the consideration of an immortal spirit; despising pain, and toil, and peril ; almost courting martyrdom ; immovable by threats of ven-

gcance, or by hope of reward; alike inaccessible to flat-
tery and to fear—but for that one man I would hold
the East in my hand to-day! For the fleet was largely
manned and officered by Christians, and all things were
arranged to deliver up the ships to me, when this fierce,
invincible, immovable presbyter poured out the angry
torrent of his eloquence and learning, urging the Christians to obey all laws of the government under which
they lived that were not contrary to conscience, and denouncing those who might engage on either side in favor
of an earthly ruler as traitors to Christ and his kingdom. Their courage shriveled up before his fierce denunciation, as if it had been smitten by the wrath of
God, and all the carefully prepared plans for getting possession of more than half the fleet of Licinius, and especially of the great galleys with three banks of oars, faded
away before the breath of this one irreconcilable and immovable man. Then the attention of the Emperor Licinius having been called to the matter, he made a lustration of his army and navy, and dishonorably dismissed
therefrom every man who refused to offer sacrifice to the
gods; and also from his civil service, and from his
palaces. And since that day there hath been no man in
the service of Licinius that is a Christian. But the emperor sent to Arius a parchment giving to him legal authority to preach the gospel publicly in his city of Alexandria, because his gospel had saved the fleet; and the
stern, uncompromising presbyter sent it back with a message that his authority to preach was from God, not from
man."

"For what reason did Arius so bitterly take sides against thee, the favorite of God, the protector of the Church?"

"It would be unjust," said Constantine, "to say that he ever did so. He did not; but his powerful influence in holding the Christians of Egypt and of Syria to strictest neutrality was the most injurious policy he could have pursued against me; but he would have pursued the same course against any other ruler in the world."

Eusebius was the fast friend of Arius, whom he admired and loved beyond all living men (for Pamphilus had already suffered martyrdom); and the great ecclesiastic, rejoicing at the praises bestowed upon his friend by the greatest ruler of men, strove to call out yet more of his opinion, and accordingly said unto him, "Couldst thou not, then, attack the moral character of Arius, and call a council to condemn him for some irregularity, and so get rid of him?"

"Nay," answered the emperor, "the man is proof against all earthly temptations. When all arrangements had been made to confer upon him the see of Alexandria, he calmly but positively refused to accept the office, saying he would live and die presbyter of the Baucalis church. Gifts of money sent unto him anonymously he poured into the common treasury of the Church uncounted, and, in the midst of opulence, lived the life of an anchorite. Seven hundred of the noblest women of Alexandria are his communicants, and constant watchfulness never detected him in the slightest impropriety with any of them. In the pestilence which decimated and terrified the great city, by day and night he ministered unto the afflicted, when even parents abandoned their children and children their parents, and the ties of blood were disregarded, until the people believed him to be invested with a charmed life that was invulnerable to poniard, poison, or pestilence.   He is the purest and the strongest soul on earth," said the emperor, with undisguised admiration, "but he hath barred my way unto the conquest of the East!"

Eusebius glowed with pleasure as he listened to the language in which the emperor depicted the character of Arius, and replied : "Only the truly great are able to do justice to those whom they have strong reason to dislike, but thou hast painted the grand and lonely soul of the Libyan even as it is.   He hath been purified by sorrow. He is all for Christ, and earthly hopes, fears and ambitions no more can move his chaste and lofty spirit."

"But," said Constantine, sternly, "however admirable the presbyter may be, I will not forget that he hath robbed me of the fleet! He hath barred my way unto the conquest of the East."

Then said Eusebius : "If the fleet of Licinius could be by some means neutralized; if that valiant tyrant could, perhaps, be induced to keep his fleet out of the war altogether, and leave the fate of the empire to be decided by the armies of the East and of the West—would that content thee?"

The handsome face of Constantine glowed with a wonderful light of hope and pleasure as he answered, eagerly : "Yea, thou most wise and infallible bishop! If thou canst accomplish this thing, soon shall the churches of the East enjoy the imperial protection as fully as do those of the Western Empire ; and, freed from the persecutions of Licinius and of the pagan priests, the Church shall triumph over all the world. But I have told thee that no more able warrior lives than the emperor; he will never forego the use of his right arm of power : thou canst not neutralize his navy."

The greatest of ecclesiastics gazed with affectionate admiration upon the greatest of emperors, and calmly answered : "I am a man of peace, and know nothing of the conduct of a war. But I do know something of the human heart, and of the secret springs that govern the actions of men. When I did visit thee in Gaul, before the war with Maxentius, thou didst tell me that I could not cast a javelin, nor smite with a sword, nor draw out a legion in battle order, but that I knew all Italy, and showed thee how to conquer Rome. Verily I know not how to sail a ship, yet I will endeavor diligently to keep the tyrant's navy far off from thy coasts. If I should fail, thou wilt quickly know the unwelcome truth ; and if I succeed thou shalt learn it immediately."

"Thou hast always succeeded," answered Constantine ; "no promise made by thee hath failed. Thou hast never once disappointed thine emperor and friend."

"For the present," said Eusebius, "I do greatly desire of thee an indefinite leave of absence, but I trust not a protracted one, in order that I may pay a visit to my beloved brother Eusebius, the Bishop of Nicomedia."

For an instant the face of Constantine was clouded.

"Within the dominions of Licinius?" he softly murmured, but in a moment he answered: "Thou hast leave to go! But tell me, bishop, why thou goest unto Nicomedia. What canst thou do there except to expose thy dear and valuable head to the fury of the emperor?"

"I go thither," said Eusebius, with a light and musical laugh, "seeking to prepare a problem over which the historians and warriors of all future ages shall puzzle their weary brains in vain. The question which will be, I trust, a riddle unto them, is briefly this: Why was it that, in the second war with the most Christian Emperor Constantine, the brave and competent commander Licinius, possessing so vast a superiority at sea, utterly failed to carry an offensive war into the very center of his rival's dominions, and, having moored his fleet safely in some secure strait or bay, left the issue of the war to be decided by the land-forces alone, in the conduct of which the most glorious Emperor Constantine was known to be invincible?"

Then Constantine sprang from his seat, and with eager, glowing face he embraced the bishop and kissed him, saying: "Canst thou, indeed, do this thing for me? If thou canst, thou art stronger than ten legions, and deservest a reward equal to their pay!"

"Thou knowest well," said Eusebius, kindly but with inexpressible dignity, "that I have served thee faithfully without reward, because I love thee, Augustus, and love the Church of Christ, and know assuredly that thine own triumph will secure the triumph of the faith!"

"Thou speakest nothing but the truth, bishop," replied Constantine, his fine face lighting up with strong emotions, "and I have loved and honored thee in my heart accordingly. Thou knowest that, whenever thou needest me, I am all thine own. But how can this miracle that shall neutralize the emperor's maritime ascendency be wrought?"

"I think," answered Eusebius, gravely and sadly, "that miracles have recently ceased throughout the world, so that even the Church of Christ hath to depend upon only human agencies, which thou knowest was not formerly the case. It is well known, however, that the old Emperor Licinius doth not doubt the truth and divinity of our holy religion, although he hateth the Christians because he hath been persuaded that they offer up more prayers for thee than for himself. Now, it hath seemed probable to me that if an authentic Christian prophecy could be privately circulated through the imperial palace of Nicomedia to the purport that the Eastern Empire would be overthrown whenever it might send a hostile fleet to ravage the coasts of Europe, his fear and hatred of the Christians would influence him to retain his fleet at home in order to forestall the prophecy. Of course, the common sense of the matter would be, as thou hast said, for him to use his vast naval strength to desolate thy coasts in Greece, Italy, Africa, Hispania, and Gaul; but, perhaps, he may not do so. The matter is not very clearly wrought out in my mind, but gradually takes shape as I consider it, and I desire to see my brother, Eusebius of Nicomedia, a wise and prudent man, to converse with him concerning it."

"Thou art a great and wonderful bishop," said Constantine. "Go thou, and may God prosper thee! Keep me well informed of thy movements, and of all events that happen. Thou shalt have orders for all supplies, attendance, and money, which thou canst possibly need for thy purposes. If thou fall into any trouble at Nicomedia, or elsewhere, have sure means of informing me, for I would risk the sovereignty of the world to deliver thee, thou incomparable friend and bishop. When wilt thou depart?'

"Within a few days, at most," said Eusebius. "And thou shalt do nothing except to grant me leave of absence. We bishops can further each other upon our journeys quite well, and I wish to go secretly and without attracting notice."

"When thou hast leisure," said Constantine, "come unto me again, and come prepared to unravel these questions concerning the celebration of Easter, and concerning the Godhead, to the very last threads of them; for I earnestly desire to be perfectly informed therein."

CHAPTER III.

A DAY or two afterward, Eusebius again sought audience of the emperor, and in a long interview, during which Constantine, with his own hand, kept copious and accurate memoranda of the conversation, the bishop carefully explained the nature of the church controversy respecting the observance of Easter, and also the nature of the abstract and peculiar ideas involved in the dispute concerning the Deity; and in the whole interview the emperor manifested the perfect thoroughness with which his calm, grand intelligence was accustomed to go to the very bottom of every matter which once secured his interest, grasping all possible aspects and relationships of the subject—the evidence upon which alleged facts might be founded, the authority upon which each opinion might rest—so that at the close of the long and studious interview he was as well informed upon the subjects discussed as were the most learned ecclesiastics of his generation.

"I perceive," he said to Eusebius, "that thou art an advocate of the opinion of Arius the Libyan, concerning what Hosius calleth the Holy Trinity?"

"Yea!" answered the bishop; "for neither do the Gospels teach me, nor can the aid of reason enable me to understand that three are one any more than that one is three; nor can I evade the fact that 'Father' and 'Son' are terms which of necessity imply that the Father antedates the Son; nor can I believe that God the Father lived in our flesh and died upon the cross. So that, whenever the 'Arian heresy,' as they call it, shall be heard before a general council, I shall be numbered among the heterodox, if it is indeed possible that any council shall ever condemn the grand Libyan's doctrines!"

"I regret much," replied the emperor, "that thy conscience leadeth thee in that direction, although the fact must never become a cause of difference between thee and me. For, while I would yield cheerful acquiescence to thy superior learning about all merely religious questions, I perceive already that the political aspects of this controversy will make it politic for me to maintain the opinions of Hosius and his party."

"What possible political significance can exist in such an abstract dispute about matters of theological faith and doctrine?"

Constantine laughed pleasantly, and answered: "Of course, a pious and learned bishop would sooner perceive the minutest ramifications of the theological roots of any question than to grasp its most palpable political outgrowth. I will tell thee, bishop, but the communication is for thee alone. As to the paschal controversy, it is a mere matter of sentiment or feeling between those who do not

17

wish to follow the Jews in fixing the time of its observance,
and desire to have some period assigned by the Christian authority, on the one hand ; and, on the other, those who are
unwilling to depart from the practice of three centuries for
any reason—but these differences can be easily reconciled.
But, as to this other controversy, it is of an essentially different kind.   Thy statement of it revealed to me the
salient fact that the doctrine of Arius is that of the Eastern Church, the doctrine of Hosius that of the Western ;
and a geographical line might almost be run through the
faith upon this question—Arius and his party upon one
side, Hosius and his upon the other—and along the line
itself many who are not the partisans of either opinion.
Thou seest, therefore, that it is really a question between
two empires, and, whenever it shall be determined, a proper
regard for the prestige of mine own empire requires me to
see that the decision shall be in favor of the Western
Church.   Dost thou now perceive one plainest and least
important point of its political bearings ? ”

“ Yea, verily,” answered Eusebius.   “ But it had not
occurred to me before ! ”

“After the matter shall have been accomplished,” said
Constantine, “many others shall also see it, but not just
yet ; for it is the business of him who is fit to rule not
only to see, but to foresee, whatever may concern his empire ! ”

“Thou alone hast seen it yet,” replied the bishop.
“ But what other political significance can the controversy
possibly possess ? ”

“Ah ! bishop,” said the emperor, “ it is the great question of our age. It involves in itself the whole field of controversy between the old civilizations and the new ; between paganism and Christianity ; between Jesus Christ and the rulers of mankind. The doctrines of Arius are the utterances of that primitive Christianity which proclaimed the fraternity of all men, condemned war, slavery, and private-property rights. It maintaineth Jesus as the king of a kingdom established in the world ; a real and actual government among the Christian communities, which may yield obedience to laws that do not fetter conscience, but does not acknowledge allegiance to any human emperor or king. Its universal prevalence would speedily render all government over the people ridiculous and unnecessary ; for Christ would be the only king, and all men brethren, free and equal, as was the case in Mœsia, under the apostolical Ulfilas, until I was constrained to send an army thither and force the Goths to give up their communal organization, and adopt the Roman laws and customs. The system of Arius, primitive Christianity, dear bishop, would leave no room for Constantine on earth. But the doctrine of Hosius, by elevating Jesus to actual Godhead, leaveth his earthly career a mere manifestation, or appearance, of the divine in human flesh ; and, since the God hath returned to his former ineffable condition, it leaveth his kingdom to be only a pure and lofty spiritual phantasm—and leaves mankind for Constantine to govern. Thou seest that there can be no rivalry between the Christianity of Hosius and the sovereigns of this world, while the faith of Arius would soon subvert all human governments, and dethrone every prince on earth. Beyond any question, the emperors, from Nero to my own times, sought only to preserve the empire by persecuting the Christians, and properly described Christianity as 'a baleful and malignant' superstition,' 'a criminal association,' 'a new society that departed from the laws and ceremonies of our fathers, inventing a new government for itself inconsistent with the imperial laws and rights.' They understood that Roman sovereignty could not maintain itself against a rapidly increasing association that proposed to abolish war, slavery, private rights of property, offices, rank, and prerogative; and they tried to stamp it out of existence. These emperors strove to defend the empire by exterminating the Christians; if they had been greater men, they would have adopted the new religion, pruned it of all doctrines that might menace the imperial authority, translating Jesus to the highest heaven, and taking for themselves his place upon the earth—as I have done. I am, therefore, the champion of the Holy Trinity, as Hosius hath defined it; and at the right time Arius must be condemned as a heretic. For I will no more suffer him to build up the churches of the East upon this basis of primitive Christianity than I would suffer Ulfilas to accomplish a similar purpose among the Gothic tribes. Dost thou now perceive the political significancy of this Arian heresy, my dear bishop?"

But Eusebius stood before the emperor pale and trembling, the cold perspiration standing in great drops upon his pallid brow. For a moment an awful mist of horror enveloped his struggling soul. Had he, then, made a terrible mistake in using his own large abilities and influence to place the persecuted saints under the protection of the grand and humane emperor? Had he betrayed the Church of Christ, and lost his own soul, in bringing about that union of ecclesiastical and imperial authority which made the kingdom of heaven an appanage of the Roman emperor, and had secured safety, peace, and glory, for the Christians by giving to Constantine the place that should belong only to Jesus Christ? Had he indeed been overreached and manipulated by this most able of mankind for his own political purposes, even while he thought himself to be using Constantine for the glory of God and for the edification of the Church? Sick, doubtful, terrified, he faintly answered: "But the things which thou sayest the doctrines of Arius would accomplish are precisely the triumph which our Lord did promise to the Church, and which he pledged his divinity to' achieve! Surely Arius must be right! War, slavery, and mammon-worship, must be banished out of the world! Mankind must become brethren in the Lord! The Church must triumph, and Christ must be the only king!"

"Not in my time!" said Constantine, with the calmness and firmness of mature and deliberate conviction; "not while I live! The empire shall be mine own. I will yield my right to no man, human or divine! Let the Church grow and prepare for future triumph over earthly sovereignty when the scepter shall be held by some more weak and nerveless hand than mine. I will govern while I live, both church and state, in spite of gods or demons!"

The bishop made no answer. A terrible error into which he had gone with glad heart and exuberant hope seemed palpably revealed to him. He was utterly cowed and humbled. With a crushing sense of self-abasement, shame, mortification, repentance, almost crime, he realized the fact that, compared with that colossal man, who amused himself by playing with the loftiest emotions of the human soul as he did with his ever-victorious legions—a man who, under his calm, grand bearing, concealed a devil of ambition that was ready to mock at all that men hold sacred, and even to hurl his phalanx against Christ himself—he felt like a child, a pygmy.

With ashy lips he murmured : " Almost thou hast defied the Son of God ! Beware ! "

Then, with a singular smile that had in its beauty and light something of lofty mournfulness, the emperor answered : " And if I should do so, dear bishop, what then ? Jesus hath no power against me except through thaumaturgy, and thou dost know that thaumaturgy faded out when the Church abandoned that communal system upon which Arius insisteth yet so manfully. I have made my choice, and will abide the issue, bishop. Thou knowest that I never was baptized. I might have been a Christian, but I preferred to reign over the Roman Empire ; and I will reign until the end."

Ah ! for him, then, with all the glad assurance born of utter ignorance that such a being could exist among mankind, the bishop had carefully freighted " the old ship Zion " with the godless furniture of Roman law and custom, its statutes of slavery, its laws and usages of war and conquest, its idolatrous system of private-property rights, titles, prerogatives, political and social class distinctions between those whom God made to be brethren, out of which idolatry the sorrow of the world had grown, from all of which Jesus had died to ransom a fallen race. He had unwittingly launched the freighted ship upon the troubled sea of earthly politics. Thinking that he would win the Roman Empire for the Church, he had betrayed and sold the cause of Christ to Constantine. Thinking that he guided and controlled the emperor, he had labored with all diligence to make himself the master's slave. He knew it now only too well—he knew that Constantine had always known it; and, appalled by the vast resources of that greatest of mankind, crushed by the sense of his amazing genius, he seemed unto himself to grow small, contemptible, and weak.

And the ship of the Church? Would she go down forever in the troubled waters, amid the stormy strife for worldly gains and power? Or would she yet, somehow, sometime, somewhere, outride the tempests, and in some unknown and distant clime reach into a safe haven? "Not in my time," said Constantine; "not while I live!" When, then?

These bitter meditations were broken by the calm, sweet voice of Constantine: "Bishop, thou must perceive for thyself that the radical polity of the primitive Christianity to which Arius cleaves unswervingly, and which Ulfilas founded among the Goths so firmly that I had to send the legions thither to uproot it, was somewhat fanatical, or at least premature, and not suited to the every-day life of selfish and wicked men. Thou must perceive, also, with equal clearness, that the splendid ecclesiasticism which I have established throughout the Western Empire in place of the primitive religion is vastly better for mankind than any system ever before attempted, and that it should be speedily extended over all the East. What future, grander developments await the Church, no mortal can foretell. For the present, I desire of thee to seek means whereby to fan the flame of this Arian controversy: it must not die out until it can be summoned before an imperial council, and receive formal condemnation at the mouths of all the bishops called into a synod by the Emperor of the west!"

"And if, when the council shall have been convened, its members shall sustain Arius, what then?"

"A religious war, perhaps," answered Constantine, "or a return unto the pagan gods; both dreadful alternatives, which the Church and the empire should regard with equal horror. But the council will never so decide. I answer for its action; only keep thou the flame of controversy burning until the proper hour arrives!"

"I will contrive means that shall not fail to do so," answered Eusebius, and, bowing low, at a sign from the emperor he withdrew, overwhelmed with the perception of that calm, relentless, almost superhuman sagacity which Constantine had permitted him to see.

"Yea!" murmured Eusebius, "I will fan this flame of controversy! It shall blaze throughout the Church! And it may even happen that Constantine, although the greatest of the human race, is not a match for God. Who knows? Thaumaturgy may be restored to the Church, or, even if, as Constantine asserteth, the kingdom of our Lord was prematurely established, the spiritual truth of the gospel will sometime educate mankind up to the ultimate reception of its socialism and politics. And to this end it shall be my task before I die to organize within the bosom of the Church sacred brotherhoods, bound by holy ties of chastity, obedience, and poverty, to keep alive forever the memory of that communal system upon which Christ founded his kingdom. At all events, there is no possibility of going backward now; and more than ever do I desire to see Constantine obtain the sovereignty of the East. And now for Nicomedia!"

That very day the bishop set out upon his dangerous mission, to concert measures by which to neutralize the naval power of the Emperor Licinius.

CHAPTER IV.

THE PROPHECY OF GAIUS.

PROCEEDING, therefore, with all diligence, not very many days afterward, the Bishop of Cæsarea arrived at Nicomedia, and straightway, by the use of certain secret means of communication which were well known to all Christians, he found, and took up his abode with, Eusebius of that city; and they together discussed at great length what means might be used to neutralize the naval power of the tyrant Licinius.

Eusebius of Cæsarea had been absent for many months, and Constantine had begun to grow impatient at his long delay, during which he had received no tidings from the bishop personally, and had heard nothing concerning him, except that he was quietly residing in the city with the other Eusebius. And the emperor, who valued his bishop highly, and enjoyed his companionship more than that of any other man, began to fear that the revelation of his own real character and purposes, which he had made at their last memorable interview, had alienated his friend forever, and thereby deprived himself of the services which he deemed to be almost invaluable. It gave him unmingled pleasure, therefore, to receive upon a certain day a written message that "Eusebius, Bishop of Nicomedia, sent by his brother Eusebius Pamphilus, craves audience of the emperor." Constantine eagerly ordered that he be admitted, and, having dismissed all others, he gave the bishop a very cordial greeting, and then said, with greatest interest and solicitude : " Tell me first of all of thy brother, my friend the Bishop of Cæsarea ! Where now is the holy and able man ? Is he well ? What doeth he ? "

The bishop was somewhat lacking in the courtly elegance that characterized his brother, but still had a certain ease born of good sense and honesty of purpose, and he answered in a straightforward and intelligent way that pleased Constantine, and enabled him instantly to " take the measure of the man," and value him at once at his full worth, a thing he was not always able to do with the other Eusebius.

" The bishop, my brother, fared well when I last saw him. We parted at Nicomedia—he to go unto Alexandria, ' upon the emperor's business,' he said ; I to come hither by his desire. He sendeth love and reverence unto thee, ' the greatest of mankind,' as he saith ; and hath sent me hither because he thought that the things which I am requested to tell thee ought not to be committed to writing, nor intrusted to any ordinary messenger. Whenever thou desirest to hear it, I will briefly narrate what hath happened at Nicomedia." ·

" I am alone with thee, bishop, to hear thy report. Proceed with thy narrative at once. But first be thou seated, and partake of such refreshments as thou wilt."

"Nay," answered the bishop, "I need naught except thine own attention."

"Then sit thou there, and count upon an eager listener."

"The business upon which thy bishop came unto me having been carefully unfolded by him, the delay therein was caused by the necessity of sending far beyond Antioch for a fitting person to accomplish that upon which we had agreed as necessary for thy service; but it hath been done. The great fleet of the Emperor Licinius hath been so far neutralized that not a ship thereof will cross the sea to molest thy coasts if there should be war. On that thou mayst implicitly rely."

"Tell me the means by which this most important work hath been accomplished; and spare thou no details of the business: my only wish now is to hear thee fully!"

"It happened more than a year ago," said the bishop, "that I received letters from a presbyter at Chalcis, far beyond Antioch in Syria, concerning a most singular youth of that village, who was an epileptic—a devout Christian, but of strange fancies and of extraordinary appearance. This lad, the presbyter informed me, during the paroxysms of his disease seemed to be possessed by some sort of a spirit of divination, and the Church there had vainly attempted to exorcise the spirit; for thaumaturgy hath recently been lost. But the presbyter himself had little faith in his prophetic powers, because he had discovered that it was possible, by strongly impressing the mind of the youth, before the paroxysms came upon him, with some peculiar and striking thought, to anticipate the subject, and often even the very words, of his supposed prophetic ravings. Now, when the bishop unfolded to me what he desired to attempt for thy service, I at once thought of this Syrian youth, and judged that he might be advantageously used therein. The sending of a messenger to Chalcis for him wrought some delay, and, when the messenger reached that place, the youth had gone elsewhere ; and it was a work of time to discover him, and might, indeed, have been impossible, but for a certain notoriety bestowed upon him by the strange misfortune under which he labored. And, after we had received the youth at Nicomedia, it was a work of time, and care, and patience, to secure his entire confidence, and train him properly for the business we had undertaken. Do I state the matter too minutely for thy patience ? "

" Nay," said Constantine ; " it is wonderfully interesting. Thou need have no fear that thy narrative will weary me : I do desire to hear thee fully."

" We found by frequent experiments," continued Eusebius, " that the paroxysms of the youth's disease were not strictly periodical, but that any sudden, strong emotion was liable to bring on an attack. We found that when we had made him memorize certain words beforehand, he was liable, on the increment of his disease, to repeat just those words in a sort of chanting tone, the melody and manner of which were very impressive, even when the words themselves were unmeaning. We found that he was ready to do or suffer anything if persuaded that it would be for the good of the Church. We kept the youth in safe retreat, carefully secluded, so that he might remain entirely un-

known in Nicomedia. We then constantly assured him
that God was able to accomplish his own designs by using
even the most humble agencies, and that no man had the
right to look upon himself as a being too insignificant to
work for the glory of his Creator; and that even he, although sorely afflicted, by zeal and faithfulness might be
able some time to perform a great service to the persecuted
Church. He eagerly inquired how that might be, and was
manifestly ready to seek for martyrdom if that had been
the duty enjoined upon him. But we carefully impressed
upon him that all that was required of him was to memorize and constantly repeat a certain form of words that we
dictated to him; to meditate upon them day and night;
to suffer nothing else to occupy his thoughts; and to wait
in faith and hope the result of this discipline. We instructed him that, if any one should ask him about the
words he might utter when the fit was on him, to say
nothing, except that he was moved so to speak; if any
should ask him whom he knew in Nicomedia, he was to
answer, 'Eusebius the bishop'; and that in answer to
every question put to him he should tell the exact truth.
We soon found that, whenever he suffered under a paroxysm of his malady, he would fall to the ground and presently repeat in that sad, wailing chant that seemed to be
natural to him, the very words which we had dictated to
him, and no others."

"What words were these?" asked Constantine.

"The words," replied Eusebius, "were as follows:
'Joy to the land of Syria! Joy to the holy ones of Egypt!
for their deliverer cometh! When the great ships shall

cross the middle sea, the tyrant's power shall fail, and a holy emperor shall add the East unto his Western Empire ! Joy to Syria and to Egypt, when the great ships shall cross the middle sea !'

" Having experimented with the lad until it seemed to be morally certain that, under the influence of a paroxysm of his disease, he would chant these words only, we directed him to go daily to the gate which opened into the grounds surrounding the imperial palace at Nicomedia, until he might see the Emperor Licinius about to come forth, and that then he should boldly force his way through the gates, at any hazard, without offering salutations or explanation to any one. This the youth promised faithfully to do ; and it happened that, the first time he went thither, he saw one whom he supposed to be the emperor, coming forth accompanied by a throng of attendants, and he rushed forward so impetuously that the emperor was compelled to give place to him ; and then a soldier knocked down the poor lad with the pole of his pike. Licinius stopped to ascertain the meaning of an intrusion so bold and unusual, and the pain of the blow and the excitement of the situation brought upon the youth one of his strange attacks, and while he lay writhing and twisting about upon the paving-stones, in a loud, weird voice, whose unearthly melody filled all the place, he chanted the words that had been taught to him : ' Joy to the land of Syria ! Joy to the holy ones of Egypt ! for their deliverer cometh ! When the great ships shall cross the middle sea, the tyrant's power shall fail, and a holy emperor shall add the East unto his Western Empire ! Joy to Syria and to Egypt, when the great ships shall cross the middle sea!' Then a centurion sprang forward, and would have slain the youth with his sword, but Licinius waved him off, and stood looking upon the singular lad with interest and wonder. And the youth flopped up off of the ground like a fish, and fell back heavily, and almost immediately resumed his wild, sweet chanting of the self-same words; and a profound silence obtained until his song was ended. And very soon that paroxysm passed off, and the lad arose, and looked about him, as if he knew not where he was nor how he came to be there."

Constantine laughed a low, joyous, almost boyish laugh, exclaiming: "A superb performance, indeed! A masterly.thing! But continue thy most welcome narrative!"

"Then the Emperor Licinius, whose features are bronzed, and hard, and cruel, looked steadily upon the abashed young man, saying in a stern, imperious voice, 'Who art thou?'

"And the lad answered, 'I am Gaius, a poor youth of Chalcis in Syria!'

"'Knowest thou to whom thou art speaking?'

"'Nay, verily,' answered Gaius, 'but I suppose thee to be the emperor!'

"'What is thy business in Nicomedia?'

"'I have no business anywhere,' said the lad. 'I am diseased, an invalid, an epileptic, and am incapacitated for business. Verily I came unto Nicomedia hoping to be cured of this fearful malady.'

"'What brought thee unto our palace-gates?'

"'I came hither to look upon the emperor, having

never seen so great a man; but some cowardly brute did strike me down with a pike!'

"'Why didst thou chant such things as thou hast done even in mine own presence?'

"'What things did I chant? I know not, for the hard blow brought upon me an attack of the epilepsy, and while it continueth I know not what I say, but speak only as I am moved to speak!'

"'What, then, moveth thee to chant at all?'

"'I know not, nor do I even know that I have done so, unless some one who hath heard me informeth me thereof!'

"'Whom knowest thou in my city of Nicomedia?'

"'None save the Bishop Eusebius!'

"'Art thou, then, a Christian?'.

"'Yea! Thanks to the boundless mercy of our Lord!'

"Then said the emperor: 'Let immediate search be made for this Eusebius, and let him be straightway brought before me. Keep ye this boy in strictest prison, but use him kindly; for it may be that he hath a demon!'

"I did not choose to be found upon that day, although the city was sifted well for that purpose. And upon the next day, Licinius caused the lad Gaius to be brought before him, and he spoke kindly unto him, saying: 'Thou art a strange and interesting youth, and I desire to take thee into my service, and to attach thee unto myself, and to care for thee well. Hast thou memory good enough to keep in thy mind for me a catalogue of more than three hundred ships?'

"'I know not,' said the lad. 'At school I learned

18

rapidly and retained well all that I acquired; but I fear that the malady wherewith I am afflicted hath injured both mind and body.'

" ' Let me test thy memory somewhat to ascertain thy capacity for the service I would have thee render. Canst thou name the stations and distances upon the road from Chalcis unto Antioch, and thence unto the sea ? '

" And the boy gave the whole itinerary correctly. And the emperor asked of him a great many questions with exceeding affability, and finally said unto him : 'Thou hast a fine, retentive memory, and I will make a man of thee. See, now, how much thou canst remember of the song which thou didst twice chant on yesterday ! '

" But the lad said : ' I know not the words at all, and know not that I did chant at all. All that occurreth when the fit is upon me is blankness and darkness, so that I know nothing, and suffer not, and if fire were put upon me, I would not feel any pain so long as the paroxysm continueth ! '

" Then the emperor gave way to wrath, and shouted furiously : ' Thou liest, villain ! Thou seekest to deceive me ! Repeat thy chant instantly, or I will put thee to torture to extract the truth ! '

" Then the boy grew very pale, and trembled, but he only answered : ' Thou demandest of me that which is impossible ! I do not know the words, and can not repeat them, though thou shouldst slay me ! '

" Then cried out the emperor, ' Bring thumb-screws hither, and torment this wretch ! '

" Then one put upon his thumb that cruel screw, and

twisted hard upon it, and the boy shrieked with pain. Then the fit came upon him, and he fell headlong upon the floor, and the torturer removed the screw. And immediately the boy began, in a clear, sweet voice that filled the great hall with music, to chant the same words again : 'Joy to the land of Syria! Joy to the holy ones of Egypt!'—and the emperor sprang forward, and with the point of a dagger he tore up a finger-nail of the boy, watching his face intently ; but the lad's countenance changed not, and he continued his chant evenly and serenely. And the emperor commanded that fire be brought to him in a brazier, and he laid a coal thereof upon the boy's naked breast, and blew upon it until the burned flesh smelled all about, but the boy showed no consciousness of pain, and continued to chant sweetly until his song was ended. And for a short space the lad lay as one dead, and then a strong convulsion contorted his limbs, and 'lifted him from the floor, and violently cast him down again ; and then once more he chanted the same words, and the emperor listened and watched him with fear and wonder. And when the attack had passed away, Licinius said : 'Let this boy be guarded carefully, but let him be treated with the greatest kindness ; for surely, beyond any doubt, he hath a demon!'

"And the lictors with great astonishment and fear led the boy away.

"And having been fully informed of all these things on the same night, by a Christian whom we had allowed to sacrifice and so retain his place in the palace, for the good of the Church, upon the next morning went I up to the gates and boldly demanded admission, declaring to the centurion on duty who I was, and that I had been informed that the emperor was seeking me throughout the city; and speedily they brought me into the presence of Licinius, and he said, 'Art thou Eusebius, the Bishop of Nicomedia ?'

"'Yea, I am he!'

"'And like all of thy treasonable sect, that lurk within my city of Nicomedia, thou art still offering up prayers for the Emperor Constantine ?'

"'Yea, doubtless!'

"'And thou dost not pray for me, nor propitiate God for me, thine own lawful emperor, at all ?'

"'Yea, daily I pray God for thee that he would soften thy flinty heart, and turn thee from the devices of wickedness unto the wisdom of the just!'

"'But thou prayest not for my prosperity, and for the glory and perpetuity of mine empire ?'

"'Nay, verily. I have no faith to pray for the triumph of the cruel and of the wicked!'

"Then said he, 'Dost thou know the boy Gaius of Chalcis ?'

"'Yea! He was with me at my house until the third day past, but he hath disappeared, and I am anxious concerning him.'

"'Is there anything peculiar about the boy ?'

"'He hath a peculiar and terrible malady called epilepsy!'

"And then attentively regarding me with his hard and searching eyes, he said, 'Doth the boy prophesy ?'

" ' When he hath a paroxysm of his disease he customarily chanteth strange things which some esteem to be prophecies ; but whether his sayings be truly prophetic or not I can not inform thee.'

" ' Perhaps thou dost remember the words of some of his pretended prophecies ? '

" ' Yea, verily ! For since he hath been with me he hath hardly ever chanted anything but a certain song which I have heard him repeat very often when the disease taketh him.'

" ' Repeat thou those words ! '

" Then with a certain show of exultation I chanted the same words that Gaius had uttered, and, when I had finished, Licinius cried out fiercely, ' Thou dost believe, indeed, that the words of Gaius are a sure prophecy, and thou dost rejoice at my threatened overthrow ! '

" I looked smilingly upon the emperor, but made no answer ; and thereupon he fell into a great rage and said unto me, grimly enough : ' Thou art a tall man, bishop ! Verily, I think thou art fully a head too tall, and this day I will reduce thee to a more proper stature by cutting off thy head ' ; and when he saw that I was unterrified by this threat, he added, ' And the boy's head also ! '

" Then gazing fixedly upon him, I did say : ' Surely thou mayst do so, for thou art a blood-soaked, merciless tyrant enough for any crime. But this deed would make thee contemptible ; for it would prove that thou art not only a tyrant, but also a fool ! '

" Then turning almost livid with suppressed wrath, he cried out, ' What dost thou mean, thou insolent ? '

" ' I mean that some years ago when the bold and eloquent preaching of the brave and righteous presbyter, Arius the Libyan, did operate to save for thee a large part of thy fleet, thou didst order that he should never be molested in the public discharge of the duties of his sacred office; wherefore, even the Christians, who knew thee to be a bloody tyrant, and a desecrator of the sacrament of marriage by an infamous law, and a violator of all the sanctities and decencies of life, still did give thee credit for intelligence. But if now thou shalt murder those who, even unintentionally, have given thee warning in time to save thy whole navy, all men will regard thee as an idiot.'

" ' How save my whole navy ? '

" ' By keeping the ships thereof upon thine own side of the Mediterranean; for the words are, " *when* the great ships shall cross the middle sea," and perhaps it may signify not until *then?* '

" ' By Jupiter Stator,' he answered, vehemently, ' I think that thou art right ! And that accursed " when " shall never happen. For this honest saying of thine, thou mayst go hence free, and take the lad Gaius with thee ! '

" And thereupon I withdrew; but I am certainly advised that his purpose holds good never to send his fleet across the Mediterranean."

" How dost thou know that ?" asked Constantine, eagerly.

" We waited many weeks," replied Eusebius, " to obtain some reliable indications of his purposes; but the Emperor Licinius is a great commander, and men drilled in military services talk cautiously even when drunk, as he frequently is, so that we got nothing. Finally, a centurion came one night to mine abode, which I had caused to be publicly known, and with great courtesy informed me that the emperor had sent him to bring me into his presence. Having dismissed all others, as if the matter were most secret, he said : 'I know ye Christian bishops love not me, and that ye offer prayers for Constantine; yet I do not think that thou wouldst lie to me. I therefore tell thee that, since thou wert last before me, I sent an embassy secretly unto the oracle at Delphi, with many costly gifts, asking of the oracle what success I would have if I should send my navy against the Western Empire; and I desire thee to read and to construe the answer of the god.' Then he gave unto me a parchment on which was written, 'When the navy of the Emperor Licinius shall pass over the sea to war with the Emperor Constantine, his empire shall be overthrown.' I read the oracle, and laughed. Then said I unto him : 'Like all of the pretended oracles of the heathen, it is simply an evasion. Of course, if two great emperors engage in war, one of them must be overthrown. This oracle saith not which of them. If the Western Empire be defeated, the priests will say, "We foretold that." But if the Eastern Empire shall be subverted, they will just as truly say, " We foretold that." '

"'Art thou certain that the language bears one construction as naturally and grammatically as it does the other ?'

"'Assuredly so ! The Latin infinitive mood with the

accusative case possesses a wonderful facility for such a construction as may signify either one thing or the other.'

"Then he gave way to sudden wrath, and cried aloud : 'Curses on the lying, cheating oracles by which so many mighty men have been lured into destruction !' And, fixing his eyes upon me, he continued, 'Was there any such ambiguity in what thy boy Gaius chanted ?'

"'Nay, verily,' I answered. 'He said, "A holy emperor shall add the East unto his Western Empire." Thou canst not add the East unto anything, although thou mightest add something to the East; but canst add nothing to the Western Empire, which is not thine own, and thou art not a "holy emperor !"'

"'It is only a cursed trick of the oracle to lure me on to ruin !' he exclaimed. 'The Emperor Constantine hath bribed the god to influence me so that he may invade and overthrow mine empire while my fleet is far away. I will keep mine own coasts safe with wooden walls henceforth, and not a ship shall cross the middle sea.'

"Then he said unto me : 'Thou seem'st an honest and fair-minded man, and henceforth thou may'st practice thy religion publicly in my city of Nicomedia without fear or molestation. So fare thee well.'

"I think that this completeth my account, except I should add that from the very beginning of this matter the Emperor Licinius hath zealously endeavored to keep it all profoundly secret, so that it is known to very few." ·

Then said Constantine unto the bishop : "What didst thou mean by saying to the emperor, 'The Christians who knew thee to be a bloody tyrant, and the desecrator of the sacrament of marriage by an infamous law'? What law was that?"

And Eusebius answered : "He hath revived the former law of Maximin, that 'no woman of rank should marry without the emperor's consent,' and for the same infamous purpose, *ut ipse in omnibus nuptiis prægustator esset;* and this licentiousness hath done more to set the Church against the emperor than even the murder of the bishops."

"How strange," said Constantine, "that men should think themselves fit to govern an empire who can not even govern their own brutal passions!"

Then the great emperor indulged in long-continued laughter, not loud nor vociferous, but quiet, hearty, joyous, and exultant. But, soon resuming his usual equanimity, he said unto the bishop : "Thou art the most welcome messenger that hath ever come unto me since thy brother of Cæsarea did first visit me in Gaul before the overthrow of Maxentius. Tell me what great favor worthy of Rome's emperor I can do for thee."

Then Eusebius, with glowing countenance, bent low, and seizing the emperor's hand he kissed it fervently, exclaiming, "Stretch forth thy mighty hand, Augustus, and free the persecuted churches of the East!"

Constantine was deeply moved, and answered : "It shall be done, bishop! Trust me, it shall be done! But I have given order for thy fitting entertainment, and while thou shalt rest and refresh thyself, think of some personal favor I can do for thee."

Eusebius bowed gravely and withdrew.

The emperor was alone, seated, buried in profoundest meditation. For a long time he was silent, and then his deep thought found utterance in murmured words: "A wonderful faith, truly, that can bind the heart and intellect of even able men like the Eusebii in absolute slavery to an idea, so that Christ and the Church are first in all their thoughts and purposes; and ease, comfort, wealth, and power, and even life and death, are trifling things compared therewith! If any God exists, these Christians surely have discovered him in Jesus. But I am sufficient for myself, and need no Deity."

Then he was silent again for some time longer. But suddenly he gave way to jubilant merriment, murmuring amid his laughter: "It was a superb farce, that prophecy of Gaius! Better than the *Legio Fulminea*. Better even than the Labarum! Surely the fine, Grecian hand of my Eusebius hath only acquired a more delicate touch with his advancing years!" And the great emperor continued to laugh merrily.

But neither pain nor pleasure ever interfered with the grand game of empire; and before midnight orders had been framed and issued by which the veteran legions of Hispania, Gaul, and Germany were to be gradually replaced by more recent levies; by which the brave and hardy Goths were put upon the most rigid military discipline; and by which all the chosen troops, upon whose skill and valor the unconquerable leader would be willing to stake the sovereignty of the world, were slowly concentrated to the eastward of Milan by a quiet, steady, unostentatious military movement that consumed months in its accomplishment and scarcely excited the suspicions of even the vigilant and intelligent agents of the Emperor Licinius.

CHAPTER V.

In the year A. D. 319, Alexander, the old and pious Bishop of Alexandria, having become imbued with that Trinitarianism which began to assume a sort of doctrinal prominence in the Western Church even from the time when Constantine had defeated Maxentius and had so become Emperor of Rome, publicly proclaimed this dogma wherever he went. During that year, upon one of his episcopal visits, he preached in the Baucalis church a sermon which gave great offense to Arius the Libyan, who was presbyter thereof, and to many of the vast and opulent congregation. Upon the following Sabbath the presbyter had delivered an elaborate discourse, in the course of which he inveighed with great force and earnestness against some "expounders of new doctrines who had grown too learned in the philosophy of the world, and too much in love with the political and legal religion which had been established in place of Christianity in the Western Empire to remain satisfied with the simple, unquestionable statement of the Gospels that Jesus Christ was the Son of God; and had gone about to trouble the faith and harass the consciences of believers by novel and dangerous speculations concerning the nature of Deity that were not taught in the Scriptures and were unknown to three centuries of Christian faith and practice." And, although Arius mentioned not the venerable bishop by name, no one doubted for whom his fierce rebuke was intended, and understood perfectly well what doctrinal deliverances he condemned as "the philosophy of the world," as "the political and legal religion which had been established in the Western Empire," and as "not taught in the Scriptures," and as "unknown to three centuries of Christian faith and practice." To this sermon the bishop subsequently replied in language of even greater vehemence; and before very long there was a continuous controversy going on between them, in which numerous Christians engaged on both sides, until it spread throughout the churches and grew into heated and sometimes acrimonious disputations. Nearly all the Romans in Alexandria took part with the bishop, and urged him earnestly in the prosecution of the controversy, while the native Christians, for the most part, clave unto Arius; and the word "foreigner," which before that time was never applied by one Christian to another (for they were all brethren), quickly crept into common use.

The superior learning, zeal, and influence of the presbyter greatly outweighed the personal and episcopal power of the bishop, and a vast majority of the Alexandrian clergy and laity sustained the views of Arius as the only true doctrine of the Scriptures, as approved by the ancient and constant teachings of the Church; and the controversy might have sunk into oblivion but for the "foreign" element, many of whom really seemed to make it their chief vocation to proclaim the great truth of "the Holy Trinity," and to utter eloquent panegyrics upon the character of Constantine the Emperor of Rome. Under these influences each party steadily maintained its own opinions, and the matter remained in this condition until Eusebius of Cæsarea, having parted from the other Eusebius at Nicomedia, had journeyed unto Alexandria to redeem his promise made to the emperor that the flame of controversy should be kept burning until a general council could be convoked to determine it. Eusebius very soon comprehended the situation, and speedily reached the conclusion that even his superior official station and the support of the "foreigners" would not enable the bishop long to maintain himself against the vast power and influence of the presbyter without efficient aid. That, he thought, could not be effectively rendered except by some man of rare abilities, who might combine in himself all the characteristics of a courtier as well as of a priest, for the "foreign element" was already largely secularized; and he very anxiously looked about him for some man fit to be intrusted with the task of upholding the hands of the venerable Alexander.

Of course our Eusebius had duly renewed his ancient friendship for Arius, whom he loved and honored above all living men, and they had many interesting conversations upon the condition and prospects of the Church, and upon the present duties of the faithful pastor. Eusebius skillfully argued in favor of accommodating priestly action to the exigencies of social and political surroundings. Arius would hear of no compromise upon any point of either faith or practice. "Pontius Pilate," he vehemently exclaimed, "was the prince of compromisers when he washed his hands of 'the innocent blood,' and delivered up our Lord to be crucified! His successors are in all things worthy of him, seeking both to win the world by their actions and to save their souls by the profession of a faith which they do not practice! How fare ye bishops under the reign of Antichrist—ye that dwell where Satan's seat is?"

"The Church hath prospered beyond all expectation. The bishops almost rank with princes; the presbyters are blessed with exceeding comfort and honor, and throughout the Western Empire the people crowd into the churches faster than they can be built."

Then the grim old presbyter's hand waved to and fro, and his grand, shaggy head darted forward upon the long, lean neck, and the sad eyes gleamed with strange, mesmeric light, and his voice hissed with sibilant sharpness as he exclaimed: "Yea, my brother! And I have heard that your prince-bishops own slaves and nourish concubines; and that 'the brethren' hold estates and offices, and fleece their brethren by the crime of usury; and that the only difference between Romans who are Christians and those who are not subsists in the fact that one class of them patronizes the imperial churches and professes faith in Christ, and the other does not degrade itself and dishonor religion by any such shams and farces! Are these things so?"

Eusebius winced at this fierce and bitter thrust, but answered : "Some abuses have crept in among us, in consequence of our wonderful prosperity, which were unknown to the severity and simplicity of an earlier age ; but we have many saintly bishops, presbyters, and people ; and the evils of which thou speakest belong not to the Church, but to the frailty of individuals."

"Thou art verily mistaken, brother ! Or what dost thou expect from a statutory religion, from an established church of which Constantine is king instead of Christ ? I tell thee plainly that a church which imperial authority hath legalized along with legalized war, slavery, and mammon-worship, is not only no church of Christ, but is that Antichrist of which John in the Apocalypse doth speak. And it shall grow continually worse and worse."

"I doubt not," answered Eusebius, "that it would have been better to have preserved primitive Christianity ; but the emperor is so powerful, and ecclesiasticism hath become insensibly so firmly established, that it is impossible now to turn back to the original system, perhaps dangerous to attempt it."

"Yea, dangerous," said Arius, bitterly. "For already he hath persecuted the saints, having waged a cruel war against the Goths to overthrow the church which Ulfilas planted among them, and force them to adopt the Roman laws and legal religion. I look forward every year to see this man of sin build a new capital, upon seven hills, above the sea, that John's description of him may be made complete. Thou must follow thine own counsel, brother. As for me, in life, in death, I am fixed in unflinching opposition to any name of blasphemy that may be used to designate a legal religion that sanctions war, slavery, and mammon-worship."

Many such conversations occurred between the bishop and Arius; but Eusebius found that the stern old man was incapable of compromise, and despised all expediency.

"Yea," he would say, "I have been told that ye Western Christians already believe that charity consisteth of alms-giving, instead of love to the brethren! . . .

"Ye foolishly dream of converting the world," he cried, "by means of a church founded upon Roman laws, whose faith is a mere intellectual assent and conviction! But ye will find that instead of securing liberty, fraternity, equality, ye have only added the bond of conscience to bind the burdens more tightly upon the shoulders of mankind, and furnished the new Pharisees with new power to oppress the poor. . . .

"Yea, verily," he said, "ye know that faith in Christ and community of property constituted the liberty of the gospel wherewith Jesus sought to make man free! But ye have imported into the very bosom of the Church all of the tyrannies, injustices, class-distinctions, and wrongs which constitute mammon-worship and the sorrow of the world; and there is no difference between your system and the old religions except that ye have substituted the name of Christ for that of Jupiter and Mars in juggling with the rights of man."

19

And when Eusebius endeavored to arouse in the stern old man some considerations of personal prudence, by intimating the probability that Constantine might some day rule the East also, the lone and immovable man sternly answered :

"Yea, he will obtain the East! For he alone of all men hath never failed in diplomacy ; hath never abandoned a purpose ; hath never lost a battle, and never will ! He hath sold his soul for earthly glory, and Satan will pay to him his price."

But although Eusebius loved to commune with the stern old man, whose stainless integrity of character he could love and honor, but scarcely imitate, he never forgot the object of his journey to Alexandria, and was constantly on the lookout for some one to whom he could assign the task of aiding the ancient Alexander in his controversy with the great and fearless presbyter. At last he fell in with a youth who was an archdeacon in the bishop's church, and who, although very young, was possessed of such remarkable genius and learning, and of such pre-eminent personal advantages, as at once to attract and astonish him, and seemed to render him the fittest person to engage. He sedulously cultivated the young man's friendship, and admired him more and more as he learned more of his character and abilities. Finally, he cordially invited the youth to make with him a visit to Constantine, and having with much difficulty obtained the consent of the aged Alexander, who loved the bright and accomplished youth with exceeding tenderness, they twain departed for Milan. When the long and tedious

journey had been safely accomplished, Eusebius promptly
waited upon the emperor, who received him with fraternal
cordiality.

"Ah, thou vagabond friend," he cried, "thou run-
away bishop, whom I had almost given up for lost, give
some good account of thyself, or thou shalt never again
have leave of absence, even for a day."

"I have indeed delayed my return beyond all expectation," said the bishop; "but I suppose that my
brother of Nicomedia hath imparted all needful information of thy lost shepherd up to the time at which I set
out for Alexandria."

"Yea, verily," answered Constantine. "And his narrative was most perspicuous and entertaining, and eloquent enough to draw my veteran legions from the remotest quarters of the empire; and even now they are
slowly but steadily concentrating eastwardly, and they
have a certain Oriental bearing in their movements which
would please thee mightily if only thou wert soldier
enough to perceive it."

Both of the great men indulged in a laugh at this
pleasant sally of the emperor, who continued: "Ah! my
beloved bishop, it was indeed most delicate and superb
work! Thou must henceforth insert into all the copies
of the Apocrypha 'The Prophecy of Gaius of Chalcis,'
but not during the lifetime of the Emperor Licinius,
else he would decapitate mankind to reach thy single
head!"

And again the emperor laughed like a boy, and the
bishop joined in his merriment.

"How hast thou fared in Egypt, bishop? And what good tidings hast thou brought me thence?"

"I have explored the position of the controversy between the Bishop Alexander and Arius as thoroughly as possible. I find that Alexander, who begins greatly to feel his advanced years, is no match for the learned, eloquent, and powerful presbyter, and that unless he receive active, intelligent support, the controversy in Egypt and Syria will ultimately die out for want of opposition to Arius. The aged bishop hath been raised too much under the influence of the mighty causes which molded the character of Arius himself, to be a fit antagonist for him; and younger blood, warm with the new age of Constantine rather than with that of primitive Christianity, is imperatively required. Thine agents at Alexandria have been zealous and faithful, but a remarkable man is needed at that place; less than genius will accomplish nothing."

"Such men are rare enough," responded the emperor; "but surely thou must have discovered at least one."

"I was much troubled to find a fit agent for such a work, and finally would not decide to fix upon the man of mine own choice without first having given thee an opportunity to see and determine for thyself; and, therefore, I brought him hither with me."

"Who is the man?"

"He is a youth, but little more than twenty years of age, but, like many of the nameless orphans whom the Church hath raised, he is very thoroughly educated, especially in the Scriptures. He hath natural genius for the ministry and for politics. When he was a child, the Bishop Alexander saw him one day baptizing other children in the bay in sport; but the old bishop was so charmed with the solemn grace and dignity with which the child performed the sacred rite, that he declared the ceremony valid and took the children into his own church, and hath raised and educated this boy with loving care and patience. He is now an archdeacon of the bishop's congregation. Thou must not despise his youth, for in Alexandria, which is perhaps the most intellectual city of the world, it is commonly believed that this youth is the most eloquent, the most intelligent, and the most beautiful of the sons of men. But I would have thee judge for thyself. If he please thee, I advise that thou keep with thee the most wise and learned Hosius, and through him instruct the young archdeacon thoroughly. I decline to meddle any further in the business, for I am both the friend of Arius and a stout believer in his doctrine, and when the time comes will be upon his side."

"What is the name of this youthful paragon," said Constantine, "who hath so mightily bewitched thee?"

"At Alexandria they commonly call him the Christian Apollo; but his name is Athanasius."

"Wilt thou bring him unto me?"

The bishop quietly withdrew, and soon returned and introduced to the emperor a youth as perfect as an artist's dream of beauty. He was one of the most perfect specimens of Egyptian manhood. Small of stature, seeming to one of the emperor's magnificent proportions to be almost a dwarf, the expression of his face was of angelic beauty. There was a hardly perceptible stoop in his figure which gave him an appearance of native humility; a hooked nose, clearly chiseled; a small, rosy mouth; a short, silky beard spreading away into luxuriant whiskers; light, soft auburn hair; large, bright, serene eyes of womanly tenderness and purity; and limbs and features delicately but exquisitely fashioned—all combined to confer an irresistible charm upon his person and manners. Eusebius at once withdrew, leaving Constantine alone with the bright and beautiful boy. The splendid youth, with a movement free alike from shame and from audacity, but full of matchless ease and grace, darted forward, sank lightly down upon one knee, grasped one of the emperor's hands and kissed it—an act of homage never exacted, and seldom looked for, from any Christian—and lifting his soft, luminous eyes toward the emperor's face, said in tones as liquid and mellow as perfect flute-notes: "I thank thee, Augustus, that thy kindness satisfieth one great longing of my heart; for I have desired above all things to look upon thy face."

The emperor was charmed with the youth's exquisite manner and wonderful beauty, and gently raising him replied: "I give thee back thy thanks, lad, for surely thou art far better worth the seeing than am I. But why didst thou kneel to me? Most Christians make it a matter of conscience to kneel to none but God only, and I have respected their scruples."

"I crave pardon if mine obeisance hath been offensive unto thee," the mellifluous voice replied; "for I did but offer to thee the homage which my heart hath taught me to be due from raw but hopeful youth to mature and glorious manhood; from one of the very humblest of the people unto the wisest and greatest ruler of mankind; from a young but sincere and earnest Christian to the magnificent protector of the Church!"

Constantine laid his hand caressingly upon the young man's glorious head, and, laughing lightly, answered: "If thy tongue so drippeth honey, lad, the bees will settle in thy mouth and some time, may be, sting thee. Art thou so pleasant to all sorts of men?"

"Why not?" responded the melodious voice. "I could love all that are good, pity all that are evil, forgive their injuries, despise their hate, and die, I think, to do them service if that could benefit mankind."

"Boy," said Constantine, gravely but pleasantly, "thou hast uttered the profoundest secret of all true statesmanship! Who taught thee that?"

"I think my teacher hath been Jesus Christ. But I knew not that this sentiment was statesmanship, for I have learned it as religion."

"Only a few of the most gifted of mankind," replied Constantine, "have been wise enough to perceive that true religion and true statesmanship are twins that can never be torn apart without fatal injuries to both of them."

"And, therefore," said Athanasius, "it follows that the wisest emperor must also be the best; and hence the people of the Western Empire should count themselves the most fortunate of mankind."

"If thou dost so believe concerning the Empire of the West," said Constantine, "perhaps thou wouldst not decline to enter the service of its emperor in thine own country. Art thou bound by ties of love or of allegiance to the great Emperor Licinius ?"

"Nay," replied Athanasius, "I am bound by no human allegiance other than to obey all laws in force in the government under which I live that conflict not with conscience. Nor have I been taught to regard one earthly sovereign as better than another, except as the policy of the human ruler may affect the Church favorably or unfavorably. Nor could any temporal advantages induce me to abandon the ministry of the Church in which I hold the humble place of an archdeacon, for I would choose even a menial service in the temple of God rather than the most exalted position outside of it."

"Then," said Constantine, briefly, "thou dost decline to enter into my service ?"

"Nay," answered Athanasius. "Thou hast thyself declared that true religion and true statesmanship coincide throughout; and I have been taught to regard thee as both the greatest ruler of mankind and as the strong, unwavering defender of the faith ; so that in place of declining any services thou mayst require at my hands, I am ready to give my life for thee ; only I can not abandon the ministry, to which conscience, inclination, and training have consecrated me ; and verily a Christian emperor hath need of faithful ministers as much as of faithful generals."

The eyes of Constantine sparkled with pleasure as he

answered : "Thou meanest, then, that thou wouldst labor as zealously for the glory of mine empire within the pale of the Church as my civil officers do in the affairs of government, or as my generals do in the military campaigns ?"

"Yea, verily !" said Athanasius ; "and if it were not presumptuous in a boy to express an opinion in the presence of one so wise and great, I would not hesitate to declare that the victories which thou shalt gain in aiding the Church shall be less costly, less bloody, and more permanent, than any which thine invincible arms can ever gain by the sword ; for thou shalt win not only provinces, but hearts ! "

" Boy," cried Constantine, "thy cunning speech unveileth the secret dream of every ruler that nature hath fitted for dominion. For he that swayeth the scepter of empire only to acquire larger means for the gratification of his own lust for wealth, ostentation, luxury, and pride, is but a tyrant, however wise and strong he may be. The born ruler lives for his people, and, as thou hast said, can not satisfy his grand ambition unless he shall conquer hearts as well as provinces."

" Thy thought is worthy of thy greatness," replied Athanasius, "and showeth me that the welfare of the Church and of the emperor must be identical in every true and proper government, so that priest and soldier both may labor for its glory."

" Wilt thou define, as thou dost understand it, a true and proper government ? "

"A true and proper government, as I conceive it

to be, is the just and wise administration of all civil, military, and ecclesiastical authority by one supreme ruler."

The splendid face of Constantine grew bright with pleasure as he heard this concise and luminous reply; but desiring still further to draw out the young man's views, to which his use of the word "ecclesiastical" (entirely new to the emperor) gave a particular value, he answered as follows: "And which dost thou think to be of supreme authority, the civil, military, or ecclesiastical power?"

"Neither of them separately," replied Athanasius. "But only the ruler, that standeth in the place of God, should be supreme. It would be gross tyranny for the military authority to dominate the civil administration; it would be gross impertinence for the ecclesiastical authority to direct the armies of the empire; it would be confusion for either of them to interfere with the domain of another. Each should operate in its appropriate sphere, and the ruler whom God hath given should direct the movements of them all. For he standeth in the place of God."

"Yet," muttered Constantine to himself, "the heretic Arius saith that it is a blasphemy for any man to seek to stand in that high place, which belongeth unto Christ alone!" But unto Athanasius he presently made answer: "Thou hast wisdom far beyond thine age; but in regard to these things thou dost not agree well with the opinions of the most wise and learned presbyter, Arius the Libyan!"

Athanasius remained silent for some moments, looking
up into the face of the tall emperor, who was watching
his beautiful countenance with interest and curiosity, and
a strange, almost indefinable expression lighted his sparkling features. The red lips parted and very slightly curled,
but not with scorn or dislike. He had the very same
expression, perhaps, that the face of some beautiful young
girl might wear if a grandmother, whom she loved and
revered, should begin to lecture her upon the observance
of some propriety which the world had outgrown since
the ancient dame had been a maiden of her own age.
At last he said: "Nay, verily. The presbyter Arius
surpasseth all living men in personal holiness; but his
holiness is stern, ascetic, forbidding. He surpasseth all
men in learning; but his learning laboreth to blight and
destroy all the rare flowers of sentiment wherewith art,
science, and philosophy seek to adorn and beautify the
faith. He is the most earnestly Christian of all men;
but his religion is hard, exacting, exclusive, and refuseth
to blend with the performance of the duties of faith the
light and human tenderness that endeareth piety unto
the hearts of common men. He saith that the kingdom
of heaven is the only government that our Lord established upon earth; that the Christian hath need of no
other; and that to own allegiance to an earthly sovereign, or blend his laws with our religion, is to betray
the Christ. He belongeth to a past age and to a van-
ishing system, and while he is one of the ablest, purest,
most admirable Christians in the world, he is not, and
never will be, an ecclesiastic. He hath been reared up

in an age of miracles and martyrdoms, and can not comprehend the world as it is, nor the Church as it must be and is fast becoming."

Constantine regarded the gifted youth with wonder and delight, and listened with joy and amazement while the fresh and silvery tongue struck out, in forms of speech as clear and beautiful as the last coins issued from the royal mint, thoughts which he had himself long cherished and acted upon, but had never been able to conceive so perspicuously as the young archdeacon uttered them. The emperor then said, "Thou adoptest the opinions of the most learned and pious Bishop Alexander rather than those of the primitive, inflexible, and turbulent presbyter, dost thou not ?"

"Only to a limited extent," answered the musical voice of Athanasius. "For our venerable bishop himself is ancient, and agreeth in many things with the presbyter. Truly, the great advantage that Arius hath over him consisteth in the fact that they have attended the same councils and witnessed the same events together, and the presbyter doth continually affirm this thing or that, and sayeth unto the bishop : 'Thou, also, wast then present; is it true, or not, as I have stated it ?' And the bishop answereth, 'That thing I deny not, for it is true.' And then, as the report of the thunder followeth the lightning's flash, the fierce presbyter's conclusion striketh and overwhelmeth him. Thou canst scarcely understand how all this may be, unless thou hast seen men and women burned at the stake thyself, and hast heard their testimony, sifting through the flames, that they obeyed Jesus Christ, the only rightful King, whence they were called *martyrs*, that is, *witnesses;* but both Alexander and Arius have beheld such things, and the influence thereof abideth with them forever."

Then answered Constantine: "I thank God this day that I have seen no such events, and that no man under mine own government, or under that of my father, the most holy Emperor Constantius, hath ever seen them. But whence, then, hast thou learned thy views of the relation that ought to subsist between the Church and the emperor?"

"Chiefly from mine own thoughts, which many circumstances have provoked to activity, especially the efforts I have made to aid our venerable bishop. Long ago, in one of our social gatherings, when Arius did press the bishop fiercely upon the point that Christians must have naught to do with any government except the kingdom of heaven, which Jesus ordained for them, I arose and asked permission to put a question, which being granted, I said, 'If Tiberius Cæsar had been a Christian, would not our Lord have rejoiced to see him rule the world?' And for some time the fierce man was silent."

"And what answer did he ever make?" asked Constantine.

"He said at last: 'And if the little foxes that destroy the vines could have asked foolish questions in Greek, would Moses have pronounced the animals unclean?' And I said: 'But the foxes never speak in Greek; it is contrary to the law of nature.' And he said to me: 'Neither can an emperor be a Christian;

it is contrary to the law of Christ, which ordaineth
equality, liberty, and fraternity for all believers.' And
those of his party thought the answer to be sufficient.
But, notwithstanding, I did follow the leading of mine
own thoughts, and many things grew out of it."

"Let not thy thoughts change their course," replied
Constantine; "for thou art altogether right. Thou
shalt be my friend: remember that thou art young, and
that the pious Alexander groweth very old; so that, in
the course of nature, thou mayst live to see the episcopal throne at Alexandria vacant; or if they have no
throne there yet, one shall some day be established. But
thou hast charmed me into the neglect of other duties.
Go, now, and come again on to-morrow at the same
hour."

Then the beautiful boy again glided forward, lightly
kneeled and kissed the emperor's hand, and smilingly
withdrew.

And for many months afterward Constantine kept the
young man Athanasius with him, and also Hosius, the
venerable and learned Bishop of Cordova; and daily
the youth passed some hours in conversation with the
emperor or with the bishop, or with both of them together; so that when he returned to Alexandria his bright
and wonderful intelligence was enlarged and enlightened
by the foremost thoughts concerning things both royal
and ecclesiastical that any men of that age could teach
him. And the youth bore with him a most kind and
affectionate letter written to the ancient Bishop Alexander by Constantine's own hand, and also a beautiful

communion service of silver for his church. And Athanasius said unto Constantine almost at the moment of his departure, "Shall I deliver unto Arius for thee any message ?"

And Constantine laughingly answered : "If the presbyter inquire of thee, thou mayst inform him that the emperor said of him, 'There are no birds in last year's nests.'"

But Arius the presbyter never asked Athanasius anything about the emperor. Even when the stern old man was told that Athanasius had been to Milan, and had for months abode in the emperor's palace, he only said : "The stature and Roman strength which enableth Constantine to cope with German, Briton, and Gaul, is fitly joined to the subtilty, beauty, and intelligence by which Athanasius typifieth the countless centuries of Egyptian civilization ; and the two, like Herod and Caiaphas, combine against our Lord."

From the date of the return of Athanasius, men perceived that the Bishop Alexander became more open and explicit in his definitions of the Holy Trinity, more pointed in his opposition to the teachings of Arius, more eloquent in his praises of any pious emperor whom God might raise up to free the Christians of the East and identify his government with the Church. And Arius, having publicly taught that the unity of the Godhead consisted in the divine nature of Father, Spirit, and Son, and not in any blasphemous and impossible conception of the identity of them, or of their union in one person, just as the human family consisteth of father, mother, and son; and having gone so far as to write in a little metrical book of doctrine that "God was, when Christ was not"; that "God was not always Father"; and that the words "Father" and "Son," "begotten" and "conceived," necessarily implied the "priority" of him that begat, and of her that conceived —was by the Bishop Alexander ordered to suspend the exercises of his functions as presbyter of the Baucalis church. And, thereupon, the Libyan called his congregation together and said unto them: "Brethren, Alexander the bishop hath issued an order to suspend me from the performance of my duties as presbyter because I do not believe, and have refused to teach, his impossible, novel, Western, unscriptural philosophy concerning that which he calleth 'the Holy Trinity,' a phrase not found in Scripture. Ye know that the title to the Baucalis church was placed by the martyr Theckla, who caused it to be erected, in certain trustees of the common Church, not in the bishop, for in those days the bishops owned nothing. Ye know that the original members of this community (many of whom still live) called me to be the presbyter, and that I have discharged the duties of that place as faithfully as I was able to do by the space of nearly thirty years. None but the trustees have authority or right to close the church against me or my community; and I am well advised by diligent searching of the Scriptures, and by the Christian practices of three centuries, that no bishop hath any authority to suspend a presbyter, and that the order made by Brother Alexander in that behalf is puerile and void. I purpose, therefore, to continue the usual ministrations of divine service, and all my pastoral work among you, until the Church shall bid me to abstain; and ye who may desire so to do, can continue to attend."

The trustees of the Baucalis church promptly refused to close its doors upon Arius, and his entire congregation remained steadfastly devoted to him; and Bishop Alexander and those who followed him denounced the Libyan as a "heretic," and began to pray for the coming of Constantine; and wherever the influence of the Roman Empire was dominant, the "Arian heresy" was condemned; and the flame of controversy grew fiercer and fiercer, and spread throughout Christendom.

CHAPTER VI.

THE ONE GREAT BATTLE OF CHRISTENDOM!

DURING the progress of these affairs, Constantine had thoroughly satisfied himself, by the reports of his secret political agents in Nicomedia and elsewhere, that the assurances which the Eusebii had given to him that Licinius would not in any event move his fleet away from the coasts of Asia were entirely trustworthy. The overthrow of the Gothic church, which had been founded and edified by Ulfilas, had been followed by a treaty of peace with that splendid people, whereby they had bound themselves to furnish, whenever the service of the emperor required it, forty thousand young men for the imperial army; these legions had long ago been supplied, armed, and thoroughly exercised, and constituted in themselves a magnificent army. The emperor had been triumphant everywhere. "Confiding in the superiority of his genius and military power," saith the historian Gibbon, "he determined, without any previous injury, to exert them for the destruction of Licinius, whose advanced age and unpopular vices seemed to promise an easy conquest. But the old emperor, awakened by the approaching danger, deceived the expectations of his friends as well as enemies. Calling

forth that spirit and those abilities by which he had deserved the friendship of Galerius and the imperial purple,
he prepared himself for the contest, collected the forces
of the East, and soon filled the plains of Hadrianople with
his troops, and the straits of the Hellespont with his fleet.
The army consisted of one hundred and fifty thousand
foot and fifteen thousand horse. The fleet was composed
of three hundred and fifty galleys of three ranks of oars.
. . . The troops of Constantine were ordered to rendezvous
at Thessalonica. They numbered above one hundred and
twenty thousand horse and foot. Their emperor was
satisfied with their martial appearance, and his army contained more soldiers, though fewer men, than that of his
eastern competitor. The legions of Constantine were
levied in the warlike provinces of Europe; action had
confirmed their discipline; victory had elevated their
hopes, and there were among them a great number of veterans, who, after seventeen glorious campaigns under the
same leader, prepared themselves to deserve honorable dis-
missal by a last effort of their valor. But the naval preparations of Constantine were in every respect much inferior to those of Licinius. The maritine cities of Greece
sent their respective quotas of men and ships to the celebrated harbor of Piræus, and their united forces consisted
of no more than two hundred small vessels. . . . *It is
only surprising* that the Eastern emperor, *who possessed so
great a superiority* at sea, should have neglected this opportunity of carrying an offensive war into the center of
his rival's dominions. Instead of embracing such an
active resolution, *which might have changed the whole face*

of the war, the prudent Licinius expected the approach of his rival in a camp near Hadrianople, which he fortified with an anxious care that betrayed his apprehensions of the event. Constantine directed his march from Thessalonica toward that part of Thrace, till he found himself stopped by the broad and rapid stream of the Hebrus, and discovered the numerous army of Licinius, which filled the steep ascent of the hill, from the river to the city of Hadrianople. Many days were spent in doubtful skirmishes; but at length the obstacles of the passage and of the attack were removed by the intrepid conduct of Constantine. . . . The valor and danger of Constantine are attested by a slight wound which he received in the thigh; but . . . the victory was obtained no less by the conduct of the general than by the courage of the hero; for a body of five thousand archers marched round to occupy a thick wood in the rear of the enemy, whose attention was distracted by the building of the bridge; and Licinius, perplexed by so many artful evolutions, was reluctantly drawn from his advantageous post to combat on equal terms in the plain. The contest was no longer equal. His confused multitude of new levies was easily vanquished by the veterans of the West. Thirty-four thousand men are reported to have been slain. The fortified camp of Licinius was taken by assault the evening of the battle; the greater part of the fugitives, who had retired to the mountains, surrendered themselves the next day to the discretion of the conqueror; and his rival, who could no longer keep the field, confined himself within the walls of Byzantium. The siege of Byzantium, which was immediately undertaken by Constantine, was attended with great labor and uncertainty. In the late civil war, the fortifications of that place, so justly considered as the key of Europe and Asia, had been repaired and strengthened ; and *as long as Licinius remained master of the sea,* the garrison was much less exposed to the danger of famine than the army of the besiegers. The naval commanders of Constantine were summoned to his camp, and received his positive orders to force the passage of the Hellespont, *as the fleet of Licinius, instead of seeking and destroying their feeble enemy, continued inactive in those narrow straits, where its superiority of numbers was of little use or advantage.* Crispus, the emperor's eldest son, was intrusted with the execution of this daring enterprise, which he performed with so much courage and success that he deserved the esteem, and most probably excited the jealousy, of his father. The engagement lasted two days ; and in the evening of the first, the contending fleets, after considerable mutual loss, retired to their respective harbors in Europe and Asia. The second day, about noon, a strong south wind sprang up, which carried the vessels of Crispus against the enemy, and as this casual opportunity was improved by his skillful intrepidity, he soon obtained a complete victory. For the current always sets out of the Hellespont, and, when it is assisted by a north wind, no vessel can attempt the passage, but a south wind renders the force thereof almost imperceptible. One hundred and thirty vessels were destroyed, five thousand men were slain, and Amandus, the admiral of the fleet, escaped with the utmost difficulty to the shores of Chalcedon. As soon as the Hellespont was open, a plentiful convoy of provisions flowed into the camp of Constantine, who had already advanced the operations of the siege.   He constructed artificial mounds of earth of equal height with the ramparts of Byzantium. The lofty towers which were erected on that foundation galled the besieged with large stones and darts from the military engines, and the battering-rams had shaken the walls in several places.   If Licinius persisted much longer in the defense, he exposed himself to be involved in the ruin of the place.   Before he was surrounded, he prudently removed his person and his treasures to Chalcedon, in Asia. . . . Such were the resources and such the abilities of Licinius, that, after so many successive defeats, he collected in Bithynia a new army of fifty or sixty thousand men, while the activity of Constantine was employed in the siege of Byzantium.   The vigilant emperor did not, however, neglect the last struggles of his antagonist.   A considerable part of his victorious army was transported over the Bosporus in small vessels, and the decisive engagement was fought soon after their landing on the heights of Chrysopolis, now called Scutari.   The troops of Licinius, though they were lately raised, ill armed, and worse disciplined, made head against the conquerors with fruitless but desperate valor, till a total defeat, and a slaughter of five-and-twenty thousand men, irretrievably determined the fate of their leader.   He retired to Nicomedia, rather with the view of gaining some time for negotiation, than with the hope of any effectual defense. Constantia, his wife, the sister of Constantine, interceded with her brother in favor of her husband, and obtained from his policy, rather than from his compassion, a solemn promise, confirmed by an oath, that, after the resignation of the purple, Licinius should be permitted to pass the remainder of his life in peace and affluence. . . . By this victory of Constantine the Roman world was again united under one emperor, thirty-seven years after Diocletian had divided his power and provinces with his associate Maximian. . . . The foundation of Constantinople, and the *legal establishment* of the Christian religion, were the immediate and memorable consequences of this revolution."

If the victory had been otherwise, the face of history might have been entirely changed: the Christian communities might have been permitted to maintain their original communal organization, at least in the Eastern Church, and Christ might still have had a kingdom upon earth. If Licinius had employed his naval superiority in offensive war, instead of keeping it cooped up under the shores of Asia, "in those narrow straits where its superiority of numbers was of little use or advantage," the probabilities are that he might have maintained his power at least in the East; but the Eusebii had "neutralized" the mighty fleet by that which Constantine denominated "the prophecy of Gaius of Chalcis," and Christianity was subverted everywhere, and the "legal establishment" of Constantine usurped its place.

Almost immediately Constantine proceeded to mark out the boundaries of the city—Constantinople—which prescient John had seen from rocky Patmos; and he traced the boundaries thereof, going on foot with a spear in his hand, and declared that in so doing he was act-ing in obedience to the directions of God; and when those who were with him remonstrated against his tracing so vast a space for a city, the emperor replied: "I shall advance till He, the invisible guide who marches before me, thinks proper to stop." And so he laid off the boundaries of the city upon seven great hills, which included the ancient site of Byzantium, and soon began to lay the foundations, and to plan and to build the palaces, theatres, circus, amphitheatre, and churches of Constantinople.

About the same time the emperor became greatly interested in the preparation of new copies of the Scriptures, and especially of the epistles of John; and he had learned clerks and skillful writers constantly employed in making copies in the new, running Greek text, which was lately come into use, and was more easy and beautiful than the uncial letters of an earlier age; and he distributed them to the bishops throughout the Roman Empire. And next he sent letters to all of the bishops, requesting them to meet in a solemn council of the whole Christian Church, at the city of Nicea, upon a designated day, in order to discuss and settle the disputed questions by which the world was agitated. And in conformity with this royal request, or order, in the year 325 was assembled the most remarkable body of men that the exigencies of political or religious life hath ever convened together in the history of the world; for it was the first œcumenical council ever called in Christendom, those which had preceded it having been assembled by the Christian bishops, of their own accord, and not by the authority of a prince or emperor, whose power was said to rule the habitable earth (Οἰκουμένη).

The letter which Constantine addressed to the bishops was as follows : " That there is nothing more honorable in my sight than religion is, 1 believe, manifest to every man. Now, because the Synod of Bishops at Ancyra, of Galatia, consented formerly that it should be so, it hath now seemed unto us, on many accounts, that it would be well for it to be assembled at Nice, a city of Bithynia; because the bishops of Italy, and of the rest of the countries of Europe, are coming, and because of the excellent temperature of the air, and because I shall be at hand as a spectator and participator of what is done. Wherefore I signify to you, my beloved brethren, that ye, all of you, promptly assemble at the city I spoke of, that is Nice. Let every one of you, therefore, diligently inquire into that which is profitable, in order that, as I before said, without any delay, we may speedily come to be a present spectator of those things which are done by the same. God keep you, my beloved brethren ! "

The reasons assigned by the emperor for calling the Council of Nicea were first and chiefly that " the Synod of Ancyra " (which had been called by the bishops without the interference of any secular authority) " had formerly consented " to meet in a general council at Nice, and that " the bishops of Italy and of Europe would be there," and that " the air of the place was of an excellent temperature," and that their coming into Bithynia would afford the emperor an opportunity to be "a spectator of their proceedings." There was no intimation given that the emperor desired to preside over their council, or to control its action, or to force its deliberations to assume any political significance whatever, or to compel it to take such action as must inevitably result in the subversion of the Christian polity and the establishment of an entirely different church system. The letter was based first upon the consent given by the Council of Ancyra and then upon matters of expediency, and in no respect did it question the absolute right of the bishops to meet where they might please, and to deliberate without the intermeddling of secular authority. So, at least, it seemed to all the bishops of the Eastern Church, except a small number who had been, to a greater or less degree, leavened by the leaven of ecclesiasticism. On the face of it the letter was as full a recognition of the freedom of the bishops, and as full a recognition of the Christian polity which had for three centuries held all property in common, as was the celebrated Edict of Milan, in which Constantine and Licinius had united in commanding the officers of the Roman world to restore the property of Christians as *communal* property, the language of that edict being as follows: "All of which will be necessary to be delivered up *to the body of the Christians* without delay. And since the Christians themselves are known to have had not only those places where they were accustomed to meet, but other places also, *belonging not to individuals among them*, but to the *right of the whole body* of Christians, you will also command all these, by virtue of the law before mentioned, without any hesitation, to be restored to the same Christians, *that is to their body, and to each conventicle separately.*"

But already the bishops of the Western Empire, with Hosius and Eusebius at their head, had come to understand that while Constantine cared little about any matter of faith, he had determined to utterly destroy the Christian polity, especially in regard to communism and the refusal of Christians to bear arms. The regulations by which their journeys were governed prescribed that they should come at the emperor's expense, and that "each bishop should be accompanied by a retinue of two presbyters and three slaves."

At and near the appointed time there were bishops and presbyters assembled from the four quarters of the world—from Persia and from Gaul, from Scythia and from Africa. There were many who were the victims of pagan persecutions, and still bore in their own persons the marks of the tortures to which they had been subjected. This one had lost an eye, gouged out by the torturer's sword or pincers; that one had the sinews of his leg seared with hot iron to keep him from escaping from the mines, to which he had been condemned for the crime of being a Christian; and the other had had the flesh scraped off his ribs by the instruments of torture. Of the whole number present, it was believed that only the eleven who came from the remotest East had escaped mutilation in some ghastly form.

Arius, although not a bishop, was there by the express order of Constantine, who could always sleep upon his vengeance, but never could forget nor forego it. The place of the assembly's sessions was a great hall in the imperial palace of Nicea. The bishops and presbyters, assembled upon the emperor's order, traveling at his expense, to the immediate vicinity of Nicomedia, then the imperial residence, into a royal palace, and fed by his bounty, were from the very first the creatures of Constantine, so far as complete control of the political significancy of religion could make them so.

The emperor had only two great purposes to accomplish in patronizing the Church and engineering the council : one of which was to make the Eastern Church as willingly and thoroughly dependent upon the imperial authority as he had already practically made that of the West, and to render it as much a bulwark of his government ; the other was to render this condition of things, in appearance at least, the spontaneous and inspired action of a free conclave of bishops.

As for the theological verity of their doctrines or practice, the royal atheist cared not a denarius. His object was to make the Church as much a part of the imperial power as a legion might be, its bishops as much his agents and servants as the military officers ; and to uproot and cast out the only essential features of Christianity which tended to segregate the Christians into a separate and distinct body in the empire, by subverting "the kingdom of heaven" with its communistic organization, that excluded war, slavery, and mammon-worship from the communities of the faithful, so that no man should feel that because he was a Christian he was therefore more free, or less a subject of the empire ! This he proposed to do by inducing the council to define the faith and prescribe temporal penalties for heresy, which were to be enforced by the emperor's authority, just as were the judgments of the magistrates against violators of the criminal laws : the action of the council was to make an offense against the Church a crime against the imperial law. Subject to the accomplishment of these purposes, he really desired that they might reach conclusions as nearly unanimous as possible ; for he was as anxious to avoid the creating of parties and classes in the Church as he was to avoid sowing discord among his other subjects.

Upon the assembling of the council, Eusebius of Cæsarea, "in metrical prose, if not in actual verses, recited an address to the emperor, and then a hymn of thanksgiving to the Almighty for the victory over Licinius." Thereupon Constantine addressed the council in the Latin language, which his dragoman immediately interpreted into Greek, as follows : " It has, my friends, been the object of my highest wishes to enjoy your sacred company, and, having obtained this, I confess my thankfulness to the King of all that, in addition to all my other blessings, he has granted to me this greatest of all—I mean, to receive you all assembled together, and to see one, common, harmonious opinion of all. Let, then, no envious enemy injure our happiness, and, after the destruction of the impious power of the tyrants by the might of God our Saviour, let not the spirit of evil overwhelm the divine law with blasphemies : for to me far worse than any war or battle is the civil war of the Church of God—yea, far more fearful than the wars which have waged without. As, then, by the assent and co-operation of a higher power, I have gained my victories over my enemies, I thought that nothing remained but to give God thanks, and to rejoice with those who have been delivered by me. But since I learned of your divisions, contrary to all expectation, I gave the report my first consideration ; and, praying that this also might be healed through my assistance, I called you all together without delay. I rejoice at the mere sight of your assembly : but the moment that I shall consider the chief fulfillment of my prayers will be when I see you all joined together in heart and soul, and determining on one peaceful harmony for all, which it should well become you, who are consecrated to God, to preach to others. Do not, then, delay, my friends ; do not delay, ministers of God, and good servants of our common Lord and Saviour, to remove all grounds of difference, and to wind up, by laws of peace, every link of controversy. Thus will you have done what is most pleasing to the God who is over all, and you will render the greatest boon to me your fellow-servant."

" The council was now formally opened, and the emperor gave permission to the presidents of the assembly to commence their proceedings " ; and the Bishops of Alexandria, Cordova, Antioch, and Cæsarea, were chosen to preside over their deliberations : of whom Hosius, Alexander, and Eusebius, were politicians thoroughly imbued with the ecclesiastical spirit and purposes of the emperor, although the last-named bishop was the warm personal friend of

Arius, and a follower of his theological tenets. Constantine himself assumed the functions of a bishop, and participated in all their debates, "directing all his energies to that one point which he himself described as his aim—a unanimity of decision" as to all merely theological disputes. For, even before the council had met, innumerable complaints of one bishop against another had been placed in his hands; so that he was satisfied that one great design he had in view was already accomplished: for this fact showed that already they regarded him as the ultimate judge—the real source of all authority in the Church (instead of Christ), as truly as he was in the state. All of these complaints, therefore, he publicly burned in their presence, with a solemn oath that he had not read any of them, and he said, "It is the command of Christ that he who desires to be himself forgiven, must first forgive his brother."

But the very strongest proof that the emperor was lying, was the fact that he made oath to his statement; and perhaps there was not a thing named in any of the complaints, that could give him a hold upon any bishop, that was not carefully preserved.

The first matter which came before this august assembly was the question whether the Christian passover ("Easter") should be celebrated on the same day with the Jewish (the fourteenth day of the month Nisan), or on the following Sunday. And the bitter feeling of many of the Christians that "the celebration of it on the same day that was kept by the wicked race that put the Saviour to death was an impious absurdity," on one side, and the

reverence on the other side for a custom which had come
down from the apostles, gave rise to a long controversy on the subject; but it was finally "determined
by common consent" that the ancient custom should
be set aside, and the more recent Christian practice established.

During these proceedings, Arius the Libyan took no
part whatever in the discussions or business of the council, but sat as a quiet and attentive spectator of their deliberations. Many of them, knowing his great erudition
and holy character, consulted him privately, and he fully
gave them the benefit of his learning and opinions. Arius
was now sixty years of age, and was greatly changed from
the bright and happy youth whom we knew at Baucalis;
greatly changed even from the broken-hearted but ever-
diligent, earnest, and eloquent presbyter of the earlier
years of his ministry at Alexandria. "He is tall and
thin, apparently unable to support his stature; he has an
odd way of contorting and twisting himself, which his
enemies compare to the wrigglings of a snake. He would
be handsome, but for the emaciation and deadly pallor of
his face, and a downcast look imparted by a weakness of
eye-sight. At times his veins throb and swell, and his
limbs tremble, as if suffering from some violent internal
complaint, the same, perhaps, that will terminate one day
in his sudden and frightful death. There is a wild look
about him, that is at first sight startling. His dress and
demeanor are those of a rigid ascetic. He wears a long
coat with short sleeves, such as the monks wore to indicate
that their hands were not made for injury, and a scarf

of only half size, such as was the mark of an austere life ; and his hair hangs in tangled masses about his head. He is usually silent, but at times breaks out into fierce excitement, such as will give the impression of madness. Yet with all this there is a sweetness in his voice, and a winning, earnest manner, which fascinate those who come across him. Among the religious ladies of Alexandria he is said to have had from the first a following of not less than seven hundred. This strange, captivating, moon-struck giant is the heretic Arius, or, as his adversaries call him, the madman of Ares, or Mars " : and the description given here of him is not that of a partisan of his own, but of a Trinitarian ecclesiastic.

Many sittings of the council passed, day after day, in which the paschal controversy, the Melitian schism, and other matters of a theological character, were discussed and determined, but the heretic remained utterly silent. He was ever ready to give aid, advice, counsel, and furnish references to authorities, to those who applied to him, but not once did he open his lips to speak to the assembly. But the purpose of Constantine to crush him wavered not, and the emperor had one rare quality—he knew how to wait.

One evening, after the close of the council's daily session, the ancient Bishop Alexander, accompanied by his young Archdeacon Athanasius, was proceeding toward his lodgings, when Marcellus, the Bishop of Ancyra, accosted him : " Hail, bishop ! From what thou didst tell me of his fierce, aggressive nature, I am astonished to find that the Libyan madman continueth so quiet. How is it that

21

thou hast called him vehement, fierce, eloquent, and con-
troversial ? "

"He hath some secret end in view," replied the
bishop, "and I can not fathom his purposes. But on to-
morrow, Athanasius, who speaketh for me in the council,
shall provoke him to some reply, and thou mayst then
judge of his quiet disposition for thyself."

"Good enough," said Marcellus. "No man can pick
a quarrel with an oyster that keepeth its shell closed."

CHAPTER VII.

THE SUBVERSION OF THE PRIMITIVE CHURCH.

On the next meeting of the council, Hosius, Bishop of Cordova, offered a resolution that the Church should make a decree requiring all the married clergy to separate from their wives and lead lives of celibacy. Some objected to this, on the ground that the practice of the Church had never prohibited the marriage of clergymen of any rank ; others insisted on adopting the rule, because clerical marriages, besides other inconveniences, would tend to make the office of bishop an hereditary one, and so elevate improper persons to that sacred place. But the chief opposition "came from a most unexpected quarter. From among the Egyptian bishops stepped out into the midst, looking out of his one remaining eye, and halting on his paralyzed leg, the old hermit-confessor, Paphnutius. With a roar of indignation rather than a speech, he broke into the debate : ' Lay not this heavy yoke on the clergy. Marriage is honorable in all, and the bed undefiled. By exaggerated strictness you will do the Church more harm than good. All can not bear such an ascetic rule. The wives themselves will suffer from it. Marriage itself is continence. It is enough for a man to keep from marriage after he has been ordained, according to the ancient custom, but do not separate him from the wife whom once for all he married when he was a layman!'

"His speech produced a profound impression. His own austere life and unblemished celibacy gave force to every word he uttered."

The resolution, or proposition, was voted down, but the discussion of it gave Athanasius the opportunity he wanted. Having arisen with that almost irresistible grace and suavity which distinguished him, the beautiful young man, in a light, musical, mocking tone, that must have been terribly irritating to a grave and reverend presbyter like Arius, spoke as follows : "I greatly marvel, brethren, that we have not enjoyed the benefit of that princely readiness and strength in debate for which the very learned presbyter Arius hath so great reputation, upon this important question. Surely a minister who is reputed to have at his beck and call, day or night, rain or shine, more than seven hundred virgins and widows in our good city of Alexandria, ought to be able, from his own experience, to give us wise counsel concerning the celibacy of the clergy. I hope that he will do so."

The brilliant, smiling youth resumed his seat, and every eye was turned upon the Libyan, but he neither rose nor answered. The grand, shaggy head bent slightly forward, and a momentary gleam shone in the somber eyes ; while a peculiar shiver passed over his whole frame, the python's idiopathic legacy, and a weary sigh exhaled through the ashy lips ; but he took not. even the slightest notice of Athanasius, nor of his flippant speech. It was manifest that all of them expected him to say something, knowing the readiness and splendor of his oratory, but he was utterly silent; and this silence, following the young archdeacon's sally against him, seemed to indicate an unpleasant state of feeling—or what did it indicate?

"He could browbeat his bishop in Alexandria," whispered a bishop to Eusebius of Nicomedia, "but he quaileth in the presence of the emperor."

But Eusebius answered: "He quaileth not for any man; but he answereth not, because to do so might be to recognize this assembly *as a council of the Church*, and that he hath not yet done by speech or act."

Then the headstrong and violent Marcellus, Bishop of Ancyra, cried out in fierce, defiant tones: "Hearest thou not the friendly utterances of Athanasius, who speaketh for Alexander, thy bishop? or dost thou carry thyself so high as to treat with contempt thy learned and venerable bishop, thou iron-hearted heretic, that thou answerest nothing?"

The Libyan turned his head slightly, and, fixing his sad eyes upon Marcellus, gazed upon him steadily, quietly, compassionately, but did not utter a word; and immediately there was a clamor throughout the assembly, some condemning the intemperate words and manner of the Bishop of Ancyra, and some the seeming insolence of Arius. Then the Emperor Constantine arose, and forthwith the clamor subsided, and the emperor said: "I have often and earnestly desired that peace and Christian charity might characterize our deliberations. The remarks and the manner of the Bishop of Ancyra are hasty and uncalled for; but the obstinate silence of the presbyter indicateth a proud and scornful mind—for it is known to all that the young archdeacon speaketh for the holy Bishop Alexander because of his age and feebleness; and if thou dost decline to notice the brilliant Athanasius because of his youth, thou must not despise thy venerable superior who speaketh through him. I command thee, therefore, to answer as if Alexander himself had addressed thee."

The emperor sat down, and a murmur of admiration and applause ran through the entire assembly. Then the mighty heretic arose, and in his sweet, incisive, penetrating voice, answered: "By command of Augustus, the emperor, whose legal subject I have become by the defeat and death of the late Emperor Licinius, I arise to declare that if any one supposeth I did fail to notice the remarks of the young, learned, and eloquent archdeacon, because of any feeling of scorn for his youth, or for his office, or because of any uncharity toward him, or any one else in this assembly, he doeth me much injustice. This, it seemeth to me, is well proved by the fact, which ye all do know, that during the weeks that ye have been assembled, I have taken no part in any discussion, ecclesiastical or political, in which ye have engaged. Because I am not an officer of the Roman government, civil, military, or judicial, and have not thought it to be consistent with the position and duties of a presbyter of the Church of Jesus Christ to assume the right to take part in the business of a royal council, seeing that my life hath been devoted to religious affairs which belong to our Lord, and not to civil, military, or judicial functions which pertain unto the emperor, I supposed that it would be as indecent and presumptuous for me to meddle with the business of the empire, by virtue of my office, as it would be for a Roman judge, or centurion, to intrude into my church and preach the gospel by virtue of his judicial or military rank. If it had been otherwise, I might have had something to say when I perceived that the royal authority offered a gross insult to Christ and to his Church by making *Elia Capitolina*, the ancient Jerusalem, the oldest and most honored see in Christendom, secondary to new Nicomedia, in order to accommodate ecclesiastical departments to the other political divisions of the empire ; nor would I speak at all except at the command of the emperor."

Having thus spoken, Arius took his seat. The words opened up plainly and unmistakably the vast difference that separated the Christianity of the first three centuries from the imperial Church of Constantine : the allegiance that belonged to Jesus alone was in process of being transferred to the emperor. It was to extirpate this very freedom of conscience, this very liberty of the gospel that acknowledged no master but Christ, that Constantine had convened the council ; and although he had known that the question must come up, and must be met, and although he had been for years, and especially since the summoning of the bishops, using every artifice, argument, and influence, and urging his ablest agents, to be prepared for it when it might come, he and his partisans had determined that it should be raised out of proceedings to be instituted against Arius upon charges of heresy ; but the

ARIUS THE LIBYAN.

wonderful adroitness with which the great presbyter had changed the face of the whole matter, and had actually put both the emperor and his council on the defensive, took Constantine utterly by surprise, and for a moment he lost even his marvelous self-control, and cried out in a voice of thunder, "Then why art thou here?"

And Arius, with scintillant eyes, but in placid, melodious tones, responded: "I came hither upon the written order of the emperor, as I supposed it to be the duty of a law-abiding subject to do; but certainly not as an officer of the Roman government, entitled to participate in royal businesses."

This calm and dignified reply still more clearly revealed to all the assembly the fact that their enthusiastic love for Constantine had too much blinded their eyes to the undeniable truth that the council was œcumenical, not apostolical—the affair of the emperor, not of the Christ. This reply was not ostensibly connected with any heretical teachings of Arius, or of any one else, and raised no question of orthodoxy at all; it struck at the very tap-roots of the whole movement. "Whose council is this?" was the question that each involuntarily asked himself, and it was manifest that the simple, unobjectionable words of the Libyan produced a profound impression upon many hearts that began to consider whether the fact that the council was royal did not imply in itself the fact that it was not Christian, but was really treasonable toward Christ; and in the midst of the solemn silence caused by such anxious meditation, the virulent and incautious Bishop of Ancyra cried out: "Who art thou that censurest the victorious and holy emperor, and condemnest the œcumenical council of the Church with thy sly, serpentine wriggle and speech ? Art thou not Arius the heretic ? Arius the defamer of the Son of God ? thou bold scorner of the Holy Trinity ! thou cunning madman ! "

But Arius only looked upon the furious bishop with a sad and pitying smile.

Then Constantine cried out: "Answer thou the bishop !"

Then, still quietly and pleasantly, with a peculiar, mesmeric light in his somber eyes, and strange, thrilling sibilation in his penetrating voice, Arius arose and said : "By the command of Augustus I answer that I have not censured the emperor, nor condemned the council. As to my being a heretic, I only reply that, if this thing be true, it is no concern of the emperor's, who hath never been ordained to be the keeper of my conscience. It is an affair entirely between the Master— Christ—and his servant Arius. For ye all do know that there is no Roman law prescribing what we must believe or disbelieve, since the persecutors lost power to enforce obedience to their laws prescribing faith in false gods, by the infliction of tortures and death, against those who for conscience' sake refused to obey. But ye know that neither Jesus nor his apostles ever denounced, nor authorized any human being to denounce, a temporal penalty for heresy ; for the Church only prescribes that ye should refuse to fellowship the obdurate heretic, or disobedient person ; and I trust you far enough to believe that if any pagan emperor, or any human au-

thority, should enact laws requiring you to believe, or to
do, anything contrary to good conscience, ye would be
faithful Christians enough to refuse obedience to such
laws, as our fathers from the beginning have gloriously
done. For this is a matter between each man and his God
only; not between him and the government which exercises dominion over him. This the Church hath held from
the beginning; and when the heathen laws did prescribe
that ye who are here assembled should do and believe
things contrary to Christ and to conscience, ye did refuse,
so that every bishop here, except those eleven who come
from the remotest East, hath endured tortures rather than
obey the human laws. If, therefore, I be a heretic, as
brother Marcellus of Ancyra ignorantly supposeth, what
have the empire or its laws to do with that? Why speak
ye of orthodoxy, or of heterodoxy, in a great royal, political assembly like this; unless, perhaps, some of ye are
willing to believe that the great and powerful emperor is
also a god, having charge of your faith and conscience,
as well as of your political condition; so that what the
law of Constantine shall prescribe as right to be believed
and done shall be your rule of faith and practice, and
not what our Lord Christ hath prescribed? For me, a
poor presbyter of the Christian Church, to assume the
right to deliberate upon and prescribe laws for the empire would be gross impudence and arrogance; for any
human authority to usurp the right to make laws controlling the faith of Christ's Church, would be as gross
a sacrilege. Was Constantine crucified for you? Or
were ye baptized into his name? And do ye hope for

salvation by faith in and obedience to him? I was not. I have come, therefore, hither in obedience to the imperial mandate, and have spoken by the emperor's command. As to the empire, I have no authority and no desire to make laws for it; as to my Christian faith, no man nor angel hath right or power to meddle therewith, or to prescribe laws for it. It is a thing between my soul and its Saviour, whom I have served all my life long in spite of imperial laws, and whom I will continue to serve, no matter what laws may be enacted. Brethren, will ye do likewise? or will ye now deny the Christ?"

For an instant the old man raised his tall form upright, the shaggy head sprang forward upon the long, peculiar neck, and the somber, sad eyes rested upon almost every face. Then quietly he resumed his seat.

Athanasius, Hosius, Constantine, and others, saw at the same instant that against the impregnable position taken by Arius no assault could prosper. They knew that constant and almost imperceptible steps had been necessary for years to seduce any large section of the Western Church from that very position, and that the church which Ulfilas had planted among the Goths had only been driven therefrom by the merciless use of fire and sword. They knew well that the line of demarkation between all earthly kingdoms and the kingdom of Christ in the world was clearly and unmistakably drawn, consisting not alone in faith and sentiment, but in a social and political policy which had been for three centuries the glory of Christianity, and had been so fearfully illustrated by recent persecutions under Licinius in the East, that the council could not be deluded in reference thereto ; and they were seeking with anxious solicitude to find some way to avoid further discussion upon the matter, which might arouse an interest in it that would dissolve the council upon the point which the Libyan urged, that the Church could not meet in œcumenical council at the order of an emperor, and make decrees to be forced by imperial law, without forsaking Christ. Long before the bold presbyter had ceased to speak, the emperor had determined in his own mind that it was necessary to gain time for consultation and for concerted action, and especially necessary to stop the discussion of this dangerous question as to the right of a *royal* council to legislate for the Church of Christ— the tendency of which was obviously to separate the Church from imperialism altogether, rather than to accomplish his determined purpose of blending the Church with imperial law and make himself head of both. As soon, therefore, as the heretic sat down, at a sign from the emperor, Alexander and Hosius adjourned the council until the following day.

CHAPTER VIII.

THE ABDICATION OF CONSTANTINE.

THERE is little doubt but upon that night so many of the council favored the views of the Libyan, that if a vote had been taken upon the point urged by him, the council would have resolved that its own organization was contrary to Christ; was an effort thoughtlessly made to put Constantine in place of Jesus at the head of the Church, and would have dissolved itself, until summoned to convene by the agreement of the bishops only. Almost the whole night was spent in anxious consultation between those bishops who were ready to maintain the freedom of the Church at any hazard, and the great heresiarch, whom they instinctively recognized as leader of the struggle in favor of religious liberty, as to the most available path of escape from the dangerous and unchristian position into which they had been led by their zeal and love for the emperor who protected the Church from persecution. Arius told them plainly that if the Church of Christ was to be governed by an œcumenical or royal council, its independence was gone; and in place of being the "kingdom of heaven" upon earth, which our Lord had organized, the Church must become a human institution—part of the empire of Constantine, or of any other prince or power to whom its members might be subject; its faith and policy dictated by Roman law, not by the word of God; its doctrines dependent upon the mutations of government, not upon the teachings of Jesus: a thing by which the cause of Christ is verily betrayed. There were none in the council who did not perceive this truth, although there were some who were for Constantine, even against Jesus himself.

During nearly the whole night, also, Hosius, Athanasius, Eustatius, Marcellus, Constantine, and others, were engaged in eager consultation, but seemed unable to find any solution of the difficulty. And the next morning Athanasius reported to the emperor that the more they had considered the matter, the more difficult and dangerous it had appeared; and that the only way to avoid serious risk of dissolving the council was to avoid all discussion upon its right to sit for the Church, and to let Arius alone as long as he might appear disposed to remain quiet. Many hearts were burdened with anxiety, and Eusebius of Cæsarea was especially oppressed with deep concern.

"And if the council when assembled shall sustain the views of Arius," he had once asked Constantine, "what then?" and the emperor had answered, "A religious war, perhaps, or a return to paganism!"

But to Athanasius and others who urged the necessity of temporizing with Arius, and avoiding all discussion of the vital points which the heretic lost no opportunity of forcing upon them, Constantine finally said: "I will make no compromise with the Libyan; it is necessary to crush that serpent's head, and I will do it ! He hath certainly evinced marvelous skill, intelligence, and daring, in forcing an issue upon us which we do not desire to determine ; he would have made a magnificent general ; but I will ruin him to-day. Rest ye all in peace."

And when the council assembled, all of them filled with anxiety as to what might occur, and many of them determined, even at the risk of martyrdom, not to take any further part in the deliberations of an imperial conclave such as they clearly perceived that one to be, the emperor arose first of all, and, with wonderful grace and ease, addressed them as follows : " Ye know my love for all of you, my friends, and my zeal for the cause of Christ. But some among you have taken offense, and have even doubted the propriety or binding force of your own decrees upon the conscience of Christians, because it hath appeared to you that the emperor hath assumed authority over you in regard to matters of faith. This is surely a grave mistake. To correct this false and injurious impression, I here commit to your presiding bishops my ring, my sword, and my scepter ; and unto you I give power this day over mine empire, to do in it whatever you think fit for the promotion of religion and for the advantage of the faithful. Ye are the law-makers of the Church of Christ, and not him whom God hath made Emperor of Rome. Proceed with your sacred business in your own time and way. If ye shall deem it to be necessary to remove even the most intangible objection of the cavilers to do so, ye can dissolve the council, return to your homes, and let the bishops reassemble when and where ye will. But if, being already assembled at some expense of time and trouble, ye deem it more expedient now to constitute yourselves into a church council, do so in your own time and manner. Farewell!"

And, having so spoken, the emperor bowed gracefully to the admiring assembly and withdrew. But almost immediately Hosius, Bishop of Cordova, proposed, and without a dissenting voice the council voted, that a deputation of bishops be appointed to inform the emperor that the Church had met in council, and to request him to return and bestow upon them the benefit of his great wisdom and Christian zeal, in aid of their deliberations; and smilingly the emperor returned.

The action of the emperor was just that of the preeminently greatest politician; and Arius, then first fully realizing the vast intellectual resources of the most consummate statesman whom the world has seen, murmured unto himself, "Again is Christ betrayed into the hands of wicked men!" And thenceforward calmly, almost indifferently, he looked forward to what he supposed to be his own impending doom; for he well knew that Constantine spared no human life that, even by chance, might seem to stand in the way of his self-aggrandizement: and if his marvelous sagacity could conceive and execute such an act as he had just accomplished, what was there of which he could be incapable?

Then the bishop Hosius of Cordova said: "Brethren, it is manifest that the technical objections which found place in the consciences of some among us, based upon the seeming authority of our most glorious and Christian emperor over us, have been thoroughly eradicated by his own most wise, pious, and unsolicited condescension, and that we sit now as an absolutely independent body for the consideration of the business and doctrines of the Church of Christ, as much as if we had come of our own motion originally from the ends of the earth, without the generous and Christian liberality of our royal friend and protector. Let us, therefore, proceed with our deliberations to secure the prosperity of the Church of our blessed Lord!"

In this sentiment all concurred; and even the dullest among them immediately perceived that the crafty act of Constantine had cut out from under the great heretic the only sure foundation upon which he might have builded, and had left him at the mercy of the emperor.

For many days the great council proceeded with its business, and sometimes their differences gave rise to excited and earnest debate, in which the easy, marvelous, persuasive eloquence and irresistible manners of Athanasius raised the brilliant youth to the highest place in the opinions of all; in which the magnificent Spaniard Hosius fully maintained the almost apostolic reverence that had long been given to his great age, vast erudition, and grand character; and in which both the Eusebii added to their former wide-spread reputation for learning, piety, and influence. Many other names, before that time almost unknown beyond the local limits of their own churches and bishoprics, became celebrated throughout Christendom for various excellences or for striking characteristics. Only the sad-eyed and seemingly broken-hearted presbyter Arius appeared to be indifferent to the course of business, and silent during the discussion of questions upon which all knew he might have brought to bear an unequaled mass of erudition, illumined by the strong light of genius, if he had cared to do so.

Gradually, little by little, no one knew how, the conviction spread throughout the great assembly that the man Arius was doomed, and that there was no possibility of escape for him; and day by day they were awaiting the institution of proceedings against him which would be the beginning of the end anticipated. None knew whence this weird impression arose, and few ever spoke of it: for no man that ever ruled on earth knew better how to create or how to guide for his own purposes that intangible, remorseless, and murderous influence to which in later times we have applied the expression "public opinion" than did the wonderful Emperor Constantine, ages before other statesmen recognized even the existence of such a force. And through the more gifted agents, lay and clerical, who were devoted to him heart and soul, the impression that the Libyan must be condemned grew imperceptibly but unceasingly stronger. Without knowing why, the enemies of the great presbyter became daily more self-confident and aggressive; without knowing why, the lukewarm and undecided souls that form a considerable segment of every large assembly, insensibly withdrew themselves from his support, and drifted more and more into the sentiment of his foes; and, without knowing why, the few, strong, brave, earnest men, who decidedly clung to his opinions and unswervingly loved the man, began to concentrate their forces and husband their resources for some desperate and decisive struggle which they instinctively felt to be approaching.

The Libyan himself had long regarded his fate as decisively settled. He had interpreted the Apocalypse as referring to Constantine, and did not doubt either the temporary overthrow of Christianity by the emperor, or the fact that he would be involved in its ruin. He looked without fear, perhaps more with a feeling of curiosity than anything else, for signs which might enable him to form a conjecture as to how long the kingdom of heaven might be banished out of the world : its ultimate restoration and final triumph over human governments he never doubted ; but he would hardly have turned his hand, or raised his head, to avoid the death which he supposed Constantine had determined to bring upon him. " If," he said unto his intimate friends, " the emperor's council carry out his wishes, I desire ye all to remember, in the future, that no Christian council hath, or hath ever attempted, to exercise authority to put any man to death for heresy. The only punishments the Church hath ever imposed stop with the refusal to fellowship an unbeliever or a wrong-doer. If Constantine condemn me, remember that he is not a bishop, hath never even been baptized, and hath no authority to decide upon what is or what is not heretical ; and the Roman law hath never, so far at least, attempted to define what a Christian may lawfully believe. Ye see, therefore, that the fact of my destruction illustrateth well the character of the council, and showeth that even the magnificent spectacle of his resignation which he so well enacted can not convert Constantine's meeting into a council of the Christian Church. And I suppose that this will more plainly appear as the matter proceedeth further."

Then answered the Bishop of Nicomedia, saying: "Brother, if thou must perish for the cause of Christ, I perish also with thee. I am an Arian, and shall claim the right to die with thee if any murder shall be done."

"And I also!" said Eusebius of Cæsarea. "And I also!" said Maris of Chalcedon; and Theognis of Nicea; and Menophantes of Ephesus; and a score of other bishops, each in his turn pressing the old presbyter's hand. Then said the presbyter: "If your resolution hold, either the policy and craft of Constantine will deny us a death so glorious, or our martyrdom will of itself reinstate the kingdom of heaven in spite of the emperor. Let us rejoice, then, in hope of the triumph of the truth!"

And having thus quietly but unflinchingly made a covenant that, if the matter should be prosecuted to extremities against Arius, they would share his fate, and thereby furnish to the whole body of Christians throughout the world a most terrible and unanswerable protest against the council and the emperor, these devoted men calmly awaited the beginning of the struggle which they knew to be steadily approaching, although they were unable to determine from what quarter it would come.

CHAPTER IX.

"I HAVE NO SUPERIOR BUT CHRIST."

WHEN the council met one morning, Athanasius produced and laughingly read a song, or hymn, which had been written and set to music by the Libyan, for the use of uneducated Christians at Alexandria, in order to enable them to memorize and keep in mind the doctrines of Christianity as he had understood them. This song was part of a little book entitled "Thalia," or "Songs of Joy," which the presbyter had written for sailors and others who had no certain means of attending regular religious services, and in it occurred the following expressions: "God was not always Father; once he was not Father; afterward he became Father; and his only-begotten is Jesus Christ our Lord."

And thereupon Marcellus, Bishop of Ancyra, moved the council to declare that this sentiment was heretical; and that the man who wrote it should be expelled from the Church of Christ; and Arius and his friends perceived that the struggle for the destruction of the presbyter had begun. For a while the council-hall was filled with clamorous and bitter denunciations of Arius: "The heretic!" "The atheist!" "The defamer of Christ!" "The

polytheist!" "The pagan!" "The Libyan serpent!"
"The ram of Baucalis!" and almost every other term of
reproach which the vocabulary of ecclesiasticism could
furnish, were shouted throughout the hall by the partisans
of Constantine. Finally, the clamor seemed to wear itself
out, and, order having been partially restored, Potammon
of Hierapolis, a confessor whom the pagans had left blind
and lame, straightened up himself and with great awk-
wardness and earnestness cried out: "Brethren, I was
reared up in Central Africa, and know nothing of philosophy, but do try to serve the Lord, and to avoid all heresy and false doctrine. I have often sung this song, not
knowing it was heresy, with my people! What is there
wrong about the song, then? Do any of you deny that
Jesus Christ is the only-begotten Son of God? or that he
is our Lord and Saviour? or will some of you now pre-
tend to believe that the Son is older than the Father?
What is wrong about the song?"

To the same effect spoke many of the friends of Arius;
and Maris of Chalcedon said: "The Gospels uniformly
call Jesus Christ the only-begotten Son of the Father, and
I have never believed it necessary or proper to go any
further than the simple, direct scriptural statement."

Finally, Eusebius of Nicomedia obtained a hearing, and,
speaking calmly and soothingly, he said: "Brethren, the
song which ye have heard read seems to be merely a metrical composition formed to aid the memory of those who
were unable to read and write, and those who had no copy
of the Scriptures, in keeping in mind certain scriptural
phrases and doctrines; and I could not be led to suspect

a great and pious presbyter of heresy upon such a cause as that. Let us proceed, then, decently and in order; and if ye would know truly what Arius hath taught as religion, call upon him to declare what he hath so taught. This seemeth to me to be the only fair and honorable course, worthy of a Christian assembly, if any one think there is cause to suppose that he hath taught anything contrary to Scripture."

This reasonable counsel at once prevailed with the greater number, and by a large vote they requested Arius to declare his teachings. Thereupon the old heretic arose, and in his strange, peculiar, fascinating tone and manner, spoke as follows: "Brethren, I have never taught anything concerning our Lord as religion, except that which is expressly laid down in the Scriptures; to wit, that Jesus is the only-begotten Son of God, the Saviour of the world. I do not know anything, and have never taught as articles of faith necessary to be believed, anything except what is thus expressly and definitively stated in the Gospels. Of course, like every man who thinks at all, I have meditated often and earnestly about the philosophy of the facts stated, and have formed in my own mind certain speculations in relation thereto which are satisfactory to mine own understanding, and I have not hesitated to declare these opinions in all proper times and places; but I have never said, at any time or place, that these merely philosophical speculations upon the nature of Deity were binding upon any man's conscience, or that they should be taught and believed as the rule of any man's faith and practice; because they have not been revealed or declared as such by the word of God. If any man allege that I have done otherwise, let him make the charge in writing and produce the proof, as was the custom at every Christian council in such cases that hath ever been held upon the motion of the bishops authorized to call a council, as at Jerusalem, Antioch, Rome, in Pontus, Gaul, Mesopotamia, and Ephesus."

The presbyter said no more, but quietly resumed his seat, and the calm, grave, and reasonable manner in which he had met and disposed of the vociferations which had assailed him, in the opinion of nearly all, left no course to be pursued with decency except to present written charges against him, and offer proofs thereof. But such a course did not by any means suit the purposes of those who were resolved upon his ruin ; and Athanasius, who at all times was able to command a respectful hearing at the hands of the assembly, without seeming to notice the challenge thrown down by the Libyan, said in his own winning and seemingly respectful way : "Hast thou not publicly and customarily, in thy Baucalis church, in Alexandria, preached things that were contrary to the views of the Bishop Alexander—contrary to his interpretation of the Scriptures, for which he did order that thou be suspended from thy ministry ; and didst not thou pertinaciously refuse to obey his episcopal order, and obstinately persevere in proclaiming thine abominable heresies ? Wilt thou now deny this ? "

Then with an effort to preserve his self-control that sent a strange shiver creeping over his gaunt and mighty frame, the presbyter made answer : "It appeareth, brethren, that this gifted youth hath been taught to believe that it is heresy to differ in opinion with the learned and pious brother, Alexander! It is very true that I and my brother Alexander have somewhat differed in opinion, but I am not advised that he hath any more authority to dictate my opinions than have I to dictate his; and I am very certain that, wherein the bishop hath differed with me, he is in error."

But Constantine cried out, "Answer thou whether thou hast preached in spite of the order of suspension made against thee by thy superior!"

And the old heretic arose again, and answered: "I had supposed that the answer already made would be sufficient for any bishop, but being commanded by an unbaptized emperor to answer yet further, I have to say that I have no 'superior' but Christ; as for the order of brother Alexander 'suspending' me from the exercise of the functions of a presbyter, all the clergy here assembled well know that it is void. The day hath not yet come when any one brother in the Church can 'suspend' another. I suppose that, under the legal religion which is to replace the gospel of Christ, a bishop will have some such authority over a presbyter as a legionary hath over a centurion, or a centurion over a soldier; but we have not quite reached that condition! As to the differences of opinion between myself and the brother Alexander and others, I will simply state that our good city of Alexandria hath a population marvelously intellectual, and greatly addicted to the study of philosophy. Hence it hath happened that many of the brethren, and some even of the bishops and presbyters, have added, unconsciously perhaps, to their faith in the facts set forth in the Gospels certain philosophical notions intended for the explanation of these facts, which notions they have derived from many teachers —chiefly from the great heathen Plato, and from his followers, the neo-Platonists, and from the school of Philo the Egyptian. The learned and pious Bishop Alexander derived from some such source (I know not what) certain philosophical views which seemed to deny utterly the separate existence of the Son of God; and which savored strongly of the heresy of Sabellius that had been condemned by more than one Christian council, and which did tend directly to the subversion of the primitive Christian communities, and to the overthrow of 'the kingdom of heaven' which Jesus did ordain, and to the substitution therefor of some such ecclesiastical system as I am told the emperor hath established in the Western Empire, in which the emperor, not Christ, is head of the Church, and in which the law prescribes what a man may believe or not believe (just as the pagan laws have always done), instead of the Scriptures. So long as brother Alexander held these erroneous opinions privately, I meddled not with them; but when he afterward saw proper to come and preach these heresies to mine own congregation, I guarded my community against this pernicious philosophy; for the Gospels and the Acts furnish the only authority concerning Christ and faith in him; and not the opinions of Sabellius, Alexander, Hosius, or Constantine. As for mine own philosophical opinions concerning Deity, I never learned them of Plato, nor of Philo, nor of Sa-

bellius, but of the most wise and pious Am-nem-hat, who
was for many years high-priest of the pagan temple at
Ombos, holding there the same position which the Emperor Constantine as Pontifex Maximus hath so long
held at Rome ; but Am-nem-hat was afterward a glorious Christian, and a holy martyr, at our city of Alexandria, as many of you know. But no man hath ever heard
me claim that these philosophical opinions constituted
any rule of faith or practice, or were binding upon any
man's conscience ; although I doubt not that the theological opinions of a most ancient and learned Egyptian
high-priest are entitled to as much respect as those of
the flamen of Jupiter, at Rome, who is now the Emperor
Constantine."

And again the old heretic resumed his seat, having
created a strong impression in his favor in the minds of all
who were not committed to the task of destroying him,
although many of them trembled for his safety on hearing
his bold and ingenious assault upon the emperor. But
Marcellus, Bishop of Ancyra, sprang to his feet, and in
loud and threatening tones cried out : " O thou most insolent and abusive heretic, darest thou to call the most
Christian emperor a pagan ? "

But Maris, Bishop of Chalcedon, stretched forth his
hand and answered : " The presbyter Arius hath said that
the great emperor is yet unbaptized, and that he is, by the
law of the Roman Empire, Pontifex Maximus, and flamen
of Jupiter ! I understand that all this is true ; and, if it be
not true, no man will more rejoice than I would to hear
the emperor now declare that he hath been baptized into

the faith of Christ, and that he is no longer high-priest of pagan Rome."

The bishop sat down, and every eye was at once turned upon Constantine. But the emperor neither spake nor moved; and almost immediately his partisans began to cry out that Arius should declare to the council what were those philosophical opinions to which he referred, which thing they did to cover up the failure of the emperor to respond to Maris the bishop; and the friends of the Libyan joined in the same cry, because they did believe that the philosophy of Arius would be found to be correct, and not heretical. And thereupon, being pressed upon all sides at once, the presbyter again arose and spoke in the following manner: "I suppose, brethren, that there hath never been any difficulty in the mind of any Christian as to the simple declarations of the gospel concerning our Lord; and that the faith of all Christians in the divinity of our common Saviour is founded upon the gospel narrative. The difficulties arise only when the mind passes on beyond the plain teachings of the gospel, and attempts to comprehend how these things may be, and to formulate for itself some creed upon the nature of the Deity. In this regard there have been maintained three great philosophical opinions, as ye do know, which may be very briefly stated as follows:

"1. That the Son of God must be a dependent and spontaneous being, created from nothing by the will of the Father, by whom also all things were made.

"2. That the Son possessed all of the inherent, incommunicable perfections which religion and philosophy appropriate to the supreme God. So that there are in the Godhead three distinct and infinite minds or substances, three co-equal and co-eternal beings, composing the divine essence, three independent Deities as to whom an effort is made to preserve the unity of the first cause by assuming the perpetual concord of their administration, the essential agreement of their will; and this I understand to be the philosophy of Hosius, Alexander, the emperor, and others for whom Athanasius is spokesman.

"3. Three beings who, by the self-derived necessity of their existence, possess divine attributes in perfect degree, who are eternal in duration, infinite in space, intimately present to each other and to the universe; and are yet one and the same being, manifesting himself in different forms, and considered in different aspects: so that the Trinity becomes a trinity of names and abstract manifestations existing only in the mind; they are not persons at all, but only attributes.

"This is the heresy of Sabellius, which Christian councils have condemned. It differeth from Athanasius in degree, but not, I think, in kind.

"Not one of these three opinions satisfieth my mind and heart. The martyr Am-nem-hat taught me when I was a boy that the original faith, which long ages ago preceded the polytheism of Egypt, Assyria, India, China, Greece, Rome, and all other heathen nations, uniformly represented the one God to be a dual, spiritual Being, and that the Divine nature must be a Triad, or Trinity, completed by the birth of a son of this double-natured spiritual God. In the gospels I read that Christ is 'the only-begotten

Son of God': a Father begets. He was 'conceived' of the
Holy Ghost: a Mother conceives. He was 'born' of a
virgin, and for our salvation did live among men. The
same holy martyr called my attention to the fact, which I
have since carefully verified, that while the Scriptures in
no place apply the word 'mother' to the Holy Ghost, the
words 'Holy Ghost' are used in them two hundred and
twelve times, and were uniformly in the Greek neuter
gender, which affirmeth nothing as to sex. He also showed
me that Moses called the one God by a name which is the
plural number of a Hebrew noun. It hath, therefore,
appeared to me to be true that, as far as anything concerning Deity can be expressed in human language, the
sacred use of the words 'Father,' 'Son,' 'Holy Ghost,'
'begotten,' 'conceived,' were intended to convey to our
minds the idea that in some spiritual sense of sexhood the
nature of Deity is that in the likeness and image whereof
man was created; and signify a divine family, so far as
earthly things can typify spiritual truth. Hence, as I did
set forth in my letter to Eusebius of Nicomedia, and to
Alexander of Alexandria, as the Church knoweth, I have
always taught that the Son is not unoriginate, nor part of
the unoriginate, nor made of things previously existing;
but that by the will and purpose of God he was in being
before time, perfectly divine, the only-begotten; that
before his generation he was not; that we believe in
one God alone without birth, alone everlasting, alone unoriginate. We believe that God gave birth to the only-
begotten Son, before eternal periods, making the divine
family a Triad, through whom he made these periods and

all else that was made; that he gave birth to the Son, not in semblance, not in idea, but in truth giving unto him a real existence; and we have refused to profess faith in the teachings of Bishop Alexander, that 'as God is eternal, so is his Son'; 'where the Father, there the Son'; 'the Son is present in God without birth'; 'ever-begotten'; 'an Eternal God, an Eternal Son'; 'the Son is your God himself.'

"But I have never taught this philosophy as an article of faith, binding upon the conscience of believers; and have required of them to profess faith in nothing except what the gospels declare."

The philosophy of Arius struck many as a novel thing. To some of them it seemed to be a rational and beautiful solution of problems which they had pondered long and regarded as insoluble, and had abandoned in despair. To none of them did it seem to be at all tainted with heresy.

But Athanasius had a definite end in view, which closed his ears to any statement the presbyter might make, although he waited courteously until Arius had concluded his remarks, and then exclaimed, "Hast thou not taught that the Son of God was created out of things not existing?"

"Never," said Arius. "Thou knowest I have taught that he was not 'created' at all, but 'begotten'; 'conceived,' not made."

"Hast thou not taught that there was a time when the Son was not?"

"Nay, verily! The word 'time' is thine own, not

mine. But I have said 'God was, when he was not.' I have said that 'before he was begotten he was not.' Else how could God beget him? But this was in the beginning, before 'time' was."

"Hast thou not taught that the Father was superior to the Son, and the Son inferior to the Father?"

"Nay, verily! I can not conceive of the words 'superior' and 'inferior' as applicable to the divine nature, or family, any more than I can conceive of thy word 'time' as applied to the divine existence. If thou canst do so, O Athanasius, thou or thy friends, and furnish a definition of the Trinity that does not deny the separate existence of the Son; nor imply identity of person in Father, Son, and Holy Ghost; or which does not set up three distinct, co-equal Gods, or which does not degrade the Son to the condition of a created Being, made, not begotten, except the definition which I quoted from the philosophy of Am-nem-hat the martyr, and have adopted as mine own, announce thou now, or when thou wilt, such a definition of the Trinity, and, if I can at all comprehend it, I will follow thee to death, if need be, in defense thereof: for lo! these many years have I sought for such a definition and found it not, except in Am-nem-hat's profound aphorism that the true and only idea of Trinity subsisteth in family—Father, Mother, Son: the Father-Ghost, and Christ!"

Then answered Athanasius: "Verily I would not dare to utter a formula of faith upon so high a theme in any hasty or inconsiderate manner. So for the present let that question rest, and I doubt not that the learned bishops who defend the deity of Christ will soon frame out of the Scriptures a definition of the Catholic faith which shall both satisfy all orthodox souls and bring thine own God-dishonoring heresies to light."

"If it come out of the Scriptures, friend Athanasius, they must omit therefrom thy newly-coined word 'Catholic,' for that word is not scriptural, nor is the idea which thou signifiest by it therein. The Scriptures speak not of the 'Catholic' Church at all, but of 'the common church,' 'the common faith,' 'the common salvation,' 'the common hope,' 'the common Saviour'; and thou well knowest that 'common' pertaineth only to the common or communal organization of Christ's kingdom. Yet, perhaps, it is natural that one so young, so beautiful, so gifted as thou art, should prefer the imperial and aristocratic designation which hath been recently adopted in the Western Empire, and despise the plebeian, scriptural name 'common' or 'communal.' For two Christians might both belong to thy 'Catholic' Church, while one of them might be a prince and the other a pauper; but the two Christians who belong to the primitive 'common' church must be brethren, equal, free, fraternal; and the difference, friend Athanasius, between 'common' (κοίνος) and 'catholic' (κατα ὅλος) is just the difference between the Christian Church and that of Constantine. I know not what the martyrs would have said of it, nor what the steadfast confessors here present may think of it; but I prefer the ancient, scriptural term 'common,' 'communal,' 'communistic' church of which Jesus Christ only is King, and in which all men are brethren, to the

23

new 'Catholic' establishment which has come in with our unbaptized emperor."

There was not a confessor present but what would have applauded these bold and truthful sentiments, the force of which we can at this day with difficulty realize; but Constantine bit his lip to restrain a terrible oath, and his face darkened ominously as he glared upon the audacious presbyter. Hosius, Marcellus, Alexander, and others of the same party, seemed to have been stricken dumb by the clear, incisive, fearless, and uncompromising declarations of Arius. Only Athanasius seemed to preserve his marvelous self-possession, and laughed musically, while, in order to distract attention from the dangerous question which the old heretic seemed determined to bring up at every possible turn of the discussion, he cried aloud: "But hast thou not commonly taught that the Father, Son, and Holy Ghost are three, and not one God, and thereby made thy heresy assume the complexion of polytheism? Hast thou not done that?"

"I have taught," answered Arius, "and I think that the Scriptures teach, that the three are not one person, but three persons; and that the Trinity is one family, in likeness whereof man was created. Eve, the first mother, was not created out of things not existing, but she proceeded out of the first man's side; not above him, not below him—equal with him, bone of his bone, flesh of his flesh; and the first human son was born of them. This to my mind in some way typifies the divine family, except that the idea of creation applies not to it. This I have stated as mine own conception of the matter, not as an article of faith. If thou knowest any better idea, state it plainly, I pray thee : I am not yet too old to learn."

Then said Athanasius, triumphantly, "I supposed, indeed, that God would presently lay bare thy heresy ; for thou dost deny the express words of Scripture that these three are one ; and thus thou art convicted !"

Once more the dangerous light gleamed in the old man's somber eyes, and that nervous twitching, which his enemies likened to the wriggling of a serpent, passed over him ; but he controlled himself wonderfully, and calmly enough inquired : "What scripture, then ? Wilt thou read it ; or tell us in what place it may be found ?"

Then said Athanasius : "I read from the first letter of John as follows : '*For there are three that bear record in heaven, the Father, the Word, and the Holy Ghost : and these three are one. And there are three that bear witness in earth, the spirit, and the water, and the blood : and these three agree in one.*' How, then, sayest thou that the Father, the Word, and the Holy Ghost are not one, in the very teeth of the Scriptures, O thou subtle heretic ?"

The reading of this scripture produced a profound sensation in the council. Many turned to their copy of John's letter to read the words for themselves, the greater number using the new and beautiful manuscripts which the munificent liberality of the emperor had caused to be transcribed and distributed among the bishops some time before ; but many also had ancient copies written in the uncial text. But Arius said unto Athanasius, "Wilt thou give to me thy book ?"

And Athanasius sent it to him by one of the pages in

attendance. The grim old presbyter received the parchment, and looked at it, and handled it, and turned it over and over in his hands with a strange, sarcastic smile, and then said in that peculiar, sibilant tone which cut and tingled like a serpent's hiss : "I perceive, brethren, that this beautiful manuscript is one of those copies which hath been supplied to many bishops and presbyters by the zeal and benevolence of our most Christian, but unbaptized, emperor ; and the book is beautifully written in the new, running Greek text which hath lately come into use. I have but one objection to it, brethren ; and the objection is, that the words '*in heaven, the Father, the Word, and the Holy Ghost: and these three are one. And there are three that bear witness in earth*'—these words were never written by John, but by some one else ; they have been added to the text within the last ten years !" And then the tall form reared itself to the full height of its gigantic stature ; the long, thin right hand swayed to and fro with a strange rhythmic motion, the huge, rough, noble head seemed to start forward upon the long, bony neck, as a cobra thrusts it forward ; the strange, mesmeric light burned in the somber eyes, and, fastening his gaze full upon the emperor, he cried out in tones that rang through every corner and crevice of the vast hall, shrill, incisive, penetrating : "These words are forgeries—every one of them ! What John wrote was this: '*For there are three that bear record, the spirit, the water, and the blood: and these three agree in one.*'"

The effect was electrical. Many trembled for the bold and eloquent man whose words and manner seemed to charge upon the emperor himself the guilt of sacrilege in forging the sacred writings; although, perhaps, none doubted that the words were forged. But Athanasius gazed upon him haughtily, and demanded: "Who art thou, madman, that dost so boldly assail the genuineness of a scripture that suiteth not with thy notorious heresy? How knowest thou that the words were never written by John?"

The presbyter's fierce excitement had almost immediately faded away, and he quietly answered: "Brethren, I know that the words are forgeries, because the rank Sabellianism which they teach is contrary to John's spirit, and would better suit the views of certain persons who desire to confound the Son with the Father in order to abolish the sovereignty of Christ over his earthly kingdom by placing some one else in his rightful place. Secondly, because ye can not find the words in any copy written in the uncial text, before the recent, running Greek text came into common use. Ye have many uncial copies here: see whether any of them contain the words. Thirdly, because, more than thirty years ago, the learned martyr Am-nem-hat, in our city of Alexandria, had in his possession the original letter of John"; and, with tremulous and mournful cadence that brought tears into the eyes of all who knew his history, he continued: "Am-nem-hat abode in the house of his great-grand-niece, the holy, the beautiful, the martyred Theckla. This blessed virgin did carefully copy the letter upon vellum, and sent it to Antioch as a gift even unto me, by the hands of Bishop Peter." Taking the book from a cedar box on the seat beside him, he continued : " Here is the copy of John's letter, written by the hand of one martyr, under the supervision of another, and delivered by a third martyr unto me, that am ready to follow them upon the glorious way whenever God so will ! Search and see whether ye can find these forged words in this thrice-sacred book ! "

A moment of profound silence followed. Constantine, Athanasius, Hosius, and all of their faction, perceived that this assault also had not only failed, but had left the powerful heretic in full possession of the field of battle ; and, at a sign from the emperor, the bishops immediately adjourned the council until the following day.

CHAPTER X.

THE COMMUNION OF THE SAINTS.

As soon as the great council assembled on the following day, Eusebius of Cæsarea addressed them, saying: "Brethren, the controversy concerning the nature of Deity provoketh much uncharity, and leadeth to no result. I have, therefore, drawn up, and now offer for your consideration, a Confession of Faith, which is no new form of doctrine, but is the same which I learned in my childhood, and during the time I was a catechumen, and at the time I was baptized, from my predecessors in the bishopric of Nicomedia; and the same which I have taught for many years while I was presbyter and bishop, before this great dispute had arisen. This confession hath been read and approved by the emperor, the beloved of Heaven, and it seemeth to me to be the truth as nearly as divine things can be expressed in human language. I have a hope, therefore, that it may be accepted by all as a sufficient declaration of our Christian faith.

"It is as follows: 'I believe in one God, the Father Almighty, Maker of all things both visible and invisible, and in one Lord Jesus Christ, the Word of God, God

of God, Light of Light, Life of Life, the only-begotten
Son, the first-born of every creature; begotten of the
Father before all worlds, by whom, also, all things were
made; who for our salvation was made flesh and lived
among men, and suffered, and rose again on the third
day, and ascended to the Father, and shall come in
glory to judge the quick and the dead. And we believe in one Holy Ghost. As also our Lord, sending
forth his own disciples to preach, said: ' Go and teach
all nations, baptizing them into the name of the Father,
and of the Son, and of the Holy Ghost.' Concerning
which things we affirm that this is so, and that we think
so, and that it hath long been so held; and that we
remain steadfast to death for this faith, anathematizing
every godless heresy; that we have taught these things
from our heart and soul, from the time that we have
known ourselves; and that we now think and say them
in truth, we testify in the name of Almighty God, and
of our Lord Jesus Christ, being able to prove even by
demonstration, and to persuade you that in past times
also this we believed and preached.'"

This creed seemed to be acceptable to nearly all the
members of the council, and Hosius said unto Arius,
"Wilt thou subscribe this creed?"

And the heretic answered: "Certainly. I can cheerfully subscribe to all that is contained in this confession
of faith; for Eusebius hath only made a formal statement of what I have taught and believed, and what the
ancient Church hath held from the beginning. Yet I
like not the creed. For the bishops all know that while

never before did a council draw up any written confession of faith, yet at every council the bishops did repeat and affirm the creed received from the apostles; and the most important item therein, next to the profession of faith in Christ, was this : 'I believe in the communion of saints'; by which the Church constantly affirmed its faith in the divine wisdom of the communal organization of 'the kingdom of heaven.' Ye have mutilated the confession by omitting this vital article in order to accommodate the faith to the imperial laws regarding war, slavery, and mammon-worship. Let the great article be restored to its proper place, and I will subscribe the creed."

Then there was a terrible clamor, greater than all that had preceded it—the partisans of Constantine boldly declaring that "the day had gone by forever for maintaining the communal organization of the Church"; that this "primitive community of rights and property was only a temporary arrangement, not designed to be permanent, and had faded away"; and, finally, that "the emperor would not permit the creed to contain an article which cut off not only the emperor and all his officers, but also every 'rich man,' from admission to the Church." But those who were determined to maintain the apostolic organization which Jesus himself had ordained were equally clamorous in shouting that to omit the article of "communion of the saints" was to adopt the Roman law, and betray the Church into the hands of the enemies of Jesus. Then Constantine ordered in the imperial guards and commanded them to clear the hall, and the bishops adjourned the council in the midst of an uproar in which the struggle was not always confined to words, but some severe blows were given and received upon both sides. The voice of the bishops adjourning the council had failed to designate any day or hour at which it should reassemble, and for some days no session at all was held; and during these days all the weight of the imperial authority was brought to bear upon the unhappy bishops to force them to adopt a creed omitting the article concerning "the communion of saints" which from the very days of Jesus had been the sacred symbol of the social and political organization of the Christian Church. Constantine declared that bishops who made it a matter of conscience to do so might continue to teach and to preach it, but that the article must be omitted from the creed; and gradually all of them were brought over to the making of this kind of a compromise with their consciences. When this result had been attained, the bishops gave out that the council would be reassembled upon the following day.

On that evening, Constantine called unto him Hosius, Alexander, Athanasius, and others of his adherents, and said unto them : " It is not expedient for me that Arius, or any other man, should be condemned for refusing to subscribe a confession of faith that omits the article concerning community of the saints. I wish that thing to be forgotten as soon as possible, and that the condemnation of this man should be founded upon some other accusation. I desire ye, therefore, to seek for some scriptural word or other which may not be repugnant to the

majority of the council, but which Arius can not subscribe. He is a man that would manifestly die and count
it great gain rather than make even the slightest con-
cession in any matter of conscience. Ye must, therefore, insert in the creed some word or phrase that he
will not subscribe, but to which the majority shall not
make any strenuous objection. It must not appear to
the Church that 'the communion of saints' hath caused
trouble."

"There is no such word or expression in any gospel,"
answered Hosius, sententiously.

"Then ye must seek for it elsewhere," said Constantine. "The creed must contain some word which he will
refuse to subscribe, and it must appear that the controversy with him is concerning that word, and not concerning the abandonment of the primitive Church polity."

"There is a word that hath lately come into use at
Alexandria," said Athanasius, "which I feel certain would
prevent the presbyter from signing any creed that con-
tains it, but I do not think that either the Latin language or the Latin brain is delicate enough to grasp
that peculiar signification of the Greek expression which
would make it repugnant to Arius, so that the Western
churchmen would not object to the use of it, but it is
not exactly a scriptural phrase."

"What is the word?" asked the emperor.

"It is the new compound, 'consubstantial' ($\delta\mu oo\upsilon\sigma\iota o\varsigma$),
which admitteth of an interpretation that would shock the
fine Egyptian thought of the presbyter, but many might
not be subtile enough to perceive it. It suiteth well the

majority of the bishops in the sense in which they understand it."

"I do well remember the word," said Constantine. "For, when I was upon the study of this controversy, I first heard it; and it occurreth either in some memoranda which I made of a conversation with Eusebius, or in a letter written unto him by his brother of Nicomedia. Let me get those papers."

So saying, the emperor opened a drawer in his bureau and took therefrom a bundle of manuscript, and after a short examination he said : "Here is the letter. Eusebius of Nicomedia saith here that 'to assert the Son of God to be of one substance with the Father is a proposition evidently absurd.' "

The beautiful eyes of Athanasius sparkled with delight, and he cried out : "That is the very word and letter that we want ! It cometh, like all good things, from the emperor, and is like an inspiration to our cause !"

"Yea," said Hosius. "The majority will receive the word well—holding that it does not necessarily imply the identity of persons ; but will Arius certainly reject it ?"

"Yea," replied Athanasius ; "I have heard his comments on the word, and I am certain that his stubborn, inflexible spirit will not bend enough to make him subscribe a creed containing it."

"Press thou not the matter too vehemently, archdeacon," said Constantine, "lest thou drive many to support him. Be mild and persuasive, for there is time enough."

So, when the council had assembled on the following

day, Athanasius said : "The learned and venerable Bishops Alexander and Hosius, and many others with them, have carefully examined the form of the Confession of Faith offered by the learned Bishop Eusebius, and they make no objection thereto : but fear that it may leave open some advantages for entrance of heresy, as is shown by this letter of Eusebius of Nicomedia, wherein he declareth that to say that the Son is consubstantial (ὁμοούσιος) with the Father is absurd. They therefore desire, in order to cut off all heretical interpretation of the creed, and vindicate the divinity of our Lord, to offer a creed containing the declaration that Son and Father are of one substance."

Immediately there was a clamor of the Arians against the use of the word ; but they, and many who were undecided, looked to Arius for advice and direction, and Athanasius said, "The bishops desire to know whether the learned presbyter Arius will subscribe the creed containing this word, the bulwark against all heresy ?"

And Arius arose, and, looking upon Athanasius with a gentle smile, said unto him : "I perceive that thy master Constantine hath at last reached the fulfillment of his desires against the Church and kingdom of my master Christ. Brethren, I have already declared to you that I would subscribe no confession of faith which omitted to set forth the article of the communion of saints ; and I perceive well that the insertion of this new ecclesiastical term is resorted to only in order to avoid making notorious the fact that the emperor hath commanded that the primitive organization of the Church shall be abandoned. As to this word 'consubstantial,' I have no objection to it in the only sense in which I can conscientiously use it, as implying that the Father and Son (like every other father and son) are beings of the same nature; yet I would not subscribe a creed containing this word, because it is unscriptural. In the sense in which it will come to be used hereafter (if not, indeed, already), it denies the separate existence of the Son; it will imply an almost physical adhesion of the persons of the Divine Family, and the actual identity of Father and Son. It hath before this time been used by incautious or heretical persons, and hath already been condemned as heretical by councils which no prince or emperor controlled, and whose voice was the free utterance of the unsecularized but persecuted Church. I will never subscribe a creed containing such a word; and have never found it necessary to go outside of the Scriptures to find words wherewith to define the Christian faith."

And Athanasius answered: "What if the word, in the exact form of it, is not in the Scriptures? Surely its derivatives and compounds are found therein; nor is it any more unscriptural than the songs of Arius written in his book 'Thalia.' What if it hath been used by heretics and condemned as heretical? That was only because it hath been used in some heretical sense, and not as we use it now. What if the use of the word might be tortured into the support of Sabellianism by some who wrest even the Scriptures to their own destruction? The rejection of it argues far more strongly in favor of polytheism—the ancient paganism from which the Church hath so long suffered ; and the word must be used, because it is the only safeguard against the very heresy of which Arius hath been suspected or accused."

And the question was long debated by others, and the council adjourned ; but there were not many that stood out firmly against the use of this celebrated word.

At the next meeting of the council, Hosius of Cordova announced that, following the sentiments of the great majority, they had prepared another declaration of the faith, upon which he hoped all might agree ; and thereupon the same was read : " We believe in one God, the Father Almighty, Maker of all things, both visible and invisible. And in one Lord Jesus Christ, the Son of God, begotten of the Father, only begotten, that is to say, of the substance of the Father, God of God, Light of Light, very God of very God, begotten, not made, being of one substance with the Father, by whom all things were made, both things in heaven and things in earth ; who for us men and for our salvation came down and was made man, suffered, and rose again on the third day ; went up into the heavens, and is to come again to judge the quick and the dead. And in the Holy Ghost.

"*But those who say, ' There was when he was not,' and ' Before he was begotten he was not,' and that ' He came into existence from what was not,' or who profess that the Son of God is a different ' person' or ' substance,' or that he is created, or changeable, or variable, are anathematized by the Catholic Church.*"

A great many members refused to sign the creed, and especially the anathema with which it concluded ; because they thought that the presbyter Arius, at whom it was aimed, neither taught nor held the views thereby imputed to him. Eusebius of Cæsarea asked for time to consider the matter, and "to consult with the emperor who had imposed it upon them"—a course which others also followed.

Constantine professed to believe that this last creed was delivered by an inspiration of the bishops directly given from heaven; and he at once issued a decree of banishment against all who might refuse to subscribe to it. "He denounced Arius and his disciples as impious, and ordered that he and his books should follow the fate of the pagan Porphyry; and that he and his school should be called Porphyrians, and his books burned under penalty of death to any one who perused them." But he gave them time to reflect upon the matter; and on the next day many stood resolved not to sign, notwithstanding the terrible threats of the emperor. In this state of fear and perplexity, when no man knew to what extremities his brutal threats to extort their compliance might be carried, and when a moody silence, born of their terror and distress, had settled upon the council, to the surprise of all, Arius the Libyan arose and addressed them as follows: "Brethren, I am well persuaded that no other opportunity will ever be given unto me to address any assembly of Christians; being persuaded that the condemnation denounced against me ariseth not from any mistaken zeal on the part of the unbaptized emperor concerning religion, but only from a political necessity that springeth from his godless and insatiable thirst for universal and unhindered power; for verily I think he knoweth little, and careth less, for any confession of faith, except as it affecteth his imperial ambition. As a man, therefore, already doomed, and soon, perhaps, to die, I desire to stir up your pure minds by way of remembrance concerning the primitive Church, which now fadeth out of the world, as it hath already faded out of the Western Empire. Brethren, centuries ago, the great Greek philosopher, Plato, in his 'Republic,' did declare that 'any ordinary city is in fact two cities, one the city of the rich, the other that of the poor, at war with one another'; and this statement is verily true everywhere on earth. For the religion of mankind hath been, in some shape, the worship of mammon, and the warfare, of which Plato speaketh, a warfare for property—for property in offices, prerogatives, lands, houses, wealth, slaves, and every shape that property can take. Ye know that the law was a schoolmaster to lead us to Christ; and that, to prevent the universal and hopeless oppression of the poor, God by Moses did ordain the statute of the year of jubilee, and the statute of the seventh year; and ye know that the prophet Isaiah did make these statutes, which secured a certain blessing for the poor every 'seventh year' and every 'fiftieth year,' typical of the continuous state of believers, in the kingdom of heaven, declaring it to be the gospel preached to the poor; and ye know that our Lord did solemnly declare that this prophecy was fulfilled in him, wherefore the wealthy and aristocratic Scribes and Pharisees, who were 'covetous,' persecuted him even unto death; even as the ruling classes at Rome, and through-

24

out the world, have done until the triumph of Constantine over Maxentius at the Milvian Bridge. Ye know
that our Lord set up a kingdom that was good news, a
gospel, to the poor of the earth, because its purpose and
effect were to abolish war, slavery, polygamy, and all unjust distinctions between men and classes of men, based
upon the idolatry of mammon. Ye know that all of
these parables were spoken with reference to this kingdom in which communion of saints, partnership of all
believers, should secure liberty, equality, fraternity, for
all Christians. Ye know that, while the apostles remained on earth, the believers had all things common,
except wives and children, disowned all government
except that of Jesus, obeyed all laws for the sake of
peace except such as conflicted with conscience, and so
builded up the Christian communes that governed themselves by the laws of Christ alone, inflicting no temporal
punishment except that they refused to fellowship the ob-
durately wicked. Ye know that they commonly wrought
miracles to prove the divinity of Jesus and the right of
the Church to preach and to teach in his name. We
learn from Philo the Egyptian, and from many others,
that 'those who entered upon the Christian life divested
themselves of their property, and gave it to those legally
entitled thereto or to the common Church,' and that
'the disciples of that time, animated by more ardent love
of the divine word, first fulfilled the Saviour's precept by
distributing their substance to the needy ; and that the
Holy Spirit wrought many wonders through them, so
that, as soon as the gospel was heard, men voluntarily

and in crowds eagerly embraced the true faith.' Ye
know that three bishops were ordained by the apostles,
even Lucius, Evodius, and Polycarp, all of whom consecrated their property to the common Church, as did
the apostolical fathers Clemens, Ignatius, Barnabas, Hermas, as also did Paulinas, Cyprian, Hilary, and countless
other well-known and notable Christians; and ye know
that such were the law and the practice of the Church until
very recent times! Ye know that thaumaturgy remained
with the Church until this divine ordinance was neglected. Ye know, brethren, that there were no slaves, no
war, no rich, no poor, no kings, no rulers, in the kingdom of our Lord, but liberty, fraternity, equality for all;
and that war, slavery, mammon-worship, which had ever
been the curse of human life, were abolished by the gospel of Christ. Brethren, already in the Western Empire
(and from this day in the East) all this is changed.
'The kingdom of heaven' is utterly subverted. Even
the bishops came hither with slaves; many of you are
'rich men,' that could not enter into the kingdom of
heaven. The Church conformeth in all things to the
imperial laws: for that man Constantine hath such
unbounded ambition and unbelief that he suffereth not
the Church of Christ to exist in the world, and hath
so founded the Church of Constantine, subverting all of
Christianity except its spiritual truth. But ye can plainly see what things shall come to pass. That man whom
ye love because it hath suited the purposes of his atheistic ambition to protect the Church against other tyrants,
hath established an imperial legal religion for the world,

and declares that he will persecute all who conform not thereto. So did the Scribes and Pharisees; so did Tiberius Cæsar, Nero, Diocletian, and the rest of his predecessors; but so Jesus and his apostles never did. I know not whether that man who doeth these things, and hath begun to found his capital, called by his own name of blasphemy, upon seven hills above the sea, be he of whom John in the Apocalypse did speak, but he suiteth well in many respects with what John did prophesy.

"Hear me yet a little further. Ye will all, or nearly all, subscribe this creed! Ye will be forced so to do! For the Holy Spirit cometh upon no council of an earthly emperor, but only of Christ's Church. Henceforth, therefore, thaumaturgy shall be lost unto the Church! Henceforth, therefore, Christianity shall be a human institution! And the faith of Christians will be first one thing, then another, as successive emperors may determine to be best. Those who now are orthodox will be proscribed as heretics, and those who now are heretics will be called orthodox; and Christian emperors will seek to exterminate Christian heretics with fire and sword throughout the world. For the millions of Armenia, and many more throughout Egypt, Syria, and Africa, and the whole nation of the Goths, are as I am—what ye call Arian. So is the brave, the successful, the popular Crispus Cæsar. So is Ulfilas, whom Constantine calleth the Moses of the Goths, whom he now proposes to ordain a bishop over the people whom he converted, and upon whom Constantine made war to force them to accommodate their religion to imperial law. So is Constantia, the sister of the emperor, the widow of Licinius; and so is the young Licinius, her son, and others perhaps of the same imperial family, concerning whom I do not know. See ye not that when Constantine shall die, and his sons shall succeed to empire, the faith of Christ which is now condemned shall be established by the imperial law as true?—And even thou, Athanasius, next Bishop of Alexandria, mayst find thyself a fugitive from thine episcopal palace (which the emperor shall give unto thee), a vagabond upon the friendless earth, a martyr for, or a renegade from, what thou now maintainest to be true!

"Brethren, I go hence to death, or banishment, or both. I care not for it. For I live in the steadfast faith and hope that, although the kingdom of heaven be now subverted by the man of sin, yet again some time, somehow, somewhere, it shall be re-established upon the foundation of faith and communism which our Lord did lay, and shall prevail; and war, slavery, and mammon-worship, shall all cease to curse the world; for all people that love liberty and hate tryants shall be Arians, and mankind shall yet realize the promise of our Lord which he confirmed by his life, by his miracles and parables, and by his death and resurrection, of universal liberty, equality, and faternity. Brethren, farewell! and the peace of God be with you!"

Then the gaunt, sad, immovable, and irreconcilable heretic walked calmly out of the hall. During the utterance of this terrible oration, many seemed awed by the solemn grandeur and prophetic earnestness of the speaker ; many were terrified at his fearless denunciation of the plans, atheism, and hypocrisy of the emperor ; and some secretly rejoiced because they supposed that his boldness irrevocably sealed his doom. Constantine himself, convulsed with suppressed wrath, grew pale with passion, and bit his lips to restrain some indiscreet expression of his jealousy, doubt, and fear, as Arius declared the numbers and strength of the Arian party in Armenia, Egypt, Syria, and among the Goths, and eulogized the gallant Crispus Cæsar, his popular and splendid son.

CHAPTER XI.

ONE JOT THAT PASSED FROM THE LAW.

ON that very night the grand, lonely, immovable pres-byter disappeared, and in that council was seen no more. But the next day came the emperor's sister Constantia, the widow of Licinius, and Licinius, her son, and Crispus Cæsar, the eldest son of Constantine, born of his first wife Minervina, and the emperor's mother, Helena, and all, casting themselves at the feet of Constantine, with tears and supplications besought him that the great, learned, and holy Arius might not be put to death. And they so vehemently urged this petition that Constantine finally seemed to give way thereto, and promised, confirming his promise with an awful oath, that he would spare the life of the presbyter. In truth, he supposed that to execute Arius would be impolitic, because it would forever alienate a very large number of his subjects, and he wished to avoid it, and also to win praises for his clemency. He there-fore ordered that Arius be banished to, and closely guarded in, a strong fortress in the wildest portion of Illyricum, until, "in the opinion of the emperor, the Arians of Armenia, Egypt, and Syria, and the Goths, might have become reconciled unto the creed of Nicea."

Crispus Cæsar boldly declared that he indorsed the opinions of Arius, and regarded the great heretic with larger love and reverence than any other man had ever gained from him ; and the emperor heard this declaration with gloom and hatred, but in ominous silence.

And one by one, under the influence of the threats of Constantine, who still held the bishops together, determined to extort the unanimous consent of all to the acts of the council, under the specious and continuous arguments and forced interpretations of the creed, used by his partisans both lay and clerical, and under the benumbing and stupefying effects of protracted weariness and hopelessness all of them finally subscribed the creed, except Arius and six others—Eusebius of Cæsarea, Eusebius of Nicomedia, Theonas, Bishop of Marmarica, Secundus, Bishop of Theuchira, Euzoius the deacon, Achillas the reader, and Saras, a presbyter—against all of whom the emperor made a decree of perpetual banishment, but gave not orders for the enforcement thereof. He was not satisfied ; especially he was dissatisfied because he was unable to extort the signatures of the Eusebii ; and he still waited, determined in some way to obtain these signatures. Finally, he caused Eusebius of Cæsarea to be brought before him, and, assuming an air of great friendliness and concern toward him, he said : "Dear bishop, I did tell thee long ago that our differences about the Arian heresy must never be a cause of quarrel between thee and me. I wish to know what difficulty thou hast (and thy brother) in subscribing the creed ?"

And Eusebius answered : "The difficulty truly is not

a very large one; it is just the size and shape of an 'iota' of the Greek alphabet."

"If it is as insignificant as that," answered the emperor, "let us quietly remove it and be friends again. Tell me, therefore, what thou dost mean."

"Hast thou here the creed?" asked Eusebius.

Constantine handed the parchment to him, and Eusebius said: "This word ὁμοούσιος is one which Arius condemneth as implying the identity of Father and Son, and my conscience suffereth not me to sign it; but the word ὁμοιούσιος, which differeth therefrom only by the one small *iota* therein, expresses exactly what I believe, that Father and Son are of like divine nature."

"And wouldst thou sign it if this letter had been written therein? and thy brother? and the others who are sentenced to banishment?"

"Assuredly!"

"It shall never be said," laughed Constantine, "that I have lost my friend and bishop for such a trifle!"

Then he pointed out the fact that a small "ι" had been dexterously inserted between "ὁμο" and "ουσιος" in both the places where the word occurred in the creed, making it the Arian ὁμοιούσιος, instead of the Trinitarian ὁμοούσιος.

"Now, bishop, give me thy signature, and communicate this arrangement confidentially unto the others, and let them come and sign also, that the creed may be unanimously signed, and all of these unseemly dissensions banished out of the established Church."

The bishop laughed lightly, but signed the confession

of faith, and not long afterward all the others did so, except Arius, who was already far upon the road to the heart of Illyricum.

Constantine had now completed his long-cherished design of subverting the social and political organization of the primitive Church, and establishing a state religion, of which he might be the head in place of Jesus Christ, in whose name he founded a system that was in open rebellion against the Saviour's whole life and teachings.

It remained only for him to have the action of the Œcumenical Council confirmed by some miraculous circumstances, and the imperial ingenuity was fully equal to the occasion; for two members of the council had died at Nicea during its protracted session, and were buried in the church: With a grand and ostentatious procession by torch-light, the sacred roll of parchment was taken to their tomb and left there through the night, the emperor himself having prayed publicly that, if the departed bishops approved the action of the council, they might in some way signify their assent to the decrees and creed thereof; and early the next morning the signatures of the dead bishops were found upon the parchment! Their endorsement was unequivocal: "We, Chrysanthus and Mysonius, fully concurring with the first Holy and Œcumenical Synod, although removed from earth, have signed the volume with our own hands."

Still, the emperor did not dissolve the assembly, and, in order to gain over the personal affection even of those who had most stubbornly resisted his sacrilegious domination of the council, he provided a magnificent banquet for the members thereof, and lavished upon them every mark of love and honor. He lodged the one-eyed, hamstrung old Paphnutius in his own palace, "and often sent for him to hear the story of his persecutions; and now it was remarked how he would throw his arms round the old man, and put his lips to his eyeless socket as if to suck out with his reverential kiss the blessing which, as it were, lurked in the sacred cavity, and stroked down with his imperial hand the frightful wound; how he pressed his legs and arms, and the royal purple, to the paralyzed limbs, and put his own eyeball into the socket." And, because those maimed and tortured members of the council who had been "confessors" enjoyed the reputation of especial sanctity and honor throughout the Church, Constantine used the same disgusting demagogy in his dealings with them all, and fawned upon and flattered them in the name of Jesus, until he believed he had stolen for himself their influence in aiding him to eradicate primitive Christianity out of the East, as he had already done in the West, and so banishing the kingdom of heaven from the face of the earth; and so nourishing in the very bosom of the Church, maintained and governed by imperial authority, the ancient crimes of war, slavery, and mammon-worship, perpetuating the bondage of the people unto the ruling classes, and giving the sanction of religion to class distinctions between men and families, based upon this idolatry, which had been always the curse of human life.

And for a whole year Constantine pursued his pur-

pose quietly, unceasingly, intelligently, by the use of a
thousand different means and agencies, to reduce the East
to a condition of ecclesiastical serfdom to his authority,
and to confirm, popularize, and consolidate his power.
But the slow, doubtful, hesitating adoption of the imperial church by the Christians of Armenia, and to a
less degree by those of Syria, Egypt, and the Gothic
provinces along the Danube, to whom he had sent back
their teacher Ulfilas after ordaining him to be a royal
bishop, inspired the emperor with misgivings of the future, and with an almost unreasoning jealousy and hatred
of Crispus Cæsar, his son, who was the favorite of all
those regions, and of Licinius, who represented the family of the legitimate sovereign thereof, whom Constantine
had dethroned and destroyed.

And the next year the emperor went to Rome to celebrate the Ides of Quintilis, the anniversary of the battle
of Lake Regillus, in which, according to the chronicles
of pagan Rome, the twin-gods Castor and Pollux had
fought in defense of the Eternal City, and brought thereto
the welcome news of victory. It was esteemed to be the
most sacred ceremony known to the Roman people. During the grand festival, Constantine, believing that after
the Council of Nicca his own ecclesiastical system was
so powerful and so securely established that he need not
longer patronize the heathen, refused to take his proper
place in the ancient ritual appropriate to the occasion,
and even exhibited his contempt for the empty pageantry of a legion of knights passing in solemn procession,
by commenting upon their appearance with that caustic,

epigrammatic wit of which few men were more thoroughly master. That large portion of the Romans who yet openly adhered to the ancient religion were insulted and furious at the conduct of the emperor, and there was a fierce riot in the streets, during which stones were hurled at the statues of the emperor, and attempts made to overthrow them.

His wife Fausta, the daughter of the fierce old emperor Maximian, inherited much of her father's cruel nature and imperious ambition. She and Constantine had three sons—Constantine, Constantius, and Constans. She had always envied Crispus Cæsar the superiority which his primogenial rights gave to him as the first-born of Constantine over her own sons, and especially had her jealousy been inflamed by the splendid reputation which young Cæsar had gained by the skill and courage wherewith he had defeated the vastly superior navy of Licinius in the straits of the Hellespont. Next to the great emperor himself stood Crispus Cæsar, not only in official station, but in the love and admiration of the world; and her own sons occupied a far less conspicuous position, which was rendered more galling to her pride by the very prominence derived from the fact that they also were the sons of the emperor. Fausta had remarked with secret joy the open aid and friendship showed by Crispus Cæsar for Arius, which fact had aroused the suspicions, as much as the victory of Crispus had excited the jealousy, of the emperor. She failed not, also, to perceive that the devotion of Constantia, the widow of Licinius, and of the Empress Helena, Constantine's mother, to this same Arius, had created a common interest and friendship between Cæsar, Helena, and Constantia, while Eusebius of Nico-media was the trusted friend and adviser of all of them, and the tutor of young Licinius. Fausta herself, the daughter of a pagan and the wife of an atheist, was as nearly devoid of religious sentiment as it was ever possible for a woman to become ; and, like her husband, thought that all faith is only superstition, which may be advan-tageously used by a wise ruler for the government of men ; and understanding better than any one else that Constantine regarded the free Arian spirit as the most dangerous element in the political future of the empire, she had cunningly employed every artifice and innuendo that could tend to inflame his personal hatred of these religious dissenters. She affected to regard the riot in the streets of Rome as arising from the machinations of the Arian recusants. Knowing that Constantine had only once visited Rome since the overthrow of Maxentius, and that he disliked the place, she pretended to desire that he should fix his imperial residence at Rome, on the ground that Milan was inconveniently situated, and that both Nicomedia and Constantinople, being in the midst of vast Arian communities, were unsafe for him.

She thought that the rioting in Rome gave her the opportunity to take some decisive step in accomplishing her long-cherished designs, and began more vehemently to press her insidious suggestions upon the gloomy soul of the atheist whom she knew to worship only himself.

"If the stone wherewith these Arian strangers who are in the city marred the head of thy statue on the

Via Sacra had smitten thee, thou wouldst have been slain at once."

"But," said the emperor, dryly, passing his hand over his forehead, "I feel not the slightest pain from the blow."

"The undirected mob is powerless against thee," she said ; "but this infamous act is but the unguarded expression of a sentiment common to the millions of Armenia, and to large numbers of the Egyptians and Syrians, and to nearly all of the Goths."

"What hath caused thee so much uneasiness from such a trifle as the throwing of a stone or two ? The royal blood should despise such visionary fears."

"But the guardsman, Pilus, who hath lately come from Illyricum, informeth me that in the garrison it is commonly reported that the heretic Arius saith that, if Christians could lawfully bear arms, the Arians of Armenia and the Goths alone could seat Licinius upon the throne of his father, and Crispus Cæsar upon thine."

"But neither Licinius, nor Crispus, nor the Arians, cherish any such treasonable designs," said Constantine.

"I fear lest thou art lulled into a false security. Ever anxious for thy safety and for thy glory, I have consulted auguries and oracles, and, although these things have no great weight with thee or with me as matters of religious faith, the oracles were always valuable portents to show the drift of popular opinion and desire ; and no great statesman can afford to despise them, for that which the multitude long after doth sooner or later come to pass ;

and all the divinations portend calamity to thee and thy house from the Arians."

"But Licinius is a boy, and Crispus Cæsar is quiet, modest, temperate, and unostentatious. He hath neither vices nor ambitions that require him to aspire higher than he already standeth."

"Thou wouldst rather cease to be than cease to rule the empire. Dominion is the dominant passion of thy lofty soul. It is the marked characteristic of thy race. There are other men mastered by similar ambition. The quiet, orderly life of Cæsar may blind the eyes of mankind to an ambition that would hesitate at nothing. Thy father was such a temperate youth that he sacrificed all common lusts and appetites to win the sovereignty of Rome, and he would not have been contented long with that if he had lived. Thou didst inherit his nature with his military genius, and thou hast lived moderately in order to gain the sovereignty of the world. Crispus hath inherited from thee the great abilities which enabled him to triumph on the Hellespont and share thy glory, or rather take to himself the greater share. He would not forego the pleasures of youth and the advantages of his great position unless he were constantly meditating upon some great design. Look to thyself, Augustus."

Such insidious counsels she constantly offered to the jealous and cruel emperor, and they bore a deadly fruit. Suddenly the gallant young Cæsar was seized, transported to the gloomy fortress of Pola, imprisoned, and then murdered, by order of "the most Christian Emperor Constantine," "the favorite of God," "the defender of the faith," his father! Almost immediately the young Licinius was snatched from the arms of his mother, and put to death by the order of his uncle, Constantine, "the first Christian Emperor of Rome."

"I have fortified my throne against all danger from Crispus Cæsar and the Arians," said Constantine unto himself.

"The road to royal favor and to future power is opened for my splendid brood of Cæsars," murmured Fausta under her breath.

"The Empress Fausta hath plotted against and murdered my gallant son Crispus, and my grandson Licinius, whom I loved. I will be revenged upon the cruel murderess or die!" was the unuttered comment of the Empress-mother Helena; and from that hour, with the slow, settled, and deliberate hatred of old age and hopeless sorrow, she sought for the life of Fausta.

The world held its breath in horror at these fearful crimes, and hardly did the historians of that age dare to commit any account thereof unto posterity. But it was impossible for the officers of the Illyrian fortress, where Arius was imprisoned, to speak of such atrocities without some knowledge thereof coming to their quiet, intelligent prisoner. When he heard of the assassination of Crispus Cæsar and of Licinius, the only comment made by the stern, inflexible, incorruptible old heretic was this: "A council of Christ's Church ought not to be œcumenical and barren; and the first one already beareth terrible but legitimate fruits."

25

The empress-mother, old Helena, continually and skillfully directed the suspicions of her dark-souled, bloody son against the Empress Fausta herself; and, when she had prepared her vengeance so that she thought it could not fail, she accused Fausta of infidelity to the emperor, with that same Pilus, of the imperial guardsmen. Many craftily prepared circumstances corroborated the infamous and degrading accusation, and quickly and secretly the emperor put his wife to death.

"Small recompense for my great wrong," murmured Helena, "but all that I can take; for the woman's beautiful sons are also mine own grandchildren."

"I have no friend on earth," mused Constantine, "except my mother and Eusebius of Cæsarea."

When the gloomy old prisoner of the Illyrian fortress heard of the murder of Fausta, upon this disgraceful charge of adultery with a guardsman, he said : "The grand name of Constantine is soaked with domestic blood and draggled in domestic filth. The royal œcumenical council beareth such strange and deadly fruit."

The officers of the fortress were held to be accountable with their lives for the heretic's safe-keeping, and vigilant spies reported to Constantine almost every word he uttered, and stole and transmitted to the emperor almost every line he wrote, and the old man's gloomy comments upon the condition of the Church, and his strange and seemingly inspired interpretations of prophecy, which he supposed to relate to Constantine and his new city of Constantinople, built upon seven hills, above the narrow straits whereto the commerce of the world resorted, doubtless aided Fausta's and Helena's conspiracies to lead him into the commission of those horrible crimes which shocked the moral sense of the world, and justified the pagans in breathless wonder as to what new atrocities would follow the legal establishment of the Christian faith —atrocities that perhaps afterward drove Julian the Apostate to struggle for the restoration of paganism. And doubtless Arius himself would long ago have perished, if the emperor had not hoped to obtain from his manuscripts and prophecies warning of every coming danger.

CHAPTER XII.

AN IMPERIAL REPENTANCE.

But, although these secret horrors, which degraded the noblest family of the empire, were kept as still as private crimes, and men dared scarcely speak of them except in terrified whispers, the knowledge thereof spread abroad, until enough was known to fill the Christian world with detestation of the emperor; and he whose governing passion had been to rule mankind, and to command their respect and reverence at any cost, found himself to be held by the popular verdict as an outcast from virtue and decency. His iron soul was proof against every shaft except this, but the wound it inflicted upon his boundless self-love was bitter and incurable. Realizing that he had outraged the moral sentiment of Christendom by these atrocious crimes, the emperor determined to overthrow what he called Christianity, and re-establish the pagan religion, charging his crimes to the blinding influences of the superstition and strong magic of the Church, and thereby win for himself the love and confidence of that large portion of his subjects who still adhered to the ancient idolatries. In pursuance of this design, Constantine applied to the flamens at Rome for purification from his domestic crimes, as the first step toward the rehabilitation of his moral nakedness and deformity; but the priests, who knew his crafty, unscrupulous, cruel, and atheistic nature, and who already had in training the young and gifted Julian, seized this opportunity to gratify their theological hate, by boldly declaring that the ancient rituals of paganism did not know any form of expiation for such fearful and unnecessary crimes as his.

Then Constantine turned away forever from heathenism, and sent for Hosius, Bishop of Cordova, who assured him that "in Christianity all sin, however great, may find forgiveness: for He saveth unto the uttermost all that come unto God by him."

"And what method must I use to secure this forgiveness?" asked the emperor.

"Only true repentance toward God, and humble, sincere faith in Jesus Christ," said the bishop.

Then, with a singular smile, Constantine looked at the bishop and answered: "Bishop, thou dost forget that thou art not now talking to a woman taken in adultery, nor to a thief upon the cross. Farewell!"

And with a wave of the hand the emperor contemptuously dismissed him.

But Constantine could not endure the popular detestation of which he knew himself to be justly the object, and as a last resort he sent for Eusebius of Cæsarea. Eusebius knew the emperor fully as well as the emperor knew him, and, of course, knew that he might as well chant psalms to a deaf ass as to recommend faith and repentance to the imperial atheist, as Hosius of Cordova had innocently endeavored to do. When Eusebius came before the emperor, Constantine spoke to him in a light, bantering tone, saying : " Bishop, Crispus Cæsar became infatuated with the idea that he was great enough to wear my sandals and to wield my spear even while I live ; and the young man met with a fatal accident. The youth Licinius, and the woman Fausta, exposed themselves to some unwholesome atmosphere, and the results of their indiscretion were deleterious to their health. These events have happened unfortunately for me, and I require thine unfailing aid in avoiding further inconvenience from them. What canst thou do for me ? "

" Could not the flamens of Jupiter give thy burdened conscience rest ? " said the bishop, quietly, but with malicious pleasure.

" No," answered Constantine, laughing. " The priests are good haters—somewhat too demonstrative, perhaps, but steady and reliable in their antipathies ; and so they took out their spite upon me the first time Fate gave them an opportunity."

" Could not the most learned and holy Hosius point out to thee the road to peace ? "

" No, indeed. That respectable idiot began some sort of mummery concerning faith and repentance ; but I cut him short. Bishop, thou wert not wont to be so difficult. I confess that, since the Council of Nicea, I have not done justice to thy superior merit, and have even felt somewhat estranged from thee. Forget all that, and let us once more be friends."

"Augustus," said the bishop, "I have keenly felt the withdrawal of thy favor, although I have complained to no one. I think that, if it had been otherwise, I could have showed thee sufficient reasons for avoiding some terrible mistakes. What is the exact difficulty which these mistakes have led thee upon?"

"The Arians are rejoiced by any occurrence that gives them a pretext for railing at me; the orthodox Christians have the unblushing impudence to attempt to sit in judgment upon the actions of the emperor that rescued them from persecutions, and affect to be shocked thereby, just as if they were fit to judge his deeds or comprehend his policy; the implacable flamens hope to make such use of these accidents as to lead the world back to paganism without my aid. The Arians hate me because I would not permit them to establish a kingdom in the empire of which I was not to be the king. Thou must find some way to conciliate the fools, for the hearts of all men are estranged from me; and, as thou hast always known, I would rather rule by love than by terror. But rule I will, while I shall live. Now, how can I regain my former hold upon either the pagan or the Christian world?"

"Thou must first of all definitely abandon the idea that the empire can ever return to paganism," said Eusebius. "The amazing progress of Christianity among the people and the rapid decline of heathenism demonstrate that the old religion hath almost ceased to be a political force, and any emperor who would seek to re-establish it is foredoomed to certain failure."

"Let that pass. Ye bishops always regard the Church as the first thing to be considered. I concede that thou art right. What then?"

"Thou must also understand," said Eusebius, with malicious pleasure, "that, while the will of the emperor is the law of the land, it is no longer the standard of right and wrong for Christians. Thy statutes may control political life, and prescribe the external forms of worship for the Church: its conscience hath passed even beyond thy control."

Constantine turned white with wrath.

"The impudent beggars!" he cried, "whom I redeemed from tortures and from death! Where, then, was their 'conscience' when the council subverted the kingdom of heaven upon earth, and they all signed the decree which abolished the earthly sovereignty of Christ? But," checking his furious anger with a mighty effort, "what next?"

"If a man hath done a crime," said Eusebius, "no matter how cruel and unnatural, the Christians understand that he may obtain forgiveness for his sin by repentance and faith, even as King David did in the matter of Bath-sheba."

"Well!" said Constantine, impatiently.

"The Christian world will never pardon thee without this repentance and faith, or the appearance of it," said Eusebius, and he uttered the last few words in a low, peculiar tone.

"And what shape might 'the appearance of it' assume?" asked the emperor, with a laugh.

"Thou mightst go in sackcloth and ashes unto the church and publicly pray to God and man for pardon!"

"And I might far sooner hang up a bishop and exterminate a sect that would seriously insist upon any such degrading terms!"

"So I supposed," said Eusebius, "and even then such a course would only be 'the appearance' of faith and repentance, not the things themselves. But thou mightst build a church and dedicate it unto the memory of Cæsar; or set up his statue, with an inscription intimating that he was the victim of a mistake, and the object of affectionate and sorrowful remembrance. Either of these 'appearances of it' might be sufficient."

"That will answer," cried Constantine. "Crispus Cæsar was a handsome man, and an excellent subject for a statue. The statue shall be of gold, and the inscription shall be, 'To Crispus, mine injured and innocent son.' Will that, think you, reconcile the orthodox? Or what else dost thou advise?"

"The Empress-mother Helena should exhibit some similar token of repentance for her hatred of the Empress Fausta."

"And what 'appearance of it' should her faith and repentance assume?" said Constantine, laughing merrily.

"Recently," replied Eusebius, "a lively interest hath sprung up throughout the Church in the 'holy places' in Palestine. If the empress should make a pilgrimage to the Holy Land, and found there a handsome church and some sacred shrines, she would cease to annoy thee, amuse herself, and do a great work toward restoring the love and confidence of Christians to thyself and her."

"Thou art a true and glorious bishop," laughed the emperor, "and thou dost never forget the welfare of the Church. The empress-mother shall go quickly on her sacred pilgrimage, and all the holy places shall rejoice. Is not that enough? Or is there yet something more?"

"This would suffice for the orthodox," said Eusebius; "but years have passed since the Council of Nicea. Time hath assuaged the bitterness of former days, which would, perhaps, have faded out altogether but that the banishment of Arius keepeth it alive. If thou wouldst reconcile the whole Church unto thyself, recall and even show some special honor to the Libyan."

"Thou hast reserved thy bitterest medicine for the last!"

"But it is necessary, Augustus. For days past thy sister Constantia, who is even now upon the bed of death, hath entreated me that I would come unto thee and ask thee to visit her, that she might make it her dying request that thou recall Arius and restore his church to him. Of course I could not come till thou didst order it." And then the bishop, fixing his eyes firmly upon the face of Constantine, with his right hand extended, said with inexpressible dignity: "Augustus, thy sister's husband, Licinius, the Emperor of the East, and her only son, Licinius, both perished by thine own order; yet her devotion unto thee hath never faltered. Surely thou canst not refuse her dying supplications!"

Constantine's face for once grew soft with a genuine

emotion of humanity, and he replied: "Surely not, bishop! I always loved Constantia. I will visit her, and do whatever she desires."

"Go to-day, then," said Eusebius, "for she hath but few hours more to live."

And Constantine went; and the long and sorely tried and deeply injured, but still faithful and loving sister, with her dying breath besought him to recall the great and holy Arius, and restore the peace and unity of the Church and of the empire; and with a mighty oath (as usual) he promised so to do.

CHAPTER XIII.

DURING the slow lapse of all the years which had passed away since the date of the Nicene Council, Arius the Libyan was almost as much dead unto the world as if he had indeed departed from this life. None, except the emperor and a few trusted officers, knew anything more of him than that he was kept a close prisoner somewhere in Illyricum, none knew precisely where; and so carefully was the secret guarded, that even unto this day the precise place and manner of his imprisonment remain entirely unknown. For a few years after he had disappeared so suddenly, there were now and then vague rumors in circulation that some of his devoted adherents had discovered the location of his prison, and were plotting to deliver him therefrom; and the same rumors indefinitely connected the names of Crispus Cæsar and of young Licinius with these revolutionary designs; and cunning Fausta had used these rumors, with remorseless skill and intelligence, to the destruction of them both. But whether these were merely vague and idle surmises, whether there was some foundation in fact for them, or whether the crafty emperor himself had invented and floated them, in order to justify the murders upon which he had already determined, will forever be unknown. For, upon the perpetration of these enormous crimes, a mist of horror overspread the empire that hid the name and memory of the Libyan from the popular gaze, and thenceforth absolutely nothing was known of him until he suddenly and unexpectedly appeared at Constantinople.

A few days after the funeral of Constantia, Constantine summoned Eusebius and said unto him : "Bishop, I swore unto Constantia that I would recall Arius speedily, and I will keep mine oath ; for reflection convinceth me that piety in this regard is true policy also.   In what manner dost thou deem it most fitting to effectuate this purpose ? "

" Do it like a Christian, like a statesman, like an emperor," said Eusebius, " with a whole heart, generously ! And let there be nothing small, or niggardly, or mean, in thine action.   A few narrow-minded ones among the orthodox may for a while murmur at it ; but the Arians will rejoice, and all Christians and all men will say it was a noble thing to do ! Therefore, let it be done in a grand and princely way ! "

" Particularize the programme which thou thinkest to be 'grand' and 'princely.' "

" Let free pardon be granted unto Arius, without conditions of any kind whatever. Let proclamation be made that the presbyter will be received into communion again, in thine own city and in thine own church, and then transferred to his old pastoral charge, the Baucalis

church in Alexandria, and so recompense his sufferings
with a triumphant return, and receive him at the church-
door in thine own person!"

"It shall so be done at once," answered Constantine.
"No apologies or explanations to be demanded or received.   Do thou immediately set a day, and carefully
arrange all the details of the ceremony as thou wilt.
I will have the old heretic here at the appointed time."

And Eusebius with a glad heart set to work to carry
the emperor's design into effect.   Some among the orthodox murmured, and on the evening before the day
appointed, Alexander, the Bishop of Constantinople, was
heard to exclaim, "Let me, or Arius, die before to-
morrow!"

But the emperor's will could not be resisted; and,
although the orthodox shuddered to acknowledge as a
brother beloved and equal one whom they had always
branded as a heretic, the secularized, imperial Church
must commit treason or obey; for the royal œcumenical
council had borne, along with other fruit, this, that a
difference of religious faith and action might very easily
constitute the crime of treason against the emperor.

On the day which had been set apart for the solemn
pageantry, Arius was brought by chosen officers to the
lodgings where the Eusebii abode when in the city; but,
designing to prepare for the long-imprisoned Libyan all
the delightful surprise which a sudden realization of the
great change in his condition might afford, the Eusebii
had not permitted any one to inform him fully of the
matters contemplated.   They even doubted, also, whether

the grand, ascetic, incorruptible old man would enter an imperial church to receive honor at the hands of an earthly sovereign unless he should be taken by surprise. When, therefore, the next morning, at the appointed hour, they took places upon each side of him, and invited him to walk with them and view the grand and beautiful metropolitan church, the ancient man went forth not knowing what special purpose was contemplated. And as they drew nearer unto the church, and beheld a vast concourse of people in holiday attire, and ranks of soldiers in magnificent array, with banners flying, and heard the mighty shouts that seemed to rend the heavens, " Glory to Constantine, the favorite of God !" " Long live Arius, the great and faithful presbyter !" the Libyan paused, and, gazing upon the Eusebii, inquired, " Bishops, beloved, what mean these mighty clamors, and these salutations of Constantine and Arius ?"

And they answered, " Father, come on with us and thou shalt gladly see."

" Not a step more, until ye have told me all !"

" It meaneth that thou art recalled, not only to Constantinople, but to the very bosom of the Church, subject to no conditions whatever ! And the emperor himself waits at the door yonder to welcome and to honor thee."

Then brake the strong heart within him of a hopeless sorrow, and, faintly murmuring these words, ' The Antichrist hath triumphed here where Satan hath his seat !' a convulsion seized upon him, and, as the two steadfast friends strove to hold him up, the gigantic form of the grand old man glided slowly down between them, and lay

prone upon the pavement, as if the spirit had gone out
of him forever.   And presently a slight contortion swept
over the great, gaunt frame ; the bony right hand extended itself upward, waving gently from side to side; the
rough and noble head darted forward upon the long, lithe
neck; a tender smile, ineffably soft and sweet, played
around the weary, patient mouth, and lighted up the somber eyes and haggard countenance with joy and beauty;
and gazing far away, as if his sight could pierce the bending heavens, he sweetly murmured, 'Jesus, and Theckla also !' Then darkness fell upon the weary face and
eyes ; the mighty limbs relaxed once more ; and he lay
still upon the rocky way.

Arius the Libyan was dead !

THE END.